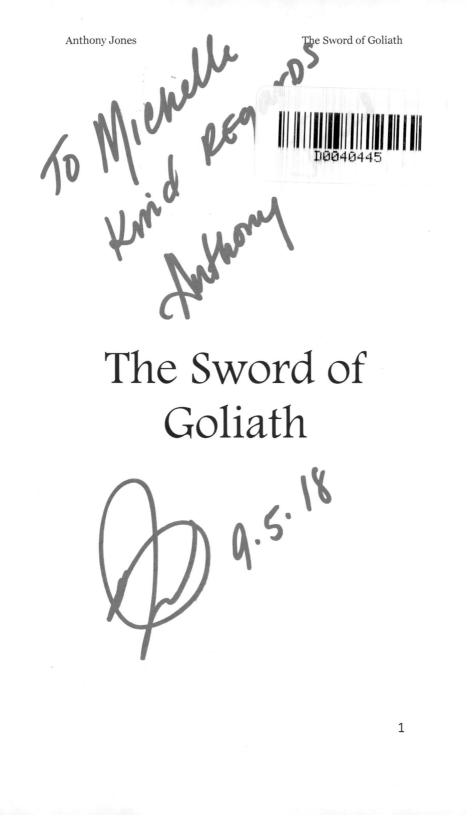

The Sword of Goliath

The Bloodline Chronicles Book I

The Sword of Goliath

By Anthony Jones

A Raven Branch Book

First Edition

Edited by Lee Ann

Cover by Dane Low

~ To my beautiful wife Sherri ~

The Bloodline Chronicles

Author's Note

Genesis Chapter 6 (King James Version)

2~ *"The sons of God saw the daughters of men that they were fair; and they took them wives of all which they chose."*

4~ *"There were giants in the earth in those days; and also after that, when the sons of God came in unto the daughters of men, and they bare children to them, the same became mighty men which were of old, men of renown."*

I have always been troubled by Genesis 6, as it lends itself to the notion that the sons of God, or Angels, engaged in sexual relations with humans and produced a hybrid Nephilim with exceptional powers.

I am a Christian man, and do not wish to offend Christians by suggesting that the Bloodline Chronicles are anything but fantasy. *The Sword of Goliath* is not meant to add or interpret biblical principles or to confuse believers. Rather, this is a novel based on fantasy and make-believe.

The *Shaddai* was a term I settled on to describe a superhuman being of the bloodline of Angels, who remained loyal to God. Although the actual meaning of Shaddai is still debatable, for the purpose of this tale, its meaning includes "Gods destroyers," or "Knights of El Shaddai." Also the "Paladin" are the selected twelve Shaddai preordained to effectively use the twelve enchanted instruments which make up a talisman of invincible power.

The appropriate name for the Nephilim offspring who rejected God are the "Grigori." The Grigori are sworn

enemies of the Shaddai. The Grigori also have a Mesa of twelve dragons who are chosen to use the twelve enchanted instruments against all that is holy.

The Sword of Goliath is the first book in a larger tale of the Shaddai's quest to assemble the lost enchanted instruments while battling the Grigori in the shadows of modern America and in other dimensions.

Πρόλογος

Prologue

Adam and Eve had everything they could want; they walked with God, and were loved above all others. They lived in a beautiful garden at peace with the animals, free to eat from the tree of life. Also in the garden was the tree of the knowledge of good and evil. Adam and Eve were ordered to stay away from this tree and were instructed that eating from the tree would mean certain death.

One day, Morning Star, entered the garden as a serpent and tempted Eve to eat of the fruit of the tree of the knowledge of good and evil. The serpent told Eve the fruit would make her wise and she would become like God. Eve doubted the serpent and was inclined to turn away until the snake said, "Eve, oh, beautiful Eve, I, but a lowly serpent, did eat of the tree and you are amazed that I can speak. How much more will the power of the tree do for you? Surely you will become a god." Eve made the choice to eat of the tree. Adam also made the choice to eat of the tree so they could become gods together.

After they sinned, the sky was covered in darkness and a voice was heard. "Adam! Adam! Why do you and the woman Eve hide from me?"

Adam and Eve were terrified and cold as the warm sun was covered in darkness.

"Oh, Lord, we hide because we are naked and the shame is more than we can bear," Adam said.

Adam and Eve covered themselves with the large leaves from the fig tree and stepped out to face their accuser.

"We have sinned, oh Lord," Adam said. "We disobeyed the commandment to stay away from the forbidden fruit and we are ashamed."

God had mercy on his creation and recognized the repentant spirit they displayed. Rather than killing them, he caused an Angel with a flaming sword to appear and cast Adam and Eve from the garden. They were told they must now work hard and till the earth; by the sweat of their brow they would grow crops and through pain they would produce children.

God loved Adam and Eve and was sad to see them dying. The Angel told Adam that God would send a Redeemer, his own Son, the Good Shepherd, to pay the price for their sin so they could escape damnation through his grace. The Angel explained the Redeemer would be born to this earth and through his sacrifice, he would obtain the keys to death, hell, and the grave.

This pleased Adam and Eve. They populated the earth outside the garden, which was now guarded by the Angel with the flaming sword.

During this time, the sons of God, or Watcher Angels, including Azazel and Semyaza, lusted after the beautiful human daughters of men and took wives of the women. Their wives bore them children. The children of Azazel and Semyaza were Giants with superhuman power, called Nephilim.

This displeased God very much and he sent Enoch, a holy man, to tell the Watcher Angels they had sinned and were to ascend into heaven no more. The Watcher Angels were saddened and made a petition for Enoch to present to God on their behalf, explaining their mistake and begging forgiveness and redemption for them and their offspring.

In a dream, an Angel told Enoch to return to the Watcher Angels and inform them that their petition had been rejected. The Angel also told him that their children were an abomination who did not fall under the covenant God had made with Adam.

The Nephilim, who were half-Angel and half-human, were considered the spawn of the unholy. Archangels Michael and Raphael were sent to bind Azazel and Semyaza, along with others, and imprison them in Nether Gloom until the end of days.

The bloodline of the angelic beings eventually reached a point where redemption could be realized. The bloodline of the Watchers who remained loyal to God were called Shaddai, meaning "Gods Destroyers". The offspring who rejected God were known as Grigori. The Shaddai were commissioned to gather the twelve enchanted instruments which form a talisman of invincible power. Also seeking such power were the evil Grigori. And thus, the battle continues.

PART ONE

Chapter I

The Prisoner

ONE

It was just another morning, waking up to the odor of ass, breath, and feet in West Block at San Quentin State Prison. Jake Stanton lay awake on the two-inch, permanently stained mattress covering the bedsprings on the rack in his eight-by-ten-foot cell. The dawn cutting the Bay fog and shining through the upper windows was lighting the first day of the rest of his life in this God-forsaken dungeon. Sounds of men snoring and toilets flushing were breaking the relative silence of the cellblock stacked five tiers high, holding a thousand men. The hundred-fifty-year-old building was coming alive, and the noise would only become louder until darkness returned again.

The regulators of this prison were as different as night and day, and just as desensitized as the inmate population. *Trust*, a word that held a completely different meaning on the streets, was not in the vocabulary of the inmates in this broken city within a city.

A plump officer in a jumpsuit uniform with faded patches on his shoulders walked along the gun rail towards the front of the housing unit. A Ruger mini 14 rifle was slung across his large belly and his pudgy pink hands gripped the stock. He was also sporting a .38-caliber revolver in a holster under the doughy roll on his left side. The two-by-twelve planks bowed and creaked with every step as the officer made his way to the worn-out chair next to an old milk crate holding a few torn newspapers.

Jake felt a shiver climb his spine and pulled the sheet and wool blanket to his chin and tried to relax.

"Chow release in west block!" a male voice announced over the public address system. "Release the back bar!" the voice said.

The slamming of doors and jingle of keys announced the release for the morning meal—if you could call it a meal. Prison food smells and tastes the same regardless of what day or even what meal it is. The funk in the housing units was testament to this fact. The rank of burning wicks and waste odor from bland, uninteresting meals along with the rot of unclean laundry and men, who were allowed a ten-minute shower every other day, created the signature stench of prison. There was nothing quite like it anywhere on earth. The smell of hot garbage at the county dump paled in comparison.

The poorly circulated air contributed to the awful living conditions. The smoke arose in the unit like fog lifting from a lake on a cold autumn morning. This smoke was a result of five hundred small burning wicks made from tightly rolled toilet paper draped in the corner of each and every cell, burning slowly, so the occupant could light a cigarette or pilot an inmate-manufactured cookstove at any time. After all, lighters and matches were against prison rules.

The smoke hung in the rafters like clouds of sulfur, burning Jake's throat and lungs with each and every breath. *Why not just issue lighters?* Jake thought. *It would sure make it easier for everyone to breathe, to say nothing of the thousands of rolls of toilet paper going up in smoke.*

Jake could hardly believe he'd landed in this awful place. *Is this a nightmare? Will I wake up one day and learn this was all a bad dream?* For a moment, Jake's brain chose not to remember why he was in prison; his mind swam more and more these days as sleep was leaving, and he was in that hazy time determining what was a dream and what was real. The palms of his hands went to his temples and he rubbed his aching head. When awareness came to him, he quickly pushed it from his mind and longed for blissful sleep. He reminisced of better days, when he was considered one of the good guys.

TWO

Jake was a strong man with a ruddy exterior and handsome features, but he was not like anyone else. Something had set him apart since the day he was born. It was nothing obvious, nothing you could put your finger on. Not different *bad*, just different. Jake often wondered if others felt the way he did. Since childhood, Jake had struggled with his identity, trying hard to fit in, but try as he may, he always felt as awkward as a chicken in a duck pond.

In school, he was one of the brightest students in the class. He rarely studied, but always passed his exams with high marks. Jake was like a sponge, absorbing knowledge and always learning new things. From age two he was mimicking his mother reading to him, holding a book to his forehead and sounding the letters into words. In no time he was on his own, killing the books, first in his nursery, then the children's books in the family room on the high shelves over the fireplace. Then the novels in his mother's library. One by one he devoured them and was hungry for more. Jake's parents marveled at his photographic memory, which allowed him, at age seven, to participate in the adult conversations around the coffee pot following the morning devotions.

Jake could recite his Sunday school lessons almost word for word, and often corrected the teacher in matters where she may have got the name wrong in a Bible story.

Jake was a mild-mannered child, one of the best babies ever, his mother would boast, but something behind his mild nature slept, something monstrous, or at least

11

something not understood. It was an anomaly, hidden in the body of a beautiful child, sleeping behind his ice-blue eyes. It was something remarkable, mysterious, and something to be feared, even by Jake himself.

THREE

Jake had few friends as a child; most of the kids his age could not keep up with his constantly evolving mind. His intelligence was far beyond the children around him, causing him to tire easily of their ignorance. The older kids avoided him and treated him like a freak.

As a loner, Jake wandered the Comstock Junior High School hallways during breaks; he usually ate his lunch alone in the school cafeteria and sat in the rear of the classroom, where he could remain anonymous. His anonymity served him well until he was fourteen years old.

FOUR

On a gray November morning, Jake's science teacher, Ms. Martin, surprised the class with a movie titled *If I had a Million Dollars*. This was a great treat for the class as Ms. Martin, despite being very attractive, even sexy— for an older woman (although she wore far too much perfume)—was known for her strict scientific ways and would rarely relax to enjoy movies or stray from the textbook.

"Pay attention, class! I am only going to say this once. If you ever want to see another movie in my class, you will be careful not to be disruptive in any way."

Ms. Martin walked back and forth at the front of the class with her hands folded together behind her back, her high heels tapping on the lab's stone tile floor. Her generous chest pointed her path, and her studious glasses framed her pretty face. She was only about four feet seven without those heels but the shoes brought her to a solid five feet tall.

"I expect you will all be on your very best behavior. It will only take one to ruin it for the rest of the class. So, consider yourselves warned, and don't make this the last movie we see this year."

Jake liked Ms. Martin; she was good-looking and dressed sexy, with short skirts and lots of makeup. She was a refreshing vision compared to Ms. Moore, his English teacher, who was an old, wrinkled hag, mean as they come, and smelling of coffee and cigarettes. She had a rotten tooth in her head reeking of gingivitis, causing Jake to hold his breath when she was close to keep his stomach from clenching.

The movie was black-and-white and starred a fat man who was conducting a study of human behavior and sense of entitlement. The movie reminded Jake of the parable in the Bible about the master of three slaves. To one, the master gave five talents of gold; to another, two talents of gold; and to the third, he gave one talent of gold. The master went away and when he returned, he called the three servants to him for an accounting.

The first servant bowed to his master and presented him with ten talents of gold; he was praised for wisdom, and granted entrance into the joy of his master's house. The second servant showed the master he had doubled the two talents of gold to four; he was praised, and granted entrance into the joy of his master's house. However, the third servant said, "Oh, master, I knew you were a hard man and would one day return demanding your money, so I was careful to bury it so I could have it to present to you once again. Behold, master, your gold."

When the master saw this, he became angry. "You knew I would return, so why did you not put it in a bank so at least it would earn interest? Why did you bury it, you fool? Depart from me and be damned!"

Jake remembered thinking the master was quite the hard man; he was very cold, and showed little tolerance for laziness. Moreover, he had an expectation of performance or duty when none was made clear. Jake would remember this, and would later strive for success in all things regardless of expectations.

Jake lost himself in the movie and was awakened back to reality by an obnoxious boy with curly orange hair seated directly behind him named Billy Parson. The boy was fooling around, causing Ms. Martin to become annoyed. Jake turned to Billy and said in a hushed voice, "Why don't you shut up? Some of us are trying to watch the movie." The boy gave Jake an evil look but shut his hole just the same. Something about Jake's ice-blue eyes frightened the boy.

FIVE

After the movie, the class prepared for third period. Jake, still wondering about the meaning of the movie, in a daydream state of mind, stepped out the door on his way to US history when brilliant light and black spotting behind his eyes pulsed pain as Billy's fist took him out of operation.

"You shut up, punk," Billy muttered as he wrinkled his nose and raised his upper lip, causing his face to look like a pig.

Jake, dazed, knees buckling, still holding his books with both arms, was trying to understand what had just happened when again the boy sucker punched him in the face. Jake went down, stars dazzling bright in his mind, books flying, loose papers lifting up like butterflies lost in the wind. Jake shook his head and looked around with tears in his eyes. He could see Billy and his gang scampering away, cawing like a flock of crows as they left. Jake collected his books, gathered what he could of the loose papers, and went to his locker.

He took a few deep breaths and tried to get it together. The blood was burning his cheeks and he felt the sting of his feelings in the back of his throat with every breath. Jake was not seriously injured, just embarrassed and hurt. Now something inside Jake welled up and he shivered. It was not anger, but a force. Something foreign began to take control of him. Jake had only felt this sensation on a few occasions in his young life, when he fell from the pier while fishing in the San Francisco Bay and almost drowned in the freezing water, or when his grandfather died. The entity dwelling inside him was coming forward.

Jake tried to push the thoughts of dismembering young Billy from his mind. He saw the whole thing in a dream-like vision. He watched himself moving in slow motion, executing perfect Kung Fu movements, methodically destroying the boy. Jake was shaking and breathing heavy; he closed his eyes, tightened his fists, and concentrated. Then, as suddenly as it appeared, it was gone. A comforting peace washed over Jake like a warm hug and he knew what to do. Thoughts of dismembering Billy left his mind, but he would not let the boy get away with the sucker punch.

SIX

Jake cleaned himself up and made it to history class without incident. The day became progressively better.

"Can anyone tell me who the primary enemy of the United States was during World War II?" asked Mr. Brocker. Hands shot up all over the classroom. Jake looked down at his drawing of a boy facing a Giant with a sword. Jake was surprised at what his hand seemed to be drawing all on its own. Jake's usual doodles were nothing more than a cluster of wandering circular marks. Here he had actually created a work of art, and it was good. "Mr. Stanton, perhaps you could enlighten us.

Jake looked up. "Japan," he said in a mild voice.

"That is correct," said Mr. Brocker. "Japan attacked the United States on December 7, 1941, by bombing our navy fleet in Hawaii." Jake went back to his drawing as Mr. Brocker turned to use the chalkboard.

15

Later that afternoon, Jake waited by Billy's locker. He could hear the obnoxious boy making fun of another kid as his followers laughed and tagged behind him. Billy turned the corner and was nose-to-nose with Jake. The look of surprise froze on Billy's face and his eyes widened like Marty Feldman in *Young Frankenstein*.

"You want some more, Stanton?" Billy cursed, tossing his book bag to the ground and taking a fighting stance. "C'mon, punk!" Billy screeched.

Jake ducked the right cross thrown by the orange-haired boy, then, with lightning speed, grabbed Billy by the shirt and swung him hard into the lockers, causing a loud echoing sound as Billy's head dented locker number 12. Before the boy could get to his feet, Jake's Redwing carpenter boot met Billy's face, tossing his head sideways, causing blood to spray from Billy's lip and nose. The growing crowd of students began to chant, "Fight, fight, fight . . ."

Billy, completely dazed and in considerable pain, had no intention of fighting at that point. The sight of his own blood caused him to weep uncontrollably. He crawled away from his opponent and made a large wet spot in the front of his bell-bottom Levi's.

A medium-built, balding man with a comb-over hairstyle hurried toward the growing group of teens. Vince Powell, the Comstock dean of boys, rushed to break up the fight, pushing students aside and carving a path through the crowd; but it was too late. Jake had managed to round the corner of the building just in time to miss being caught fighting on school grounds, an offence usually punished with a three-day suspension. Not to mention what Jake's father would do. This simple incident would return to Jake time and time again, and he would use it to measure all future enemy encounters.

SEVEN

Jake was not known for being a fighter; he was hardly known at all. His mild nature had followed him most of his life and he'd never had to get physical with anyone— until now. Jake was not afraid, he just steered clear of trouble when it came to violence. Jake would feel a stir inside when violence was imminent. He did not fear personal injury, rather he feared what he might do to his opponent, or feared what the stir inside him may do.

The fight rumor circled the school and the facts were distorted to the point where most people believed Jake was some kind of a black belt karate expert, resulting in the usual bullies keeping their distance. This single incident provided Jake with a new identity and quickly changed his social status. Jake developed a more outlaw attitude despite his once overpowering peaceful disposition. His clothes went from polo shirts and corduroy pants to Levi's and leather jackets.

Girls came and went for Jake; nothing lasting more than a few months. That was, until he met the girl of his dreams, one who would change his life forever; Teresa Burke, the most beautiful girl he had ever seen. Her long, blond hair reached past her petite backside and neared the back of her knees. She was five foot two, her eyes were blue, and oh, what those blue eyes could do. *Love at first sight*, Jake thought. As if it was yesterday, Jake recalled when she transferred to his high school during his freshman year. He was only fifteen so he was still taking the bus, but he would imagine what it would be like once he had a car and the courage to ask her out.

EIGHT

"Release the fourth tier!" shouted the officer over the public address system. This was followed by a crack and clank of the large steel bars moving away from the cell doors, then multiple bangs as the doors flew open and orange jumpsuits filled the tier like a stream of California poppies in a strong wind.

The inmates poured down the stairwell towards the entrance of the housing unit. *Just another spoke in the broken system,* Jake thought as he joined the flow of two hundred inmates now stepping through the big steel rotunda doors and spilling into the fog on the West Block yard. The cool salt air was refreshing. Jake drew it deep into his lungs then exhaled hard in an effort to force out the funky building air trapped inside his body. The seagulls screamed with excitement as they flew over the orange river of men, occasionally dropping the stinky, processed remains of what the very same prisoners had left them the day before.

A smirk, almost a smile, washed across Jake's face as he noticed the sudden appearance of black-and-white bird crap dripping from the tall inmate's newly shaved head in front of him. The slimy goo had struck the tattoo of a clown face, resulting in the effect of black-and-white tears.

"Disgusting!!" shouted the tattooed skinhead as he used his hand to transfer the slime from his head to his orange jumpsuit.

"You know, that's considered good luck," said the chubby, shorter inmate to his left.

"Yeah, right, what great luck. I am in prison, on my way to eat the awful, with bird crap all over me. I would hate to see what you consider *bad* luck." The taller man stepped over the painted yellow line toward the outside sink and toilet on the yard. He was stopped by a gray-haired officer who resembled an older version of Clint Eastwood, and every bit as grumpy as the old man he played in the movie *Grand Torino*.

"No stopping. Move along. This area is closed," the Clint Eastwood lookalike said.

"Are you kidding me?" the skinhead replied as he pointed to the bird crap on his hand and jumpsuit. "I just want to wash up before I eat!" he barked.

"Keep moving, no stopping, this area is closed," the officer repeated, almost in a robot voice, not looking in the inmate's direction, rather looking at everyone and everything except the protesting inmate.

"Can't you see I got bird crap on me?" the skinhead repeated.

"You have two choices," the officer said. "Keep walking or go to the hole. What's it gonna be?" Never looking directly at the inmate, the officer moved his head from side to side, taking in the mass movement. The tall, soiled skinhead turned on his heels and rejoined the movement, keeping in stride with the rest of the orange river and fading into a sea of orange jumpsuits now moving into the south dining hall.

Jake knew the officer was not purposely being a prick; he was looking for the crime or sleight of hand this birdbrain inmate was running interference for. He knew the guy could be up to something. He had been beaten many times in the past with tricks like this; an inmate approaches an officer as a distraction, and meanwhile, someone is getting stabbed or passing off drugs, kites (small notes), or weapons. A dirty jumpsuit or a little bird crap is a small price to pay to prevent an attack or make a possible drug bust.

Over the years, this officer learned, the release to the dining hall is no time to engage in non-emergency dialog with a reception center inmate.

Jake took his tray from the blind feeding slot and shuffled to the next available stainless steel seat at the table and planted himself. This was reception, no segregation here; blacks sat with whites, Crips with Bloods, south with north; that was just the way it was. You sat where you were told or you did not eat. Not that you would miss much; the nasty smell of Jake's tray was steaming to his nose and the awfulness was a constant reminder of good meals lost and taken for granted.

NO FOOD LEAVES THE DINING HALL proclaimed the sign above the exit. This sucked; however, on the bright side, most of the food served in the dining hall was not worth taking anyway.

"You gonna eat that?" asked the young, dirty inmate to Jake's right, pointing to Jake's cracked hardboiled egg with his chin. Both his hands were working to woof down the oatmeal and potatoes mixed together on his tray. The potatoes were cold and undercooked, but would provide the much-needed nourishment to stay strong and on guard in this den of thieves. Jake nodded and picked up the sorry excuse of a piece of toast, more like a piece of stale bread, and began to spread it with jam. Hard-boiled eggs were a rare treat in prison and well coveted, as they were easily concealed when leaving the dining hall and good for trade on the yard.

Everything was money in prison. Food, cigarettes, drugs, cash, stamps, envelopes, even state-issued medical cotton blankets, as they are much more comfortable than the standard rough wool. Tobacco, now outlawed in prison, sells for more than marijuana. Heroin was a close third. The most valued item in prison is a cell phone and charger. Some inmates were even keeping up with their Facebook page from their prison cell thanks to new iPhones and mini computers. E-mail and unmonitored phone calls provided inmates the ability to mastermind drug deals, as well as reach out to the streets when needed.

Officers were always tossing the cell looking for the electronic devices as they were being made to look like fools on the prison blog sites by the inmates. On occasion, Jake would overhear the officers discussing the blog sites, naming them and alleging all manner of foul play. Here the inmates were given a forum to make their grievances known or just rant. Occasionally, the information posted would lead to an arrest of a crooked cop bringing in drugs and contraband for money.

"Three minutes!" a loud voice announced as Jake was mopping up the last of the oatmeal from his tray. Inmates were being excused to take their tray, first to the trashcan for a three-tap offload, and then to the tray cart where they stacked their now empty tray and marched in a line to exit the dining hall. Jake took time to study the larger-than-life painting covering the dining hall walls as he walked to exit the building. He had always been amazed at the painted walls in the San Quentin south dining hall. He heard that, should San Quentin ever close, the painted walls would be shipped to the Smithsonian Institute for their historical value. Each of the four dining halls was painted by the same inmate in the 1960s and depicts different stories of California.

What is known only to a few is that the artist inmate who painted the murals also included hidden messages and optical illusions in each of the painted walls. Jake liked to watch the airplane follow him from one end of the dining hall to the other, turning as he walked, always pointing forward and never leaving his sight. Jake also noticed the opiate poppy field and the demon that held this painter prisoner and took his life away.

As the last of the fourth tier exited the dining hall, they made their way slowly back across the concrete yard beneath the screaming gulls, who bombed them like fighter pilots attacking enemy boats entering protected waters.

NINE

When back at West Block, the inmates climbed four flights of stairs and returned to their cells. Jake studied the officer on the gun rail and made mental notes of his actions—or lack thereof—and what distraction seemed to catch his attention.

On the first tier was a rather attractive female officer, Summerfield, standing behind the desk near the public address system and phone. Inmates were approaching her in a line to request a trust withdraw slip or a sick call slip, mostly to get a better look at her tight jumpsuit uniform. Her beauty also seemed to hold the attention of the gunman as he was leaning over the rail undressing her with his lustful eyes.

Jake passed by cells on the tier and noticed everything from drugs being sold to an in-cell assault taking place right under the nose of this unsuspecting gunman. Jake would remember the name of the lazy officer: R. Armstrong. If ever he had a chance to get away with something, it may as well be in the presence of Officer R. Armstrong. Not all of the cops in this hellhole were as clueless as Armstrong. Jake also made note of the very alert and impressive officers who actually took pride in doing their job well. On more than one occasion, Jake had observed Officer Avery save an inmate's life.

Jake stepped into his cell and the tier officer walked by and spiked the door locked. Jake sat on his bunk, pulled the egg from his pocket, and began to peel the shell and toss it into the toilet. When he finished, he removed the packets of salt and pepper from his pocket and opened them both with one bite of his teeth. He sprinkled the salt and pepper on the egg and took a bite; without looking, he repeated the seasoning and finished it. He picked up the coverless paperback book on his bunk and began to read.

The man in black fled across the desert and the gunslinger followed . . . Jake went on reading until sleep took him and he escaped into another world deep inside his mind.

TEN

In his dream, Jake was home with Teresa, and happy to hold her in his arms. She was kissing his face and rubbing herself against his leg. He was excited beyond all love when something shook him. He jumped to his feet and saw a dark shadow move across their bedroom towards the bathroom. As he went for his gun in the nightstand drawer, he felt pain on the top of his head and warm blood pouring down his forehead before all went black. He awoke with Teresa's name on his lips. Jake, dazed and in pain, found himself handcuffed in a hospital bed. Here he was met by two Sonoma County detectives who showed him pictures of his beautiful wife, bloody and hacked into pieces. At the sight of this he screamed: "NO! No! No! No! No!"

Now he was awake in his cell, sweating in his bunk at San Quentin, trying to remember what had happened and why he was in this awful dungeon. When he collected himself, he pushed the disturbing memories from his head and drifted back to an unrestful slumber. This nightmare would repeat itself at least once a day, torturing Jake with turmoil resulting in sleeplessness.

ELEVEN

Jake was again awakened to the sound of his cell door being un-spiked. He sat up and noticed the same female officer that he had seen handing out inmate forms earlier, escorting an inmate.

"This is you," she said while motioning for the inmate to enter Jake's cell. A man with shoulder-length hair, about twenty-five years of age, standing about six feet tall, with a medium build, entered Jake's cell.

"Name's Stephen," the man said, and extended his hand to Jake.

"Jake Stanton," Jake replied as he shook his hand.

Jake assisted Stephen with his belongings, including the fish kit containing tooth powder, a toothbrush with half of the handle cut off to discourage repurposing as a weapon, two sheets, one wool blanket, and some hand soap.

Once the men were inside the cell, the female officer locked the door. Jake reached over and pushed on the light so Stephen could make up the top bunk. Jake lay back down on the lower bunk and went back to reading *The Dark Tower: Volume 1—The Gunslinger.*

"Good book?" Stephen asked.

"So far," said Jake.

"It's the first of the Gunslinger series by Stephen King. I'm a big King fan but never read any of the Gunslinger series," Jake said.

"I have read them all," Stephen replied. "I am so pissed at King because of how he ended the series I can't stand it."

"Oh yeah? Well, don't tell me how it ends, I'm kinda getting attached to this Roland character, although he just let my namesake die," Jake continued. "The boy, Jake, in the book just said, 'Go ahead then, there are other worlds than these,' and Roland let him fall into the abyss," Jake explained. "I'm almost done with this book, then I want to get the next volume."

"If you like the first, you will love the next book," said Stephen. "It's called *The Drawing of the Three*, then *The Wastelands*, then *Wizard and Glass*. Like I said, I have read them all."

"That is one positive thing about doing time. It will make a man take the time to read a book," Jake added, remembering his childhood and the hundreds of books he'd consumed until he became distracted by life at age fourteen and stopped reading altogether.

"Violation?" Stephen said in a questioning manner.

"Negative," Jake said.

"I'm three years into a life sentence. Just lost my latest appeal and doomed to repeat reception center here at Quentin."

"Yikes!" Stephen exclaimed.

"That explains why we are in the same cell. I just got three strikes."

"Wow, sucks to be us, eh?" Jake smirked, and peeked over the pages he was reading to add a sardonic look in Stephen's direction, just in time to meet him returning the same.

"Couple of unlucky coconuts about to join the all-male society where you always want to remember, never drop the soap in the shower," Stephen said. Jake smiled. The two talked all afternoon and most of the night.

There was an instant connection between them that was remarkable and unexplainable. It was as if they had known each other all of their lives. Jake listened to Stephen tell of his fall from grace behind his need to be rich and famous. He thought robbing banks was the fastest way to get ahead in this world. After all, "That's where the money is," Stephen explained.

"I would have got away with it too, if only I'd left the state. Instead, I lingered to meet up with a girlfriend and the cops were waiting at her house.

When it was Jake's turn to tell of why he was in prison, he started by saying, "I'm innocent. I'm here because it was easier to convict me than to find the true killer of my wife, Teresa." Jake's eyes welled up as he told the story of his beautiful wife being murdered and him not being able to protect her.

"I'm haunted daily by her ghost." His voice was shaking and cracked as he continued. "I was found, unconscious, in my home, with her blood on me."

Jake drifted back beyond that fatal night to the part of his life that was good and as close to normal as he had ever been.

TWELVE

Jake told how he'd met Teresa in high school. When he first looked into her blue eyes with doe-like lashes, Jake knew what it meant to drown in someone's eyes. Her twin sister, Sherri, was every bit as sweet as Teresa and beautiful but looked different to Jake, even though they were identical. Jake was in love; he could not imagine being any luckier than the moment she accepted his first date invitation to the homecoming dance at Healdsburg High School. And on that October night, under a full moon, after the game against Cardinal Newman, in his 1972 Dodge Polara, Jake kissed Teresa for the first time. If ever there was a soul mate for anyone, he had found his. She was soft and hot under his touch. She wanted him, and he came alive. He could feel his muscles tighten under her small hands, and their embrace made them one breath and one person.

Jake was a different man when he was with Teresa. She became his reason to live and he, hers. He stopped smoking and attended church with her every Sunday. They took long rides on his motorcycle, stopping in small towns for lunch. They would talk about what their dream home would look like in the foothills of Sonoma County. Teresa's family owned a horse ranch near Windsor and she barrel raced in rodeos at least once a month. Jake sat on the fence taking pictures and watching her ride.

On weekends they sometimes took her horses on rides to Lake Sonoma in the green valley of Sonoma County. On some occasions they would bring a blanket, a packed lunch, and fishing poles. They'd lay on the blanket looking up at the blue sky while their horses cropped grass nearby, and planned their lives together. A dream could not have been better.

After high school, Teresa went to college at UC Davis to study medicine, and Jake went on to earn his general contractor license like his father, who was now a building inspector. They were married on a beach in Maui, and planned on having children once she completed her internship and became a doctor. Jake was building custom homes in the hills of Marin County, catering to the rich; at the same time, he was building their dream home in the oak-covered foothills of Santa Rosa.

Jake designed the house on five acres of green hills in an elite Santa Rosa subdivision called Loch Haven. The estate included a four-stable barn and a large workshop. The home was completed in the winter of 2003, and Teresa and Jake moved in under clouds of rain. They spent the first night on the floor in front of the fireplace in the family room lit with candles.

***

Six months had passed, and they were putting the finishing touches on the home furnishings when everything went wrong. Evil invaded their lives and darkness fell upon them.

THIRTEEN

Jake told Stephen the whole story. "The spring wind was blowing the night air through the open window of the master bedroom where Teresa and I were making love. I heard a sound and jumped to my feet. I saw a shadow moving across the room toward the bathroom and remembered going for my loaded Ruger 9mm I kept in the nightstand drawer. I was struck over the head, and everything went black. I woke up handcuffed to a hospital bed three days later, with a concussion and nineteen stitches in my dome."

Stephen noticed how hard it was for Jake to tell of his beloved's gruesome death. Jake's voice cracked and his eyes held standing tears as he continued.

"The killer, or killers, knocked me over the head and covered me in blood before dialing 9-1-1. It was the kind of thing you would see on *20/20* or *60 Minutes*, only this time, the husband is innocent." Now a single tear traced the cheek of Jake. "I loved my wife and would never put hands on her. But the evidence against me was overwhelming. I was spared the death penalty by the grace of God and because my in-laws knew I would rather die than harm their daughter. To me it appeared only the prosecutor and the jury were against me." Jake rubbed his eyes with the heels of his hands and sighed.

"Anyway, here I sit after three years of appeals, back in West Block at San Quentin, waiting to be endorsed and released to the main line." Stephen sat back against the wall facing Jake, listening to the sad story and reflecting on the pain in Jake's voice and face.

FOURTEEN

"Good night, my brown brothers!" shouted the shot caller for the Northern Structure on the back bar of the tier. And so went the nightly shut-down call that caused the general roar in the housing unit to quiet. Jake thought it strange, how everything in prison seemed to be about respect; it was so overstated, considering most of the inmates were locked up for some form of disrespect. Nevertheless, it was just another anomaly to the never-ending strangeness of living in prison.

FIFTEEN

"Jake, do you play chess?" Stephen asked.

"Not very well, but I'll give it a shot," Jake said. The two played chess and talked the night away, growing as close as brothers.

The next day was more or less a repeat of the last, with an announcement blaring over the West Block public address system. "Good morning, campers, time to rise and shine for the morning meal. Today's menu includes pancakes, sausage, a side of eggs, and that life-giving coffee San Quentin is famous for, yum, yum, gotta have it!" yelled the fat, goofy-looking Officer DeVito, who was much more a clown than a peace officer. He always wore the CDC windbreaker and baseball cap, even inside on hot days. One would think he never washed the jacket by the sweat-stained rings near the arms and the odor that followed him like Pigpen's dust cloud in a Charlie Brown cartoon. His ball cap covered a balding head with stringy hair cropped at his neck growing in a horseshoe shape.

"Release the back bar!" he yelled into the microphone. The big steel bar slowly moved and the doors slammed open with a bang.

Jake and Stephen moved onto the tier and walked to the dining hall along with the rest of the orange mob. Jake noticed Officer Armstrong on the gun rail and caught him peering down on Officer Summerfield, the same female officer who had escorted Stephen to his cell the week before. As usual, Armstrong was asleep at the wheel. Jake watched as inmates were mugged, drugs were sold, and cells were robbed under this lazy gunman's nose. The days turned into weeks and weeks into months, and they both remained in West Block.

SIXTEEN

"Jake, you ever think about getting out of here?" Stephen asked.

"All the time," Jake said. "I think we will likely be getting out this month and released to the general population," he continued.

"No, not out of West Block, you bonehead, out of prison!" Stephen said.

"I know what you meant," Jake smiled. "I was making a joke. I know you hear me talking in my sleep; it wakes me up sometimes. I'm always thinking of getting out of prison. I feel I'm supposed to do something other than time in this dungeon, and lately, I think I'm supposed to be doing something with you."

"Ahhh, the dreams. You have been having dreams, eh?" Stephen looked into Jake's eyes.

"Yes," he said. "You too?" Jake asked.

"No, the dreams are for you, and the time is coming when you will know why the dreams were necessary," Stephen said, eyes never leaving Jake's.

Jake thought, *I must be talking a lot in my sleep; how else would he know about the dreams?*

SEVENTEEN

Jake lay on the bunk with the mirror attached to the tightly rolled paper arm, allowing him to view the officers' station on the first tier. He could see three officers and two inmates in the reflection; the officers were Lindy, Summerfield, and DeVito. Lindy had an inmate on the wall spread-eagled and Summerfield was providing cover. DeVito was reclined on a tall stool leaning against the wall, pushing Cheetos into his mouth while watching the pat down. *DeVito is like a kid at a matinee*, Jake thought.

As Lindy made his way up the second leg the inmate screamed, "That's my balls, you punk!" and turned around on Lindy to retaliate for an unwanted squeeze that caused considerable pain. Summerfield took her pepper spray and sprayed the unsuspecting inmate like you might spray a cockroach with a can of Raid. DeVito jerked and his chair slipped out from under him, sending his snack into the air, creating the illusion of an orange snowstorm. Jake was reminded of the Keystone Kops as he took it all in; he laughed until tears were streaming down his cheeks. *You can't buy that kind of entertainment*, he thought. Stephen asked him what was happening and Jake took a breath and told him, and they both had a good laugh.

That night, after the evening meal, Stephen asked Jake about his dreams. Jake said, "I suppose I'm keeping you up. I don't mean to. I keep dreaming about the night I lost Teresa. I haven't been able to sleep through the night, and keep waking up in a cold sweat. I'm truly sorry if I'm waking you."

"Not at all, Jake." Stephen sat up on his elbow. "I think I know how to help you with the dreams, if you will let me try."

"What do you have in mind?" Jake asked.

Stephen reached into his pocket and brought out a gold coin on a chain. "Have you ever been hypnotized?" Stephen asked.

"As a matter of fact, I volunteered when Teresa and I were on Pier 39 in the summer of '02, but it didn't work. I was the only one in the crowd who was not quacking like a duck."

"Mind if I give it a try?" Stephen asked.

"Give it your best shot; I don't much believe in it though."

Stephen started to move the coin back and forth and told Jake to watch the coin. A moment later, Jake felt awesome; he felt more refreshed than he'd ever felt in his life.

"See, I told you," Jake said. "I just can't be put under."

Stephen smiled and put the coin back in his pocket.

"How about another game of chess?" Jake asked. Stephen got out the board and began to put the pieces in their places.

"I have been mapping the building and the prison, and noting the habits of the officers. I have noticed you doing the same, Jake. What do you think about planning an escape?" Jake could hardly believe his ears; he was not a career criminal, but even he knew one never talks about escape unless you completely trust whom you are talking to. Jake also knew for a fact that nobody trusted anybody in prison.

"God knows I hate this place and I sure do not want to spend the rest of my life here," Jake said.

"You don't have to," Stephen replied. "You can come with me if you wish." Jake looked into Stephen's eyes; he was dead serious.

He means to escape, and now he has invited me to join him! Jake thought. "Let's do it," Jake said after a long pause. "But how?"

"Let me worry about that, my friend," Stephen said. The two were moving chess pieces, killing opponents with incredible speed; one would take the other as fast as they could reach and make a move. The game ended with Stephen in checkmate three minutes after the game started. Stephen smiled.

"I have a plan. For now, let's get some sleep. Bay Side has yard tomorrow. I want to show you something there."

Jake lay awake for a long time thinking about what Stephen had said. He tried to think of the last successful prison break he had heard of. He had trouble coming up with anything other than the series on the Discovery Channel: *"I Almost Got Away with it."* The key word was *almost*; but what did he have to lose? He was serving a life sentence for something he had not done. He may as well be guilty of something if he was going to do the time.

EIGHTEEN

It was almost dawn when Jake fell asleep and traveled back into Dreamland, where he could still hold his Teresa. They were on horses this time, riding to the lake; he could almost taste the jasmine in the air as they rode in the hot summer sun. It was so real; he knew he was dreaming, but he seemed in complete control and completely awake, almost as if he were having an out-of-body experience, like when he was about to fight Billy Parson. Whatever it was, he was far from prison and with his soul mate.

"Chow release in West Block!" It was DeVito, waking up the unit with his smartass remarks over the loudspeaker. Jake was yanked from Teresa's arms and pulled into DeVitoland for another bland, awful meal.

NINETEEN

After the meal, Stephen and Jake walked to the fence facing the San Francisco Bay and looked out at the Larkspur Ferry speeding to the city. The boat held tourists standing on the upper deck with their cameras and binoculars looking at the inmates, much as one would view animals in a zoo. San Quentin was historic; however, the cameras were pointing at the inmates gawking back at the boat like monkeys in a cage. Some of the inmates returned waves from the crowd on the boat and others whistled at the females, who were little more than a frame of a person in the distance. Jake laughed in his head as he watched the inmates making gang signs to the women on the boat; they somehow believed that they were cool and the women wanted them. *What idiots*, Jake thought.

"That's our ticket out," Stephen said. "Hope you like boats."

Jake looked at the large boat cutting into the water and shrugged. "Sure thing, Stephen, whatever you say. Only that boat is on the other side of the fence with the razor wire and gun towers with sharpshooters," Jake said with a sarcastic tone. "Oh yeah, and there is that little thing called clothes and, oh yeah, a boat ticket," Jake continued.

"Oh, ye of little faith," Stephen said, looking back at the boat. "That's what makes it a challenge. If it were easy, what fun would that be?" The two locked eyes and smiled.

"Hey, I'm up for whatever you have in mind. After that breakfast, I'm willing to risk anything," Jake said, poking his fingers through the fence. Relaxing his arms, he stared into the city beyond the boat and bay.

TWENTY

Jake walked over to the part of the yard reserved for the white inmates and began his workout with Stephen standing behind him, his arms folded. This was how cellmates watched each other's back on the prison yard. Jake would return the favor for Stephen when it was his turn to put his face to the concrete ground and exercise to remain strong and capable.

The yard can be a dangerous place in prison. Jake remembered when he first arrived and made the mistake of doing some pushups in the corner of yard belonging to the Northern Hispanic inmates. It resulted in three white inmates beating him with a lock in a sock, nearly taking out his right eye. A hard lesson to learn and a mistake he would never make again. He was lucky the whites disciplined him with the lock in a sock. If the Hispanics did it, they would have used a blade, and likely would have done permanent damage.

There was no orientation by inmates or second chances when walking the prison yard. If you chose to learn by doing, you were likely to learn the hard way. Prison lessons were quickly learned and not soon forgotten. Jake had witnessed his share of killings for things as small as losing a bet on a football game and failing to pay up in a timely manner.

The biggest problem was, you never knew whom you could trust and for how long. Jake had seen cellmates in a gang live together for months, and for a reason often never revealed, one was told to kill the other. Failure to follow orders was a death sentence. How many times did the place go on lockdown over stupid housecleaning by gang leaders? It was really something to see. If a gang member was caught with an informational kite (small note), he was certain to be punished by the others. Sometimes it was a simple three-on-one beating, but other times it was a razor to the throat and bleeding out while whistles were blowing and officers were running. At any rate, the prospect of living his life in this place was not appealing.

TWENTY-ONE

Jake and Stephen followed their tier back into West Block for yard recall. Once back in the cell, Jake shivered from his arms to his scalp at the thought of escaping with Stephen. Just to dream of one day being free was a reason to sleep. And sleep he did. For the first time in what seemed like ages, Jake slept, with Stephen over his head. Jake had had cellmates in the past but had never slept deeply. Trust was everything, and for some reason, Jake trusted Stephen. He could not explain why this guy was different; he just felt peaceful, and knew Stephen was a true friend. And in this place, that was something you rarely found.

Chapter II

The Awakening

ONE

Jake woke to a light flashing in his eyes at about 2:00 a.m. The rookie, Officer Lindy, was conducting his count and trying out the new mini mag light he'd just bought. Jake made a mental note of this, as normally the cops simply walked by the cell and briefly paused with the lights out. Lindy was doing it right. He was counting living, breathing flesh.

Jake heard Stephen breathing steadily and rolled over to return to the blissful dream of not being in prison when he heard Stephen.

"You awake, Jake?" he whispered.

"Yeah, Lindy's new toy just beamed me in the eyes," Jake replied.

"I know, where did he get that lightsaber? It blinded me when he hit me," Stephen whispered.

"Yikes, that would do it, I felt the heat," Jake replied.

"I want to show you something, but I have to dismount to do it," Stephen said.

"What's up?"

"Did you see the gun rail officer tonight?" Stephen asked.

"Yes, I did, but I didn't catch his name. Who is he?" Jake asked.

"His name is D. Tower," Stephen said, jumping to the floor in his socks and making a muffled thump on the hard concrete. Jake sat up in bed opposite Stephen.

"Jake, do you trust me?" Stephen asked. "I mean, do you really trust me?" Jake looked puzzled as he took in Stephen's expression.

"I guess so," Jake said. "Why?"

With a slight uncertain tone in his voice, he whispered, "Because I need to put my hand on your forehead for a moment and I don't want you to freak out."

"OK, I'm starting to freak out, Stephen. Why do you think you need to touch me?"

Jake, a certified heterosexual, took a little pride in being able to identify homosexuals; in his prison time, he had been approached on more than one occasion by a lonely cellmate who asked him if he swings that way. Jake was quick to let it be known he prefers women and has no interest in experimenting. Jake had nothing against them, providing they kept it to themselves; more to the point, providing they did not touch him. He was relatively certain Stephen was not a homosexual; however, prison will do strange things to a man over time. More than one straight man turned to the other side once locked up for a few years, and after all, they were good friends. *And now he wants to touch me,* Jake thought.

"It's not what you think. I just need to show you something," Stephen whispered.

Jake heard himself say, "OK, go ahead."

Stephen put his hand on Jake's forehead, much like a preacher at a halleluiah healing revival. Jake felt gooseflesh climb up his legs to his head and back down again. Then, without warning, Jake felt something else, something he had never felt before; it was as if someone had dumped a bucket of warm honey—that's right, honey—over his head, and it was slowly dripping down his face and the back of his neck until it covered his whole body. Something was in him, something was around him, something was holding him, and he could not move.

But Jake didn't want to move. He was submerged in a warm feeling of peace, like Christmas morning as a child. It was a feeling of safety and delight, like being in the arms of Teresa, feeling loved and held, and the tingling sensation of pleasure all at the same time. Stephen pulled away with a sudden stroke and collapsed exhausted, drained of all energy; his arms and legs were like lumps of clay. Jake's eyes were closed and he had tears pouring down his face. After a long pause, Jake opened his eyes as the feeling faded.

"What did you do?" Jake asked. "What happened to me?"

"I woke you up from your slumber," Stephen said. "I wanted you to know who you really are."

Jake looked at Stephen for a long time. He noticed something different about him. He could see a glowing light above his head and tried to determine where it was coming from. *Is it a reflection from the tier light? Is the moon shining in the cell and reflecting off the heavy gloss paint on the wall? What is it?* Jake thought. Jake rubbed his eyes with the palms of his hands. He looked again; while the light was blurred, it was still there, glowing like a bulb coming from nowhere. Suddenly, he noticed the gunman walking by on the gun rail following the counting officer, Lindy, who was likely on the fifth tier by now. Jake noticed the same type of glow above his head, only the color was green, not white, like the glow over Stephen's head.

"OK, so what kind of acid trip is this?" Jake asked. Stephen was now sitting up with his back to the steel bars on the cell door with the white glow shining over his head.

"No drugs," Stephen said. "What can you see? A glowing light above my head? Kinda like a halo?" Stephen asked.

"Yes," Jake said, pausing, "that is exactly what I'm seeing. What is going on?"

"Have you ever read the Bible, or gone to Sunday school, Jake?" Stephen asked, looking into eyes filled with disbelief.

"Yes," Jake said. "I'm familiar with the Bible and I completed six years of Sunday school, but I have never seen or heard of anything like this before."

"The book of Genesis, chapter six, talks about the 'Sons of God considering the women of the land finding them fair, and they laid with them and behold Giants walked the earth.' Do you recall?" Stephen questioned.

"As a matter of fact, I do recall that section, and I always wondered what that meant," Jake replied.

"Well, the descendants of those Giants are still here on earth," Stephen explained, "and some of them make up a subculture in league with evil, while others are from the holy bloodline aligned with God—"

"Wait a minute," Jake interrupted. "Are you trying to tell me you are a descendent of an Angel?" Jake was wide-eyed and looked frightened.

"Actually, I'm trying to explain that *you* are a descendent of an Angel, Jake. I assumed you had already put it together that I'm a Shaddai when you checked out my halo," Stephen said with a half-smile.

Jake's stomach was doing backflips. As he turned towards the wall, he saw the white glow over his own head in the mirror. His hands went for it at once and only passed through the air, feeling nothing.

"Oh, you can't touch it, and try not to look so crazy. You and I are the only ones here who can see it, and it will only appear at night." Stephen's smile was becoming more pronounced.

"I'm an Angel?"

"Not exactly, Jake. You are descended from an Angel, but mostly you are a human from the holy bloodline of Seth, son of Adam, God's first creation." Stephen continued, "We are both descendants of the same bloodline. I was assigned to you at birth and have watched you grow up; well, at least most of your life," Stephen said, looking as peaceful as a shepherd caring for a lamb.

"I was born in 1827, and was about your age when I learned who I was. I was awakened by my guardian, David," Stephen explained.

Jake's face turned white; his brow dropped and he looked angry. "Where were you when Teresa was killed? Why did you let her die?" Jake said with a grim look and shallow tone. "If you are my guardian, where were you when I needed you most?"

"Jake, I was there when this terrible thing happened in your life. I was alerted when the killers turned to finish you and by the grace of God was there to save you before the killers took your life. There are limits to what I can do, as you will soon learn, and there are dangers still facing you even now, in this prison. In case you have not noticed, I'm just as locked up as you are. I don't have the power to make the doors fly open and allow us to walk away. It is by the grace of God that I was allowed to wake you, and by his grace we will escape this place." Jake relaxed his anger and looked at the floor. "There is a plan and a purpose for all that happens," Stephen said. "You will come to understand this, and it will make you strong."

***

The officer on the gun rail passed another time. "Do you see the color of the glow above Officer Tower?" Stephen asked. "It's green, the color of the fallen, the damned. He is the enemy, only he doesn't know it, just as you didn't know you were Shaddai."

"But how?" Jake asked. "The Bible speaks of God destroying the earth with a flood and all the wicked died in the waters. How was the blood of evil allowed to escape the flood?" Before Stephen could answer, Jake followed his question with the conclusion, "All of Noah's sons were from the line of Seth."

Stephen explained, "The blood of the Nephilim was in Ham's wife. She carried the line through the deadly flood. The wife of Japheth also carried angelic blood from Semyaza, and we are her descendants." Understanding started to seep into Jake's mind.

Stephen continued, "Look at the glow over Officer Tower with the corners of your eyes, but don't look at it directly." Stephen looked very serious as he explained this to Jake.

"There are others in this place, and one who knows who you are. We must avoid him and escape before he can stop us and hinder our mission."

"Mission? What mission?" Jake looked confused; his eyebrows moved as high as they had ever been on his head. "I'm sorry," Jake said, "I'm still trying to get my mind around this. I have known you for less than three months, and I hear you talking about escape, then you tell me I'm a descendent of an Angel. I have been housed with some nut jobs on psych meds in the past; one even told me he was from another planet, so give me a moment to think about this."

"I'm not a nut job, Jake, and you know it," Stephen said. Jake did know it; however, it seemed appropriate to point out the obvious, if for no other reason than to buy some time to adjust to this bombshell. In fact, ever since the hallelujah forehead push, he'd felt something going on in his mind and in his body; a knowing, a peace that he finally knew why he felt so out of place all his life.

He was awakening to his purpose on this earth. Suddenly, he wondered how he was able to stand not knowing all these years. There was also something else: he knew Teresa was in a better place, not a mythical mansion in the clouds like you may hear in a Sunday sermon or at a fake funeral; but a knowing, an actual knowing that she was alive and living. Her earthly body, while beautiful, was of little consequence, because it was only a holding shell of her spirit and soul. Teresa's true beauty lived on, in a real place, with green meadows and tall trees, majestic mountains, and even horses. A true dream home, paradise, where peace and love dwell, where family and loved ones who have passed on live in harmony together in a wonderful town or city by a blue ocean. Jake knew in his heart of hearts that life was good where she was. Jake could feel the tears in his eyes as this was made known to him. He fell to his knees and gave thanks. Stephen placed his hand on Jake's back as he wept.

The night passed, and not another word was spoken between them. However, they were communicating all night; Jake with his many questions, and Stephen with his all-knowing answers. It was hours before Jake realized he was not moving his mouth and sound was not emanating from his body. Rather, they were communicating telepathically. Jake heard Stephen's voice as though he was speaking aloud as he sent his voice through the air but it could only be heard by him and Stephen. Stephen eventually told Jake to get some rest, as they had much to discuss in the morning. They fell asleep.

TWO

In his dream, the moon was the color of burnt orange and hung very low in the sky. Jake was at home, in the bedroom. Teresa stirred and jumped out of bed and turned on the light. The shadow disappeared. Teresa ran to Jake and embraced him. Jake stood in shock as the dream—or nightmare—was changing. She covered his face with kisses and he could feel the tears wet on his chest as she hugged him. Teresa held him tight; this was no dream. He was here, this was real.

Teresa took him by the hand and walked him from the bedroom into a kitchen. The house was different; it resembled their place at Loch Haven but was larger. Teresa started the coffee maker. "I miss you, Jake. I miss you so much."

"Is this a dream?" Jake asked. "It feels so real!"

"It's real," Teresa said. "I'm here, we are talking. Ask me anything and I will answer. I have always been here, and now finally after three years you can see me. It seems an eternity!"

"I'm sorry, Teresa. I'm sorry I was not there for you. I'm sorry they hurt you. I'm so sorry," Jake said in a shaking voice.

"Jake," Teresa said, "you have to stop blaming yourself for what was out of your control. You could do nothing for me on that night as we were attacked by monsters, actual monsters, who are pure evil. My body was killed but I felt nothing; no pain, no fear. I was taken by Michael before my body was touched. Nothing they did to me caused me pain except leaving you behind. I'm safe now; I'm with your family."

"My family?"

She smiled, and Jake relaxed. "Your other family, a bloodline not known to you when we met. Life is not what we thought, Jacob." She was the only one who could get away with using his Christian name, other than his mother. "You are special, and you will soon learn what I mean by special. I'm at peace. We can be together again, and it's not like any dream you have ever known." Teresa walked around the kitchen and pushed up on her toes to reach two cups that hung on the wall. She poured the coffee and smiled her glowing smile that removed all the fear from Jake's heart and made him feel strong. She kissed his cheek where the tears were tracing lines in his face. He closed his eyes, feeling safe.

"Am I really here with you?" he asked, holding her tight. "If so, I never want to wake up. I want to stay with you forever."

"I'm always here," Teresa said. "And we can be together whenever you want." She looked him in those ice-blue eyes. "You and Stephen have a mission to complete." Jake was surprised at the way she was talking. *How did she know about Stephen?* "They will try to destroy you and they are getting closer by the day." *This is crazy,* Jake thought. But deep inside he was starting to accept it and it was not crazy, it was destiny—his destiny—and he knew it.

***

When Jake awoke, he felt like a different person. He shook Stephen awake and they got dressed. Stephen smiled at the sight of knowing on Jake's face. Today they were moving to North Block, the general population, and among new dangers.

Chapter III

Reaping Minds

ONE

Jake and Stephen stood with four other inmates in the West Block yard with their property and bedding rolled into a bundle, awaiting the escort that would take them to North Block. Officer DeVito crossed the yard to the line of inmates near the rotunda doors.

"OK, roll call," DeVito said. "Sound off and give me your CDCR number when I call your name. Dashane."

"E-44628," the tall, dark, and ugly cowboy-looking inmate answered.

"Dearborn."

"D-55323," the short black inmate answered.

"Stross."

"E-12516," Stephen said. As their names were called, the inmates picked up their bundles and stepped into a single-file line. Officer DeVito escorted the inmates through the South Block rotunda doors and then on the upper yard towards North Block.

The column marched along in a single-file line carrying their bedrolls containing all the property they possessed. As they passed the upper yard shack near the canteen, Jake noticed a tall inmate being escorted toward the legal law library with a green glowing light above his head. Later he would learn this was Richard Ramirez, also known as the "Night Stalker." The officer escorting the inmate held the handcuffs while two other officers— one with an MK forty-six pepper spray aimed directly at the inmate's head and the other with a forty-millimeter launcher—conducted the escort as if they expected the Night Stalker to spring from his cuffs and disembowel them at any moment. Jake tried to view the halo with the

45

corners of his eyes as Stephen instructed; however, he caught himself looking directly at the glowing light. It was compelling.

"Escort!" Officer DeVito yelled, and four inmates who were walking in their direction stopped and turned to face the wall as the column marched past. When the group reached the North Block rotunda, Officer DeVito instructed them to wait against the wall as he opened the great steel door leading into North Block. An attractive black female officer by the name of Leone took the paperwork from DeVito. She conducted another roll call to ensure that her paperwork matched the inmates coming from West Block. She handed each inmate a new copy of the California Code of Regulations Title 15, as well as the North Block rules and policies. She then introduced the North Block inmate clerk, Rusty.

Rusty began his orientation speech. He explained the program in the unit and told them when the phones would be available, when they could use the showers, and when they would go to the lower yard or library. As Rusty talked, other inmates pushing large laundry bins were taking sizes and providing each inmate their clothing allotment. Both Jake and Stephen were given two towels, three pairs of blue denim pants and shirts, seven pairs of socks, seven pairs of white boxer shorts, seven T-shirts, and one pair of boots. In addition, each inmate was handed a thick, gray winter coat and a set of bright-yellow rain gear that when properly donned would create a Gorton's fisherman look. All of the clothing was marked CDCR Prisoner. It was nice to climb out of the orange pumpkin suits and into some real pants for a change. *It's amazing what you take for granted, the simple things*, Jake thought. The counselor schedule was posted on the wall and assigned to the inmates via the last two digits of their CDCR number. Both Stephen and Jake were assigned to Counselor Lewis.

TWO

"Stross and Stanton!" called Officer Leone. "You are in four north fifty-three. Take it to your cell and the tier officer will lock you up. Don't be anywhere except in front of your cell or you will be out of bounds, understood?"

"Yes, ma'am," Jake answered. Stephen and Jake walked up the four flights of stairs to the fourth tier. On the yard side of the unit were cells marked one through fifty, and on the Adjustment Center (AC) side were cells marked fifty-one through one hundred. The AC side of the unit was usually reserved for inmates who were on C-status or refused to work. This was not the case with Stephen and Jake; they simply had not been assigned a job yet. Nevertheless, they were housed with mostly non-program inmates.

As Stephen and Jake arrived at their assigned cell, they were met by Officer Spearman, a tall, thin black officer who could have made a living as a standup comic. Spearman was always making jokes and had everyone around him laughing.

"Welcome to the Ritz," Spearman said while demonstrating to Jake and Stephen a small bow, as if he were a doorman in an expensive hotel, holding open their cell door. "Would you care to see the room service menu?" Jake and Stephen smiled as they entered the cell and the door was locked behind them. Jake noticed a slightly different odor in the housing unit; also, it was not quite as loud as West Block. This unit was not as rowdy. Sure, it had a significant hum of white noise, but compared to West Block, it was like night and day. As Jake started to place his bedroll on the lower bunk, he stopped.

"I suppose we should flip for the lower bunk, or perhaps I should yield to your age and sleep on top," Jake said with a smile.

"Nonsense," Stephen said as he placed his bedding on the top bunk. "The last thing I want is to get comfortable in this place. You sleep on the lower as usual." The two began making their bunks up and placing their clothing in the shelving units, along with their shaving supplies and a few snack items they had purchased at the institutional canteen. Jake placed the photo of Teresa, his beloved, in the springs above his head so he could look at her when he lay down.

Once settled in their new cell, the questions began again. Jake could feel himself evolving inside and he wanted to understand what was happening. Stephen explained that the Angel bloodline was both good and evil. "We are made of body, soul, and spirit," Stephen said. "The soul is cherished by God and coveted by Lucifer, or the devil, also known by many other names, like the Prince of Darkness, Morning Star, or Son of Dawn. His disciples included fallen Angels like Zoltar, Loki, Azrael, and many others. Their creed included the opposite of God, our Father, and is based in wrath, greed, sloth, pride, lust, envy, and gluttony—the seven deadly sins. The prophets tell us of the end of the world, but after the end, the real battle begins."

Jake looked intrigued as Stephen explained, "Armageddon is the earthly battle that destroys mankind. The battle of the heavens is one led by God's army and his saints. We are in that number, Jake, and you have something special to offer."

"Why me? What is so special about me?" Jake asked.

"Everyone is special, Jake, but you hold the key to the location of the Sword of Goliath," Stephen said. "When you have awakened to a level of comprehension, you will know where the enchanted weapon is located." Jake's intrigue was turning into all-out curiosity. "That's why they want you," Stephen continued. "Zoltar and his followers will try to enter and read the secrets of your mind. We must be careful he gets nothing. The enemy is everywhere, so we also must be careful not to wake them up by mistake."

Jake looked concerned. "By mistake?"

"You remember how I woke you up, Jake?"

"How could I forget," Jake replied.

"Well, that is like tossing a cup of ice water in a sleeping man's face. Even the heaviest sleeper will usually spring awake." Jake smiled. "As we use our powers, or even look at their halo, we are shaking them, and run the risk of waking them up," Stephen explained.

"We must be on our guard and be careful not to wake the evil in our midst who are descendants of the Grigori. You would know these things as time goes on, even if I didn't tell you." Stephen looked deep into Jake's ice-blue eyes. "I see the light behind your eyes, and soon you will have the power to visit the Crossing. This will amaze you beyond everything I have told you."

THREE

"Chow release in North Block!" the voice called over the public address system. The door swung open, and Stephen and Jake stepped out of the cell wearing their new gray jackets. They started down the stairs, following the other inmates to the north dining hall. As they entered the dining hall they could see how the inmates segregated themselves when allowed to sit wherever they wanted. After collecting their trays, they stood for a moment, looking around, then moved near the white inmates' tables and sat together at a table meant for four.

"Not as bad as Reception, eh?" Jake mentioned as he cut the Salisbury steak lookalike and sampled some instant potatoes with a half-smile on his face. Stephen returned the smile and gave thanks to God for the food. Following the meal, they headed for the lower yard.

FOUR

The sun was almost gone and burning red against the low clouds beyond the fog line over the wall on the lower yard. Stephen and Jake walked down the concrete stairway leading to the blacktop near the receiving and release section of the prison. On the left was the gymnasium, currently used as a dorm to house about three hundred overflow reception center inmates. In front of the gym was the handball court. Beyond that was the basketball court, then the dirt track and patches of grass making up the lower yard. Jake and Stephen walked beside the 150-year-old brick building and stood on a six-foot-by-four-foot rusty sheet of steel with hinges on one side and a lock hasp on the other.

"Where is the lock?" Jake asked. Stephen looked around to ensure the wall post officers were not paying special attention to them and said, "It has been missing for years. Inmates and officers have walked and stood where we are now and for some strange reason, never noticed the missing lock." Stephen put his foot on the edge of the steel cover and attempted to lift it with the rim of his boot. The steel cover rose slowly and then returned to the closed position as he removed his foot. *"Perhaps they simply didn't know this steel cover is all that stands between us and a tunnel to the bay,"* Stephen said without moving his lips or making a sound. Jake grinned as he realized they were again communicating telepathically. *"We must leave at night,"* Stephen said, *"after the last count and when the prison is on first watch status. That's when we'll have the best chance for success."*

"I agree," said Jake. *"We'll have a better chance with fewer staff. However, during that watch we'll have been counted and locked up inside our cell. How, pray tell, do you expect us to get out?"*

"I'm working on it," Stephen said. *"For now, we plot and plan inside our minds and keep it all confidential."*

FIVE

The men sat on a three-foot brick wall overlooking the lower yard. Four pigeons were milling about, getting close and cooing for a snack. Stephen rolled his tongue and whistled what sounded like perfect San Quentin pigeon dialect. A rusty white pigeon walked to Stephen and climbed onto his boot. Stephen quickly picked up the bird and with lightning speed, attached a small note to his leg with a rubber band. Then he said something to the bird and turned it loose. The bird circled three times, gaining altitude, and flew south towards San Francisco. "What was that?" asked Jake.

"That was a message to friends in the city. From now on we must live as if every movement is being watched and protect our thoughts, lest the enemy invade our minds."

"Invade our minds?" Jake questioned. "What do you mean, invade our minds?"

Stephen looked at Jake and noticed the sincere wonderment on his face. "Jake, my apologies. Sometimes I forget you don't fully understand who you are. It will likely be weeks before you have even a fundamental understanding of the change that is taking place in your mind and spirit." Stephen regarded Jake with a comforting look. "Our powers allow us to read the thoughts of others. This act is called *reaping*, and is a craft for Shaddai. Nevertheless, evil descendants of the Grigori can also master this ability. Therefore, we must be on guard lest others with the power reap our thoughts. Moreover, the craft of sowing thoughts by planting suggestions in our minds is to be avoided at all cost." Jake's face assumed an understanding expression. "To be on your guard, you must plant a thought in your mind that will warn you of onlookers. I have chosen my memory of David waking me as the guardian of my mind. When attempts to reap my thoughts occur, he appears to warn me and keep me safe. I recommend you choose a memory that you trust as the guardian of your mind; anything from this moment on will be suspect as a planted thought. I can help if you wish."

Jake shook his head. "I have already chosen my memory and guardian, and the safeguard is in place."

"A wise choice," Stephen said. "She would never allow harm to enter or expose you to danger. I expect you have met with her in your dreams as well?" Stephen asked.

"How did you know?" Jake replied.

"Like I said, you will understand the fundamentals in a short time." Stephen put a hand on Jake's shoulder. "She has told you of the place she is in, a paradise, unlike you can imagine." Jake nodded. "She is with your family, your bloodline that has crossed over, and is available to you when you dream. They can help you from where they are, but they are unable to enter earth, just as you are not able to ascend beyond the Crossing while in your body." Stephen dropped to his haunches and picked up a small twig and started making symbols in the dirt.

"You will have a difficult time distinguishing reality from dream, and I caution you not to lose yourself in your dreams, as your dreams are a doorway to another place. Not the final place, only a visiting area." Stephen made a loop under two straight lines with the twig.

"There are other doorways for our kind leading to places of old. We are not completely human, and therefore can still enter the garden where the tree of life and the tree of the knowledge of good and evil grow side by side. The garden is guarded by an Angel with a flaming sword. This is the symbol of our bloodline," Stephen said, pointing to his drawing of two lines with a loop under and three dots on top, resembling a type of brand not unlike the type used to mark cattle or other livestock.

"This symbol will mark the path to the doorways I speak of." Once Jake had a good look, Stephen scratched the drawing from the earth. Jake noticed inmates on the yard looking in their direction and talking to each other.

A group of about eight white inmates approached Jake and Stephen from across the yard. Stephen reached out in a reaping technique to a large, bald inmate in an attempt to make contact with his mind. Two of the inmates were followed by a glowing green light above their head. "They mean to talk to us, my friend."

"I know," said Stephen. "They will be asking for our paperwork to ensure we are not sex offenders or snitches. Did you bring your 128-g with you?"

"Never leave home without it. What about the two Grigori in the group?" Jake asked.

"Just don't look at the halo and block your thoughts from them, and they will be none the wiser. They are still asleep to who or what they are," Stephen replied.

"Welcome, brothers," the large, bald inmate said as he approached. Jake caught himself checking out the tattoos covering this man from head to belly, including a pair of devil horns above his shaven eyebrows and three teardrops from his left eye. The six other inmates took positions as if they were performing a rehearsed ritual. Two stepped up on the stainless steel seats at the yard table, establishing an elevated position. The others posted to the four directions with their backs to the conversation.

"Thanks for the greeting," Jake said. "Something we can help you with?"

"I'm Tiny," the enormous walking tattoo said. "I have the keys to North Block and the lower yard for the woods. Where you from?"

"Sonoma County," Jake said. "But I guess you already knew that. I showed my 'g' to your partner in West Block."

Tiny smiled, revealing his missing front incisor. "That was West Block. I'm checking papers for the main line. So if you want to walk this yard, I need to see your

53

paperwork." Stephen took out the goldenrod paper from his shirt pocket. It was the inmate copy of a CDCR 128-g that included his case factors and sentence. Jake did the same. As Tiny looked at the two reports, his expression resembled a Titanic survivor who watched from the lifeboat as the ship sank. "Oh crap," Tiny said with his shaved eyebrows raised. "You're both doing all day, eh?" Stephen and Jake maintained their posture. "Sorry to see that. Anything you need from now on goes through me; drugs, smokes, cell phone, bets, protection, etcetera. Understood?"

"Like you said," Jake responded, "we're doing all day. I expect nothing from you or your friends and will not be using drugs or anything that may aggravate my sentence. I'm trying to get my points down to a low level and my privileges up to a high level, so I shall ask for nothing and promise nothing. I will show respect and expect the same."

Jake looked into Tiny's green eyes.

"That just about sums it up for both of us," Stephen added.

Tiny's grin evaporated. "Understood," he said, then turned to walk away. The short inmate with a green glow above his head who was standing on one of the seats jumped down next to Jake. "You two got balls the size of coconuts. I'm surprised you can walk," he said in a hushed voice before following the rest of the group across the grass to the area reserved for white inmates only.

"What did you learn from reaping their thoughts?" Jake asked.

"It was small potatoes. Our friend, Tiny, is very worried he is going to be attacked by his own crew. He has made some judgment calls for the woods that have proved to be less than popular. His organization thinks he has grown weak and lazy, so they intend to take him out."

54

"Where did you get that from?" asked Jake.

"The other Grigori in the group; the tall, strong-looking fella. He has a piece in his sock and is waiting for the order to take out Tiny. When it comes, he must rush at him and stab as long as he can. He must withstand pepper spray, and can only stop after the second shot is fired from the gunman. If he stops before the second shot is fired, he will be in the hat himself." Jake looked amazed.

"So you were able to reap the mind of both Tiny and this other guy during that short interaction?" Jake asked.

"Jake, I entered all eight men's minds, and planted thoughts in Tiny's mind. He left thinking we were juiced in with the folks at Pelican Bay."

"Holy . . . ahhh . . . holy," said Jake. "That was remarkable. Perhaps our plan to escape will be easier than I thought."

"Don't count on it, Jake. When we use our powers, we interrupt the continuity of the energy around us and it leaves a kinda signature footprint, if you will, and footprints can be tracked." Stephen looked back at the white group who were still checking them out.

SIX

"Yard recall!" the voice announced over the loudspeaker. They moved toward North Block. Once in their cell, they made ready for shower release. "Shower release on four!" the great voice bellowed. Jake and Stephen had their towels ready and moved quickly toward the showers when the bar moved and their cell opened. As with the yard and the dining hall, each race had a number of showerheads specifically for them. Jake and Stephen stood and waited for their turn to hop under the water and scrub for a few minutes. Officer Spearman was up on the fourth tier yelling down almost as soon as they arrived.

"Get closer to the water, fellows! They will move! The closer you get, the more they will move!" Jake and Stephen rinsed, wrapped their towels around themselves, and walked back to their cell and finished dressing.

Jake asked, "So how do we know which Shaddai are awake and which ones are asleep? I'm awake and I'm able to see the halos, but I have no idea if they see mine."

"Oh, but you already know, Jake. Just like you know I'm awake and can bear witness with my spirit, so you will know them by their spirit." Immediately, Jake knew exactly what Stephen was saying. The halo over Stephen was much brighter than the ones over the others and he could discern his awakened spirit.

"So far we have seen only sleeping Grigori, and most will die in their sleep," Stephen said.

SEVEN

"Good night, my brown brothers!" a loud inmate voice announced. The tier shutdown had begun. "We'll talk more later," Stephen said. He took Jake's mirror attached to the long paper sleeve and looked down the tier. He could see fish lines going in and out of the cells. Attached to the lines were notes and tobacco. Stephen pulled the mirror in and closed his eyes.

Chapter IV

North Block Pecker Woods

ONE

That night, Jake's dream took him to a place on the coastline that looked similar to a place where he and Teresa would vacation. He was here, standing on a cliff holding Teresa, and remembering everything.

"I'm sure I will never get used to how real my dreams have become," Jake said. They kissed as the sun melted into the ocean with flaming colors that can only be realized in dreams. They were not camping this time but staying at a resort called The Inn at the Tides. The room was enormous, with open-beam knotty-pine cathedral ceilings, three bedrooms, two bathrooms, and a hot tub in the center of the great room. Jake was amazed at the detail. That night they dined on seafood at the five-star restaurant in the hotel, with a view of the under-ocean aquarium.

"I never want to leave, Teresa," Jake said, holding her hands across the table. "This is heaven to me. To be with you in this beautiful place, what more could a man ask?"

"It's nice, Jake, but nothing like paradise. I cannot describe how peaceful it is where I am and do it justice. I'm so happy to be with you and will stay with you as long as you wish, but where I am is perfect, and only missing you." He took a moment to swim in her blue eyes. "I'm so sorry they put you in prison, my sweet. It must be awful."

"Who did it, Teresa?"

Teresa recalled the night they were attacked. "I remember you getting up and I looked into the eyes of the one they call Borackus. I was so afraid. Suddenly, I was pulled from my body and taken to a bright mansion, where Michael told me I was safe. It's hard to explain, but I felt like I was coming home, and the love from everyone was so real. The only pain I felt was losing you. Michael told me you were from a very special bloodline and born to help defeat the evil ones." Tears began to well in her eyes. "I wish I had the answers you need," she said.

"You have everything I need," Jake replied. They walked to their room and made love in the large tub, and then again on the bed before drifting off to sleep in each other's arms.

TWO

The next morning, Teresa and Jake walked to the cliffs where they could watch the ocean together. "We have to talk, Jake," Stephen said as he walked along the path tracing the cliff and approaching them.

"I'm dreaming you, right?" Jake said.

Stephen smiled. "Yes and no. We're asleep in our cell at San Quentin, but we're both here as well. Hello, Teresa."

"I'm sorry," Jake interrupted. "Do you know each other?"

"Yes," Teresa said.

"How is that possible?" asked Jake.

"It's that whole body, mind, and spirit thing we talked about. Our bodies are at San Quentin, but our minds and spirits are right here, right now, and time is different here. We can spend days here and only moments will have passed in our cell. I have known Teresa for years," Stephen said with a smile. "When she was taken by Michael, we had a lot of time to get to know each other. She has been a big help in planning the escape we'll undertake." Jake was amazed as Stephen told of this place and again felt understanding growing inside him.

"We have some time now, Jake," Stephen said, "so let's get you up to speed. I know you have tons of questions; however, even as you sleep, you are awakening to who you are and what our purpose is."

Jake looked at Teresa. "Go ahead, I will be here whenever you wish," Teresa said, holding both of his hands.

"Wait a minute," Jake said. "This is *my* dream. Shouldn't I get to direct what we do?"

Stephen gave Jake that over the horizon look. "How do you know you are not in *my* dream?"

"I guess I don't," Jake said. But he did understand, and knew this was where he belonged. Never had he felt this way before. Never had he been so sure about anything in his life. Teresa kissed him and disappeared.

THREE

"Jake, you should know what powers come with awakening," Stephen began. "You understand the reaping craft, and you have the telekinetic patterns down cold. But some things are for us alone, and even your beloved is not to know." Stephen went to his haunches and Jake did the same. "Our bloodline are warriors," Stephen said. "When the Almighty directs us, we act without question. You will feel a quickening, a call to arms, and you will become his hand, so you must master the weapons of the Shaddai. The sword, the bow, the dagger, and the sling are the weapons we use, as well as hand-to-hand combat."

Jake produced a half-smile. "The weapons are a bit primitive, don't you think? What good is a bow or sling or even a sword against guns, bombs, and rockets?" Jake asked.

"Funny you should ask. When I mentioned the weapons of the Shaddai, I was not referring to the garden variety version of a sword or even a sling." Stephen reached into his hip pocket and drew out a leather sling. He then gathered three stones about the size of golf balls and loaded one of the stones into the sling. With the same lightning speed as Jake had witnessed once before with the pigeon, Stephen sent the stone in the direction of a pile of rocks on the cliff about three hundred yards away. There was a bright light and a roar of thunder on impact, carving out a section of the mountain about the size of a football field. When the dust settled, Jake was standing, mouth open, and physically shaken.

"What was that?" Jake exclaimed. "Is it because we're in Dreamland?"

"No, my friend. This is a small sample of the power of the Shaddai," Stephen explained. "The explosion you witnessed was mild compared to a war throw. It's not the stone but the energy directed—with God's purpose—that destroyed the target." Jake looked amazed. "This craft is learned, as was the telepathy. You will do fine," Stephen said as he handed the sling and remaining two stones to Jake.

Jake loaded the sling and raised it over his head as he witnessed Stephen do. When he let go, the stone flew toward the ocean and splashed about fifty yards out, making about the same splash as a golf ball might. There was no explosion; it did not even go in the direction he was aiming.

"Again," Stephen said with authority. "This time, remember who you are and He that sends you."

Jake felt the quickening, much as he did before the fight with Billy Parson in the eighth grade. He loaded the sling again. When he released the stone it took flight twice as fast and far as the one Stephen had tossed. The impact was devastating; the thunder crack shook the earth and carved the mountain from the cliff, pushing it into the ocean. Jake could feel the smile washing across his face as he looked at Stephen, who was now wearing a look of surprise.

They practiced for what seemed like weeks. "When do we go back?" Jake asked. "Will our bodies even be living after such a long time?"

"Let me show you something," Stephen said.

FOUR

Jake felt someone shaking him, saying his name. "Jake, wake up." He opened his eyes. He was in his cell. Stephen was standing over him, smiling, and turning his watch sideways, showing the time and date, 11:30 p.m., Friday, October 21, 2006.

"What?" Jake said. "We have been sleeping for two hours? We were in Dreamland for weeks it seems."

"I told you," Stephen said. "Time is different in dreams. Go back to sleep." Jake rolled over and in less than a minute he was fast asleep and standing next to Stephen on what resembled the California coastline. This time they were near a ranch house with a large barn. Above the entrance of the barn door, burned into the wood, were two lines with a curve underneath them and three dots above them. "We have much to do," Stephen said, and walked into the barn, with Jake following. In the barn was a large padded boxing ring and hanging punching bags, as well as multiple weapons hanging on the walls. On one side were different-looking swords positioned in accordance with their length. The opposite wall held a number of different-looking bows, and hundreds of arrows of all sizes. The barn had a sitting area with a picnic-style table made of high-gloss knotty pine. A cooler sat on the table containing a six-pack of Budweiser on ice. Stephen tossed a beer to Jake. "Enjoy, my friend. We're about to spend some time training you for what we'll encounter when Zoltar's servants locate us in North Block." Jake twisted the top from the ice-cold beer bottle. As he drank, he could not believe how wonderful it felt going down his throat. It was as if he was experiencing this sensation for the first time and loving it.

"Ahhh," Jake sighed as he put the beer on the table. "I could get used to this."

Stephen gave Jake a look of compassion and understanding. "Soon you will realize our full purpose.

Enjoy these moments and cherish them, for we're destined to battle incredible evil and before we're done, your faith will be tested."

"Stephen, something has been on my mind," Jake said. "You are about a hundred and sixty years old, only you don't look a day over twenty-five. How does that work?"

"The garden, Jake. It's where we must get to when first we leave the prison," Stephen said. "Now that you are awake, you are aging more quickly than you did while you slept. In the garden is a tree. The tree of life has the fruit that will arrest the aging process. I have eaten the fruit and remain twenty five in the flesh and appearance. You, on the other hand, must get to the tree in the next six months or you will age to death."

"How do we get to this garden?" Jake asked.

"We must escape the prison, then travel to a secret place under Chinatown in San Francisco."

Jake took another long drink from the bottle and set it down on the table. "Are you ready to discuss the plan to get out of the cell?" Jake asked.

"I have been receiving what I assume are signals you are sending me. You have determined that Armstrong is on the North Block gun rail on Thursday and Friday, third watch. We both know he is asleep at the wheel. We could do whatever we need to and he would not be the wiser," Stephen said.

"Agreed," Jake nodded. "I'm trying to come up with the plan to get out of the cell undetected. Ideas?"

"We dig," Stephen said. "We must dig in the rear of the cell that opens to the plumbing chase. From there we climb to the roof, then down the wall to the lower yard and into the tunnel. From there we're out to the bay and onto the Larkspur Ferry before the morning meal." Stephen smacked his hands together as if to dust them off.

Jake looked confused. "Dig? The cell is made of concrete and steel. How will we dig through that?"

Stephen tossed Jake another beer. "Well, my friend, we're about to join the hobby craft and we'll be allowed tools in our cell. Thick paint is covering walls that have grown weak from years of salt air and fog, so the digging will be much easier than you think. We must make some false heads so we can get past the evening counts, providing we go on a night when we know Officer Lindy is not working. We should be able to get past the counts."

Jake looked hopeful. "You really have planned this out, haven't you?" he said.

"Actually the plan was finalized by Teresa, your beloved. She told me how you are somewhat of an artist and could create the false heads, and even place a painting over the hole we'll be digging in the rear of the cell." Jake felt more confident than ever they would be able to pull it off.

FIVE

"Early morning unlock in North Block!" the voice announced. The nightmare began. Jake was rising to another day in San Quentin. Today he and Stephen were starting their new jobs and would be apart for the first time in months; more than months, if you count the many weeks they'd spent at the Crossing. Time was different there, but the miserable ten hours they were in San Quentin during the day was like an eternity in hell.

"No time for feeling sorry for yourself, Jake. Today you start work in the laundry," a voice said in his head. It was not Stephen, but it was familiar, someone from his past. It was the voice of his grandfather, Aaron, who had died when Jake he was nineteen. He remembered the funeral, looking at his dead grandfather in the coffin and thinking, *Why did you leave me?* Jake heard the voice then say, *"I will never leave you."* It was the father of his mother who carried the bloodline. Jake's father never

knew and his mother never knew the Angelic bloodline was from Aaron. Aaron was awake. *He was the one who pulled me from the freezing water when we were fishing at the pier in San Francisco. I called him while I was underwater and he heard me, and saved me.* Jake was suddenly remembering everything, and now it all made sense to him.

"Stanton," the officer said, who held the pass for Jake listing his new job assignment. "You Stanton?"

"Yes," Jake stood up.

"Last two"

"Seventy-six," Jake replied, and the officer opened the door. Stephen had already reported to his assignment in the barber shop so Jake was on his own. "Here is your pass. Don't lose it. Give it to your supervisor in the laundry. You can go to early morning chow if you want, but be at the laundry at 0800 hours or it will be a write up," the officer said as he shut the cell door.

Jake made his way down the stairs and heard the voice again, *"Be on your guard, Jake, you are in danger."*

Jake reached out to Stephen. *"You there?"*

"Always," Stephen replied.

"I'm hearing the voice of my grandfather, Aaron. He is telling me to be on my guard," Jake said.

"Then do it," Stephen commanded. *"Your grandfather has crossed over, however, he is our bloodline, and will help you to pay attention,"* Stephen explained. *"Teresa is available to you in dreams and can guard your memories, but Aaron can speak to you directly at any time, as can I. So when he speaks, you should listen."*

"Thank you, my friend," Jake said. *"How is the new assignment?"*

"I'm learning to cut hair. So far I have only had to cut them to a bald head. I'm a little nervous that someone will ask me to take a little off the top," Stephen said.

"Good luck with that," Jake laughed.

SIX

Jake made his way across the lower yard through the fog to the large locked doors at the rear of the building marked LAUNDRY. Jake knocked on the door; there was no response. He stood with his back to the building, looking at other inmates walking through the fog across the lower yard to their assignments. Three inmates were approaching him; Jake felt a quickening, and the hair on the back of his neck was standing on end. He reached out with the reaping technique and heard voices.

"Who the hell is this jerk?"

"Better not even speak to me."

"Ahhh, fresh meat."

"Come on, baby, we can get it on in the towel section."

"That's him. That's the one Zoltar said to look out for."

Jake took a breath; he felt gooseflesh climb his neck. *This guy knows Zoltar,* Jake thought. *I have to disrupt his thought process.* Jake decided to plant some thoughts of his own. He concentrated and projected his thoughts: *"That is the fool who killed Coulter White in a knife fight at Pelican Bay . . . That is the fool who killed Coulter White in a knife fight at Pelican Bay . . . That is the fool who killed Coulter White in a knife fight at Pelican Bay . . . That is not the one Zoltar is looking for . . ."*

"What's up?" the largest of the three inmates said to Jake. *This is the one who knows Zoltar, and maybe even me,* Jake thought. "Just waiting to start my new job," Jake said.

"My name's Jones, everyone calls me Slowpoke."

"Stanton," Jake responded, and accepted the extended hand and shook it.

"Where you from?" asked Slowpoke.

"Sonoma County," Jake replied.

Slowpoke looked Jake up and down. "Did we do time together?" he asked.

"Not sure," Jake said. "I have been up and down the state, did a SHU term at the bay, so it's possible," Jake said. The eyes widened of all three inmates and they were visibly impressed with Jake.

"Let me show you what you will be doing," Slowpoke said. "I have been in Laundry for two years. Our supervisor is a cool dude, lets us kick back once our work is done. You'll like it here." Jake could hardly believe this was the same guy who was just thinking he was the one Zoltar was looking for. *He seems like a nice guy*, Jake thought.

"*On your guard!*" his grandfather's voice said again. Jake shook his head and continued meeting the rest of his new work crew, including the one they called Sweet Cheeks, a homosexual transgender black inmate with breasts. A Filipino staff member named Umba showed up in a truck.

"There's the boss," Slowpoke said.

Jake was put to work sorting a mountain of smelly laundry. He was placing the colors in a pile and the whites in a pile, then Sweet Cheeks would collect his piles and put them in the machine. Jake worked for hours without making much of a dent in the pile as the truck kept bringing in more smelly laundry and adding to the mountain.

SEVEN

"You there, Jake?" Stephen called.

"Right here, buddy," Jake said, while he kept on working.

"Just had my first unhappy customer," Stephen continued. *"I carved a few ruts in his hair with the clippers so he will likely not be on our fan list, but that's not why I called. I have spotted a Grigori who is tracking you."*

"What?" Jake exclaimed. *"How bad is it?"*

"Not as bad as it could be. He is a reception center inmate, so he is out of our reach," Stephen said. *"He was under escort to West Block. I held back so he didn't know I saw anything. He was trying to contact an inmate named Borackus and I picked up on his footprints."*

"Understood," Jake responded.

"I have heard of Borackus," Stephen said. *"I think he works in the kitchen, on the reception side. He will likely be endorsed to the main line soon, Jake."*

"Good work," Jake said. *"I too have had an encounter with one who may know Zoltar."*

"Ahhh, you mean Slowpoke," Stephen said with some excitement in his message.

"You are good," Jake said. *"Thanks for looking out for me. See you back at the cell."*

EIGHT

As the occupants of four north fifty-four arrived back at their cell, they noticed they had visitors: two officers were inside their cell searching everything. Jake and

Stephen stepped back and stood about one cell down as the larger of the officers exited the cell. "Get comfortable, fellas," the officer said. "We're gonna be here a while." Jake noticed that the security squad officers in their cell wore a slightly different uniform, with green and black patches on their shoulders. *Did they know something about the plan to escape? It would be bad to be separated from Stephen, and worse to be shipped to a higher security facility. What was it Stephen told me? I have six months to get to the tree of life.* Jake started to sweat.

"Try not to look so nervous, Jake," Stephen said. *"This is why we keep our plan in our head and never take notes."* Suddenly a loud buzzing noise sounded from the building next door.

"Alarm in the AC!" a voice said over the radio on the officer's belt, then over the loudspeaker: "Alarm in the AC! Alarm in the AC!" Both officers bolted out of the cell and past Jake and Stephen, then ran down the stairs in response to the alarm. Stephen and Jake entered their cell and began the long process of cleaning up the mess. The picture on the rear wall remained in place and untouched, a nice oil painting Jake did of the ranch house near the cliffs on the California coastline, the sun melting into the ocean on the horizon. Had it been moved, the security squad officers would have seen the paint scraped off the wall and a very small hole.

"We caught a break," Jake said. "What if they come back?"

Stephen smiled that shepherd-like smile and said, "Have a little faith, Jake. We are the good guys, remember?"

Jake smiled back. "You're right, Stephen, we're the good guys. Thanks." They continued cleaning the mess left by the search, including pouring the shampoo back into the bottle from the plastic baggie; the officer had done this to see if anything was hidden inside.

NINE

Because they were now working and had a privilege card, Jake and Stephen were allowed to shower with the kitchen workers. "Way better than showering with the tier, eh?" Jake said to Stephen as he was drying off from a leisurely twenty-minute shower.

"Ahhh, yes," Stephen said as he was dressing for the evening meal. They returned to their cell, which was now left unlocked during times of movement. Jake had purchased a combination lock that would remain on the cell door while they were out. "Tonight is Thursday, so Armstrong will be on the gun rail. We should be able to get some work done on the rear wall," Stephen said.

"Hope so. He has called in sick the last two weeks and Tower has worked overtime. He is alert and on his J-O-B," Jake said as they tossed their shower rolls in the cell and locked the cell door before heading for the north dining hall for the evening meal.

TEN

As Jake and Stephen walked out the North Block rotunda, they could see six inmates moving towards Tiny from behind. The tall inmate with the shank walked alongside Tiny and put his arm around him as if they were long-lost friends. As Tiny reacted and stepped away, the tall inmate pounced on Tiny and started stabbing him in the kidneys, back, and neck area, over and over. Blood was spraying from the neck wound. Tiny shrieked and screamed, and the nearby pigeons took flight. The loud buzzing alarm sounded and then: "Get down! Get down!" was heard over the speaker. Stephen and Jake dropped to a prone position and watched as the responding officers sprayed what looked like a garden hose portion of pepper spray at the stabbing inmate, but he didn't slow down; he kept stabbing, again and again. Then the thunder crack of the big gun above their heads went off; still the inmate rose and fell, stabbing big Tiny with every stroke. Again the gun cracked, and smoke was rising among the inmates trying to move away from the incident. Only after the second shot did the inmate toss the knife and prone out. Tiny pitched forward and hit the blacktop dead, the last of his blood pumping from the severed artery on his neck. He died with a look of confusion on his face, eyes open as if to say, "Wait, just wait, let me explain." But he had breathed his last breath as leader of the woods. By now, the medical unit was near and the security squad officers were placing the tall assassin in handcuffs. Jake and Stephen watched as the medical staff rolled Tiny into the Stokes litter and lifted him into the medical vehicle.

ELEVEN

It was two hours before Jake and Stephen were escorted back to their cell. "We knew he was going to stab Tiny. Should we have warned him?" Jake asked.

"It would have made no difference," Stephen said. "He would have been just as dead, only we would have to explain why we knew he was going to get hit. Likely they would have thought we were in on it."

Jake raised his eyebrows. "Yeah, you're right. How would we know he was about to get stabbed?" Stephen agreed. "What now?" Jake asked.

"We're on lockdown until they investigate. Tonight we get to work on the rear wall." He pointed to the gun rail with his chin. There was sloppy Armstrong, sitting on the chair with a newspaper to his face, his gun sitting on the chair next to him.

"He's not even wearing his gun," Jake said.

"I know, let's get some work done." They took out their tools, including the case-hardened leather tools and the hammer that went with them, and started chiseling the hole larger. The in-cell TV was loud enough to cover the noise but the toilet flushing was even better. They filled it with dirt and busted concrete and flushed it away.

Within a few hours they had a hole they could put their head through.

"That's enough for tonight," Stephen said. "Let's get some rest."

Chapter V

The Enemy

ONE

Jake was exhausted. He was asleep when his head hit the pillow. He longed for Teresa, to hold her, kiss her, and love her. He knew she was a call away in his sleep. However, he found himself standing on the cliff on the coast alone this time. He was looking down at the waves breaking against the rocks and marveling at the beauty, the salt air in his face, and the breeze that carried the familiar aroma of seaside star jasmine. Then he felt the presence of the Good Shepherd, standing beside him and taking his hand. He wanted to look up and see his face, but for some reason he could not stop looking at the waves crashing and splashing against the rocks below.

"Do you trust me, Jake?" His voice was gentle, as if caring for a newborn lamb. Jake tried to swallow but could not; the rocks looked smaller now. "Do you trust me, Jake?" he said again.

"Of course I do, Lord," Jake answered. He continued to look down and noticed he was about ten feet above the ground, floating in the air. Jake was astonished at the sight of his boots hanging above the ground and felt the smile wash across his face.

"Do you trust me, Jake?" he said again. Suddenly, Jake felt the wind in his hair and the ground was no longer ten feet down, it was like he was looking out from an airplane.

"I trust you, Lord," Jake said. Then he was released. He was falling, faster and faster. The ground was rushing up to him at an incredible speed. Jake extended his arms but they were not arms at all, they were wings, and he was not a man, he was an eagle. He was not falling, but soaring!

He climbed higher and higher, and heard the voice say, "Behold, my child, in whom I am well pleased." That feeling of love was in and around him like when Stephen first put his hand on his forehead and awakened him.

"I'm your servant, Lord, and will obey." Jake soared towards the cliff and then up again through the clouds. As he dipped and rose, he remembered his life and what it felt like to trust and be trusted. He was prepared to lay down his life for his cause. A feeling of purpose and direction consumed him. Thunder crashed, and he was back on the ground standing on the cliff, looking down at the waves smashing against the rocks. The hand that took his hand now was all too familiar; it was his love, Teresa. He held her in his arms, kissing her passionately. When they parted she looked up at him; she could see the tears in his eyes. "I missed you," he said.

"And I, you, my love," she replied.

TWO

Jake awoke in the ranch house alone in bed. He was refreshed, rested, and restored. He could smell bacon cooking and could hear Stephen talking to Teresa. But he heard more, another voice; it was the voice of his grandfather. Jake recognized the pipe tobacco smell as his grandfather's brand. He got dressed and joined them in the great room next to the kitchen. Stephen was sitting on a bar stool and his grandfather, Aaron, was sitting in the recliner, puffing his pipe. Jake went to him and hugged him.

"Grandfather, you're here!" When Jake knew him in life, he had been missing his right leg from above the knee due to a diabetic amputation. Now both legs were whole.

"Hello, Jake," Aaron said.

"Your leg!" Jake marveled.

"Yes, I'm all here," Aaron said.

"It was so nice to hear your voice, but to see you . . ." Jake said, smiling. "Teresa, you know my grandfather?"

"I do," she answered. "He and I—and the others—have talked much about you, Jake."

Jake looked at Teresa. "Others?"

Teresa poured coffee. "Your family who have crossed over are many. Your uncle John and aunt Julie visit me often. Also your cousin Ronald."

Jake smiled. "Ronald? Wow, I can't wait to see them!"

"And you shall, Jake," Stephen said. "Most of our bloodline crossed over while still asleep in their knowledge of Shaddai, having never known who or where they came from."

Jake put his arm around Teresa.

"Can I talk to you, Jake?" Aaron asked as he got to his feet.

"Of course, Grandfather," Jake said.

"Let's take a drive." They walked out the back door.

Teresa said good-bye on the back deck with a kiss. "She tastes like a peach, Grandfather," Jake said as he got into the passenger side of the red pickup truck and rolled down the window. Jake was amazed. *This was the truck, the same old 1965 Chevy he gave my mom when I was a kid,* he thought.

Jake waved to Stephen and Teresa, who were both standing on the back deck of the ranch house, or home, as he had come to know it. The house and ranch were on about fifty acres of beautiful land in the outer foothills of Bodega Village, the small town they visited on occasion. Stephen and Teresa were still waving as Aaron and Jake headed down the dirt road and out of sight. Jake noticed a pack on the seat and opened it enough to see some breakfast sandwiches inside. He also noticed the fishing poles and folding chairs in the back of the truck beside the tackle box.

THREE

"I miss you, Jake," Aaron said. "It's so good to see you again. Now that you know where you come from, I can visit you, but I fear for you," Aaron said in a concerned voice. "You have a difficult task ahead of you. Escaping that dungeon is only the beginning of a very dangerous path. The enemy you will face is pure evil. I'm here to let you know, you don't have to continue." Jake turned and looked at his grandfather. "This is your opportunity to go back," Aaron said

"Go back?" Jake asked.

"Not back to prison," Aaron said, "but back to your life with Teresa."

Jake looked confused. "What are you saying? I can go back?"

"God always gives us a way out when we choose to follow him. Your test was when you were taken high and asked if you trust him. Without hesitation or fear you answered with trust; even when you were falling to the earth, you trusted him. As you spread your arms, they became wings. God will provide you a different path, one that is not quite as exciting sometimes, but one of relative peace. He will never force us to follow him. Inasmuch as you are awake now, you can be put to rest again and live a long life."

Jake listened to his grandfather; he knew he was telling him this for a reason. "Grandfather, you mean I can return to my life with Teresa, before the nightmare started?"

Aaron looked into Jake's eyes. "With God, all things are possible," he said. "God always gives us a choice."

Jake scratched his head, then his hand went to the side of his jaw, a habit he picked up from being around Stephen. "What would happen to you and Stephen?" Jake asked.

Aaron pulled up to the lake near some large oak trees and parked. The place was beautiful, with the green grass, wildflowers growing randomly in the fields, and the smoky mist lifting from the perfectly still water on the lake. Beyond was a beautiful sunrise with orange and red clouds above the purple mountains. "We would be just fine, Jake. You can return to your life and your home. The same home you sold to pay for the legal fees during your trial."

By now they had gotten out of the truck and were setting up their fishing site with the folding chairs, blanket, and the pack of food. Aaron took his fishing pole out and began casting his croppy jig in the lake and slowly reeling it in as Jake stared into space, wondering. Jake thought, *Why would I be put through all of this only to go back?* A warm breeze blew through the leaves above them. He looked at the wild horses cropping grass in the distance and watched a flock of geese fly overhead crying their earnest adjures.

Then Jake heard the words again in the Good Shepherd's voice, "Do you trust me, Jake?" and he remembered the feeling of soaring above the ground as an eagle and the feeling of awakening to the touch of Stephen's hand on his forehead.

"I have changed, Grandfather. I'm not the same person I was," Jake began. "I'm Jacob, Grandson of Aaron, brother of Stephen from the bloodline of Seth, and I know my destiny is to stay on the path."

Aaron smiled as he casted his line again. "OK, Jake, but it will not be without its sacrifices. This was the time for you to get out; there is no turning back after this moment. Before you're through, you may view your time in prison as a walk in the park."

Suddenly the clouds blew in and covered the sunshine. An eerie darkness fell upon them. Jake saw what looked like a large man-sized bat fly across the sky. The warm breeze turned to a cold wind and the leaves above them detached and fell like dying butterflies.

FOUR

"He is here," Aaron said, and dropped the pole where he stood. Jake reached into his hip pocket and withdrew the leather sling. He selected two stones from around his feet and raised them to the sky with one hand. With his eyes closed he said, "God, grant me strength and bless the stones I hold to you." A creature landed in the lake and stood knee-deep in front of Jake. His eyes were yellow and his flesh was green. He was naked, and looked like a winged man only with bat wings instead of feathers. He grinned a set of teeth that looked filed into points, and displayed the forked tongue of a red snake. His hands were large and he had claws as fingernails. He was facing Jake, but Jake could see a tail moving behind him. In his childhood nightmares, this was the boogie man, the goblin under the bed, the beast in the dark closet waiting to devour him in his sleep; the enemy of light and destroyer of all that is good and holy.

"You should have turned back when you had the chance, pilgrim!" the creature screamed in an inhuman voice. An odor from the monster hit Jake like a 2x4 to the face. "I'm Zoltar, brother to Morning Star and Master of the Dark. Bow to me and live!"

Aaron stepped towards the creature and the monster looked at him and shrieked a sound so loud and terrifying, the energy knocked Aaron backwards into the truck and he fell to the ground. Jake loaded the sling and the monster took flight. The speed of the creature was incredible; he was like a supersonic jet breaking the sound barrier, or perhaps the crack was thunder from the dark clouds forming like a hurricane. Jake could not tell. Within seconds the monster was once again on the ground facing him, this time on a patch of mud to his left. The creature laughed.

"You are small and weak. You will never be able to stand against me." Jake looked around and could see many other shadows behind the creature. They looked like an army of monsters with swords, spears, and shields in their claws. Jake could smell the stench of rotting flesh. "I will take you apart and swallow your soul for eternity!" Zoltar screeched.

Jake stepped forward. He could feel the power of the Good Shepherd inside him. He was reminded of the day he stood up to Billy Parson in the eighth grade, and a smile appeared on his face. "You come against me in this place, with sword and spear and javelin." He remembered what young David said to Goliath, the Giant, when faced with impossible odds: "But I come against you in the name of the Lord Almighty, whom you have defied," Jake said with authority. "It's not by sword or spear that the Lord saves; for the battle is the Lord's, and he will give you into my hands!" Jake shouted.

The monster bent forward and started at him. Jake stepped to his left as a matador might step to miss the charge of the oncoming bull. His sling swirled above him and with the speed of a blink, tossed the stone. The stone lit up the darkness; the sound was as deafening as thunder crashing. The ground began to shake. The area the creature was standing on was destroyed in an explosion; only smoke and an enormous crater remained. The sun chased away the darkness as bits of ash and pieces of rotten green flesh rained down and hit the still water of the lake.

"Are you OK, Grandfather?" Jake asked.

"I am now" he said. Aaron got to his feet and dusted himself off. "I have never seen the face of Zoltar, I have only heard stories," Aaron continued. "You did good, Jake. God is with you and you displayed great courage. But we have not seen the last of Zoltar."

"He survived the explosion?" Jake asked.

"Zoltar is a fallen Angel. He can be killed, but not in a traditional way. Explosions will only temporarily stop him, as will mortal injuries that would normally kill a man. But after a time on the earth he heals himself and becomes as powerful as ever. This is why we must gather the twelve instruments. The Sword of Goliath is the one you must recover."

Jake looked bewildered. "But I don't have a clue where this sword could be," Jake said.

Aaron smiled. "Oh yes you do," he said, "and soon you will know it."

Aaron and Jake talked all afternoon. They ate the food Teresa had packed them. Jake could not get over how wonderful the food was here. They managed to catch some fish; the fish were beautiful. They looked like a cross between a large mouth bass and a rainbow trout. The smallest they took was about three pounds.

As the sun began to set, they loaded the truck and headed back to the ranch house. On the drive back, Jake looked out over the rolling, green hills covered in beautiful wildflowers and considered the confrontation he'd had with Zoltar and what his grandfather had told him about going back. He smiled. He thought about himself and Stephen back in their cell, sleeping, and wondered how much time had truly passed; ten minutes, an hour? After all, time was different here, wasn't it?

FIVE

As Aaron and Jake reached the ranch house, they saw Stephen and Teresa riding horseback near the barn. Jake and Aaron got out of the truck and walked onto the deck as the riders approached and dismounted.

"Welcome home," Teresa said as she gave Jake a loving kiss.

Stephen walked around the back of the truck and picked up the stringer of fish. "This will make a tasty supper," he said, and carried the catch to the outside sink on the deck. Jake stood beside Stephen and cleaned the fish. "What was it like?" Stephen asked. Jake looked up. "Confronting Zoltar; what was it like?"

"He tried to scare me off my path," Jake said. "I felt the Good Shepherd inside me and all my fear was abolished." Jake cut into another fish and pulled the guts from the meat. "What are Morning Star and Zoltar thinking?" he continued. "Do they really think they are a match for the Good Shepherd?"

"They stopped thinking a long time ago, Jake, when they rebelled against him and embraced evil. They are damned and full of hate. They exist to pull as many souls as possible to share the hell to which they are damned. They are kinda like a shark, a predator that must stay in motion feeding on other life to exist. To stop even long enough to think is to die," Stephen explained.

"What about their appearance?" Jake asked. "The smell and sight of them is disgusting."

"What you saw is what evil has done to them, kinda like what drugs and alcohol abuse will do to a human if left unattended." Jake remembered some shot-out drug addicts in West Block that looked sixty-five but were only twenty-eight. "Morning Star and Zoltar were part of the choir of Angels, beautiful in appearance; Lucifer was the most beautiful of all Angels." Stephen rinsed the fish and placed them on a clean cutting board. "The vile things they have become seem right to them."

"And the smell?" Jake asked.

"Corruption and evil smell the way they should, as death, rotten flesh, and dead men's bones," Stephen said.

"My grandfather said to kill an Angel, one must remove his heart or head," Jake said without looking up from the sink.

Stephen looked at Jake; he knew the comment was leading to another question and smiled. "You want to know what it would take to kill a Shaddai."

"It would help," Jake said.

"Well, like I said, we're not Angels, but we're not human, either. The sleeping Shaddai will die the death of any mortal man." Stephen looked over at Aaron, who was sitting and talking with Teresa on the deck. "But one who is awake and has eaten from the tree of life will live until he is mortally wounded from one of the twelve enchanted instruments, or the Good Shepherd decides to call him home, whichever comes first."

"You've mentioned the enchanted instruments before. What exactly are they?" Jake asked.

"Well," Stephen said, "There are twelve instruments of enchanted power which, when properly used against the Shaddai, may cause death. They also will destroy Grigori and fallen Angels. Three swords, one spear, a bow, a sling, a trumpet, a cup, a whip, a staff, a jawbone, and a dagger," Stephen explained.

"What makes the instruments so special?" Jake asked.

"The three swords were blessed and used to lead kingdoms. You recall the Sword of Goliath?"

"Yes," Jake answered.

"The other two swords are known on earth as that of King Nebuchadnezzar of Babylon, and Prime Minister Zaphnath-Paaneah, or Joseph, of Egypt."

"I see," Jake said. "So let me guess; the jawbone is the one used by Samson, the sling is the one David used against Goliath, the trumpet was used by Joshua when battling over Jericho, and the staff was the one carried by Moses when he led Israel from Egypt?"

Stephen grinned. "You did pay attention in Sunday school, very good!"

"The dagger?" Jake asked.

"It belonged to Abraham and was to be used on Isaac, his son, during a ritualistic burnt offering to God."

"Ahhh," Jake understood. "And the whip?"

"The whip," Stephen continued, "was used by the Good Shepherd to cleanse his father's temple." Stephen put his hand to his jaw. "The bow is that of Jonathan, son of King Saul and beloved brother of David," Stephen explained. "The Roman spear that pierced the Good Shepherd's heart and the cup of Christ, or Holy Grail, make up the twelve."

Jake displayed an understanding look then asked, "Do we know where the twelve instruments are now?"

"We have three of the twelve," Stephen answered. "The Sword of Nebuchadnezzar of Babylon, and the Whip of Christ. Also, we have the Dagger of Moriah, taken by Gabriel the very day Abraham's hand was stilled from slaying Isaac. Part of our quest includes finding the rest. The world has changed, and many of the bloodline have turned against the Light, having been deceived by the enemy. Zoltar and his followers are seeking the instruments as well; that is what led them to you, Jake."

Jake and Stephen entered the house and were at the kitchen sink giving the fish another rinse. "It's believed the location of the Sword of Goliath is hidden in your mind. While you were asleep, the only way Zoltar could obtain the location was through a mind extraction," Stephen explained.

"Mind extraction?" Jake asked.

"Yes, while you slept, he could simply kill you and consume your brain."

"What!" Jake exclaimed. "Did you say consume my brain, like eat it?"

"I'm afraid so, Jake. The ones who went after you in the spring of 2003 knew the general location but not the exact person who possessed the knowledge of the sword. They started with Teresa and were about to kill you when Daniel and I arrived." Jake sat down on the bar stool and rubbed his eyes with the palms of his hands. "We no sooner entered the house than they fled."

Jake looked at his boots. "So Teresa was killed because of me?" Jake said in a shaking voice.

"Jake, you must not blame yourself. This is God's plan. We walk by faith, and praise him in all things." Jake knew he was right. He also knew he had a chance to go back and had decided to press on.

He looked at Stephen. "So why don't I know where the sword is now?"

"Oh, you know, only it will take time for you to learn how to use your mind as you awaken. We could take a short-cut. I could hypnotize you and extract the location that way."

Jake laughed. "You already tried, I can't be put under, remember?"

"It's true, I have tried—and was successful. I wanted you to get some rest. I will not try again. I think we're better off to leave the location a secret for now."

"Successful?" Jake said.

"Why do you think you have been waking up so refreshed lately?" Stephen said.

SIX

"I'll get the barbeque started," Teresa said as she and Aaron entered the kitchen area.

"The fresh catch of the day should be delightful," Aaron added.

"Your grandfather told me about your encounter with Zoltar," Teresa said. "Are you all right?"

"The more I think about it, the more I think it was meant to be a simple introduction or a test of some kind," Jake said. "It was quite effective. The time had come for me to meet the boogie man that has been tormenting me my whole life."

"Not to worry, Jake," Stephen added. "We are well prepared for his kind and will finish him in due time. For now, let us not dwell on the darkness. Let's enjoy the moment with family and good food."

"Amen," Aaron said.

Teresa had prepared the table and opened a nice bottle of wine while Jake and Stephen ran the grill. Aaron puffed his pipe on the deck and looked off towards the lake where Zoltar and his disciples had confronted them. Jake liked the smell of his grandfather's pipe; it reminded him of childhood holidays. Aaron noticed a water dish and a small food dish with a lid on it. He thought it odd for a cat dish to have a lid and asked Teresa about it.

"When did you get a cat?" he asked, pointing at the dishes with his smoking pipe.

"Grandpa, you have not met Conchita?" Teresa asked.

"Is that your cat?" Aaron asked.

"Not a cat, Grandpa, a young white napped mangabey. She is an Old World monkey and is very special."

"Special?" Aaron asked.

"Yes, she has about a thirty-word vocabulary and can speak fluent sign language," Teresa explained.

"So she is a talking monkey. I have heard of such in Sion but never outside the holy city," Aaron said

"She comes from Sion, Grandpa, a gift from Michael."

Jake smiled. "A gift, that's one way of putting it. Conchita takes lots of attention and I get jealous sometimes. We both fight for attention from Teresa."

Teresa smiled and wrapped her arms around Jake. "You know there is no competition."

"Where is the little monkey?" Stephen asked.

"She is sleeping in my room," Teresa said.

"On my pillow," Jake added.

It was true; Conchita had come to love Jake's pillow. Jake assumed each day when he would awaken in San Quentin that Conchita would take over his side of the bed. Actually, she hardly took any room at all. She was a miniature mangabey and weighed about two pounds. She had tiny little fingers, small, dark-brown eyes, and oversized pointy ears. The fur on her head was soft and stood on end like an old man with a crew cut. She was quite adorable, but what made her so special was that she could say words. In her tiny little voice she could say about thirty words; some in Russian, but most in English. She could sign many other words.

Jake was astounded when he'd first met Conchita, but like everything else remarkable about being at the Crossing, he simply added it to the list of incredible phenomena.

As if she heard her name or sensed people talking about her, Conchita emerged from the bedroom. In two lightning-fast moves she jumped to the counter and then onto Jake's shoulder.

"Jake," she said in her tiny little voice, "home, home." She then kissed his cheek. Jake reached up and scratched her neck; she tilted her head and closed her eyes in enjoyment.

"Conchita, meet Grandpa," Jake said, and pointed at Aaron.

"Pa, pa," Conchita replied, and waved her little hand in a princess wave. Aaron smiled and returned the wave. Jake handed Conchita a peanut and she took it to the table to dine.

Teresa completed the table setting and Stephen brought the perfectly grilled fish to the table. They all took their seats. Aaron took Jake's hand and the hand of Stephen, who was already holding the hand of little Conchita, linking them to Teresa and Jake, for grace. Aaron gave thanks for the fish, their safe return after the confrontation with Zoltar, and the gift of seeing his grandson again. When all was said, they each said amen. Even Conchita spoke this closure to prayer, although she would have no part of the fish. Her plate contained a nice salad covered with sweet sauce and macadamia nuts. After the meal they all sat on the deck and talked about the prison and the escape plan.

Chapter VI

Count Time

ONE

Jake and Stephen were nearly finished with the hole in the rear of the cell. Jake had made two papier mâché heads with incredible likeness to their own. The hole in the rear of the cell became a wonderful hiding spot. Jake had also made a cover for the hole out of the same material, and with some soap and paint, you would never know the hole was even there. Despite this, the painting of the California coastline hung over the area as double insurance to ensure it would not be discovered. The heads were completed with hair Stephen smuggled back from his assignment at the barbershop. Because his false head would need long hair like his own tresses, Stephen found himself convincing a young inmate that his locks should go so he could get a tattoo on his scalp. The inmate agreed, so Stephen didn't have to cut his own hair, a sacrifice he would have made if the young inmate held out.

With the heads complete and the hole ready to test, Jake and Stephen decided to make the next move. They had to go through the plumbing chase and get to the roof. The only problem was that the roof door was locked. This meant they needed a key to open the lock. Jake had discovered that the locks in the prison were all marked with a number next to the keyhole. This made it easier for an officer to determine which key out of the many on their ring was the correct key for that lock.

That night, they decided to test the fake heads and go to the roof door to get the correct number. At about 10:30 p.m., after the count cleared, they made their move. Jake went first. Before going through the hole, Stephen placed the heads on their beds next to the rolled-up clothing under the blanket, creating the illusion of two sleeping inmates. Once through the hole, the painting went up and they were out of sight.

TWO

"It's dark," Jake whispered.

"Ya think?" Stephen said, then clicked on his Zippo lighter and made his way down the chase hallway. When he reached the end, he looked back at Jake and pointed up. Jake started up the ladder and could see by moonlight his way to the sixth tier. Stephen followed. They crawled on their stomachs towards the door. Stephen pointed at the officer on the upper gun rail; it was Armstrong. He was sleeping and snoring loudly. If he woke up, he would look right at them. They rounded the corner and were out of sight of the sleeping gunman.

"There's the door," Jake whispered. "Check the lock."

Stephen took out the Zippo again and lit it; N12 was the number. They waited for about an hour to pass, then went back the way they came.

Once at the entrance to the cell, they waited again until they heard the keys moving past the cell and going down the stairs. While they were on their haunches, rats were moving around their feet. One started biting Jake's boot in what seemed to be retaliation for invading their space. Jake kicked him into the concrete wall and heard him scream in pain before releasing the boot. The other rats seemed to agree they were outmatched and gave way to the strangers.

Once Stephen believed they were in the clear, he removed the painting and they climbed back into their cell.

"I hate rats," Jake said.

"Why is that?" Stephen asked.

"They are just nasty," Jake continued.

"Nasty how?" Stephen asked.

"Are you serious? They carry diseases."

Stephen smiled and looked at Jake. "Have you ever caught a disease from a rat?" Stephen asked. By now they had placed the phony heads in the hiding spot after carefully rolling them in blankets to ensure the rats didn't chew on them.

"Well, no," Jake said.

"But you hate them just the same, eh?" Now Jake started to think about it. Why did he hate rats? They'd never done anything to him, but for some reason he was repulsed by them. "Conditioning," Stephen said. "For years you were conditioned to hate rats. You didn't even see any rats but you hated them." Jake was examining his boot that was chewed on by the rat. "I tell you this because this is what the Grigori think of the Shaddai. They think we're misfits or rats," Stephen said with a serious look on his face. Jake sighed. Other than the single incident of the rat biting his boot, he had never so much as touched a rat in his life. He'd had hamsters and guinea pigs as pets when he was a child; were they not closely related to the rat? His friends even had rats as pets, and other than the giant balls they grew, he was told they make good pets.

"I never thought about it, Stephen, but you're right. I shall try to look at things differently. What about snakes?" Jake asked.

"I hate snakes," Stephen said, and they both laughed.

THREE

As they took turns rinsing in the sink, they communicated telepathically. "*So what did you think of big Armstrong on the gun rail?*" Jake asked.

"*I think he is lucky he doesn't walk in his sleep or he would likely be a bloody puddle on the cement floor,*" Stephen said.

"*I know, huh?*" Jake replied. "*We can only hope he will be on duty the night we go, and hope Spearman is our tier officer. He works a swap on first watch every Friday."*

"True, Spearman never shines his light into the cell during the counts, so he is perfect."

"What about the key?" Jake asked.

"We can try to get a copy from Officer DeVito. I'm working on a plan," Stephen said as he hopped up into his rack and folded his arms over his chest. *"He works in North Block every Tuesday and Wednesday, third watch, and he has been hinting around how he likes the way I cut heads."*

"Nice," Jake said.

"I think I could talk him into bringing the barber tools to our cell. I would give him a haircut and you can clay the key," Stephen suggested.

"I agree, that would work," Jake said.

"Get some rest, Jake, see you at the ranch." They both drifted off to sleep.

FOUR

Jake woke up in Teresa's arms. "Miss me?" Jake asked.

"Every moment you have been gone," Teresa said.

"Miss me, miss me?" Conchita said in her little voice.

"Oh yeah," Jake said, "I missed you." He scratched her neck and Conchita snuggled up to Jake, placing her head under his chin and hugging his neck. Jake hugged Conchita back.

"Can you take me to Bodega later?" Teresa asked.

"Anything for you, my dear." Jake got up and walked down the hall leading to the guest wing of the home. Conchita rode on his shoulder with her tail wrapping his neck like she was a piece of clothing. Jake knocked on the door.

"Come in," Stephen said. Jake opened the door and saw Stephen making his bed.

"Stephen home, home," Conchita said.

"Hello, little one," Stephen said.

"Dobra uothra," Conchita said.

"Ahhh, you get her Russian voice," Jake said.

The room was enormous, like the rest of the house. It contained a large sauna and tub, as well as a small weight room with free weights and an exercise bike. Stephen moved from the bed and started his workout.

"I'm taking Teresa into town later. You have plans?" Jake asked.

"As a matter of fact, yes. I would like to come along if you don't mind. I expect trouble."

Jake scratched Conchita and she closed her eyes in pleasure. "Why do you think that?" Jake asked.

"I have been picking up signals about trouble. Trust me on this one, Jake," Stephen said as he completed a set of curls with his free weights.

"You know I trust you, Stephen, and welcome your company. What about Teresa? Should she stay here?" Jake asked.

"No, I expect the trouble we'll meet is for her eyes as well," he said.

FIVE

Jake had begun to adapt to his new life here at his home on the ranch: training with Stephen, riding horses with

Teresa, and visiting family members who had crossed over. He believed he could spend eternity here and be happy. Time is so different; he would be at San Quentin for about ten hours, working in the laundry, eating in the dining hall, talking with Stephen in their cell, and when they went to bed, he was here, for weeks, eating, sleeping, living with his family and his love, like a home in a dream, only it was real. Here is where he belonged; here is where he was happy.

On most occasions, the night before he would wake up in his cell, he would dream; not like a dream he had come to know, but like he did before the awakening, the kind of dream that's hard to remember. Bits and pieces of what it was about would tug at him hours after he woke, but were too hard to put together. Jake didn't pay it much mind, as it only happened once every three weeks or so, and always the night before he would wake up in the cell.

SIX

After breakfast, Stephen and Jake, along with Teresa and little Conchita, piled into the Ford F-350 and headed for Bodega Village. The town was small, and Teresa knew most of the residents. This was where she requested to stay after meeting with Michael in the holy city. Michael explained she had crossed over and could ascend to heaven at any time. Teresa told Michael she felt she could help Jake better from here, and asked to live at the Crossing in Bodega Village. Michael agreed and provided the ranch, and even little Conchita to keep her company. He explained how she could contact others who have crossed over and how to navigate around in this new place.

Teresa had been here for years now; she had become part of the community. Uncle Lester pastored the church in Bodega Village and she saw lots of her family on Sundays when the small town held the weekly potluck. The food and company were divine; often visitors from Sion came and shared in the fair day. The festivities included outside music on the grass with flat-top guitars and stand-up basses. Jake sat in on many occasions playing guitar with his cousins like they did on the other side at family reunions, only without the drama that used to happen between relatives who seemed to fight at the drop of a hat over the stupidest things.

Time was the conversation in the truck; specifically, how little time was left to prepare for the escape from San Quentin. Jake asked Teresa what she did with herself when he was awake on the other side. She smiled. "Well, on Mondays I usually visit Sion and enjoy the music in the center square put on by the choir of Angels, and I always try to see Michael." She looked into Jake's eyes as if she was about to tell him the great secret she had been keeping, then, blinking it away she said, "Mostly, I'm on the ranch with your family; Aaron, John, Daniel, and always Conchita." Jake smiled. She looked away from Jake and took in the landscape as they drove.

What she wanted to say was, "*I go to a place where I wish you could come. I spend time with someone you really should meet. Where I go and who I am with makes up a large part of my life.*" A few times Jake tried to talk to her about this place because her eyes were telling him something, but he changed his mind. Something inside him knew it was not the right time. Time was so different at the Crossing, and was of little consequence there. However, time was growing short for Jake on the other side. He didn't want to worry Teresa about it, but he was growing gray hair more and more each day. It was as if his body was aging at about one year for every hour he was awake. It started the morning after Stephen gave him the holy roller forehead push. Now, when he was awake, he could feel the aging process rushing through his body. He thought it stopped when he was asleep, but each morning as he looked into the mirror expecting to shave a twenty-seven-year-old man, he was facing someone well into his forties.

⟩ SEVEN

The truck pulled into the parking lot at Uncle Lester's church and they got out to say hello. As they started towards the house, Lester was coming out to meet them. "Good day, young people," Lester said, waving his hand. "What brings you to town?" Uncle Less always referred to folks as "young people," even when he may only have had a year or two on them.

"Good morning, Uncle Less," Jake said. "Teresa has some business in town. We could not go past your home without saying hello."

Lester gave everyone a Christian hug.

"How have you been, Lester?" Stephen asked as he hugged the older man.

"Not bad, Stephen. Only troubled sleep lately. Have you discerned any problems around?" he asked. Part of what made the Crossing, which included towns like Bodega Village, different from Sion or other holy places was its location on the outer rim of the restricted holy land and not off limits to evil.

The residents of such towns and villages were all believers and could ascend to heaven at any time they chose; they only stayed behind to assist others or meet Shaddai who visited in dreams. The Antichrist had no business there, but it was not off limits. The meeting with Zoltar and his disciples was a good example of why a fallen Angel or Grigori would visit. For the most part, this area had God-fearing people who enjoyed country living, fishing, animals, and beautiful ocean views. Other towns at the Crossing included Eagle Mountain, the Grasslands, and the town of Cornerstone on the other side of a small mountain range. The Crossing had a few scattered hotels, stables, and inns between the small towns, including the Inn at the Tides, where Teresa and Jake stayed the first time he visited.

Stephen dropped to his haunches. He took a small twig and drew three circles joined by a triangle in the dirt. "Look familiar?" he asked Lester.

"It does," Lester said. "It's what I have been seeing in my dreams lately."

"It's the mark of the Sword of Goliath," Stephen said. "Someone or something is getting close. We are running out of time; we must get to the sword before the others."

Stephen scratched the drawing away as the sky darkened. A cold wind followed, and Jake pulled the sling from his pocket and stepped closer to Stephen. A man stepped from the back door of the church and walked towards them. "Get in the truck, Teresa," Stephen said. Teresa got in the truck and pulled the door closed. Conchita held her arm tightly and was shaking. Jake pulled a stone from his pocket; it was the remaining stone he had from his last encounter with Zoltar.

"No need for all that now," the man said. "You already sent Zoltar to the pit and I'm here to talk, not fight."

"That is far enough," Jake said. "Talk. We can hear you from there."

"My name is Borackus. Like you, I'm at San Quentin. I have come to make a truce." Jake started towards the man and Stephen grabbed him and pulled him back. "Wise move, pilgrim," the man said.

"He killed Teresa!" Jake yelled. He tried to move but Stephen's touch had left him motionless.

"What truce?" Stephen asked.

"Tell us where the sword is located and we shall let you live."

Stephen laughed. "You're a vacant shell!" he shouted. "What kind of idiot calls himself our opponent? Like Saul of Tarsus in the darkness, you kick against the stone and it pains your foot, yet you're too stupid to turn away!"

The man looked behind him to ensure his back-up was with him. Five other men walked from the rear of the church. Lester began to pray, while Teresa and Conchita watched from inside the truck.

"Send his friends back to where they came from, Jake."

Jake felt the quickening. The stone he had loaded sailed into the center of the five thugs and a thunder crack shook the earth as they disintegrated into thin air. The eyes of Borackus were as black as doll's eyes. He drew a sword. Stephen pulled a sword concealed in a back sheath; it was unknown even to Jake. The blades met and fire flew from the contact. The speed was a blur as Stephen met every attack of the sword and drove the man backward. At one point Stephen had him off balance and instead of taking his head, he sliced off his left ear. The man ran into the tree line, screaming.

The darkness cleared and Teresa ran to Jake. She kissed him and held him while trembling. Conchita jumped to Stephen and hugged his neck. "Stephen, home, home," she said. Lester raised his hands and gave thanks.

"Why did you let him live and not kill him?" Jake asked.

"He is immortal," Stephen said. "This blade would not take his head even if I wanted it to. But I did mark him." Stephen pointed the tip of his sword at the bloody ear lying in the dirt. "And he will be easy to identify when we get back to San Quentin."

"You mean he will be missing the ear even though his body is on the other side?" Jake asked.

"The ear will remain here, as would yours if he had taken it at the Crossing." Jake understood. "What happens here goes back with us," Stephen said. "Even death. You're awake, Jake, and you're understanding more and more each day. However, you have not yet tasted from the tree of life." Stephen looked at Jake with that caring gaze. "You're most vulnerable at this time, Jake." Jake nodded. He thought about what might have happened if Stephen had not stopped him from rushing Borackus. The sword he was hiding would have surely killed him. "This was a desperate move on their part," Stephen said. "Because you sent Zoltar to the pit, this idiot is making decisions on his own."

Jake looked at the gruesome ear in the dirt.

"I hope we have a chance to capitalize on the time Zoltar is in the pit," Jake said.

Stephen grinned.

Chapter VII

The Escape

ONE

Later that evening, Teresa and Jake took the horses for an evening ride. They rode along the coastline to the place they loved to sit and watch the sun melt into the ocean. The clouds this evening added a splendor to the view. "What's bothering you, Jake?" Teresa asked as they sat under the tree where Jake had carved their names.

"I'm getting old," he said. Teresa smiled. "You don't understand, babe. Back on the other side, I look like my dad. I didn't want to worry you, but I feel strange, knowing I'm twice your age." Teresa wrapped her arms around his neck and kissed the corner of his mouth. He rolled over with her on top of him and they kissed again. Teresa sat up, looking into his blue eyes.

"You're you, Jake, old or young. I love you, make no mistake about it. Nothing your body is doing on the other side will change the way I feel about you." Jake smiled and kissed the corner of her mouth in response. He laid back to take in her long lashes as the sun set for the night. They made love in the tall, sweet grass. Their horses, Pylon and Brandy, cropped grass nearby, keeping watch.

TWO

That night, Jake dreamed he saw a sword and it was glowing like a light. The sword was in what could only be described as a dark mud hut. The sword was beautiful; on one side of the handle was the image of an eagle. The other side of the handle was marked with a triangle containing a circle at each point. Gold talons held a crystal at the end of the sword's hilt. As Jake walked towards the glowing sword, he could see a shadow standing in the corner of the dark dwelling. The shadow had a green glow to it; Jake felt that the guardian of the sword was evil. Then he saw a basket filled with fruit he had never seen before. He was amazed, as the fruit was glowing like a white light. He looked above the sword and could make out words in a language foreign to him, perhaps angelic script. Somehow, he knew the words meant "Land of En-Dor." When he woke, he was in the cell and Stephen was shaving.

THREE

"Bad dream?" Stephen asked.

"I'm not sure. I think I saw the Sword of Goliath."

"What did it look like?" Stephen asked.

"In my dream, I saw a sword glowing like a light that blazed brightly. The hilt was in the shape of an eagle with folded wings. On the end of the hilt was a round diamond or gemstone held by golden eagle talons. Each side of the sword had etchings of different things. I remember on the left side was the face of an old man and on the right side was a symbol." Jake took a pad of paper and drew the mark. Stephen quickly took the paper and after looking closely, he set it aflame with his Zippo, then flushed it down the toilet.

"That's it. That is what we have been waiting for," Stephen said with a smile that lit up the cell. Jake took his place in front of the mirror and gasped. He could hardly believe what he saw: his hair was white and his beard was long. He had to use scissors to cut it away so he could shave. He looked nothing like his work ID card and wondered how he would be able to process through the gate to get to the laundry.

"Do you know where it is?" Stephen asked.

"No," Jake answered. "I see it and know what it is, but I'm not sure where it is. I will though, I can feel it. I know I will be able to find it when the time comes."

Stephen did that crazy whistle sound and two pigeons landed outside the cell. Stephen rolled a note and the pigeon entered through the food port. Stephen attached the note to the pigeon's leg. Jake marveled at the way the birds seemed to mind Stephen; he had a way with them. Jake noticed this when Stephen first met Conchita, she took to him right away. It took weeks for Jake to get to know Conchita. Stephen seemed to have a way with animals. Once the pigeon had the note, the bird flew to the rafters in the unit, then out a broken window and headed in the direction of San Francisco.

FOUR

"Workers chow release!" a voice said over the loudspeaker. The bar moved back and the doors swung open with a bang. "See you after work," Stephen said.

"No breakfast?"

"I have some people to see this morning," Stephen said, "so I will pass." Jake nodded and headed to the north dining hall. As he hit the first tier, he heard his name. Jake looked back; it was Slowpoke. "What's up?" Jake asked.

"I was calling but I didn't think it was you. What happened to your hair, man?" Slowpoke said. "You look hella shot-out, dude."

"I'm sick. I'm having some more tests but they think it's cancer," Jake explained.

"Ahhh, dude, sorry to hear that." Jake kept pace with Slowpoke while sending mental messages to the inmates and staff that were checking him out. *That dude Stanton got sick and that is why he looks different . . . That dude Stanton got sick and that is why he looks different . . . That dude Stanton got sick and that is why he looks different . . . That dude Stanton got sick and that is why he looks different . . ."*

Jake was reaping at the same time and they all started to look at him with a different thought in their head. *Now I just have to get through the gate*, he thought. *My ID looks like I could be my father.* "Stanton 76," Jake said, and the officer moved his gate pass from the inbox to the outbox. Jake kept walking without looking back.

"*On your guard, Jake,*" said a voice in his head.

"*Is that you, Grandfather?*" Jake asked.

"*Jake, be on your guard, Borackus is seeking you,*" Aaron said.

"Understood," Jake said aloud. Two inmates looked back at him; Jake smiled and kept walking. He arrived at the laundry early and stood with his back to the building until Mr. Umba showed up and unlocked the back door. Jake worked the day with one eye on the job and the other checking his six constantly. "*You there, Stephen?*"

"*I'm here, Jake.*"

"*I received a message from my grandfather,*" Jake said.

"*I know, Jake, he warned me, too.*"

"*He said Borackus is seeking me.*"

"*He is. He was transferred to East Block last night and is on our main line,*" Stephen said.

"*What do we do?*" Jake asked.

"*We go tonight.*"

"*Tonight? What about the door? We still have no key,*" Jake said.

"*I will take care of the key, we go tonight.*"

FIVE

After work, Jake made his way to North Block, looking at every inmate, and prepared for trouble around every corner. There was no sign of a one-eared inmate. When they were back in their cell and Officer Spearman locked the door, Jake breathed a sigh of relief. They showered in the cell that night by taking a "birdbath" in their sink and skipped the evening meal. Stephen started breaking up some peanuts from their shell's, then a pigeon flew into the food port and hopped to Stephen's rack and started to eat the peanuts. Jake watched as Stephen took the bird and removed a small piece of paper. As he unrolled the paper, a key fell to the mattress. "The key," Jake said. "But how?"

"I was able to trace it when DeVito fell asleep in my barber chair. I was going to make a clay mold, but DeVito was out so I simply traced the key on a pad of paper and sent it to our friends in the city. Tonight, we go."

SIX

Suddenly a loud alarm sounded in North Block. It was different from the regular dryer buzzer alarm that goes off when an officer pushes the emergency button. This was more like the sound of a police car. "It's a fire alarm," Stephen said.

"Fire alarm in North Block!" a voice announced over the loudspeaker. "Evacuate to the upper yard and line up by tier for accountability!"

"Great, this is one time I was hoping we would be locked in our cell," Stephen said. Jake and Stephen walked in single file and organized themselves by their tier with their ID cards out. Jake looked over towards East Block; they were exiting their building as well. *Holy crap*, Jake thought, *that's the building the earless idiot is in.* He kept watch over the exit, looking for any sign of the evil Borackus.

"*Wake up, Jake.*" It was Teresa. She was guarding his mind.

"Thank you, my love," Jake said, and continued to watch the exit. He viewed lots of halos exiting the building; they all looked asleep to him. Then, as if he knew before he knew, the bright-green glow of a halo exited the rear of East Block. "There he is, Stephen," Jake said.

"On your guard, Jake. Remember your lessons." Borackus exited the building at a quick pace with five other Grigori at his heels; he was looking left, then right, then zeroed in on Stephen and Jake.

They were all armed with shanks, running, all six, right at Jake and Stephen, as if they were late for a bus. Whistles sounded from overhead and officers yelled, "Get down! Get down!" All the inmates in the yard dropped to the prone position except Jake and Stephen and the approaching assailants. Borackus was leading the pack and rushed with no regard for the verbal commands to stop. Jake and Stephen took a defensive stance. When Borackus collided with Stephen he was tossed head over heels, landing on his back. The others crashed right behind him with similar results. Jake and Stephen moved with lightning speed, throwing kicks and blocks as perfectly as Bruce Lee himself. The lessons with Stephen in the arena at the ranch came to Jake and he knew what to do. Over and over he blocked kicks and punches and potential stab wounds as the attackers tried to kill them.

By now, the responding officers had fired warning shots and tossed gas grenades to try and stop the riot. However, the assailants kept coming. The officers formed a tactical skirmish line and actually created a rescue circle for Stephen and Jake, as it was obvious they were the victims of this savage attack. One by one the assailants were wrapped up by responding staff and placed in handcuffs. Even the earless Borackus was cuffed and escorted to administrative segregation for his brutal attack.

Stephen and Jake were also placed in cuffs and escorted to holding cells for participating in the riot. However, when Captain Johnson arrived, he released them after conducting interviews and receiving their signed word they had no enemy concerns on the main line. Jake thought it highly unusual for them to be released after being involved in such an incident. He then realized his friend was a master at sowing a thought in the mind of the unsuspecting. How close had they come to being discovered as escape risks? If they were placed in segregation, the hole in their cell would surely be discovered.

SEVEN

It was about midnight when Stephen and Jake made it back to their cell, and the two were relieved to know Borackus and his minions were locked up in segregation for at least ten days. They cleaned up and lay on their bunks, waiting for Officer Armstrong to fall asleep.

"Jake," Stephen said, "Don't drift off, not even for a moment. I need you fresh and ready to move quickly."

"No worries," Jake replied. Stephen used the mirror to look at the gun rail. He could see Officer Armstrong with his feet up, relaxing in his chair. Then he saw Officer Spearman coming down the tier doing his count. Stephen pulled the mirror back into the cell, and he and Jake faked sleep as Officer Spearman counted and walked on by.

"It's time," Stephen said, then dismounted and removed the painting.

The men worked quickly and silently, all the while communicating telepathically.

"*Ready?*" Stephen asked.

"*As I will ever be,*" Jake replied. The men entered the chase. Jake pulled the painting back over the hole and Stephen lit the Zippo. The men moved toward the ladder at the end of the tier, up the ladder, and then on their stomachs, moving slowly towards the door leading to the roof. Officer Armstrong was asleep, breathing deeply and releasing a snore louder than most of the inmates in the building.

At the door, Stephen took out the shiny new key and slipped it into the lock. The door opened with a creaking sound, and Jake and Stephen entered the roof. From there they had to cross the building and then reach the lower yard without being seen by the armed wall posts overlooking the perimeter. They were in luck; a thick fog had drifted in from the bay, providing perfect cover. The watch commander had not yet put up additional staff for an official fog line. Across the roof and down the wall to the yard, both men hung their body length from the rail, then dropped about ten feet to the ground. As they moved toward the handball court, Jake noticed a green glow in one of the wall posts. He was hoping it was a sleeping Grigori and not one waiting for their escape.

Stephen lifted the steel cover and Jake dropped into the dark hole. Stephen followed, then closed the hatch. Again, Stephen lit the Zippo and the two made their way through the tunnel and out to the bay. They sat at the mouth of the tunnel and began to blow up their flotation devices made from the raincoats Jake had brought back from the laundry.

When they were inflated, they began kicking out to where the Larkspur Ferry boat would pass slowly in the canal leading to the open water. They stopped at the buoy and held on, waiting for the boat.

The morning ferry lights came on and the large three-story boat was moving in their direction. Jake was thinking how nice it would be to get out of the freezing water. It reminded him of the time he and his grandfather were fishing and he fell into the water and nearly drowned.

"*Steady, Jake,*" his grandfather's voice came to him.

"This is our passage," Stephen said. "Daniel is on board with our supplies. He will be tossing two ropes for us to grab so be ready, Jake."

Jake's body was cold and much older and weaker than Stephen's, however, when the ropes were within reach, he grabbed on and started climbing. Daniel pulled Jake aboard in the darkness. Stephen climbed on right behind him.

"In here," Daniel said. Jake and Stephen stepped into a staff restroom and stripped out of their wet clothes. Daniel took their wet clothes, along with a bucket of fish guts, and dumped them over the side to attract the sharks. Stephen and Jake pulled on dry, warm clothes and cleaned themselves in the restroom before exiting and going in with the other passengers. The boat was nearly empty on the lower deck so they took a table near the window and sat with Daniel and Liea, who had hot coffee waiting for them. Stephen introduced Jake to his friends. Jake, with his white hair and tired face, looked like he could have been their grandfather.

EIGHT

"So you're the friends in San Francisco that he has been sending the birds to," Jake surmised.

Liea smiled. "We have heard so much about you, Jake. Alas, it took us months to get Stephen locked up in San Quentin with you, and now you're here." Jake detected an accent from Liea but could not place it; Russian, perhaps.

"Yes," Jake said. "I assumed Stephen made up the bank robbery story just to get to know me."

"Nyet," Liea said. "He took down the Federal Reserve Bank in San Francisco," she continued.

"You're kidding!" Jake exclaimed. "Do we do that?" Jake asked. "Rob banks, I mean?"

"Not anymore, Jake. I already did," Stephen said. "I didn't hurt anyone, and the money is federally insured. Also, they sent me to prison for it," Stephen explained.

"How did you end up in state prison for a federal crime?" Jake asked.

"That's where planning came in," Liea said.

"I used a gun and I took down several other banks the same day so they figured they could get me on the three strikes law in California by making it a state crime," he explained.

Jake smiled. "So you were telling the truth the whole time, eh?"

Looking at Liea, he said, "Yep." Stephen put his arm around Liea. "I got arrested right outside her house." Liea kissed the corner of Stephen's mouth and then he turned to her and kissed her properly.

"I see," Jake said. "And the money?"

"Eighteen million," Stephen said. "Untraceable cash, in twenty, fifty, and hundred dollar bills spread over twenty different hiding places." Stephen grinned at Jake.

"Are they still looking for the money?" Jake asked.

"They stopped about two years ago. My lawyer was successful in catching the investigators with illegal phone taps on Liea's phone. Last year the feds settled with Liea for two million in a harassment case she filed. I have a good lawyer," Stephen continued.

"So you two are worth about twenty million?" Jake asked.

Liea looked at Stephen. "It's all for the cause, and the twenty million is a drop in the bucket compared to what Tony and Ron are worth," Liea said as she looked back at Jake. "Our search for the Sword of Goliath will be expensive." In the light Jake had not noticed the white glow over Daniel's head, but in the reflection of the glass window it was unmistakable. Liea, on the other hand, had no such glow.

"So what is our next move?" Jake asked.

"We need to get you to the garden before you pass on of old age," Stephen said. Jake looked at his reflection in the window and gasped. He looked as frail as George Burns in his final days. Jake turned away from his reflection as he could not stand the sight. As the ferry sped toward San Francisco, they took one last look back at San Quentin. Jake noticed the light above the gas chamber was flashing red. This was a distress signal to the on-grounds officers to report to work, an emergency was taking place.

"The light," Jake said. "Is that because of us?"

"I don't think so," Stephen replied. "I think something else is going on, something involving Borackus. Do you feel it?"

"I feel it," Daniel said. "Borackus has taken a hostage; he is trying to escape. People are dying," Daniel said in a shaky voice.

"I didn't expect this," Stephen said. "They will likely discover we're gone very soon. Borackus will be seeking you, Jake."

Chapter VIII

The Tree of Life

ONE

As the boat docked at the pier in San Francisco, Jake and Stephen got off with Daniel and Liea. They walked through the ferry building to the parking lot on the north side, where Daniel had a truck waiting. From there they drove through the city, arriving in Chinatown as the sun was coming up. Jake and Stephen were exhausted; they followed Daniel from the parking lot to an old hotel built around the turn of the last century. Jake stood next to the staircase with Liea while Stephen and Daniel talked to an old Chinese man at the desk. Stephen motioned for Jake and Liea to come closer. The old man pulled back a curtain that was covering a brick wall. Near the top of the curtain, chiseled into the brick wall, were two small vertical lines with a curve under them and three dots above. This looked like the marks Jake saw on the barn at his ranch at the Crossing. Jake was puzzled.

Daniel walked into the brick wall and disappeared. Jake's look went from puzzled to thunderstruck. Stephen pushed him towards the bricks. His instinct wanted to resist, but Stephen's strong and persuasive arm shoved him right through the wall. Jake heard a sound like a hand rubbing a balloon. It was dark for a moment, then he found himself standing on a red carpet in front of an elevator that still looked like the old hotel. The doors opened and they all stepped inside.

The elevator went down, and as it did, Jake said, "The wall, what was that?"

"It was a doorway, Jake," Daniel said. The elevator stopped and when it opened, Jake could see a small lobby with five doors. They were marked one, two, and three, but the fourth door had no number, only the same markings Jake had seen on the brick wall and the barn. The fifth door had different markings, which Jake had never seen before. It was a capital letter E only backwards. It also had three dots above the letter. Stephen handed Jake a key and said, "You have Room Two, Jake. Get some rest."

TWO

Daniel walked to the door marked One and used the key to enter. Stephen went to the door marked Three, opened it, and went inside. Jake walked to his room and stopped. He walked to the other door with the Shaddai mark on it and tried to open it but it was locked. He tried his key but had no luck. He did the same with the other door with the backward E but could not open it. He put his ear to the door and heard sounds; he could hear crying and yelling, like someone was in great pain. Jake put his ear to the other door; he could hear birds singing, and laughter. For a moment he thought about kicking in the doors, but he then thought he should consult Stephen. Finally, he decided to do what he was told and went to his room, opened the door, and went inside.

THREE

The room was old but elegant; it had a country feel to it. The room was surprisingly large and had a parlor with a large mirror that greeted Jake as he entered. The man Jake saw in the mirror, at the ripe old age of twenty-seven, was hunched over, with white hair and a long, white beard. In the short ninety minutes it took for the ferry to reach San Francisco, Jake went from looking like George Burns to the old man on the Monopoly card. He felt completely exhausted. His bones ached with every step. Jake got undressed. He wanted to take a hot shower but simply staggered to the bed and passed out.

FOUR

Conchita was pulling Jake's hair with her little hands. "Jake, home, home." Jake sat up in bed while Teresa was getting dressed. Conchita hugged his neck and Jake scratched her where she loved it. "We did it, we're out," he said.

Teresa favored her beloved with a smile. "I know, I'm so happy. I was so worried when you were in that awful place. How is Stephen?"

"He is good. We had a run-in with that idiot, Borackus," Jake said.

"I felt that when he tried to reap your thoughts," she said.

"We're in San Francisco at the moment. Stephen is trying to get me what I need, Teresa. I'm not doing very well on the other side." She walked to him and gave him a proper welcome. Jake held her tight. "I'm good when I'm here," he said, "but if you could see me on the other side, you may not think I would live another day."

"You're here now. Come and have some breakfast," she said.

Jake could smell the pipe smoke and knew his grandfather was present. When he got to the great room he was delighted to see Daniel and Stephen sitting with Aaron. "Where is Liea?" Jake asked. "She is in San Francisco. Jake, Liea is not Shaddai; she is a human. She could only be here as Teresa is." Jake understood. *Teresa was here because she was dead, and I'm only here because I'm Shaddai and have been awakened,* he thought. "Well, we're out of the dungeon, God be praised," he said.

"Amen," Aaron said.

Then, as if to mimic Aaron, Conchita yelled, "Amen!" in her tiny little voice. She was sitting atop Jake's shoulder with her tail wrapped around his neck. They all laughed at this outburst from Conchita. She was so adorable; it was hard not to laugh.

Teresa set the table for breakfast and everyone ate their fill. As Teresa cleared the dishes, Daniel and Jake rose to help. "That was wonderful," Daniel said. "Teresa, you have a beautiful place here. I visited the north crossing near Eagle Mountain long ago before my wife ascended. It's spectacular as well, but this area is truly beautiful."

"Thank you, Daniel. Michael set me up here about five years ago and I just love it," she said. Jake was trying not to be rude, but at the same time, he wanted to know about this ascending thing; what did it mean? And why had Daniel not seen his wife in so long? He and Teresa had almost talked about it a few times, but for some reason he decided the time was not right. Perhaps it meant she ascended and left him behind, kind of like when she crossed over at death. Jake didn't want to think about it right now.

"Jake, can I see you on the deck?" Stephen asked.

"Sure," he said, stepping out to where his friend was standing.

"I need your complete attention for the next part of our mission."

Jake looked into Stephen's face.

"I can see you're troubled." Stephen put his hand on Jake's shoulder. "You know all things happen for the good for those who love the Lord."

"I know this," Jake said.

"You were given an opportunity to turn aside from this mission; you could have gone back. You could have had Teresa with you and your old life back," Stephen explained.

"I know," Jake said.

"You do know, Jake, more than you want to know." Jake thought for a moment. The questions he was about to ask were a waste of time, as he knew the answers. He didn't like them, but he knew them just the same. Teresa would ascend in time and leave him; when he lay to sleep on the other side he would not be here with her. As Daniel's wife, who lived in the north part of the crossing near Eagle Mountain, had eventually left Daniel, Teresa would leave him. He didn't know when, only that it would happen sometime in the future. Teresa knew it too; this is why there was never a good time to talk about it, because it meant the end of their being together. Who wants to discuss that? She was hiding something else too, but what? Jake was not yet able to put his finger on it or was not willing to do so. Jake needed to change the subject.

"Stephen, tell me about the garden. I know we talked about it some time ago, but I want to know everything," Jake said.

Stephen picked up his coffee cup and took a sip. "You will. Daniel is saddling the horses. You, Daniel, and I are taking a ride to the Grasslands. I want you to meet someone," Stephen said.

"The sword?" Jake asked.

"Yes, the sword, and everything you can remember about your dream." They walked back into the house. Teresa hugged Jake. He looked into her beautiful eyes and thought, *How can I ever leave you?* "Stephen wants to take a ride," Jake said.

"I know, Grandpa told me. I made you some sandwiches for the trip," Teresa said.

"You're so awesome," Jake said.

"You know it," Teresa said back with a full smile, the kind of smile that could light up a room and fix any problem he thought he may ever have. Jake said good-bye with a passionate smooch and they saddled up.

FIVE

Jake noticed the saddles were equipped with a sword, a short bow, a full quiver of arrows, and two daggers. In addition, the saddlebag held a sling and stones. He didn't say anything about the weapons; after all, he had spent many weeks with Stephen on horseback training missions with this type of setup, and Jake was a firm believer it's better to have a weapon and not need one than to need a weapon and not have one. He waved to Teresa and Conchita before they rode towards the mountains.

As they rode, Stephen began to describe the garden. "The entrance and the perimeter is flaming with white fire, the hottest flame in the universe, and the Angel at the gate is armed with a flaming sword." Stephen pulled his sword and pointed it towards the sun. "It has more animals than any zoo you have ever visited, so don't get nervous when you're approached by a tiger or a bear; they will not hurt you," Stephen said with a look of excitement.

"I can't promise I will not be alarmed by wild animals," Jake said.

"They will not bite," Stephen said again. "They are incredible, and as tame as the day is long." Daniel looked back at Stephen and Jake, wondering what the hell they were talking about. "The waterfalls are magnificent and the trees, mountains, grass, and bushes of fruit are everywhere," Stephen said, sliding his sword back into the saddle sheath.

"So tell me, Stephen, what does the fruit taste like? You know, the fruit from the tree of life, that is."

"My friend, that is one thing I'm not able to describe and give it justice. You can eat anything in the garden and feel like you could conquer the world; anything, that is, except the fruit of the forbidden tree," Stephen explained.

"It's still there? The tree Adam and Eve ate from, the tree of the knowledge of good and evil is still in the garden?" Jake asked with a look of disbelief on his face.

"Of course it is, why would it not be?" Stephen said.

"Well, because it served its purpose, why keep it around?" Jake said.

"Jake, the tree is there, the rule is there, and we must obey," Stephen explained. "The select few Shaddai who are allowed to enter the garden must stay true or they too will die."

"You mean some Shaddai have eaten from the tree even now?"

"Yes, and even some Angels trusted with caring for the animals have been tempted and failed, and died. The same deceiver who tempted the woman is still there; that's why I hate snakes," Stephen said. Jake smiled as he remembered their conversation about the rats.

They were getting higher up the mountain; when they looked back towards the ranch, it was nothing more than a small speck in the distance. Jake thought of the view when he was with the Good Shepherd, holding his hand, and when he let go, only to turn him into an eagle so he could soar across the sky. He had come a long way from that day in the eighth grade when he was nose-to-nose with Billy Parson and watching his life change. He also remembered his confrontation with Zoltar, and how he felt when the Good Shepherd filled him with strength, and when Stephen put his hand on him in that prison cell with the hallelujah forehead push and he knew everything was going to be OK. He knew even if he was left behind and Teresa ascended to heaven, where she deserved to be, he would be OK. Pylon gave a neigh as they reached the top of the trail at the entrance to the wooded area.

Chapter IX

The Prophet

ONE

The three travelers were heading into a thickly wooded area. The horses seemed nervous. The sun was nearly blocked out because of the trees. Jake looked down and saw what looked like a large bird track, only the size of a horse's hoof print.

"What is it?" Jake asked.

"Lumpa tracks," Stephen said.

"Excuse me, did you say lumpa?" Jake asked.

"That's right, lumpa," he said.

Jake had noticed some strange animals at the Crossing but he figured it was all part of being at the Crossing. Stuff was bound to be a little strange when you were living with your dead wife and a talking monkey.

The only dangerous stuff he could remember was the Zoltar encounter or the Borackus meeting, but he had never ventured too far from Bodega Village, or anywhere past the fifty-acre ranch. Now in the mountains to the north there were lumpa tracks. "What's a lumpa?" Jake asked.

"It's like a flying lizard, I guess. It breathes fire when fully grown, but the ones around the Crossing rarely reach adulthood," Stephen explained. "The wizards near the Grasslands usually kill them for their sulfur breath when they are young."

"I'm sorry," Jake said, "did you just say wizards, like Gandalf *Lord of the Rings*-type stuff?"

"I did say wizards but they are not like on TV or in the movies," Stephen said. "They are much worse. Most are evil Grigori offspring and must remain on this side of the

Crossing. Most are nasty, wicked things that serve little purpose other than terrorizing humans whenever they can."

Jake looked left, then right, then above and to the rear. "So let me try to get my head around this. Wizards are evil Grigori offspring and they live near the Grasslands where we're going?"

"I know it sounds a little crazy," Stephen said.

"Not at all, Stephen, par for the course," Jake deadpanned. Daniel broke out in a loud laugh.

TWO

As the riders came out on the other side of the woods, they could see a large valley with tall, colored grass. Some was light green, some dark green, some almost purple. Jake took notice and marveled at the beauty. On the edge of the woods was a small brick dwelling that backed up to a grass and rock-covered hill. The house was old, with a chimney spouting smoke. Nearby was a small stable and a few horses cropping grass. Through the front yard was a brook with crystal clear water. Jake could see trout moving about in the stream. As they approached the house, Stephen yelled, "Hello in the house!" There was no response. They dismounted and tethered the horses to the hitch near the stable.

An old man came out of the house wearing a tattered robe. Across his shoulders was a white serape with Hebrew markings. "Greetings," said the old man. Jake thought this guy looked a lot like he did when he saw his reflection in the hotel on the other side.

"Hello, Samuel," Stephen said.

"Is that you, Stephen?" the old man asked. "Come close, my eyes are not what they used to be."

"It's Stephen and Daniel, and I brought a friend." Jake took a good, long look at the old man. Could this be

117

Samuel, the prophet from the Bible? After all, he was in a strange spiritual place, so why not?

"Come in, come in," the old man said and opened his door. As he entered the brick house, Jake noticed shelves on every wall covering every inch from floor to ceiling. He could see two hallways from the front room and decided this place was much larger than it looked from the outside. The house backed up into the mountain, and only the front was above ground; the rest of the house was inside of the mountain. The shelves in the entry room were filled with old weapons and what looked like antique objects. The wall on the far side of the room also had shelves from floor to ceiling. The shelves were filled with books; old books with leather bindings stacked one on top of the other, hundreds of books.

"This is Jake, from the bloodline of Seth, same as I. He is Shaddai, and had a vision of the location of the Sword of Goliath."

"Ahhh, the sword, the enchanted sword of the twelve that form the talisman," the old man said. Jake extended his hand to the old man and he took it, then greeted the men with a hug.

"Samuel, like King Saul and David, Samuel?" Jake asked.

"The same," the old the man said. "I serve the God of our fathers and still have work to do. My name, meaning 'God has heard,' was given by a very Godly woman, who pledged me to our Lord's service while I was a young boy. There is much meaning in names. Like yours, my son. Jacob is a noble and renowned name."

"I guess I never thought of it as such." Jake could not stop staring. *High Priest Samuel*, Jake marveled. "I'm so pleased to meet you, Your Grace."

"We're all God's children," Samuel said. "Please have a seat, let me serve you a drink. I don't get many visitors here." The old man poured from a strange container. Jake smelled the drink and then took a small sip. It was some kind of juice or wine, it was like nothing he had ever tasted, but like most things at the Crossing, he enjoyed it and accepted the strangeness with no questions.

"Michael has sent us on a mission to find the Sword of Goliath," Stephen said.

"Yes, time is growing short. Soon the days of men will end and the saints will prepare for battle." The old man sighed, as if saddened at the prospect of another war.

"Tell him your dream, Jake," Stephen said, "and we shall heed his counsel in the matter." Jake and Daniel were sitting on a bench on one side of the table, and Stephen and Samuel were in chairs across from them on the other side of the table. The table was large and made of a hard wood. It was beautiful, the kind of table fit for a castle or palace of kings. Each leg was detailed with carvings of Angels and ended in a foot of some kind of animal. Samuel had provided wooden cups for their drinks. The cups also had detailed carvings. Jake took another sip and started to explain his dream.

"In my dream I saw a sword glowing like a light that blazed brightly. The hilt was in the shape of an eagle with folded wings. On the end of the hilt was a round diamond or gemstone held by golden eagle talons. Each side of the sword had etchings of different things. I remember on the left side was the face of an old man and on the right side was a symbol. The symbol had three circular points joined by lines, making a triangle. The sword was hidden in a hut or dwelling and a woman was watching over it. The woman was very old, and the dwelling was a mess. Among the mess was a basket, and in the basket was a strange fruit that was glowing like a light. I saw the words in a language I could not speak but understood Land of En-Dor. Then I awoke."

Samuel put his hand to his head and said, "The sword you saw in your dream is the sword you seek. It is the same sword that took the life of Goliath and Saul. The woman who guards the sword is the witch of En-Dor. She is the medium who called on me at the request of Saul many years ago. I informed Saul he would surely die the next day." Jake guessed he could look no more amazed than he did at this very moment. "You're correct, she is old; perhaps more than three thousand years old," Samuel said.

"The witch lives eternal from the fruit in the basket, the fruit of the tree of life. The serpent in the garden provides the fruit to the enemy. As you know, once the fruit leaves the garden it is weakened. The enemy uses the fruit to maintain immortality; nevertheless, it is temporary. The enemy must continue to partake from the glowing fruit to arrest the aging process. The old woman must keep a stockpile of the fruit.

"The end of days is growing close and the sword is calling to be found. Others will no doubt wish to obtain the sword so you must be on your guard. Now hear me well; the fallen and Grigori wish to kill the Shaddai and destroy the peace among believers. You must travel to this place and face the evil woman and retrieve the sword before it falls into the hands of the enemy. You will travel by boat, and trust none outside the bloodline. God will bless your journey. Remain true and he will bless you all the days of your life." Samuel put a hand on Jake's hand and one on Stephen's as he said this. Jake could feel the stir inside and now it warmed him.

The men broke bread and ate together. They drank the wine from the wooden cups. Jake asked Samuel many questions and he answered them all. By nightfall, the men accepted the hospitality of Samuel to pass the night in his home. Jake watched much movement in the woods and could hear night birds sounding the alarm of distress; he worried about the horses.

THREE

Samuel walked Jake back to another room. Jake was astounded at the size of this home. It looked like a little hut from outside, but inside it was enormous.

They passed many doorways and halls in the corridor as they walked. The floors were made of marble and the hall was lit by what appeared to be electric lamps on the walls. Also hanging on the walls were works of art; paintings of people, some of landscapes, and some of seascapes. Some of animals Jake didn't recognize. He admired the paintings as they walked through the corridor with no windows.

Finally they entered a room that opened into the mountain. The room continued the marble floor for about two thousand square feet and ended stepping down into an underground river with a large waterfall pouring into the pool around the marble floor. Plants, ferns, trees, and green moss grew everywhere, but the sky was nowhere to be seen. It was like an indoor atrium with vegetation growing up to an invisible ceiling. Jake wondered how such plant life could grow without sunlight. In the middle of the room was a marble pillar about waist-high, which looked almost like a birdbath filled with water. Samuel and Jake walked to the pillar and looked into the water.

Jake could see his reflection and the old man's reflection standing beside him. He watched the reflection fade. In its place he saw the sword, the same sword he saw in his dream. It turned, and he could see the markings on both sides. The vision faded and he saw the old woman of En-Dor; she was wearing a black robe with a large hood. At her feet was a lizard-looking creature with wings, about the size of a large dog. The vision faded again, then Jake saw Teresa. She was riding her horse and was very happy. Behind her was another horse or pony carrying a very small rider. When this faded he saw a little star-shaped hand, like that of a little girl. He could make out that she was waving. He could not quite see her face, as she was fading in and out. Then he saw her in her little dress and her shiny shoes and the white glow over her shoulder-length blond hair. Her eyes, like ice-blue pools, sparkled as they met his.

"Who is she?" Jake asked. Samuel gave Jake a comforting smile from under his long white beard and said, "She is your bloodline, Jacob, and your destiny." Jake felt the gooseflesh on the back of his neck, the warm kind like when Stephen had given him that halleluiah forehead push back in the cell at San Quentin. "Your bloodline, your destiny."

Samuel was holding a strange container, like the one he poured the juice from. It looked like a container you might find on *Gilligan's Island* made by the professor. He filled the container from the birdbath and closed it. Jake followed Samuel out of the waterfall room and back to Stephen and Daniel, who were poking around on the shelves in the front parlor.

Jake had received a lot of information from the prophet; some he would not be able to stop talking about, and some he would hold onto until the time was right. The old man had taken him to the waterfall room for a reason, and Jake would keep his own council on what he saw in the birdbath.

FOUR

The bedrooms were as amazing as everything else in this place. They had large beds with feather mattresses and pillows. Jake marveled at the beautiful velvet bed curtains. The artwork on the walls was old and resembled what one might see if they entered the Vatican, paintings from the Michelangelo time period. Each room had a sitting area with furniture and books. The books were old, and would likely be something one would find in a museum back home, but here they sat neatly on a bookshelf, one in each room. Jake picked up a book and thumbed through it for kicks. The book was titled *The Crossing*. It appeared to be a novel but was lacking the name of the author and publication date. Jake put the book on the nightstand, intending to take another look after a shower. However, when his body stretched out in that featherbed, sleep took him immediately.

FIVE

All three men awoke before the sun came up and began preparing for the journey back to the ranch. Normally, Jake only dreamed when he was on his last night at the Crossing, but on this night, he had the dream about the sword. He then had a strange dream about Teresa; she was in the distance, trying to hide something from Jake. He tried to circle her and get a better view but she turned one way, then the other. She was very polite, and Jake found it frustrating that she would not share what she was hiding. Finally, he gave up and awoke.

Samuel was praying with an old leather-bound book, asking for God's blessings. Stephen put together some biscuits and eggs and they sat together one last time at the wooden table, drinking from the wooden cups and dining on wooden plates with wooden spoons.

SIX

As the sun lifted over the trees, the men saddled their horses and said good-bye to the old prophet. Jake was amazed at the things he had seen and heard. He had so much to be thankful for, he thought. Then his mind drifted to Teresa and the dream and his smile faded.

"Take the lead, Daniel," Stephen said. "I will bring up the rear."

"Jacob!" Samuel called. "Take this." Samuel handed him a leather bag marked with two short vertical lines with a curve underneath and three dots on top. Jake could see that the container Samuel had filled from the birdbath was inside; also some papers and a book were in the bag. Jake didn't examine the contents of the bag but simply looped the leather handle over the saddle horn and said thank you. The horses started for the trail, Daniel in the lead, then Jake, and Stephen in the rear.

"What is bothering you, Jake?" Stephen asked.

"What makes you think I'm bothered?" Jake responded. Stephen looked into his face and Jake grinned. "I suppose I'm bothered by a lot of things," he said. "This land, this place, our escape from San Quentin, my body back on the other side that looks more and more like death every moment, and the lumpa prints on the ground the size of pie plates." Jake pointed at what looked like a giant bird print in the dirt.

"Would it help if I told you they only come out at night?" Stephen replied.

"It's a start," Jake said. But Stephen knew nothing Jake had said was bothering him, not really. What was bothering him were his thoughts of Teresa, thoughts of losing her, or perhaps his thoughts of what she was hiding from him. But Stephen said nothing more; he went on riding and enjoying the beautiful view. As they came to the heavy woods, something was different; the trail had changed.

"Is this the way we came?" Jake asked.

"It is," Stephen said, "but someone or something in the night has changed things."

Daniel pulled the short bow and nocked an arrow. Stephen did the same. Jake started to pull his bow and saw something rushing from the tall grass. Pylon reared and Jake tumbled off the back. As he hit the ground, he could see a green monster rushing at him. It had yellow eyes and a pig's face with razor-sharp tusks. Just as Jake was about to be run over by the beast, it pitched forward and skidded face first in the dirt just in front of Jake.

"Yikes!" Jake yelled. The monster had two arrows planted directly in his neck. "I thought you said lumpas only come out at night!"

"They do," Stephen said. "That's not a lumpa, Jake, it's a hoggal. They are like pigs but they are much better eating. I'll tie him on the back of my mount; this will be a great treat tonight. I'll show you how we cook hoggal at the Crossing. We're going to Uncle Lester's church tomorrow; this will be a splendid dish to bring to the potluck," Stephen said. Jake dusted himself off and they started back toward the ranch.

Chapter X

San Quentin

ONE

The alarm was screaming and staff were responding to Carson Section, where it was reported an inmate had jumped from the fourth tier to the gun rail and captured a mini 14 rifle and a .38 revolver.

"Alarm in South Block!" the voice announced over the loudspeaker.

"What happened?" Officer Spearman asked.

"The inmates took over Carson Section," Officer DeVito replied.

Spearman and DeVito were outside the South Block rotunda door behind the trash dumpster. Other officers were running down the gun rail towards South Block with automatic weapons.

"What?" Spearman replied.

"The same inmates we locked up behind the riot on the upper yard. It was crazy! I was trying to escort inmate Borackus to the cell and he pulled away and busted the cuffs. Then he ran to the fourth tier, jumped across to the rail and took the weapons off black Smitty. I never seen nothing like it. He tossed Smitty over the rail, he's dead. Smitty is dead!" DeVito said, on the verge of tears.

"Take it easy, DeVito, here comes the SERT team." Officers in full riot gear with automatic weapons were crossing the upper yard in two columns on a double-time march. Behind them were emergency vehicles, including two fire trucks and an ambulance with SAN QUENTIN FIRE DEPARTMENT written on the door. The men on the trucks were dressed in yellow coats with yellow fire hats. Walking and bringing up the rear was the watch commander, Lieutenant Brady, and Mr. Allen, the head of the San Quentin education program. He looked as scared as a lizard in a chicken coop, just waiting for the next disaster to rip him in another direction.

TWO

"I want you all in the sergeant's office," inmate Borackus ordered. "And drop your keys and weapons in that trashcan on your way in." He spoke with the rifle pointed at them.

"Take it easy, we're going to do whatever you want, Mr. Borackus," Sergeant Walters said as she dropped her pepper spray and baton into the fifty-five-gallon trashcan and put her hands in the air. "Just get your fat ass in there! And you can drop the Mr. Borackus bull crap. Up till twenty minutes ago I was *inmate* or *ass out* or whatever low-scum names you used." Sergeant Walters moved into the office along with Officers Yeager and Viale.

"Oh my God," Viale said. "Did you see Smitty? His head is busted wide open." Yeager just kept his hands up and went into the office.

"Get the keys, Bumpy," Borackus ordered. "Let the fellas out on three. Leave the rest of the punks to rot." Inmate Richards, also known as Bumpy, did what he was told. Bumpy made his way to the third tier where the other four of the crew were held. He un-spiked the cell doors and let out four inmates otherwise known as Shadow, Ryder, Jersey, and Slowpoke. As the four inmates moved to the first tier, Slowpoke could see the door on the gun rail being opened.

"Borackus, they're coming through the gun walk door!"

Borackus pulled Sergeant Walters from the office. "I'll kill her if you come in!" he yelled.

The door shut and the phone began to ring. "What?" Borackus yelled into the receiver.

127

"My name is Captain White, I'm the hostage negotiator, and I want to talk about your needs, wants, and desires," White said.

"It's really simple," Borackus said. "I give you two hostages and you give me two inmates from North Block. That's the deal and it's non-negotiable."

"That sounds doable," White said. "Which two inmates in North Block?"

"Stanton and Stross. Have them here in ten minutes and I won't kill the bitch."

Captain White told Lieutenant Brady to get the inmates. Brady called North Block and ordered the desk officer to make ready inmates Stross and Stanton for transfer to Carson Section. Officer Childress said he would have them in five minutes.

"Holms!" Officer Childress yelled. "Grab inmates Stross and Stanton out of four north fifty-three on the double, time is everything!"

Officer Holms went to cell four north fifty-three. "Wake up, you two, you're moving now," Officer Holms ordered through the closed cell door. Holms could see no movement inside the cell. He took his flashlight out and shined it into the cell; the sleeping inmates made no movement. Holms opened the cell and stepped inside and turned on the light but no light came on. He looked closely at the beds and noticed the inmates were simply dummies made from rolled blankets and fake heads. He pushed his alarm and the North Block buzzer sounded, blue lights flashing over the doors. Officer Holms ran down the stairwell and met Officer Childress on the second tier. "Chili, they're gone. Escaped!" Officer Holms exclaimed.

THREE

"Time is up, White! You just got an innocent sergeant killed. Maybe now you'll take us seriously!" The door to

Carson Section opened and Sergeant Walters stepped out and turned to her right. She was looking at Captain White and about sixty other staff members armed with automatic weapons in tactical positions, guns trained on the door. Also about twenty armed responders on the gun rail looked down at her. Her eyes told a story of helplessness and despair. her hands went towards her face in a praying motion, then the cracking thunder of the revolver shot a bullet through her right ear. The bullet exited the other ear, taking the ear and brains across the rotunda and splattered the white-painted concrete wall with a high-velocity blood pattern. Sergeant Walters pitched forward and landed dead on the rotunda floor, blood instantly pooling around her head, her legs kicking in reflex, then shaking before finally stopping and joining her brain in death.

"Damnit!" Captain White shouted. "What is wrong with you? We were bringing the inmates to you, punk!"

Borackus located a bullhorn in the Carson Section equipment closet and used it to reply. "I said ten minutes, *ten minutes*, you idiot! You should have taken me seriously—and the vulgar names you're calling me are unprofessional. So let me make myself perfectly clear; you have ten minutes to get me Stross and Stanton or Officer Yeager is next!"

Captain White turned toward Lieutenant Brady. "Where the hell are Stross and Stanton?"

Brady looked white as a ghost. "They're gone," he said. "Escaped. The officer found two dummies in their racks."

White's hands went to his temples; sweat was pouring from his brow. He took the bullhorn and pleaded with Borackus. "Please don't kill anyone else! We have a problem and need more time. Please give us more time!" White begged.

"You have a problem all right," Borackus answered. "You have six minutes!"

Lieutenant Street approached White. "We have a tactical plan of entry and could move in sixty seconds," Street explained. White was on the phone with the warden; he described what had happened so far and explained the critical deadline they were working with.

"Take them," Warden Windom said. "We can't stand by and let them execute our staff. We're unable to give them what they want. We have an emergency situation with the escape, two dead staff members, and we're about to lose two more. Take them now with whatever force is necessary, including deadly force. Do not waste another minute."

Captain White hung up the phone. He wiped the sweat from his forehead. "Lieutenant Street."

"Yes, Captain," Street replied.

"Go for it. Shoot to kill if necessary. Do your best to avoid harm to the hostages, but take that asshole out," White said.

"Yes, sir."

Lieutenant Street gave the signal over the secured radio channel. "Operation Raven is authorized, move on my command." The men in tactical suits with automatic weapons moved on the gun rail and the ground at the same time. They moved close to the doors leading to Carson Section. "Go Raven." Suddenly the power was out and the lights were off. The doors blasted open and explosions from concussion grenades went off. Blasts from rifles with night vision and small arms fire were heard.

"Target down, target down!" the radio on the hood of Captain White's truck reported. As the smoke cleared, Officer Spearman and Officer DeVito could see Officers Viale and Yeager running towards the fire trucks on the upper yard. "They're all dead!" Yeager reported. "They're all dead!"

FOUR

Warden Windom was walking with a group of administrators towards the emergency command post. Captain White approached her and reported the status. "Good call, Warden. Targets are all down and the remaining two hostages are safe."

"What about the escape?" the warden asked. "Have we activated the emergency escape procedures yet?"

"Not yet, ma'am," White reported.

She turned to the administrators with her. "Activate emergency escape procedures now," she ordered.

"Yes, ma'am," Chief Deputy Warden Long replied. Moments later the green light above the gas chamber turned red and started flashing. It was about seven in the morning before the escape triangle was in place. Photos of the escaped inmates were posted at all the bridges in the bay area, as well as the airports and train stations; even the ferry boat stations had a copy.

FIVE

Six body bags were brought into the Marin County Coroner's Office morgue and placed on autopsy tables. Medical Examiner Tina Harris was on duty and accepted the case. She carefully opened the first body bag containing inmate Borackus. The foul stench made even her professionally trained nose wince. She took the spray hose and washed the naked body containing multiple bullet holes through the chest and head. She turned towards her instruments on the table, noticing a shadow on the wall. She turned as Borackus grabbed her head and twisted her neck, killing her instantly. Borackus went to the other body bags and released the evil Grigori; all except Shadow. He used his finger dipped in blood to mark Shadow with death. The five fitted themselves with the clothing located in the next room and walked out the door. In the shadows was a figure that spoke in a low voice.

"Where is the location of the sword?" the voice asked. It was Zoltar. Slowpoke, Bumpy, Ryder, and Jersey bowed and dropped to their knees.

"Stanton escaped, master," Borackus said. "But we'll find him."

"You failed me three years ago when you killed his wife, and now you have failed me again. There will not be a third failure. Know this, maggot! If he reaches the sword before we do, you will not live to see what I do to him!" Zoltar said, then disappeared.

"Get up, you pathetic pussies. You kneel to me, not my master," Borackus said.

SIX

The next day the search was on for the two escaped inmates from San Quentin. It was all over the news. Stephen and Jake's pictures were shown almost as much as Borackus and the other four inmates who had mysteriously disappeared from the county morgue, where the medical examiner was found dead. Sherri, Teresa's twin sister, was watching the news in disbelief. She had visited Jake only last month and had no idea what he was planning. A knock on her door shook her back to reality. Sherri went to the door and noticed a tall, good-looking gentleman in a suit.

"Good morning, Ms. Alexander," the man said. "My name is Inspector Jericho, Sam Jericho. Mind if I have a word with you?" he asked.

"Do you have ID?" she asked. He showed her his badge. "Come in," she said. "Can I get you some coffee?"

"Yes please, black."

Sherri went to the kitchen with Sam right behind her. "Please sit down," she said, pointing to the table as she passed by to get the coffee. "What is this about?" Sam noticed the small TV in the kitchen tuned to the news report about the escape.

"I'm here because of your brother-in-law, Jake Stanton," he said. "Have you seen him lately?"

"Inspector—" she started.

"Please call me Sam," he interrupted.

"Inspector, I just saw the news this morning. I visited Jake last month and I knew nothing about his escape, I swear."

"Would you help him if he asked you?" he asked.

"I love Jake. I think he is innocent and was railroaded by the system. I don't know what I would do if he contacted me."

"Ms. Alexander," Sam started, and then took a light sip of his hot coffee. "Ahh, this is good coffee. In my line of work we often get the 7-11 brand and it's awful."

"Thank you." She favored him with a half-smile, then gave him a sardonic look. Sam knew it would be useless to press her for information.

"Please do yourself and him a favor, Ms. Alexander, and call me if he contacts you." He gave her his card and she put it on the refrigerator. "Thank you for your time," he said as he turned towards the door to leave. He turned back towards her, not unlike Colombo might do as he was questioning a witness on TV. "Oh, one more thing. I'm not only investigating the escape of Stanton and Stross, I'm also investigating the homicide of the medical examiner, Tina Harris, and the disappearance of five dead inmates from the Marin County morgue. I have reason to believe the dead inmate case is related to Jake somehow."

"Why would you think that?" Sherri asked.

"Because they were killed after they took over a unit at San Quentin and demanded to trade hostages for Stanton and Stross. When the institution could not produce them fast enough, the inmates killed a female sergeant," Sam said.

"But why would they want Jake?" she asked.

"I was hoping you could help me with that one," he said.

"I have no idea," Sherri said. "Thank you for stopping by."

Sam took another sip from the coffee cup. "I guess that means it's time to go" he said, handing her the almost full cup. "Thank you again for the coffee, and please remember what I said."

Chapter XI

The Garden

ONE

As Jake awoke from a nightmare, he found himself alone in the dark, covered in sweat. He was in the hotel room in Chinatown and his body ached as if he had spent the weekend skiing at Tahoe. Every muscle cried with pain. He tried to get up but decided against it when he could hardly move his legs. He felt the long beard on his face and knew he had to move. He reached for the light and the room lit up. He got to his feet and made his way to the bathroom. After about twenty minutes in the hot shower he shaved and got dressed. *"You there, my friend?"* Jake said telepathically.

"I'm here," Stephen said. *"How are you feeling?"*

"I've been better," Jake said.

"Meet me in the hall in about ten minutes," Stephen replied.

"Jake, it's Daniel."

"I'm here, Daniel."

"I have something for you," he said. *"Can I come in?"* "Sure," Jake answered. Daniel entered the hotel room with a bag hanging from his shoulder.

"The bag," Jake said. "The bag Samuel gave me when we were at his place in the Grasslands; but how could it be here?"

Daniel smiled and handed the bag to Jake. "We're in a very special place, Jake. You recall your lessons with Stephen, and what he told you of the markings on the wall—or rather, the door?"

"Yes, I have seen the markings on several things lately, even here," Jake said, and held up the bag where the brand was visible.

"Samuel meant for you to have that bag, Jake, so he sent it across and I collected it for you. This bag is able to travel from the Crossing to this side, and anything placed inside the bag will make the trip also." Jake still had not examined what was in the bag. He knew the container with the birdbath water was in there, and he expected a note to him on some of the loose paper, but until it was opened he would never know.

There was a knock on the door. It was Stephen. The three men stood beside the bed as Jake turned the bag upright and dumped the items on the bed. Jake saw the container with the water from the birdbath, four loose papers, a book, and a smaller bag made of buckskin that was tied shut. First Jake took the papers; it was a note from Samuel. Jake read it aloud.

***

Dear Jake,

You have committed to a path of righteousness and God will help you, but you must surrender to him and be cleansed. As with all his prophets and servants, expect to be purged clean through fire and emptied of all corruption, for as surely as those who went before you were cleansed, so shall you be cleansed before being used for his purpose.

As Moses was cast out of Egypt and crossed the great wilderness to lead the children of Israel, he was cleansed; as Jonah, the prophet, was swallowed by a great fish and lived in the belly of the whale before telling of what God will do, he was cleansed. Even as your namesake, Jacob, wrestled with the Angel before he was blessed and renamed Israel, he was cleansed of all corruption so he could be filled with righteousness.

Be not discouraged or put aside by trials and tribulations, for the road you have chosen is a difficult one. Wide is the path and easy the road that leads to destruction, but narrow is the path and hard is the way that leads to the Lord. I have enclosed the map to En-Dor. Careful that you're prepared when you meet the woman who dwells in this place of dead bones.

Be blessed,

Samuel, son of Hanna

Jake picked up the book. It was the book he had placed on the nightstand back in the guest room in the Grasslands called *The Crossing*. He would surely read it when he had a moment.

Jake opened the deerskin purse and dumped the items on the bed. Out of the purse spilled twelve gold coins and still another leather purse. When he dumped the last purse out, what landed on the bed amazed all three men. It was a small wedge of what appeared to be an apple or some kind of fruit, only it looked as fresh as if it were picked that very moment. Moreover, the slice of fruit glowed with a white light brighter than the sixty-watt bulb above their heads. Stephen picked it up and handed it to Jake. "This is for you." Stephen had tears in his eyes when he said, "It's fruit from the tree of life." Jake took the wedge and looked into the mirror on the closet doors with their reflections. He studied the two young twenty-seven and twenty-five-year-old men standing next to a ninety-year-old man who could barely walk. Jake had a rough time making them out, as his ice-blue eyes were faded to gray.

Jake put the fruit in his mouth and opened his eyes. He watched as the old man in the mirror faded away second by second. His back straightened, his shoulders widened, his white hair turned gray, then dark brown in less than thirty seconds; before he had even swallowed the fruit he

137

was the Jake Stanton who had met Stephen in West Block at San Quentin State Prison. The pain Jake was living with disappeared and he felt like he did when they were at the Crossing with Teresa. He was young again, and he was ready to stand against Zoltar and Borackus. He hungered for it.

TWO

As the three walked into the parlor where the elevator and the five doors were, Jake thought about what he had heard behind the doors.

"Where is Liea?" Jake asked.

"She will meet us at the Presidio later," Stephen said. "I didn't expect Samuel to provide the gift to you so I planned to take you to the garden. Liea cannot go there." He continued, "I think, had you not received the gift from Samuel, you would not be alive today, Jake."

"I think you're right," Jake agreed. "The doors, with the markings, what do they mean?"

"Why do you ask?" Stephen said.

"Because last night the marks were on the other doors; that mark was on that door, and vice versa," Jake said as he pointed to the brand markings on the doors.

Stephen smiled. "You're correct, Jake. The doors will not open for anyone." Jake gave Stephen one of his famous confused looks as if to say: how do we get the door open? Stephen read him loud and clear. "The door will open for you when you open it for the right reason, kinda like what Samuel was saying in his letter about cleansing yourself. No sin is allowed in the garden, Jake. That is why humans are not able to enter until after judgment day."

"Well then it's a good thing I was given the gift from Samuel because I'm black with sin. My soul is stained with sin and I'm as filthy as rags."

"That's it, Jake," Daniel said. "Truth and confession." Jake looked at the doors. He put his hand on the left door and closed his eyes. He was flying in the air like when he was an eagle at the Crossing. He could see a park and people laughing and playing. Jake was standing on green grass watching a father push his child on the swing. Across the street was a church, and people were walking out with smiles on their faces. He could hear people talking; some were speaking other languages but he understood them. He watched as children were climbing on the monkey bars; others were playing tag and still others were boarding the small train in the park where an old man wearing a hat with the name "Bob" written on it was helping the children onto the train. Jake could hear Teresa but didn't understand what she was saying. The sun was shining brightly and the smiles were everywhere. Then suddenly he was back in the parlor in front of the doors.

Jake said nothing. He put his hand on the other door and again he was flying. It was dark and he heard crying children. He was at the same park, only this scene was quite different. Here, the father was picking the crying child up from the swing and another man was confronting Bob and the children looked scared. A cool wind was blowing and leaves were tossed in the dark wind. Jake felt the quickening inside him, like when he was in the eighth grade and he was facing Billy Parson, or the times he confronted Borackus and Zoltar. There was a sense of impending doom.

Then Jake was back in the parlor and he heard a voice, it was his grandfather. "*Choose a door, Jake.*" The left was the sunshine and the right was the cold wind. Jake didn't hesitate. He opened the door leading to darkness and confronted the man who was trying to kidnap the child on the swing. The sword in Jake's hand sent the man to the grave. Then he turned to Bob; realizing he was a pedophile, Jake slayed him.

As the wind blew stronger, Jake called on Zoltar, whom he sensed was in the park; but the evil fallen Angel fled as the light of the Shaddai stood in the park. The sun appeared and the children were relieved that the evil hiding behind the fake leadership had fled. Jake had chosen wisely. He was answering the calling and was filled with righteousness. He heard the voice again as he did when he was an eagle: "This is my servant, Jacob, in whom I am well pleased."

Daniel and Stephen were standing beside Jake; they were near another door.

"Why did you choose the door leading to darkness, Jake?" Stephen asked.

"I'm a knight in the army of the Lord. My code requires me to stand against evil, regardless of the odds. I took a leap of faith."

"You speak true, Jake. Now you're ready to enter the garden."

THREE

Stephen reached for the door and opened it. The light was brilliant. The three went through the door and Jake's eyes were filled with amazement. He was standing on plush, green grass; the trees and bushes were covered with fruit. Animals were everywhere: lions, bears, elephants, dogs, tigers, and monkeys. Jake saw a monkey that looked just like Conchita. Jake saw the Angel at the gate with the flaming sword as he walked along a path next to a stream and was amazed at the clear, clean water. He could see fish swimming in the stream. "Are we really here?" Jake asked.

"Indeed, my friend," Stephen said. They walked to the center of the garden, stopping regularly to pet and show affection to the animals. Jake hugged a white tiger who was as docile as his own dog had been. Jake felt privileged to be in such a place, and soon they were looking up at the tree of life. The tree stood tall; *it is covered with enough fruit to feed the world*, Jake thought. Stephen stood on his tiptoes and pulled what looked like an orange but was the color of a red apple from the tree. He handed it to Jake. The fruit glowed brightly. Jake took a moment to admire it. It felt hard with ripeness; he took a bite. The apple-orange exploded in his mouth. It was beyond incredible, and Jake thought he was dreaming. He took another bite, then another; no core, no rind, nothing to throw away. In another bite the fruit was devoured and Jake was glowing. Then he saw the tree of the knowledge of good and evil. Jake felt the tree calling to him; it was like a long-lost lover wanting to embrace him after a lifetime apart. The pull was incredible. *"Come to me, Jake, I'll give you rest,"* the voice in his head said. Jake resisted and then pushed the thought from his mind. He said, "I'm Jacob from the bloodline of Seth, and loyal servant of Michael and the Lord our God, so get behind me, Satan!" Immediately the feeling left him.

Daniel was helping himself to some of the fruit from a nearby bush, and Stephen also ate from the tree of life. The garden was like heaven on earth; nothing could impact the joy and peace they were feeling as they dined on the tastiest fruit one could imagine. They ate till they were full, then sat back on the grass near the stream with the animals. The grass was like a silk carpet. Jake took note that the garden had no insects at all. Not an ant, spider, gnat, or fly could be seen or heard.

"No bugs?" Jake asked as he turned to Stephen.

"Nope, no bugs," Stephen replied. "Bugs came after the garden, a necessary answer to processing death," Stephen said, as a smile began to form on his face.

"Think about it; bugs serve no purpose in a life, only environment," he continued. "And here, the plants self-pollinate. No need for bees." Jake liked it when Stephen would share a smile; it seemed smiles were not so common this side of sleep these days.

"Well, that's just fine with me," Jake said, and laid back on the grass and closed his eyes. Jake felt he was at home; not the homes he'd lived in as an adult, but like his childhood home. No worries lived in his mind here, only peace. As he relaxed, he drifted to sleep.

As usual when he slept, he was instantly at the ranch and Teresa was in the bed next to him. It was such peace of mind knowing he was no longer aging on the other side. Never had he felt so strong in body, as well as spirit. With his eyes still closed, he rolled over and placed his arm around her and cupped her breast. She responded to his touch and turned to kiss him. Not like a good morning peck of a kiss, but fresh and moist and loving. His renewed body came alive and they made love like it was their first time before drifting into to a restful, deep sleep.

FOUR

Conchita was on the bed, pulling at Teresa's hair. "Resa, Resa come, come," she said. Teresa and Jake got up and Teresa went with Conchita to investigate what the matter was. Conchita was simply announcing the arrival of Aaron and Uncle Lester. Teresa made coffee as Jake took a hot shower. Then Jake entertained the company as Teresa showered and made ready for the day.

Aaron lit his pipe and asked Jake to tell of his visit to the garden. Stephen and Daniel walked in and greeted Aaron and Lester. When asked about his choice of doors, Jake smiled. "I did what came naturally," Jake explained. "The first door held a false sense of security, and nothing about our way abides falsehood."

"Well put," Daniel said. The men talked away the morning while Teresa made breakfast for everyone.

PART TWO

Chapter XII

Inspector Jericho

ONE

The rain pelted the ground and puddles; the large raindrops caused a roar under the loud and frequent crashes of thunder outside the Marin County Sheriff's Office. Sam Jericho was thumbing through photos of six dead inmates and one dead medical examiner. The only body left in the morgue was inmate Richards, otherwise known as Shadow. He'd suffered three bullet wounds to his chest and one to his head. In blood, on his forehead, was what looked like hieroglyphic markings that meant nothing to Sam. The phone on the desk startled him back to reality. "Inspector Jericho," Sam answered.

"This is Ruth Springer, Inspector, you called and left a message?" the voice on the other end of the phone said. He had reached out to Doctor Springer, a Stanford University expert on the occult and strange religious occurrences.

"Yes, Doctor, I'm investigating a homicide and was hoping I could meet with you and discuss some markings on a body that appear to be of a religious nature," Sam said.

"I would like to help, Inspector, but I have a class this afternoon. Can we meet later, say around six o'clock?"

"Six is good," Sam said. "I'll come to you at the university. Thanks again."

"No problem, Inspector. See you then."

Sam hung up the phone and opened a file on his desk marked Stanton and began to read through it. He looked at the gruesome photos of Teresa's body, what used to be a very beautiful woman. He noticed there were no other suspects pursued, even though the house had multiple prints lifted. Some of the prints were even in the victim's blood and had to have been made after the murder occurred. He discovered the prints were run in the Automated Fingerprint Identification System (AFIS) and came back with no known match. He continued to read the file and made a mental note to run the prints again when he had a moment.

"What do you see, Sam?" Sergeant Morales asked. "You got that look on your face like you just discovered who shot Kennedy again."

"Kiss my ass, John. I think this Stanton file stinks."

John Morales walked over and sat in the chair across from Sam. "Is that the Sonoma County wife murder file you had me pick up?" John asked.

"As a matter of fact, it is. It looks like our colleagues in Sonoma County did a pretty sloppy job at investigating. It says no autopsy was conducted on the remains; and take a look at the file in the print section," Sam said as he tossed the file to Sergeant Morales.

Morales stopped to check out the bloody photos, then moved to the print section and noticed the same thing as Sam. "What kind of lawyer did this guy have?" John asked. "How did he manage to get all day with this messed-up report? Even my cousin Ernie, who is about as stupid a lawyer as you could imagine, would have been able to raise reasonable doubt with this print file."

"Keep reading," Sam said. "The print file never made it to court. It was buried during trial and didn't show up until after the third appeal. Check out the dates."

"Holy crap, you're right, Sam. This guy got railroaded!" John said.

"Hey, John, do me a favor. I'm meeting with a doctor out at Stanford tonight. Can you run the prints again for me?"

"Sure, no problem, Sam," John said, and took the print file and put it in his briefcase.

TWO

The rain was not showing any signs of letting up. The 101 freeway was flooding in San Rafael so Sam had to take a back road to get around it. His wipers were on the highest speed and were working frantically to stay ahead of the downpour. Sam tried to find some music on the radio with no luck. He settled for an AM talk show to take him across the Golden Gate Bridge to San Francisco.

As he pulled through the tollbooth, he noticed the eight-by-ten-inch photos of Stanton and Stross. The look in Jake Stanton's eyes was not that of evil. The file told him that Jake was a law-abiding citizen, well respected and loved by family and his community. He was reminded of the victim's twin sister, who believed he was an innocent man.

Sam decided to take it one minute at a time; for now, he would try to discover what the crazy blood marks on the only remaining body in the morgue meant, and who killed his favorite medical examiner.

THREE

The thunder rolled like it was right on top of him as he got out of his car in the parking lot at Stanford. The walk from his car to the entrance may as well have been underwater because he could not have been wetter if he had taken a swim through the parking lot. He shook off the rain as best he could and made his way to Doctor Springer's office. He opened the door and was met by her receptionist. "Can I help you?" the little old lady at the desk asked. Her desk was very neat and was surrounded by little ceramic dogs, all of the cocker spaniel breed.

"Yes. I'm Inspector Jericho with the Marin County Sheriff's Office. I'm here to meet with Doctor Springer."

"Just a moment." The woman pushed a button on the phone and announced, "Doctor Springer, I have an Inspector Jericho to see you." Placing the phone down she said, "Inspector, would you please take a seat? Doctor Springer will be right with you." Sam turned and sat in one of the wooden chairs that looked like it could be a collector's item.

"I see you like the cocker spaniel," Sam said to the woman.

"Yes, my sweet Julia was the best dog ever. She died three years ago and I just could not bring myself to get another dog, but I keep her memory alive with my glass dog collection." Jericho offered a sympathetic smile and decided to refrain from the small talk. He looked around the room and noticed pictures of pyramids and hieroglyphic writing.

"Inspector Jericho, the doctor can see you now. Please go through the last door on the left."

"Thank you." Sam walked to the rear of the building, checking out the strange art on the walls.

FOUR

"You must be Inspector Jericho," the woman standing in front of him said as she extended her hand to meet him.

Sam managed to say, "Yes," but was in a state of shock at the beautiful woman standing in front of him. She was about twenty-eight, five foot three or so with long, dark hair and a white lab coat. The first thing he did, as with all pretty women he saw these days, was check out her wedding ring finger. He felt she noticed him doing this and turned to comment on the artwork on the walls in a desperate effort to clean it up. However, he could feel the blood burning his face.

"Does this artwork mean something special?" he asked, pointing to the painting of the pyramid behind him.

"All artwork means something special. This is a painting of Zoltar's resting place," she said, pointing to the painting he was looking at. "Zoltar is a fallen Angel and must return to the earth whenever he is mortally wounded in battle. This is where Zoltar lies and heals himself before returning to walk the earth again."

"Wait a minute," Sam said. "Did you say mortally wounded? Doesn't that usually mean dead?"

"Usually, yes," she said, "but the fallen Angels and their descendants are immortal and can only be killed if they lose their heart or their head, or if they're killed with an enchanted weapon."

Sam scratched his head. "So what did you mean by descendent?" Sam asked.

"We're only now learning about them, however, we have determined there is a subculture of humans called the Shaddai and Grigori that carry the DNA of angelic beings. We are still in the testing phase. Some of our research indicates that these beings are stronger than the Angels themselves and possess incredible powers. Please sit down, Inspector." Sam took a seat in another old wooden chair across from her desk. He was fascinated with what she was saying but still intoxicated by her beauty.

"The Shaddai, which we think means the enlightened or renowned, have a certain DNA strain that often goes unnoticed in blood tests, while other times the same DNA glows like a light under the microscope. It has baffled the strongest minds in the field," she continued.

"Incredible," Sam said. "So tell me, Doctor, could an individual look human and be one of these Shaddai?"

"Yes, they look the same as you and me, only they have superhuman DNA, which, if activated, glows life even if the body appears dead." Sam was smiling in disbelief at this statement. Doctor Springer read this in his face. "Look, Inspector, this is only now beginning to unfold.

147

Perhaps I got ahead of myself sharing too much too fast."
She pulled papers together on her desk and pushed them
into a drawer as if to hide what she was working on.
"What is it I can help you with?"

Sam pulled the photos of the dead inmates out and
placed them on her desk. "The five on the right are
missing, as if they walked out of the building after killing
the medical examiner. The sixth was left behind with this
marking on his forehead in the medical examiner's
blood."

Doctor Springer took the photo and looked closely at the
writing. She wrote down something on her yellow legal
pad and looked up at the inspector; she was as white as a
piece of chalk. "'A gift of death to my master Zoltar,' that
is what the markings mean in angelic script," she said.

"Zoltar, like in the painting, Zoltar?" Sam replied.

"The one and only," she said.

"Looks like I came to the right place," Sam said. "Please,
Doctor, tell me everything you know about the Shaddai,"
Sam asked, this time with concern on his face instead of
disbelief.

"OK, but remember, this is all very new to us, and we
have been seeing much more suspicious activity lately."

"Understood," Sam replied.

"The Bible tells us in Genesis six about the Watcher
Angels who lusted after the human women and
conceived children half-human and half-Angel, with
superhuman powers. The Bible refers to them as
Nephilim or Giants. This is part of what led to God
flooding the earth." Sam had a half-smile on his face as
he listened on the edge of his seat. "Didn't you ever go to
Sunday school?" she asked. Sam stopped smiling.
"Anyway, the Nephilim were again found in Canaan,
when the children of Israel were led out of Egypt by

Moses. The last of the Nephilim or Giants were killed when David killed Goliath—"

Sam interrupted, "I remember that part. But you say the descendants of Angels cannot be killed unless by an enchanted instrument or weapon. David killed Goliath with a stone and his sling," Sam insisted.

"David hit Goliath with the stone," she said, "then killed him with the Sword of Goliath, which is one of the enchanted weapons." Sam marveled at her narrative that made sense to him as she told it. The more she talked, the more he wondered if the dead inmates who miraculously vanished from the morgue were, in fact, descendants from Angels.

The cell phone on Inspector Jericho's belt played the Journey song "Don't Stop Believing." He quickly grabbed the phone, feeling embarrassed that Doctor Springer heard the corny ring tone. "Inspector Jericho," he answered. "Yes, I'll be right there. Give me an hour with traffic."

She was smiling. "I love that song," she said.

"I'm a little embarrassed. I'm a Journey fan and I know it's kinda corny," he said.

"Not at all," she replied. "In fact, I have tickets to see them at the Cow Palace next month." Sam looked impressed. *Well, we may have something in common after all*, he thought. "I would kill to be there," Sam said. "But my work keeps me pretty busy. You have been a great help and I would like to continue this conversation," he said.

"No problem, any time."

"I have to run. They have the surveillance video of the morgue. Can we meet again?"

"Yes, of course," she said. "Let me give you my personal cell."

"Excellent, I'll call you later tonight. Maybe we can meet sometime tomorrow and you can finish your story," he said.

"I would like that," she said. Sam could feel a spark of chemistry between them.

"OK, back into the rain. Be safe, Doctor," Sam said as he got up to leave.

"Please call me Ruth."

"OK, Ruth, and I'm Sam."

"Nice to meet you, Sam."

FIVE

Sam made his way through the rain to his car and headed back to the office. He was thinking about the incredible story Ruth had told about Angels, Grigori, and Shaddai. *Was it possible the dead inmates simply got up and walked out of the morgue?* He thought. The video would be very interesting, and he could hardly wait to view it.

SIX

As Sam entered the sheriff's office, the phone on his desk was ringing. "Inspector Jericho." Sam pulled the wet coat from his shoulders and hung it on the rack behind his chair as he listened to Sergeant Morales tell of the fingerprint he ran in AFIS. "It hit, Sam, the print. It belongs to Jessie Borackus, the same dead inmate missing from the morgue. What the hell is going on, Sam?"

"I don't know, John, but I intend to find out. Come back to the office as soon as you can, I want you to see a video," Sam said.

"On my way."

Sam plugged the DVD into the computer on his desk and booted it up. At first just snow, then a shaky vision of inside the morgue. The video showed the dead inmates being placed on the autopsy tables in body bags, then the medical examiner entered the picture, placing her instruments on a tray and setting up her tape recorder microphone. She walked out of the picture, then reentered and unzipped the body bag holding Inmate Borackus. She put her hand over her nose and mouth and made a face of disgust. She removed the body bag and rinsed the body. As she did this, blood from the wounds spilled into the drain trays on either side of the table. In the rear of the picture there was movement, as if the body bag holding the inmate at the top of the screen was being removed. This was odd, as the medical examiner was alone in the morgue. Suddenly the video cut off and nothing more was captured.

"You have got to be kidding me!" Sam exclaimed. He tried to rewind and watch it again. The results were the same. At the point he thought something should happen, no video. Sergeant Morales walked into the office and shook the water from his raincoat.

"It's really starting to come down out there," he said. He noticed Sam sitting at his desk with a sick look on his face. "So what is on the video, Sam?"

"Take a look and see for yourself," Sam answered. John pushed play and watched the video that Sam had viewed seven times.

"What the . . .?"

"I know. Just when you think you have something, the video cuts off," Sam said.

"Sam, look at the body bag at the top of the screen," John said. "Watch how it moves all by itself."

"What makes you think it moved all by itself? Perhaps an assistant is moving it."

151

"Negative, buddy," John said. "I checked it out and confirmed; she was alone in the building and the door was locked from the inside. The movement of that body bag is happening because maybe the inmate is not dead," John said.

"The reports from Quentin show Doctor Bouie pronouncing all six inmates dead."

"I know what the reports say, I read them. I even checked the time of death and noticed the bodies were on scene for three hours before they were placed in the bags. We have a dozen photos of each of the dead bodies," John said.

"I'm not saying it makes sense, only one of the bodies must have been alive. That person must have killed our medical examiner and turned off the camera, then took the other bodies with him when he left," John continued.

"That's one theory, I guess," Sam said.

Sam turned to the Stanton file.

"Now the next crazy twist," Sam started. "The unidentified fingerprints in the victim's blood just happen to be from one of the dead inmates who was killed trying to get at Jacob Stanton in the prison. This is the same Stanton who happened to escape from North Block on the same night this Borackus was killed, and the same Stanton who was convicted of killing his wife. The same Stanton whose victim's family believe he is innocent. Now it all makes perfect sense," Sam said with a heavy measure of sarcasm. "Get me the file on inmate Borackus. I want to see what he was in prison for."

"You got it, boss," John answered.

SEVEN

Inspector Jericho sat at his desk reviewing the Stanton file and also the Bible, specifically Genesis chapter 6.

"Here is the file on Borackus. The son of a bitch had a clean record until three months ago, when he was busted for a 288 rape. He pleaded guilty to the charge and accepted a three-year deal. The same prison Stanton was serving his time in, coincidently," John said.

"I think not a coincidence," Sam said. "According to prison records, Borackus tried to attack Stanton with a weapon and was being locked up into Administrative Segregation when he broke out of his cuffs and took over the gunner. So let's assume for a moment it was not a coincidence. Three years ago, Borackus makes a move on Stanton and kills his wife, framing Stanton for the crime. Then when he knows where Stanton is incarcerated, he gets himself locked up so he has another opportunity to kill Stanton, only Stanton escapes again. Borackus is killed in the incident—or perhaps we're made to believe he is killed."

"Wait a minute, boss," John said. "What do you mean by made to believe he is killed?"

"Earlier this evening, I met with a Doctor Springer," Sam started. "Dr. Springer happens to be an expert on the occult. She told me about the Shaddai, and Grigori humans who are from the bloodline of Angels, and who have superhuman powers. Dr. Springer told me the only way the Shaddai or Grigori can be killed is with a special weapon or enchanted instrument."

"Come on, boss!" John said. "You don't believe in that stuff, do you?"

"I believe in what the evidence tells me, and so far the evidence is telling me something extraordinary is going on here," Sam said.

"Do me a favor, John, send this file to the Sonoma County District Attorney and point out that the print file was not used in any of the appeals," Sam said.

"Will do, boss. Where are you going?"

"I've got to see a man about a horse," Sam said with a sardonic look. "Actually, I need to do some more research. I'm meeting Doctor Springer at the library."

Chapter XIII

The Map

ONE

Jake woke up in the garden next to Stephen and Daniel; it was a warm, spring-like day. The three walked about the garden admiring the animals and beautiful vegetation, as well as the high waterfall. On top of the rocks near the waterfall they could see a man; he leaped and drifted like a leaf to the ground and walked over to them.

"Greetings, Michael," Stephen said. "Jake, meet Michael, whom we serve."

"It's an honor," Jake said, and bowed a knight's bow with his left leg extended, heel planted and low at the waist, as Stephen had taught him.

"The honor is mine, Jake. You have impressed many among the elders in Sion," Michael said. "You have gone through much undeserved persecution, yet you continue to stand strong in your faith."

"I had a good teacher," Jake said, looking at Stephen.

"I suppose you're right about that," Michael replied. "You have a difficult path ahead of you. The sword is calling out to be found, despite the old woman of En-Dor's efforts to keep it hidden. Go with my blessing, and this."

Michael handed Jake a white cloth bag with a dagger in a leather sheath. He then touched his forehead as Stephen had long ago in their cell. Jake felt the sensation again, that of peace and love, like warm honey dripping over his head and his body. When he looked up with eyes full of tears, Michael was gone.

The three were no longer in the garden; they were standing in the parlor outside the five doors and the elevator where they entered the garden. The musky smell of old wood and mold from the hotel filled their noses. The three took the elevator to the surface where they heard that strange sound again, like flesh rubbing against a full balloon, as they passed through the brick wall. Then they were on the other side of the red curtain facing the old Chinese man, who was smiling with his eyebrows high on his forehead.

TWO

Jake looked at Stephen and asked, "Where to next?"

"We're going to the Presidio to meet Liea," Stephen said.

Daniel handed Jake his leather purse. Jake removed the dagger that was in a leather holster and attached it to his belt, then tied the strap around his upper leg. They exited the hotel.

The men stepped into a waiting taxi. "Please take us to 1248 Market," Daniel told the driver.

"Jake, what did you think of the garden?" Stephen asked.

"It's impossible to describe," Jake answered as the taxi moved through the traffic in the pouring rain. "How can I thank you for the experience?"

"I expect you will want to choke me before this night is over," Stephen laughed.

"Why do you say that?"

"Jake, the dagger Michael gave you in the garden—" Stephen started.

"I know, it's like yours. I have strapped it to my leg like you taught me."

"The dagger is nothing like the one I wear, Jake, or like the ones I trained you with. Your dagger is very old and very powerful. This is only the second time I have seen it. Michael has had that dagger since the day Gabriel took it from Abraham as he was about to sacrifice his son, Isaac."

"What are you saying, Stephen?"

"The dagger on your belt is the Dagger of Moriah, named after Abraham's altar. The Dagger of Moriah is one of the twelve enchanted instruments. This weapon will kill Zoltar or any descendant within the bloodline, including us," Stephen continued.

"Really?" Jake asked with a heavy sigh. "I would feel much better if you would carry it."

"Never think it," Stephen replied. "Inasmuch as Michael gave the blade to you, so shall you use it for his glory." Stephen was gracing Jake with one of his better you than me looks.

As the taxi made its way down side streets to avoid traffic jams, Jake lost track of all direction.

"Are we going the right way?" Jake asked.

"We must meet Liea at a warehouse in the Presidio. We'll also meet others who will help our cause," Stephen said.

THREE

The taxi pulled into a parking lot and the three travelers got out. Daniel paid the driver while Jake and Stephen made their way under the overhang of the building to get out of the rain. Daniel joined them, and Stephen opened the door. The men shook off the rain and went towards a lit office in what appeared to be an auto body shop. The smell of Bondo and paint filled the air. Jake could see Liea and two other men inside the office; both men had a glowing white light above their heads.

As the three entered the office, Liea went to Stephen and embraced him. Stephen looked very happy to see her; it had only been two days for Liea, but weeks had passed for Stephen. The time at the Crossing and in the garden was different, and his heart had grown lonely for his lover's embrace. "You look so different Jake." Liea said, "So young!"

"I feel much better, I was nearly at the end of my path" Jake said.

"Jake, this is Tony and Ron McNabe. They're brothers, and will be helping us with the logistics of our quest."

"Like the garden, the direction Samuel has indicated we should start has been moved to another dimension and is able to stay hidden from most locating instruments," Stephen explained. "Tony and Ron are excellent navigators to places in other dimensions."

Jake opened the leather purse and took out the map Samuel had given him. It was written in a strange language and meant nothing to Jake, but Tony and Ron seemed to know precisely what it said. They read and spoke to each other in that strange language, often pausing to smile and laugh. Jake felt he could reach into their minds if he wanted and learn the language, however, he remembered what Stephen had taught him about respect. Jake was satisfied to wait until they decided to invite him into the conversation.

Tony turned to Jake. "I'm sorry, how rude. The map is in angelic script and tells of an ocean in the south Atlantic near Skaggs Island. We will travel by ship."

"Great," Jake said in that dreading tone.

"You don't like ships?" Ron asked.

"The last time I was on the ocean I got so seasick I thought I would die," Jake explained.

"Not to worry," Ron said. "We have something for that. Liea, would you be kind enough to hand me that pack?" Ron pointed to a small backpack on the shelf over her head.

Liea retrieved the pack and handed it to Ron. Ron took out a small bottle and handed it to Jake. "Take a taste of this when we board and you will feel great."

Jake took the small bottle and pulled the cork and smelled it. "Smells like coconut."

"Tastes even better," Ron said.

"So where do we board this ship?" Jake asked.

"First we buy it," Liea said, and pulled the painting back from the wall. It opened like a door on hinges, exposing the face of a safe. Liea started to turn the dial first left, then right, then left again, stopping at specific numbers until she heard a metallic click. Then she turned the handle and opened the safe. Liea removed several plastic containers filled with cash.

"How much?" Liea asked.

"Three million," Ron replied.

"The buy is all set up. We deliver the cash and the ship is ours," Tony stated.

"Wait a minute," Jake said. "Won't that look a little fishy if we show up with three million cash? I'm sure the government tracks such large transactions."

"Jake, Tony and Ron are worth billions. They own hotels in twenty-five different countries. This transaction is simply the tax and transfer fees required by the Arab prince they bought the ship from. The ship is four hundred million," Liea said.

"Wow," Jake said. "You guys must travel in style."

"The ship is great, and expensive," Tony explained. "But most importantly, the ship was blessed with the navigation system for traveling trans-dimension. The star maps on board have seven different galaxies outside of our earth. The new galaxies were mapped from other voyages in the Bermuda Triangle. This ship is the only vessel that has been able to navigate back."

"The ship is currently in port on Angel Island near the naval vessels. Her name is *Delilah's Secret* and she is as beautiful as her name," Ron added.

"If we expect to be ready to depart tomorrow, we must make our way to Angel Island," Stephen said.

"The Ferry likely has our picture so we need to travel by charter boat," Jake stated.

"Agreed," Stephen said. "Liea, can you arrange for transport by boat from the Grotto to Angel Island?"

"Consider it done," she replied with a warm smile that welcomed the challenge and adventure.

"*On your guard, Jake!*" a voice in Jake's head commanded. It was Aaron; he was warning Jake of danger.

"Stephen, I received a warning from my grandfather," Jake said.

"I feel it too," Stephen said. An arrow whizzed past Jake's head and stuck in the wall next to him.

"Look out, Stephen!" Liea yelled as another archer from the rafters was drawing down on him.

Stephen leaped to the forklift nearby and started it up. Jake jumped on and they lifted the forks to the top of the office and used the forklift as a ladder to elevate their position. Once on top of the office, Jake and Stephen could clearly see their attackers. It was Slowpoke and Bumpy from the prison; there was no sign of Borackus or the others.

Jake pulled out the dagger and took a defensive posture. Slowpoke swung from the rafters to the top of the office and pulled out a sword. Stephen was squared off with Bumpy, who also had a sword. The men circled each other, and Jake's mind went back to the lessons he had learned: *When facing an enemy who has the advantage, consider retreating and when equally matched, fight.*

This had gone on long enough. These two didn't know Jake held an enchanted weapon; his dagger looked like any other short blade, and if they felt they had the advantage with a sword, all the better.

Jake dodged the wild swings of the sword by the crazed individual at the end of it. After the fourth failed attempt Slowpoke was tiring, and as he brought the heavy sword in a swinging downward motion, Jake stepped to one side, rolled past Slowpoke, and slid the dagger into his neck, burying it to the handle.

The man's eyes bulged. He let out a screeching shriek of pain and fear. Instantly he knew he was touched with an enchanted blade.

Slowpoke pitched forward, falling to the ground, dead. Bumpy saw this and retreated towards the window where they had entered. Like a fleeing cat who was hissed from the yard, the creature sprang to the rafters; in two leaps he was out the window and into the storm.

Jake and Stephen jumped to the ground and studied the body of Slowpoke. The body turned ghost-white as the last of his blood ran from the neck wound.

"How did they know we were here?" Jake asked.

"We're leaving footprints," Stephen said. "Traceable footprints. We got lucky; the two idiots we just fought were likely a search party with recon instructions, only they got greedy and tried to move in on us themselves."

"The others are now likely contacting Zoltar, so we have to get out of here," Daniel said.

"He's right, let's go," Stephen agreed.

"I know a place," Liea said. Liea led the way to the parking lot where her car was waiting. The four got into the car and sped away while Tony and Ron followed in their truck.

FOUR

Liea pulled into the parking lot of the Hyatt Hotel at Fisherman's Wharf.

"I'll get the rooms," Liea said. "Wait here until I come and get you."

The three men relaxed in the car until they received the all clear sign from Liea. They followed Liea into the elevator that took them to the twelfth floor.

"Jake, you're in room 1248 and Daniel, you have the adjoining room. We will be right across the hall. Get some rest while I arrange for the boat to take us to *Delilah's Secret*," Liea said.

Jake entered his room and pulled off the bloody clothes. Jake reflected on the fatal wound he'd executed on the inmate who taught him his job in the prison laundry. He had never taken a life before. *It was him or me*, he thought as he stepped into the shower and washed the dried blood from his hands.

Jake was amazed how hard it was to get the blood off. It was like washing paint from his skin with thinner. Even after he scrubbed his hands three times with soap he could still see the crimson color in the palms of his hands. Jake dried himself and put on the white terrycloth robe that was hanging in the closet and climbed into bed. The rain was still pouring when he fell sleep.

Chapter XIV

Abigail

ONE

Teresa was rubbing his back when he opened his eyes at the Crossing.

"You were having a bad dream, Jake," she whispered in his ear.

"I feel much better now," Jake said, and rolled over and kissed her. "I missed you," he said, hugging her tight.

"And I, you, my dear. It seems ages since you were here last," Teresa continued. "I was hoping you would come home today. I have something I want to talk about."

Jake felt the blood leave his face. He thought, *No, it's a bad time to discuss anything negative. I just killed someone, I'm on the run from the authorities for escaping Quentin, Zoltar and his minions are trying to kill me, and all I want is to be with you. Please don't tell me you're leaving, please!* However, Jake never uttered a sound; he just regarded her with a smile and tried his best to make it a comforting smile, like the ones he would receive from Stephen in his hour of need.

"What is it?" Jake asked.

"I have been keeping something from you, Jake." Jake could see the tears welling in her blue eyes.

Jake heard himself say, "I know, my love, but it's all right." Jake's words were like a warm hug, full of compassion and forgiveness.

"Come with me, then, and meet our daughter," Teresa said.

Jake's eyes widened. He didn't expect this at all. He expected her to say she was leaving him and ascending to another place, never to return to the Crossing.

Jake stood up and Teresa led him by the hand to the sliding glass door. Jake saw a beautiful little girl with his grandfather, riding a small horse and laughing.

"She is your bloodline and your destiny," said the voice of Samuel in his head. Then Jake saw the little star hand waving in the birdbath.

"Her name is Abigail," Teresa said. "Isn't she beautiful?"

"How can this be?" Jake asked.

"I was going to tell you the night we were attacked that I was three months pregnant."

Jake's eyes welled up as he watched his little girl riding her horse and laughing with her great-grandfather. "So she—"

Teresa interrupted, "She is our daughter, Jake, and she has grown up here at the Crossing. She has been staying with my dad and his sister in Bodega Village when you come home."

Teresa looked into Jake's ice-blue eyes. "Michael always tells me the day before you will arrive and I send her to her grandpa's house. Abigail has a room there, and also here."

"Here?" Jake said.

"The room off the master suite, the one with the baby doll curtains and the white pearl furniture; that is her bedroom. I thought you had enough on your mind with your training and the escape. I hope I did the right thing."

Jake hugged his wife. "I have so many questions! I'm very happy you told me, and you're right, I have had a lot on my mind," Jake said. "I was afraid you were going to leave me again. I heard what Daniel said about his wife ascending and I thought that was what you were keeping from me."

"Jake, I'll be here as long as you need me. And you speak true; one day it will be time for me to go, but that will only happen when the time is right."

Jake kissed her tears from her cheeks. "I can't lose you again, Teresa."

"You can never lose me, Jake. Come on, it's time for you to meet your daughter." Teresa opened the slider and walked onto the back deck, followed by Jake.

"Abigail!" Teresa called. "Come to Mommy!"

The girl turned the horse and trotted to the deck and dismounted. Jake marveled at her perfection. The little girl ran up the steps and hugged her mother.

"Daddy's home," Teresa said, and looked towards Jake.

"Daddy!" the little girl yelled and ran to Jake. He went to his haunches to meet her and she hugged his neck as if she had known him all her life.

"That's my horse, Rainbow," Abigail said, pointing to the painted pinto who was white with brown markings and a pink muzzle.

"She is beautiful, sweetheart, just like you," Jake said. "How old are you?" he asked.

"Five," the little girl answered. Jake looked at Teresa.

"Time is different here, my love," Teresa said with a smile.

Jake picked up his daughter and held her for the first time. So many thoughts rushed through his mind, but the Good Shepherd's voice stopped everything.

"Do you trust me, Jake?" In that moment, Jake knew everything was going to be OK. Jake carried his daughter into the house and Conchita ran to greet them.

"Abby, Abby, home," Conchita said.

TWO

Aaron came inside after putting the horse away and said hello to Jake, who was in the middle of a tea party with Abigail and Conchita. Daniel and Stephen joined the party as Teresa served some juice in the teapot. That night, Jake read his daughter a bedtime story and she went to sleep with Conchita by her side.

Jake made love to his beautiful wife and took comfort in the realization that they had no secrets between them. Jake still felt a little nervous about the fact that she would one day ascend and leave him behind, but understood that day would not come until he was able to handle it. Now that he was a father, he wondered what it would be like to lose his little girl as well. He pushed that thought from his mind and sleep took him.

THREE

Jake and Teresa spent the next three days with Abigail, playing every game she could think of. Jake started teaching her to play guitar as she showed aptitude to learn.

On what Jake thought was Saturday, he and Abigail helped Teresa in the garden. Teresa was always trying to grow her own vegetable garden on the other side but never could get a healthy crop. This time, it looked like she would succeed. Jake dug a trench from the clear-water stream that flowed through the ranch to provide water for her garden. Also, Jake and Stephen turned the stream to fill the river rock wishing well they built for little Abigail. Jake told Abigail to find a smooth stone and toss it into the well whenever she missed her daddy and he would come to visit.

Abigail collected as many smooth stones as she could find and put them in a jar in her room. Every time they took a walk or visited town, Abigail would be on the lookout for a new smooth wishing well stone.

That Sunday, at Uncle Lester's church, when the children shared what they were thankful to God for, Abigail said, "I'm thankful my daddy is home." Jake felt his heart melt in that moment. That night Jake read Abigail her favorite bedtime story until she fell asleep in his arms.

FOUR

The next morning, Jake took Abigail to the barn and saddled Brandy, Pylon, and Rainbow.

"I ride all by myself in the rodeo, Daddy," Abigail said.

"I bet you do," Jake said. "So where will we go today?" he asked.

"Mommy said we're going to the waterfalls by the river to have a picnic," Abigail said.

"Sounds like a great day," Jake said as he put Abigail up on Rainbow, then walked the horses to the hitching post near the deck.

"*Are you there, Stephen?*" Jake said telepathically

"*Always, my brother,*" Stephen answered.

"*I'm having a feeling of impending danger here today. Are you picking anything up?*"

"*I am, Jake.*"

"*Do me a favor and shadow us today,*" Jake said.

"*I'm way ahead of you, brother. Daniel and I are ready to travel.*"

Teresa came out carrying a picnic basket.

"Ready for a fun day, Abigail?" Teresa asked.

"Yes, Mommy."

Conchita hopped on the saddle with Teresa and they set out for a family picnic. Teresa was leading, then Abigail, followed by Jake. They were heading into the sun and their shadows were long behind them.

Daniel and Stephen gave them about a ten-minute head start then rode behind them to keep a watchful eye. Jake had the Dagger of Moriah concealed in his boot. He had been wrong about this feeling in the past and hoped he was wrong again, but this was no time to be taking chances.

FIVE

The trail took them through rolling hills filled with wildflowers and the smell of lilac in the air. Also through some wooded areas where animals that looked similar to deer and zebras were running in the wild.

They came across several hoggals when they got near the stream but they trotted past without incident. In the distance, Jake could hear the waterfall.

"This is truly a place of beauty," Teresa said. "I have seen the falls three times before, and each time it's better than the last."

This would be Jake's first visit to the falls but he had heard about them from his grandfather, who loved to fish the river downstream. Aaron told of a six-pound fish that broke the line after he had him on the bank, then flopped back into the water. Jake loved to hear his grandfather's fishing stories.

Jake noticed a cool wind coming up through the canyon and thought it strange on such a warm day. *"Are you there, Stephen?"*

"We can see you from where we are, Jake," Stephen said. The three came out of the woods in view of the waterfalls.

"How beautiful!" Jake said.

"I know. Have you ever seen anything like it?" Teresa agreed.

Jake thought about the waterfall in the garden but said nothing. Abigail rode to the water and let Rainbow drink.

"Good idea, Abby," Teresa said, and did the same. Jake took Pylon into the water with the other horses. Jake noticed the cool wind again and immediately registered possible danger.

Stephen picked up on this and sent a message to Jake, letting him know they were close by.

Teresa spread the blanket and put the basket out and pulled off her boots. She walked down to the stream and stepped into the cool water with the soft, sandy bottom that provided a massage effect on her feet. Abigail wanted to get wet as well so Teresa pulled off her riding boots and rolled up her pant legs. Jake considered this and remembered the dagger in his boot and decided to leave his boots on.

Conchita sat with Jake on the blanket, munching on a piece of apple and offering Jake a taste.

"Some, some," Conchita said as she offered her snack to Jake.

"I'm good, Conchita," Jake said. Nevertheless, every time she took a bite she offered some to Jake.

Jake watched as his beautiful wife and daughter played in the river near the waterfall.

The sound of horse hoofs stomping through the woods above them alerted Jake and he looked up. Jake saw his grandfather on horseback with his fishing pole and stream creel.

"I decided to join you, Jake," Aaron said. "I wanted another crack at that six-pounder I lost downstream." Aaron dismounted his horse, which joined the others cropping grass nearby.

"Hello, Grandfather. I'm just relaxing with my sweet Abigail and her beautiful mother," Jake said.

Aaron set his fishing gear near the picnic quilt. "Jake, it's a hard thing to be without the one you love. I have been without your grandmother for ten years now, and the ten are from the other side—and you know time is different at the Crossing," Aaron said.

"I know, Grandfather, and Grandma misses you as well, I'm sure," Jake said.

"I was a little worried about you guys so I thought I would come and see that you're good," Aaron said.

"Grandfather, I have felt something on the breeze today, something dangerous," Jake said.

"Trust your instincts, Jake. I too have felt some disturbance in the wind."

Clouds were rolling in quickly; Jake felt it was Borackus and Zoltar. The skies darkened and a sound of thunder shook the ground.

"Teresa!" Jake yelled, but she didn't hear; then it was too late. A monster swooped down and knocked her into the water.

"Jake, the little girl!" Stephen yelled as Zoltar grabbed little Abigail.

"Mommy! Daddy!" Abigail screamed.

Aaron ran towards the beast, who let out that horrible screech that sent him falling backward.

Jake was facing Zoltar once again. This time the monster held his baby daughter and was threatening to rip her to pieces.

"Don't hurt her! What do you want?" Jake yelled.

"The sword, pilgrim! I want the location of the sword!" Zoltar demanded.

The stench was overwhelming; Jake was thinking about the terror on Abigail's face and him failing to protect her from this green devil.

"Let her go!" Jake demanded. Jake removed a piece of rawhide from his leather bag; it was the map that Samuel had given him. Jake saw the one-eared Borackus on horseback behind Zoltar. At the sight of the map, the monster gave the little girl to Borackus. Abigail was crying and screaming. Teresa ran toward Borackus but Zoltar pushed her back with his sonic scream. She hit the dirt near Aaron.

"I have the map here!" Jake held the map out and Zoltar curled his lips back from his shark teeth in an evil smile

"Let her go!" Jake ordered

Borackus let the girl drop to the dirt and Abigail ran to her mother. Jake heard another scream from Zoltar. Stephen and Daniel had released arrows that pierced Zoltar in the chest. The monster took flight. While Jake looked up, Borackus snatched the map from Jake's hand and turned his mount back across the river.

Teresa went to Jake. Abigail hugged Jake and was crying.

"What was that thing?" Teresa asked in tears.

"It was Zoltar," Jake said. "And he has the map." Jake mounted Pylon.

"Grandfather, watch over Teresa and Abigail," Jake said as he turned Pylon and chased after Borackus.

"Jake!" Teresa yelled. However, it was too late. Jake was focused on the map and heard nothing.

"He is in the wooded area," Jake said as Stephen and Daniel joined him. The three Shaddai opened the horses to a full run. Jake could see Zoltar in the air circling down to the ground about a hundred yards ahead. Stephen and Daniel were pulling arrows and releasing

171

them in battle formation, their mounts keeping perfect pace. Jake was closing in on Borackus when an arrow hit the villain's horse and he went down. Zoltar landed over Borackus and sounded his sonic scream.

Jake could feel the force, but Pylon pushed through while Jake gripped the saddle. He leaped from his horse and rolled to the dirt with Borackus.

The map fell loose. Zoltar picked it up and took flight again. Borackus pulled his sword and cut Jake across the leg. Jake went to his boot and found himself in a fight much like the one he'd just had with Slowpoke.

"We have your map, and soon we'll have the Sword of Goliath!" he screeched.

Jake ducked a down stroke and used the roll-out technique to avoid another swing. He locked arms with Borackus and managed to force the sword loose from his hand. As the sword hit the dirt, Jake pulled the dagger and pointed it in the direction of Borackus' face. The tip of the dagger was almost making contact with his left eye; only the strength of the villain's arms prevented the blade from entering. It was an arm wrestling match with the blade moving close, then away, as they struggled.

Borackus got a good look at the dagger as he moved it from his face, pushing it lower towards his neck. Jake positioned himself on top of the evil Grigori. The two were eye-to-eye and the dagger was moving slowly away from Borackus.

"The dagger, is it . . .?"

"Yes," Jake huffed. "It is the Dagger of Moriah and has the power to end your breath."

Borackus became distracted by the dagger. His eyes were fixed on it and he developed a great O with his mouth that added to the fear washing over his face as Jake continued to push the dagger closer and closer to his throat.

Borackus tried with all of his might to push the blade away. He watched the dagger moving slowly towards his throat, then it pierced the skin on his neck and moved inside, carving through his airway and jugular. Jake heard a gurgling sound as blood rushed into the wound and filled the lungs. With a final push Jake shoved the dagger hilt-deep into the neck of the one-eared villain. The look on the villain's face appeared to say: *Wait a minute, I'm not ready to die. Wait, wait!* But die he did, in the dirt, at the Crossing, a mile past the waterfalls, under a clearing sky.

Stephan and Daniel stood beside Jake as the creature breathed his last and final breath.

"You're two for two, Jake. Michael was right to give the dagger to you," Stephen said.

"I lost the map!" Jake cried. "Zoltar will know the location of the sword!"

"The location of the Sword of Goliath is not on Samuel's map," Stephen said. "If it were, we would have gone to the Grasslands and got the map a long time ago. That map will send Zoltar on an incredible wild goose chase. It will keep him on our trail, but it will not get him near the sword," Stephen said, helping Jake to his feet.

"Remember, Jake, all things happen for the good for them that love the Lord."

Jake looked confused. Stephen and Daniel were smiling a grin like the cat that ate the canary.

"The map was a decoy?" Jake asked.

"The map is real; that is to say, it will keep Zoltar right where we want him. Only it will not take Zoltar to the sword," Stephen said.

"Soon you will know the location, Jake. You and you alone; that is why it was hidden inside the bloodline, as were all the lost enchanted instruments."

Jake looked toward the sky as they mounted their horses.

"Let's get back to your family," Stephen said.

SIX

They met Aaron, Teresa, and Abigail, who were already riding back to the ranch. "Are you OK?" Teresa asked as she examined Jake's leg wound which had closed and was barely a scar. I am fine, how are you and Abigale?" Jake asked. "We are OK, just shaken is all."

As they rode Jake thought, *What if he comes back? What if Zoltar comes to the ranch when we're not here?* But he already knew the answer. The ranch is sacred ground; no evil can enter that protected land. Jake took peace in knowing his family was safe. Zoltar was chasing his tail and Borackus was dead.

"As Borackus died at the Crossing, what happens to his body on the other side?" Jake asked.

"Borackus is on the other side with a fatal neck wound and will likely be discovered soon," Stephen explained. "He is dead, killed with the Dagger of Moriah. His corpse is likely rotting as we speak."

Chapter XV

The Body Count

ONE

Inspector Jericho sat at a table in the Marin County Library listening to the rain pound against the glass window. The large book in front of him was titled *Angels and Demons*, by Doctor T. S. Pratt. Sam was trying to concentrate on the book but his mind kept wandering to the beautiful Dr. Springer, who was choosing another book from the shelf. As she returned to the table, Sam was fighting to keep from looking up from his book. Her perfume filled the air, and he guessed it was one of those drive-the-man-crazy fragrances from Victoria's Secret.

"Look at this, Sam," Ruth said in a hushed library voice.

Sam kept his all-business face together but he felt she may be interested in him as well. He wanted so badly to turn the conversation personal. *Do you have a boyfriend? What's your favorite movie, book, color? Keep it together, Sam*, the voice named reason in his head said. *She is a doctor,* the voice continued. *You're a twice-divorced cop lost in a love affair with the job, so get your head together and let her help you with the case. Cut the romance!* Sam called it the voice of reason, but he knew it was the voice assigned to his first wife, Cindy. They had been so young, but Cindy was not as carefree or careless as Sam.

Cindy was the responsible one who paid the bills on time and pushed him to grow up. She didn't know it then, but her constant push caused Sam to eventually join the force. That was when she lost him, gone at all hours of the night, fighting crime and leaving her alone with the cat.

After a time, Cindy gave up, divorced him and married a tax consultant, and Sam was left with her pushy voice visiting him whenever he found himself undecided.

"What am I looking at?" Sam asked in his low whisper. He looked up to meet her extraordinary dark eyes.

"This is the Prophecy of the Dark Angel, or Zoltar, which means 'Dark Angel' in the Greek. He is what we would refer to as a fallen Angel. Zoltar is related to the Ishim Choir Angels, which were considered the most powerful of all Angels," Ruth explained.

Sam just stared, vaguely aware that Ruth was providing important information.

"Zoltar followed Lucifer to earth after the first war in heaven, and then it appears he made contact with Semyaza and Azazel, the Watcher Angels, after they were imprisoned in Nether Gloom."

Ruth looked up from the page she was reading. Now it was her turn to pretend there was no chemistry between them; her eyes met his for a split-second then ran back to the page.

"The prophecy speaks to the twelve enchanted instruments being hidden in the bloodline of the hybrid humans, or enlightened ones; here it also calls them the renowned or Shaddai."

Sam cleared his throat and tried to think of an intelligent question to ask. *You're so out of your league*, the voice of Cindy said inside his head.

"So let me understand something," Sam started, trying to put a sophisticated look on his face. "This Zoltar is immortal, as are the evil Grigori and Shaddai, who are from the bloodline of Angels, meaning they can't be killed unless they're wounded from one of the twelve weapons?" Sam said with a tone of disbelief.

"According to ancient script and some really old books, we have determined some of the enchanted instruments are actual weapons, like the swords or spear or even the dagger, but the twelve include things like the jawbone

Samson used to kill an army and the trumpet Joshua used in battling for Jericho."

Sam was in deep thought when his cell phone started playing "Don't Stop Believing." He could not answer it quickly enough. *I have to change that ring tone,* he thought as he answered. "Inspector Jericho. What? Are you sure? I'll be right there."

"What is it?" Ruth asked.

"Looks like we found one of the missing bodies from the morgue," Sam answered. "Would you like to come along?"

"Are you sure I should?" Ruth replied.

"We have some crazy things going on with this case, Doctor. If you don't mind, I think you can help us."

"All right," she agreed.

"Please wait here and I'll pull the car around, no sense in both of us getting soaking wet."

Ruth thanked him with a smile that showed her perfect teeth. Sam was amazed by her eyes, her hair, even her beautiful body, but now found himself attracted by her pearly white smile. *Keep it together, Sam!* Cindy said inside his head. *She is a professional and is only helping because it's the right thing to do. She didn't sign up for this to be hit on.* Sam made it to his car and turned the key in the ignition. He knew better, but he tossed the trash from the front seat of his car and brushed the seat off just the same. He didn't want her to think he was a pig.

TWO

"Where are we going?" she asked as they drove from the library parking lot.

"The city, a body shop warehouse in the Presidio. Don't worry about your car, this is the best part of town," he continued.

"I'm not worried," she said. "The car belongs to the university, one of the perks of working for the Stanford."

"A Mercedes 500 SL; that is some perk."

Ruth regarded Sam with a coy look. "So, what does your wife think about you working day and night tracking killers?"

Suddenly Sam felt the blood run to his face and pulse. "My wife?" he said with a question in his voice.

"I'm sorry, I didn't mean to pry. I just saw the ring and—"

"Oh, no, never mind, pry away. Truth is, I'm not married; well, not anymore. The ring, ahhh, well, it's kinda a habit." Sam played back his response in his head and bit the inside of his cheek, angry with himself. *Pry away? Who talks like that?*

"What about you? You married?"

"Nope," she said, and simply held up the hand she had seen him staring at on more than one occasion. "School, work, and more work. Not much time for marriage."

"I suppose that's my answer as well," Sam said. "I was married twice but the job and the hours I keep were a bad match for a successful marriage."

"What about kids?" she asked.

"No kids," Sam said. "But I did get custody of the dog in my last divorce. He is a ninety-pound German Shepherd."

Ruth smiled, and Sam was hooked.

THREE

As they pulled into the parking lot, the rain stopped. There was a feeling of freshness in the air that often follows a great downpour. Sam caught himself rushing to open the car door for Ruth and then escorting her beyond the yellow crime scene tape.

Sam and Ruth approached the body lying on the cement floor in a pool of blood.

"Who found him?" Sam asked.

"The cleaning crew for the offices." Sergeant Morales pointed with his chin to three individuals sitting inside the well-lit office, never taking his hands from his pockets. "They're giving a statement to the uniformed officers now," Morales continued.

"This is impossible," Sam said. "Inmate Jones? This is the same inmate who was lying dead in the morgue five days ago."

Sam's hand went to his chin and jaw as if he were in deep thought. "How does he bleed out a second time?"

"If he was shot in the San Quentin incident he may have been faking his death," Dr. Springer said. "But the wound in the neck is a fatal wound and looks to be created by an unusual weapon." She continued pointing to the entrance wound with her gloved hand. "Look, the flesh appears burned around the wound in the neck."

Sam went to his haunches and leaned over the body. She was right; the edges of the entrance wound looked as if it was made with a burning-hot blade.

"Let's get some photos of this wound," Sam ordered. He took another look around the building. "What is this place?" he asked.

"The building belongs to McNabe Enterprises Incorporated, or MEI," Sergeant Morales said. "However, this section is leased to Helms Auto Repair.

We have already contacted Robert Helms, the owner. He's on his way here from San Jose. He told us the building is owned by MEI and he's been here seven years."

Sam pointed to the broken skylights in the roof. "No glass inside on the floor of the building; it appears no forced entry. I want to reach out to the owners and any employees who may have a key to this place."

"You got it, boss," Sergeant Morales said.

"Why here?" Sam wondered aloud, and walked around the forklift. "Can someone lower the forks on this machine?" he asked.

A uniformed officer started the forklift and lowered the forks. Sam stepped on the fork and motioned for the officer to take him up. When it reached the top of the offices, Sam stepped off. He noticed footprints in the thick dust.

"John, get a crew up here and process this area. We have footprints, and I'll bet a dollar to a dog biscuit some of the prints belong to our dead friend down there." Sam reached into his pocket and produced a small camera and started snapping shots near his feet. He put the camera back into his pocket and came out with some white rubber surgeon gloves and pulled them on each hand.

Sam bent and picked up what looked like an old samurai sword. He stepped onto the forklift again and the officer lowered him to the ground.

"What do you make of it, Doctor?" Sam showed the sword to Ruth.

"This looks very old, but I would have to take it to the lab to make a determination of just how old."

"John, let's get this sword printed now so the good doctor can take a look in her lab."

"Yes, sir," Morales said.

Sam and Ruth moved toward the office and Sergeant Morales walked to the CSI lead.

"You guys have been here for three hours. Did anyone think to check the roof of the office where a thirty-six-inch sword was just lying around in a mess of footprints?" The investigator was looking at his feet. "My God!" Sergeant Morales added as he turned to follow Inspector Jericho.

The phone on Sergeant Morale's belt began to ring.

"Homicide, Sergeant Morales. Where is this? I'll let him know." Sergeant Morales turned to Henry Moses, the senior crime scene investigator.

"We have another one," he said. "Check out 9012 Lombard, the Best Western Motel, Room 12."

"We have all of our agents in the field tonight, you know that, right?" Moses replied.

"I know all of us on duty staff are out, so let's wake some people up. Overtime is authorized." Moses nodded his head and took out his phone.

"Hey, Sam!" Sergeant Morales called. Sam and Ruth turned to see an unusually pale Sergeant Morales. "I think we found another one of our missing morgue bodies."

"Where?" Sam asked.

"At the Best Western on Lombard, Room 12," he said.

Sam turned to Ruth. "I know it's getting late—"

"I wouldn't miss this. Take me with you," Ruth said.

"Let's go then."

FOUR

When Sam pulled from the parking lot, he turned on his emergency lights that flashed red and blue from behind the front grill of his Crown Victoria. Ruth felt a little special as the city traffic pulled over and let them pass. She thought how nice it would be to have such power over drivers when she was late for a lecture or meeting at Stanford. She supposed this was but a small benefit Sam Jericho enjoyed as he waded through the scum of society for his county salary. She wondered what that salary might be; maybe eighty, ninety thousand a year.

Sam finally broke the silence. "Do you have to work early in the morning?"

"I'm taking the weekend off," she said. "No school on Saturday."

"Ahhh, of course not. One day bleeds into the next with me. I wasn't thinking," Sam said with a little embarrassment in his voice.

"No worries. I'm actually enjoying spending time with you tonight, Sam."

Sam felt his cheeks blush. "I'm sure you have much better ways of spending your Friday night, given you're an attractive, single woman."

Now it was her turn to be embarrassed. "Oh, I don't know. It's pretty exciting actually, tracking one of the subjects I teach about. You have to admit, finding a body within six hours of death after the same body was dead for five days is a little interesting."

"I don't know that I would use the word *interesting*, but it's strange, that's for sure. Very strange."

"Don't stop believing," Steve Perry sang. Sam quickly grabbed his phone but could see Ruth was smiling. *I have to change that crazy ring tone*, he thought.

"Inspector Jericho," Sam said into his cell phone. "Who is on the scene? I want that place sealed now." Sam closed the phone and hooked it on his belt. "Sorry about that, we're a little shorthanded tonight. I just learned the body we're going to see is inmate Borackus, the same body killed at San Quentin five days ago. The on-scene investigator reports he has been dead for about two hours," Sam explained as they pulled into the motel parking lot.

The rain had started up again but not heavy. Sam again opened the door for Ruth and they walked to Room 12.

"What have we got?" Sam asked the uniformed officer at the door.

"At about 2250 hours, the couple in Room 11 reported hearing a loud scream, almost like an animal, maybe a cat in extraordinary pain. They called the manager, who did a welfare check on the room and found this guy," the officer said. "No identification, but his face was all over the news this week as being involved in the San Quentin incident."

Sam walked into the room with Ruth. On the bed in piss-stained underwear was inmate Borackus. He looked as if he was told he had just won the lottery but would never see a penny. He was missing his left ear and had a wound on his neck almost exactly like the wound on the other body they just saw.

"Look at this," Sam said. "The flesh is burned around the wound, just like the last guy."

"The door was locked from the inside." Sam was doing that walking around looking and talking to himself thing again.

"No evidence of forced entry, and no weapon." Sam's hand went to his chin. "The body bled out without moving." He turned and looked at the body. "He started bleeding and stopped bleeding right where he is."

Sam walked to the door where the manager was looking in behind the yellow police tape.

"When you entered, you say the chain lock was secure?" The motel manager looked like an older version of George Costanza from Seinfeld.

"That's right," he said.

How did the killer get out? Sam wondered, double checking the windows and ceiling, and looking in the closet. Sam discovered a small backpack in the closet. He put on his gloves and picked it up and set it on the open ironing board near the TV.

"I'll be right back," Sam said to the uniformed officer at the door.

Sam and Ruth walked next door to meet the neighbors.

"My name is Inspector Jericho, and this is Doctor Springer."

"How do you do?" Ruth said, and shook their hands.

"You say you heard a noise at about eleven o'clock. Can you tell me about it?" Sam inquired.

"It was horrible. It sounded like a cat screaming in pain," the woman said. "We both jumped up, and Melvin called the desk."

"The manager is only a few doors down and he came right away. Then we heard the man in the next room had passed away," Melvin added.

"So how long from when you heard the noise did you see the manager, would you say?"

Melvin looked at his wife, Maud. "What, three to five minutes?"

"If that long," Maud said.

"Thank you both, you have been very helpful. If you can think of anything you may have left out, please call me. Here is my card."

Sam and Ruth returned to the crime scene.

Sergeant Morales and the CSI team arrived in the parking lot. Sam and Ruth were going through the backpack on the ironing board. Sam lifted a book and a writing tablet from the backpack. Also in the bag were an eighteen-inch dagger, a sling, and an address book. The book was titled *The Twelve Instruments* by R. F. None. The writing tablet had some notes in blue ink that looked like an address. It was poorly written, but Sam read the following:

June 12, 2003

Borackus, the following are the instructions from Zoltar.

Remember to destroy this note after reading. I should be assigned the case.

Jacob and Teresa Stanton, 9135 Loch Haven Drive, Santa Rosa, CA, 95707. Sword of Goliath.

One has the location in their brain, make them talk by torturing if they still refuse to give the location, bring Zoltar their heads.

Take care, brother ~ g

"The address book looks like it belonged to Jacob Stanton," Sam said. "This is the guy, Borackus. We just got an AFIS hit on his fingerprint that puts him in the Stanton residence at the time of the murder."

"I was reading of a Grigori named Borackus. He is a direct descendent of the Watcher Angels," Ruth explained.

"Well, he had some help," Sam said. "No way he could keep the print file out of court on his own." Sam handed the book to Ruth.

"He has a note instructing him to murder Teresa and Jake Stanton in June 2003, the same month Ms. Stanton was killed. The note also tells him he should be assigned the case."

"So who?" asked Ruth. "The prosecutor? The investigator? Perhaps Zoltar has someone in the Sonoma County investigation team? Look at this book, it lists all the enchanted instruments and predicts the years they may be surfacing in the minds of the bloodline."

FIVE

Sergeant Morales and Inspector Carter of the Sonoma County Homicide Division walked into the crime scene.

"Sam, I want you to meet Inspector Carter, he is from Santa Rosa."

"Nice to meet you, Inspector," Sam said. "What brings you to our jurisdiction?"

"He investigated the Stanton murder. Remember, Sam, you told me to send the print file to the Sonoma County District Attorney?" John said. "Well, it got us some much needed help."

"How's that?" Sam asked.

"Sonoma County has provided Gary to assist us in our investigation. He is also hunting Stanton," John continued.

"Gary, eh? Gary with a 'g'?" Sam said with a sardonic look.

"That's right. We've been looking for this guy too," Gary said. "I always suspected Stanton didn't act alone, it was just too gruesome. What's in the bag?" Inspector Carter asked.

"Take a look, Gary with a 'g'. Is it OK for me to call you Gary?" Sam slid the handwritten note into his front pocket. Ruth's eyes were wide and she looked very nervous.

"Gary Carter," Inspector Carter said to Ruth.

"Oh, I'm sorry. Gary, this is Doctor Springer. She's helping out on this one too," Sam said, his smile more pronounced.

Ruth could see Sam was enjoying this. She, on the other hand, was terrified. She suspected Gary with a "g" was the author of the note and likely an agent of Zoltar himself.

Chapter XVI

Delilah's Secret

ONE

Jake woke to the sound of the phone in his room ringing. He jumped up in surprise.

"Hello?"

"Good morning, sleepyhead, it's Liea. I have some clothes for you. They're in the bag outside your door." Jake opened the door and took the bag. He showered and got dressed.

"Are you there, Stephen?" Jake reached out telepathically.

"Right here, brother."

"I can't believe I have a daughter. Isn't she beautiful?" Jake said.

"She looks like her mom," Stephen said, laughing. *"Are you ready to go? Liea has arranged transportation to the ship, and Tony and Ron are already on board."*

"I'm ready. What about Daniel?"

"He's in the lobby. Let's go."

Stephen, Liea, and Jake got in the elevator. Jake could not get his baby, Abigail, out of his mind. It was obvious by the grin on his face.

"What are you smiling about?" Liea said with a half-smile on her face. "You know we're far from home free."

Jake looked at her and his smile grew larger. Liea was nearly laughing when she said, "The braver the bird, the fatter the cat."

"He's thinking about his daughter," Stephen said.

"Daughter?" Liea looked confused.

"At the Crossing, babe."

"Ahh, I forget sometimes you guys spend my nights in another world."

The four walked to Fisherman's Wharf and made their way to the boat harbor.

"That is our charter," Liea said, pointing at a boat with a picture of a swordfish on it. The captain was a large man who looked a little like John Goodman.

"Welcome aboard," the John Goodman lookalike said. The four took seats inside the cabin and had a cup of coffee on the short trip across the bay to Angel Island. The captain docked the boat in port and the group thanked him. From the dock, Jake admired the enormous *Delilah's Secret*. He could not believe how big she was; five stories high! She looked like a mini cruise ship.

Once aboard, Jake was amazed that such a small crew was able to operate such a large ship. Ten crew members for a 300-room ship was unbelievable. The captain was Ramon Cook, of the bloodline of the Holy El Shaddai Knights, who were tracking the twelve enchanted instruments; the rest of the crew were all Shaddai dedicated to the quest.

TWO

Captain Cook showed Stephen and Jake the most important parts of the ship. Jake was certain it would take a week of Sundays to see the whole thing so they limited the tour to the bridge, the engine room, and the weapons armory. On the bridge and alone for a moment, Jake stopped Stephen.

"You remember what Samuel told us, to trust none outside our bloodline?"

Stephen smiled. "Jake, you're correct to be suspicious. However, tonight your concern should be lifted. We will have a look at the halos. If the green glow is on this ship, we'll discuss our next move."

"I'm sorry, Stephen," Jake said. "It's just—"

"Never apologize for speaking your mind, Jake. I trust you, Ron, Tony, Liea, and Daniel right now. The crew will have to earn our trust."

Stephen pointed at the ship map on the wall. "This is where our sleeping quarters are located. The top deck has the penthouse rooms so we'll be traveling in style."

"This ship can be operated in four different locations on board, according to this," Jake said.

"Amazing," Stephen agreed. They returned to the top deck for the departure briefing. All ten crewmembers, along with Tony, Ron, Stephen, Liea, Daniel, and Jake, were present. The crew was standing at parade rest formation on the right side of the room. The captain stood in front of a small lectern.

"OK, listen up. We're honored to have the new owners of *Delilah's Secret* aboard today." He extended his arm with an open hand towards Tony and Ron and said, "Anthony and Ronald McNabe."

Everyone clapped their hands. Captain Cook then turned towards the crew, who were dressed in black uniforms. "Let me begin by introducing the crew of *Delilah's Secret*. Executive Officer Darrel Armstrong. Darrel has been part of my crew since I became a captain. Next is the ship's officer of communication, Sandra West; Security Officer Timothy Reynolds, navigator, Julia Rhymes, Chief of the Boat Duncan Jones, and Lieutenant Commander Francis Galloway."

The captain turned to a large black man in uniform.

"I have the pleasure of employing the best engineer to sail the high seas," Cook bragged. "Raymond Brooks has been on *Delilah's Secret* from the day she was christened."

"Next we have able seamen John Wesley, Windy Butler, and Frank McKinney, who will be providing meals and cabin services." Cook turned to his crew. "Let me present our distinguished guests; Stephen Stross, Jake Stanton, Daniel Jackson, and Liea Levity."

Again everyone clapped their hands.

"We'll assemble at 0900 on this deck for the daily briefing. If weather prevents this, we'll meet in the Alpha Briefing Room," the captain explained. "Evening meals will be in the Donner Dining Room, and all other meals will be in the Port of Denmark Dining Room on Deck 4. Any questions?"

The crew moved together and stood at attention.

"If the guests would like to order in they need only call the galley from the phone in their suite. If you have any questions, please don't hesitate to ask a crew member; they're completely at your service," Cook said.

"Thank you, Captain," Tony said. "We appreciate your assistance with this voyage."

The captain dismissed the crew with orders to prepare to get underway. Jake was still marveling at the size of the ship and how it could be operated with such a small crew.

Well, it's not like they have a boat full of guests to tend to. We are a small party, after all, he thought.

Stephen approached Jake on the upper deck. "Let's go have a look at the armory."

"Good idea," Jake agreed. "We missed that on our short tour earlier, even though it was on the list."

Stephen and Jake walked down the stairs on the starboard side of the ship to the second deck where the armory was located. Just outside the armory was a glass office belonging to Security Officer Reynolds. He was inside finishing his inventory reports.

"Good afternoon, gentlemen," Reynolds said.

"Good afternoon," Stephen replied. "Would you be kind enough to let us in the armory? I would like to check out some small arms weapons."

"Right away, sir," Reynolds said, and used his key to open the barred door. As they entered, Jake was amazed at all the guns and ammunition in this room. It had to be about four thousand square feet of space, with an extended ceiling requiring a twenty-foot sliding ladder to reach the top shelves. The shelves and walls were covered with small arms—and some not so small.

Jake noticed some rocket launchers, bazookas, and .50-caliber machine guns that included mounts for the ship's upper decks. Officer Reynolds noticed Jake looking at the mounts.

"Once we get under the San Francisco Golden Gate Bridge I'll be moving the deck weapons into place," Officer Reynolds explained.

"I see," Jake said. "And this?"

"That is a surface-to-air missile launcher. We have ten that will be in place before nightfall, and all with electronic guiding systems that I can control from that chair."

Jake looked at the chair in the glass office he was pointing to. He noticed a wall of small television screens and lots of lights, buttons, and switches on a control panel.

"Very impressive," Jake said.

"We have the capability of tracking aircraft, missiles, submarines, ships, boats, and just about anything you can imagine. We even have seven nuclear warheads with a twenty-thousand-mile guidance system on board," he explained.

"How did you get that?" Jake asked.

"Bought them from the Russians after the Cold War," Reynolds replied.

"This is like a battleship," Jake said.

"Beg your pardon, sir, but we could dispatch a fleet of battleships in about eighteen minutes," Reynolds said.

"I'll sleep better knowing that," Jake responded, and turned to Stephen, who was collecting a couple of .40-caliber semiautomatic handguns.

"Take this, Jake. Keep it close." He handed him a handgun with four magazines like the one Officer Reynolds wore on his hip.

"So why the gun?" Jake asked.

"A simple show of arms most people understand. We'll continue to use Shaddai weapons in battle," Stephen explained.

THREE

Jake and Stephen went back to the upper deck to watch the ship go under the San Francisco Golden Gate Bridge. Jake looked out to the horizon and into the fog bank and remembered Teresa and Abigail, and how much he loved and missed them. As Jake and Stephen admired the view, the crew started mounting the weapons Reynolds told them about. In about thirty minutes the luxury ship looked like a warship, complete with satellite equipment mounted atop the control bridge. Liea joined them on deck and Stephen put his arm around her and gave her a proper kiss. Jake guessed he now knew what Stephen must feel like when they were at the Crossing and Jake was loving on Teresa. He smiled at this thought and went back to watching the beautiful view of the sun moving westward over calm seas.

Just when the captain was about to open it up and put some speed to the ship, two United States Coast Guard cutters were hailing them to stop and prepare to be boarded. Jake and Stephen went to the control bridge. Tony and Ron were already there.

"What do we do?" Jake asked.

"Come with me," Officer Reynolds said. "We have the best hiding place you can imagine."

"Take them to the fishbowl," Captain Cook said.

Stephen and Jake went with Reynolds to the elevator outside the bridge. Jake was amazed at the number of rings on the elevator. He knew the ship had five decks but the elevator rang seven times on the way down. At the bottom, they got out and followed Reynolds to the front of the ship, where a hidden door went through a false wall. Inside was everything you might find in a bomb shelter. Two beds, a television, a radio, a small kitchen with a refrigerator, and a small bathroom with a shower and toilet at the rear. The room had plenty of food for two people to spend about a month very comfortably. There were two round windows that looked under the water; Jake could see fish and sharks swimming outside the round windows.

FOUR

"What do you think is going on?" Jake asked.

"Not sure, but the United States is at war. Perhaps our guns on the top drew some attention to us," Stephen said.

"Could it be our escape?"

"I suppose, but the coast guard? Seems a bit much for only us," Stephen said. "But I suppose it could be."

Jake reached out with his mind to gather information. He was looking through the eyes of Captain Cook. Jake had mastered this technique and was able to sneak in without ever letting it be known he was there. He didn't poke around in the memories—that would be disrespectful. However, he did pick up on thoughts from time to time. Just didn't intentionally go deep and reap the minds of his friends.

FIVE

"I'm Captain Cook. Why have you stopped us?" Cook had eight of his crew positioned in and around the weapons stations with M-16 rifles in the high port position but on the ready.

"I'm Commander Books of the United States Coast Guard," he said. "Why the show of arms?" he asked.

"Commander, this ship is in international waters and in a defensive position to protect our cargo. We are within our rights to show arms," Cook said.

"What is your cargo?" the commander asked.

"Do you have a warrant?"

"No," Books said.

"Then you're not entitled to search our ship. I'll ask you once more, why did you stop us?"

"I wanted to know if you have seen these men. They escaped from San Quentin last week." Cook was looking at eight-by-ten photos of Jake and Stephen.

"Can't help you."

"Would you allow us to look around? We can detain you while we obtain the necessary warrant," Books said.

"Very well, you may take a look. Mind your men and take care on board, there are lots of expensive breakables," Cook said.

The coast guard commander motioned for his crew to come aboard for the search. The sun was now down and night had fallen. Jake, through the eyes of Captain Cook, noticed a green glow over the head of Commander Books. He also could see many other green halos boarding for the search. Jake tried to get an actual count but Cook looked away.

The ship had cameras everywhere, and Jake remembered Officer Reynolds pointing out his control booth in his office.

"Turn the cameras on to record," Jake planted the thought in Officer Reynolds' mind. Officer Reynolds went to the control panel and started recording on all cameras.

After about two hours of searching, the coast guard returned to their vessel and released *Delilah's Secret*.

Once the ship was well underway, Officer Reynolds went to the fishbowl and got Stephen and Jake.

"They're gone," Reynolds said. "They had photos of you and were looking for you."

"Thanks for the asylum," Jake said.

"My pleasure," Reynolds responded. "I'm excited to be a part of this voyage and to assist in the hunt for the Sword of Goliath."

Jake looked at Stephen. "They were briefed by the captain. I didn't know how much he shared," Stephen said. Jake smiled and they went to the elevator.

SIX

The evening meal was beef tips with wild rice and asparagus. *The food is spectacular!* Jake thought. *How long ago was it that Stephen and I had dined on mystery meat in the north dining hall at San Quentin?* They toasted their mission with wine as they dined.

"How far to our destination?" Jake asked.

"We'll be there in about four days at the speed we're going," the captain said. "Providing we don't run into bad weather."

"Bad weather?" Jake asked with a look of nervousness.

"I don't think it will hit us, but the coast guard report is calling for thirty-foot swells and strong winds to the north of us. I'm hoping we'll miss it," Captain Cook said, and raised his glass again. "To favorable weather." Everyone joined in.

Once alone in his room, Jake went the leather bag Samuel gave him and removed the strange container holding the water from the birdbath in the waterfall room. He took out a cup and filled it. He looked into the cup and saw himself looking back, then the vision blurred and another vision was there. It was Teresa and Abigail, waving a final good-bye. Jake shivered at the thought, then the vision changed. This time he saw the sword; it was wrapped in a cloth and hidden under the earth in a mud hut of a witch. When the vision faded again, Jake saw the witch. She was sitting at a vanity looking into a mirror. Jake noticed her reflection in the mirror was that of a princess; she had long hair and a young, beautiful face. When she turned to face Jake, she was hideous; her face was that of a corpse. Jake could feel that the sword was calling out but she was using her power to keep it hushed. Jake poured the water back into the container and sealed it.

Chapter XVII

The 12 Enchanted Instruments

ONE

Inspector Jericho pulled onto Highway 101 north and crossed the Golden Gate Bridge with Doctor Ruth Springer in the passenger seat.

"What are you going to do about Inspector Gary Carter, Sam?" Ruth asked.

"Nothing just yet," Sam said. "I intend to feed him enough rope so he can hang himself. We both know he was involved in the death of Teresa Stanton. Now he's snooping around our crime scene to try to find out what, if anything, we know about the cover-up. Would you like to stop in San Rafael for a nightcap?"

"Do you know a place?" she asked.

"As a matter of fact, I do." Sam pulled off on Sir Francis Drake Boulevard and parked at a place called The Marin Brewery. Sam was careful to get the car door for her again.

As they entered the brewery, Sam took the normal look for danger and located the exit routes before sitting in a booth at the window.

"What would you like?" Sam asked.

"The house chardonnay will be fine." Ruth pulled her coat and gloves off. "I'm going to powder my nose," she said.

When Ruth returned from the bathroom, her drink was waiting for her. Sam was sipping on a whisky and Seven. "I hope you don't mind, I ordered some snacks."

"Sounds good."

"So tell me about this book," Sam said as he took out the book titled *The Twelve Enchanted Instruments*.

"I have never seen that book," Ruth said. "The books I studied were *The Three Swords* and *The enchanted Twelve* by T. S. Pratt, who also wrote *Angels and Demons*. This appears to be another published reference guide of the same instruments," Ruth explained. "Let's have a look and see if it holds true to the books I studied."

Ruth opened the book and started to review the chapters listed.

Sam looked into her eyes and hoped she could not see how he was falling for her.

"The first sword was that of Goliath, the Giant, who was killed by young David," she started.

"That is the one I remember from Sunday school," Sam said.

"Next is the sword of Prime Minister Zaphnath-Paaneah, or Joseph of Egypt. He was one of the twelve children of Israel born of his second of four wives, Rebecca, who bore two sons, Joseph and Benjamin," she explained. "Israel favored Joseph over the other ten sons, resulting in his jealous brothers selling him to a merchant traveling to Egypt."

Sam smiled and took a sip of his whisky.

"Later, Joseph was sold to Captain Potiphar, and was soon minister over everything Potiphar owned. Joseph was wrongfully accused by Potiphar's wife of trying to have his way with her and was cast into the royal dungeon."

"Wait," Sam said. "Wrongfully accused?"

Ruth smiled and blushed. "She made up the story about Joseph forcing himself on her sexually."

"Hold everything!" Sam exclaimed. "This guy was a 290?"

Ruth punched Sam in the arm.

"No." She sipped her wine. "I said *wrongfully* accused."

Sam rubbed his arm. "You hit hard!"

Their eyes met and they shared an uncomfortable moment. Sam leaned forward and kissed Ruth lightly. As he started to back away she leaned forward and kissed him back, this time with the passion they both were feeling.

"I'm not looking for a relationship right now," Ruth said. Sam held her eyes with his. "Meeting you could not have come at a worse time," she continued.

Sam said nothing.

"I can't get involved," Ruth said.

Sam leaned forward and kissed her long and hard. He felt his passion rise inside and hoped she felt the same. A thought crossed his mind to get a room at the attached motel but he resisted. He felt something different with Ruth, and didn't wish to muddy the waters with sex too soon. He returned to his drink.

"Ruth, I'm so happy I met you, and I'm more than a little attracted to you, as you know. However, I need you to help me with this case; you're the expert."

Ruth smiled, then gave him another small kiss.

"Of course, I'll help you," she replied.

"Perhaps we should stay professional while we work the case," Sam suggested.

"OK."

"So, Joseph worked hard, and God blessed him in prison with the gift of interpreting dreams," she explained.

"Wait, are we done talking about—"

Ruth interrupted, "Hey, cowboy, you're right, let's stay professional. Now, do you want to hear about the twelve instruments?"

"Yes," he said, and Ruth went back to the book. "When the king had a dream, he sent for Joseph to interpret the meaning. He was so impressed with the wisdom of Joseph that he appointed him prime minister over Egypt, and he was given the Sword of Kings."

"And the third sword?" Sam asked.

"The third is that of King Nebuchadnezzar of Babylon, also known as the Sword of Lilith. Nebuchadnezzar was another wise king who took advice from Daniel the prophet. He was later tricked into making an image and forced his people to bow to it. However, Daniel's friends, Shadrach, Meshach, and Abednego, refused, and were tossed into a fiery furnace."

"I remember this story," Sam replied. "God delivered the three, and the king repented of his sin."

Ruth nodded.

"What about the trumpet?" Sam asked.

Ruth smiled. "It's written that this is the trumpet Joshua used when fighting the Battle of Jericho."

Sam looked interested.

"According to legend, the trumpet, when properly used, has the power to bring destruction from heaven and stop time," Ruth explained.

"Wow, just think what it would be like if you could stop time," Sam said.

"Some other instruments have the same power, like the Staff of Moses. It cannot only stop time, it can release hell on earth if properly used; the same with the Jawbone of an Ass used by Samson."

Sam turned the page that explained the Whip of Christ; he noticed she was reading a language that looked to him like a bird walked through ink and across the paper.

"Next is the Holy Grail, the Cup of Christ. Then the spear used to pierce the heart of Jesus. Also known as the Lance of Longinus, sometimes referred to as the Holy Spear," Ruth continued.

The waitress brought a platter of fried rock shrimp.

"Another round?" she asked.

"Yes please," Sam said. Ruth continued to go through the book and explain the other items as they dined on the snack platter and killed two more rounds. She was on the Dagger of Abraham when she stopped and began reading to herself.

"What is it?" Sam asked. She didn't look up from the book; she appeared lost in the language on the page.

"What did you find?" Sam asked again. Ruth looked white as a ghost.

"It says here when the blade of the dagger enters an immortal, it's like it was dipped in hell's sulfur, as the flesh will burn on entry and exit."

Sam now went pale.

"The wounds on Borackus and Jones seemed like the blade was dipped in hell's sulfur all right," Sam said. "Let's get out of here."

Sam drove Ruth to her car. "Are you OK to drive?" he asked.

"I had three glasses of wine in three hours, I feel fine," Ruth said.

"Call me when you get home so I know you made it safe," Sam instructed. Ruth smiled and drove away.

TWO

Sam pulled into his parking space at the Marin County Marina and made his way to his home on the water. His was the second-largest houseboat in the marina. After his second divorce, he used his share of the equity in the home to put a down payment on a floating house. It was really quite charming. He had a yard across the dock where Rusher, his dog, had plenty of green grass to run on. The lower section of the houseboat was made up of a large living room and kitchen, with a laundry room leading to the lower sundeck. On the starboard side was a bedroom and bathroom section Sam had turned into his office.

Here he had his desk, computer, and much of his reading collection. Most of his books were on shelves, but he also had a lower cabinet filled with true crime mystery and Steven King novels. The second story was the sleeping quarters, with two large bedrooms, each with a private bathroom. The master bedroom opened to the upper deck that included a hot tub and sauna next to his weight room. The top of the houseboat was a sundeck with a small kitchen and built-in Bar-B-Q. Sam was a neat freak by nature; however, Irena came daily to walk Rusher and once a week to clean the home and do the laundry. Sam was gone so much the home rarely needed much more than a dusting from time to time, but she was not complaining.

Sam took down a glass and poured two fingers of whisky, then he walked into his office and started reviewing the Stanton file. As he read, he made notes of what were clearly mistakes on the part of the prosecution. He worked through the night, and by the time he was sleeping in bed, he had completed a brief that exposed the Sonoma County DA for suppressing evidence, specifically the fingerprint file. In addition, he included a copy of the handwritten note, which clearly looked like the handwriting in the investigation reports of the arresting officer, Gary Carter. Sam ended the brief with a summary of facts explaining the relationship between Inspector Carter and Mr. Borackus. He placed a copy of the brief, along with the original note from Carter, in his safe, then he put three copies in envelopes addressed to the State Attorney General, the Inspector General, and the governor's office.

Chapter XVIII

Bodega Village

ONE

Jake woke to the sound of a little girl singing the muffin man song near his bed; it was Abigail playing with Conchita. His beloved was still asleep next to him when he got up and took Abigail and Conchita to the front room.

"Hi, sweetheart," Jake said to Abigail. "Let's let Mommy sleep a while, she seems tired," he said. "Would you like something to eat?"

Abigail smiled. "I want pancakes, they're my favorite."

"Pancakes it is," Jake said, and began moving about the kitchen gathering what he needed to cook breakfast.

Stephen walked into the kitchen. "Good morning. What's for breakfast?"

Abigail ran and hugged Stephen.

"We're having pancakes, my favorite!" she said.

"That's my favorite, too!" Stephen said. "Need some help, Dad?"

"Sure; you guys get the eggs and I'll get the mixer," he said.

The three worked together and prepared pancakes, bacon, eggs, toast, and hash brown potatoes. Jake made up a plate and took it to Teresa in bed, with juice and coffee. Her eyes said everything, her mouth didn't have to move; she was thanking him and telling him she loved him at the same time. Her eyes were also saying time grows short, soon we'll not be together; but Jake didn't want to think about that. He wanted to go on living this second life with his family, his wife, and now his beautiful daughter. He didn't want to think of losing them even for a moment.

TWO

After breakfast, Jake and Teresa took a walk to the stables with Abigail. They ended up at the pond near the clear stream that flowed through the ranch, and Jake again talked about the beauty he saw there.

Teresa gave Jake her serious look. "One day you will see *true* beauty. This is nice, but compared to Sion and beyond, it's simply a reflection, like that you see in the pond."

Jake looked down at the water and could see their reflections looking back but it was not as clear as when he looked at her.

Then Jake realized: she had seen beyond the Crossing. She knew what awaited her and was staying there for him. A tear welled in Jake's eye as he considered her sacrifice. *She's living a lesser life for me,* he thought. Teresa embraced Jake and kissed him. *She will never leave, not as long as I hope to see her when I put my head to rest on the other side. She will stay here, at the Crossing, waiting for me.*

They went back to the stables and took the horses for a ride. Abigail pointed out everything along the trail. Conchita rode on Jake's shoulder with her tail curled around his neck, and like Abigail, pointed her little finger and said, "That, that, look at that!" in her little monkey voice. The family finished the day with a fire pit and some music with the guitars.

That night, Teresa and Jake made love like never before. Jake could not imagine a more intimate moment. But when they drifted to sleep, Jake had a nightmare. It was not Zoltar or the enemy that frightened him, it was waking up at the ranch all alone. The place was dusty and the food spoiled. No horses in the stables—or any animals, for that matter. The place was completely deserted. Jake awoke in a cold sweat, calling for Teresa. She took him in her arms and hugged him. The night passed with Jake never returning to sleep.

THREE

Stephen and Aaron were on the backyard deck talking about the mission. Stephen was telling Aaron about the coast guard stopping the ship and them hiding in the fishbowl. Jake stood near the door with Abigail in his arms and Conchita on his shoulder; Abigail was feeding Conchita peanuts, and laughing when Conchita would put the shells on top of Jake's head. When Aaron looked up and saw what she was laughing at he joined her, and soon everyone had a good laugh at Conchita, which was very common. *Nothing quite as adorable as a five-year-old girl playing with a little talking monkey,* Jake thought.

Lately all he was doing was trying to face what his life would be like if he lost his family again. He didn't think he could go on. He knew she would one day ascend and leave him behind, like when she died and he lived on the other side. How many sleepless nights did he bear alone with the thought of his beloved brutally slain before him? Even the satisfaction of revenge was nothing compared to the feeling of loss and loneliness he'd endured. Jake imagined that must be true hell, to be separated from your loved ones forever, alone and lonely. Who can bear it? How would he go on without Teresa and Abigail? The thought tortured him and he was consumed by it.

That night, as Jake lay in bed, he felt the presence of another; not the enemy, but his Redeemer. Jake closed his eyes. He heard the voice again. "Do you trust me, Jake?"

He was embarrassed and ashamed. "I trust you, Lord," Jake said.

"Then let them go and trust in me," the voice said.

207

"Thank you, Lord, and forgive my weakness," Jake said, and drifted off to sleep. His dream was filled with fun times with Abigail and Teresa; he slept deeply and restfully.

FOUR

The next morning, Jake awoke to Abigail and Conchita pulling his arms. "Come on, Daddy, today is church."

Jake got up and put his hands to his eyes and rubbed them.

"Good morning, babe!" Jake yelled to Teresa, who was in the shower.

"Morning, sweetheart!" she yelled back. Jake went to the sink and brushed his teeth and shaved as Abigail and Conchita played in their room.

"You two, out of here!" Teresa ordered. "Daddy needs to shower, let's go!"

Jake showered and dressed for church. Stephen and Daniel were in the kitchen putting the finishing touches on the breakfast they made for everyone.

"Jake, your grandfather went in early. He wanted to help Lester set up for the afternoon potluck," Stephen said.

"I think he wanted to brag about the fish he caught yesterday," Jake laughed. "He finally landed that old six-pounder that got away near the falls. I kept telling him I was going to catch him so he spent every spare moment fishing for that big sucker." Jake's eyes met Teresa's and caught her checking him out, then she smiled that light-up-the-room smile.

"Today is the Bodega Village Horse Show, and Stephen said we get to take the horses to town, Daddy."

Jake looked at Stephen and he shrugged.

"You can drive if you want. I'll ride with her," Stephen said.

"Never," Jake replied as he picked up Abigail. "I would love to ride to town, but we'd better hurry if we want to make it to church on time."

"She will be riding the barrels like Mommy did," Teresa said.

"How exciting! And I'll be on the fence rooting for you to win, sweetheart," Jake added.

FIVE

"I had a nightmare last night," Stephen said.

"You?" Jake looked surprised. "You never have bad dreams."

"I know, that's why I think this means something."

"Well, do tell," Jake prodded.

"We were in port at an island with a harbor large enough for *Delilah's Secret* to enter. Daniel was asking some locals about other travelers who may have come through. Then the wind blew cold and we were attacked by Zoltar and his army."

"Attacked?" Jake asked.

"Well, arrows from an elevated location flew, then Zoltar and two other creeps faced us. One of the two was Bumpy from San Quentin, the other was a Grigori they called Derrick. He had the map Samuel gave you and was demanding the key."

Jake looked puzzled. "Key? What key?"

"I'm not sure, but I think we need to find out."

"So what happened to Zoltar and his army?" Jake asked.

"Come again?" Stephen said.

"The dream, what happened in the dream?"

"Oh, yeah, Captain Cook and the crew blew them to hell with the artillery aboard the ship."

"Well, that's a good thing then," Jake said.

"I'm sure that part was the dream, Jake. I think we were meant to focus on the key to the map."

"But you said the map was a decoy so it was no big deal that Zoltar got the map."

"It is. The map will not lead anyone to the Sword of Goliath. However, I think now we'll not only capture the sword but we'll put an end to the witch of En-Dor, and I think my dream was meant to tell us to return to Samuel."

"So let me get this right; you dream about an attack by Zoltar and his army and you think it means we need to learn how to kill a witch?"

"Pretty good, huh?" Stephen said with a smile.

"All right then," Jake said. "Let's get to church."

Teresa and Daniel drove the truck with the potluck food for after church and Jake and Abigail, along with Stephen, rode their horses over the rolling, green hills, taking the short-cut to town. Uncle Lester delivered a fine message of how we're saved by grace through Christ and how we're to love one another even as Christ loved the church. Following the service was the traditional potluck lunch that was held every week. Jake noticed new faces at the church, and often noticed a face or two missing from the crowd. Jake wondered what happened to the missing faces; did they ascend and leave their family behind? The haunting fear of losing Teresa and Abigail stayed with him. Yes, he trusted the Good Shepherd and knew he was doing the right thing, but the thought of being left behind still hung in the back of his mind.

Today was special: Abigail was to participate in the barrel races for the first time. She was amazing; only five years old, but born to ride a horse. *Like her mother,* Jake thought as he sat on the fence watching his little girl wait her turn to ride. How many times had he sat there watching Teresa race back home? Seemed like only yesterday he sat on the fence cheering for his beloved, and now it was his daughter. She was a natural breaking out of the gate and turning around each barrel, and then sprinting to the finish line. She was nearly a blur as she crossed the line. With only four other contestants in her age group, Abigail took first place and was awarded a large trophy with a horse and rider on top. It was a time to remember; his little girl, only five years old, and already finishing first place. Jake was very proud.

SIX

Jake and Abigail rode home from town side by side, talking about the race and the beautiful trophy she'd won.

"I'm going to put it in my bedroom," Abigail said.

Jake smiled. "I think it would look good in the great room over the fireplace so everyone who enters the house can see it."

"Oh yeah, Daddy, that would be great!" Abigail said. "Are you leaving soon, Daddy?"

"What do you mean, sweetheart?"

"Mommy said you would be leaving soon and we would miss you," Abigail said with a sad look on her face.

"Honey, Daddy will never leave you. Sometimes Daddy must go to work but I'll always come home," Jake said in an effort to reassure his little girl.

"I just don't want you to go. Mommy is sad when you're gone."

"I'll stay for as long as I can." Jake felt a lump in his throat when he swallowed.

"Let's race to the barn!" Abigail took off, leaving him in the dust.

SEVEN

Stephen and Daniel were in the tack room making ready to travel to the Grasslands while Jake spent some alone time with Teresa.

"Be careful, Jake," Teresa said.

"I'm always careful, beautiful," Jake replied, picking her up and holding her like a bride crossing the threshold. He kissed her softly and then lay her on the bed.

"Do we have time?" she asked.

"Let's make time," Jake said, and they pulled their clothes off and made love. It was sweet and lasting. Jake felt like it would have to last him a long time. Teresa shared this thought; it may likely be their last time together. When they were finished, she kissed him sweetly and he regarded her with his smile. This time his smile said, it's OK, my sweet, I understand you must leave me.

"*Are you there, Jake?*" It was Stephen, calling telepathically.

"*I'm here, partner.*"

"*It's time to go if we hope to be there by dark,*" Stephen said.

"*I'm on my way, see you at the barn.*"

The three men saddled up and said good-bye. Teresa was holding Abigail and they were waving. Jake remembered the reflection in the water Samuel had given him. *This is good-bye,* he thought. It was not a final farewell like he imagined in the vision.

They rode northeast and their shadows grew longer as the sun dropped lower in the western sky. Jake looked back as he did the last time they traveled this path and took in the view of the beautiful valley all the way to the coastline. The men said little until they hit the heavily wooded area.

"OK, I see lumpa tracks. So how dangerous are they, Stephen?" Jake asked.

Daniel and Stephen laughed and kept riding.

EIGHT

As the riders came into the Grasslands, they heard some strange sounds in the woods. Samuel was outside tending his animals as they approached.

"Stephen, Jacob, Daniel," Samuel said, "I have been expecting you. Please come in, make yourselves at home. Enrick will tend to your horses. It is so rare I get visitors these days, it's time he earns his money," Samuel laughed.

"We don't want to impose, Your Grace," Jake said.

Samuel smiled. "Jacob, you could never impose. I trust you need my help, and I'm here for you."

"As a matter of fact, we're here about another dream. Only this time it was Stephen who had the dream," Jake said.

"Let me get you something to drink. Please come in the house and sit down, my children," Samuel said.

Daniel took the horses to the corral and helped Enrick with the grooming. Stephen and Jake went inside the house with Samuel. Jake looked at the shelves covered in old artifacts and marveled at what it would be worth in his world.

As he snooped, Jake came across a covered basket with what looked like mushrooms inside. The mushrooms were covered in a spice mixed with cinnamon and gave off a pleasant odor. He motioned for Stephen to take a look. Stephen put his head in the basket and took a long smell and smiled.

"Smells good," Jake said. Samuel was getting the wine from the cellar.

"Samuel!" Jake called. "Stephen and I were checking out your collection of artifacts you have in the front room."

"Yes, I know, I have been meaning to organize the stuff but I never seem to have the time. Most are gifts I received over my lifetime."

"Gifts, you say?" Jake said. "What about the large basket of mushrooms on the second shelf?"

"Mushrooms?" Samuel asked, then laughed aloud. "Nay, it's not mushrooms, but three hundred Philistine foreskins provided by King Abenadad. He gave them to me for conducting his daughter's wedding. I meant to move that to the cellar," Samuel said.

Stephen and Jake winced at the thought of poking their heads in the basket. Jake was happy to drink and put the thought of cinnamon-spiced foreskins from his mind. Stephen looked a bit pale but eventually smiled at the thought of poking his head in the nasty basket.

"Supper will be ready soon," Samuel said. "Enrick makes a tasty rabbit stew with dumplings. There will be bumbleberry pie for afterward. Now, tell me your dream, Stephen, and let God reveal the meaning."

"In my dream, our ship went in to port at some island rich in beauty and under a sky of two moons. Jake, Daniel, and I left the ship. I had Samson, my childhood pet falcon, on my shoulder. I thought this strange, as he died when I was fourteen years old. Nevertheless, he made the landing with us and we stood in the center of a village or town. Daniel was asking the locals if other travelers had been in this port lately. Suddenly the wind blew cold and Zoltar and his army were before us. Zoltar stood facing Jake and me with the map you gave Jake. He was demanding the key to the map. Jake and I looked at each other and could not understand what he meant by a key. Then I was shaken awake by the bite of my pet bird."

"Ahhh, the ship you saw in your dream is your ship, and you will indeed port at an island called Opole," Samuel said. "You will be on your guard because Zoltar and his army will attack you. When Zoltar faces you and your party, he will ask for the key to the map he took from you. You will give him this." Samuel held out a crystal on a chain. "This fits the space on the map he stole and when the sun shines through the crystal at noon it will show the location of the island of Icarus, which is a very special place. It means the island of dead man's bones. This place has a special chemical in the air that turns immortals into mortals. Therefore, it will turn Zoltar and his followers into weak mortals."

Jake and Stephen shared a look of delight.

"He will come after you, angry as ever, but when he finds you—and he will—all those he commands will be easy prey for you to kill. Stephen, pay close attention to what I say and be ready for the deceiver."

"We'll be more than ready for this monster's trap," Stephen said with confidence.

"Stephen, I beg you, don't get angry with me, but what you love is making you blind. Be on your guard," Samuel ordered.

"Yes, Your Grace," Stephen said.

"After you meet Zoltar, waste no time. Head for En-Dor. Jake will know the way by then. You must kill the witch. Her weakness is her vanity. It would be best to catch her off guard," Samuel explained. "If you can, destroy her reflection and she will be dead. However, if she's ready for you, then use the sword or the dagger provided by Michael."

Jake bowed before Samuel. "How can we thank you for all you have done for us, Your Grace?"

Samuel put a hand on Jake's back.

"It's not I who help, but Him whom we serve."

That night they enjoyed a meal of rabbit stew and dumplings. Later, Samuel took them to the waterfall room and they gazed into the birdbath. When the reflection changed it was them sleeping on *Delilah's Secret*. Then they saw Teresa and Abigail playing in the yard on the ranch, then the vision changed to Liea. She appeared to be praying for Stephen, but then turned as if she knew she was being watched. The image then blurred. They then watched the reflection turn to a bird in flight; finally the vision showed the sword. It was as clear as ever and it was calling to them.

That night when they slept in Samuel's house, Jake didn't dream; he awoke refreshed and felt strong. They had an early breakfast before riding back to the ranch the next morning.

Chapter XIX

The Stanton File

ONE

Sam Jericho was angry as he thought about the Stanton file. The brief he'd drafted was meant to expose the corruption of the Sonoma County District Attorney, Anita Moore, as well as the investigator, Gary Carter, whom Sam suspected was the author of the handwritten note instructing Borackus to murder Teresa Stanton and frame her husband, Jake.

Sam wondered how deep the corruption ran. *Was the DA involved?* Sam decided to start with the lawyer. He pulled the address up for Albert Stoll and found him on College Avenue in Santa Rosa. After seven unreturned messages, Sam drove from Marin to Santa Rosa to see if this attorney even existed. As he drove, Sam was listening to the AM talk show from Sacramento; they were discussing the bodies found in San Francisco. One caller suggested the killer was the Angel of death and that he saw him leap from a warehouse window.

TWO

It was about two o'clock when Sam pulled into the offices of Rankin and Stoll Attorneys at Law. Sam stepped over the large mud puddle in the driveway of the old Victorian house. The lobby smelled of mold and musky wood mixed with perfume after a rain.

The woman at the reception desk was likely attractive at one point in her life, before the booze and drugs took their toll on her looks. She was plump, and had no business wearing the cashmere sweater that was at least one size too small for her. Her tanned cleavage was out of place under a powdered face with blue eyeshadow.

"Good afternoon. I'm Inspector Jericho with the Marin County Sheriff's Office. Is Mr. Stoll available?"

The tired receptionist looked Sam over. "He has been in court all morning. Is he expecting you?"

Before Sam could answer she crossed the room with her hand out. "My name is Arlene."

Sam shook her hand.

Sam heard a car door shut and then someone walk along the porch.

"You're in luck," Arlene said. "Mr. Stoll just arrived."

Sam looked over his shoulder and noticed a tall, thin, balding man with a Tom Selleck mustache and thick, black-rimmed glasses entering the office.

"Mr. Stoll?" Sam asked.

"Yes, can I help you?"

"I think so. My name is Sam Jericho, I'm with the Marin County Sheriff's Office. I wonder if I can have a word with you about one of your clients from about three years ago."

"Pleased to meet you. Come on back to my office. Arlene, coffee please. How would you like your coffee, Inspector?"

"None for me, thanks," Sam said.

They walked into the office and Mr. Stoll moved around the desk and sat in the large chair. "Please sit down, Inspector."

Sam took a seat in one of the red velvet chairs. He was certain someone spent a month of Saturday's seeking yard sales for just such a pair.

"Now, how can I help you?"

"I'm investigating a case where you were the defense attorney. Does the name Jacob Stanton mean anything to you?"

Mr. Albert Stoll turned white as paint and looked like someone had just kicked him in the gonads.

"I'm sorry, that name doesn't ring a bell. I represent so many people . . ."

"Well, this guy was up for murder one and was sent to San Quentin for life," Sam added. "Ring any bells?"

"I do recall the case, it was awful. Sometimes we learn that our clients do terrible things. This one was exceptionally brutal, as I recall," Albert said.

"Oh good, I'm pleased you recall. I have the file here and I had a few questions."

"I do hope this won't take long. I have another appointment, you see," Albert said in a shaky voice.

"Well, I tried to call and make an appointment about six or seven times with no luck. I'm afraid I must spend a moment with you, Mr. Stoll. It should not take long. What can you tell me about your defense of Mr. Stanton?"

"I'm sure it's all there in the file." Albert pointed at the file in Sam's arms.

"Well, let's see. This file has a separate fingerprint file but I see no argument or even the fingerprints being submitted as evidence."

"Wow, that does seem odd," Albert said, now trembling.

"You know what I think?" Sam said. "I think you omitted this file and I think someone paid you to do it."

"That's ridiculous, and I resent the implication," Albert said in the same shaky voice. His chair appeared to be heating up as he moved from side to side; sweat began forming across his nose.

"Ridiculous? Really? What if I told you I have copies of bank records that show a very substantial deposit in your account at the same time this file was omitted?"

"I knew it!" Albert yelled. "I knew it would never work. I told him I didn't want to go along with it but my partner, Rankin, made me do it!"

"Do what?" Sam asked.

"Go along with the frame-up!" Now Stoll's face was buried in his boney hands. "We were paid off by the District Attorney to drag our feet on the defense." Albert was now crying. "I never wanted to hurt anyone. They said he was guilty. His accomplice was some guy named Borackus. We took money to lay down, he was as guilty as hell."

"Quit your whimpering, Albert, and write down every name of everyone who participated in the frame-up," Sam ordered.

"It was Rankin, my partner; Anita Moore, the DA; Gary Carter, the investigator; and some guy they call Morales. That's it, that's all I know."

Sam's face dawned an astonished look. "Did you say Morales? Do you have a first name?"

"I don't remember. He just joined the team last week." Albert put his face in his hands and cried.

"Try to remember."

"I told you, that's all I know. He is working for Carter. He called him Sergeant," Albert confessed.

"Are you sure?"

"Yes, Sergeant John Morales, that's it. He is part of Carter's new crew."

"Let's go, Mr. Stoll. I'm placing you under arrest for conspiracy."

Albert got to his feet. Sam placed Albert in handcuffs and walked him to the reception area. Arlene stopped him.

"You may want this," she said, and handed Sam a CD.

"What is it?" Sam asked.

"It's a complete recording of the confession you just obtained," she said. "The office is wired."

Sam smiled at her and took the CD.

"Arlene, why?" Albert asked.

"I can't stand you or your partner. You both treat me like crap."

"Where is Rankin?" Sam asked.

"He's in court," she said.

Suddenly, Arlene pitched forward and took a step. Blood drained from the corners of her mouth and dripped on her sweater. The look of surprise on her face was eerie as she put her fingers to her mouth and her broken teeth fell into her hand. She looked at the teeth in her bloody hand with surprise; her knees buckled and she went down. Sam pulled his gun and looked around. A silent shot struck Stoll in the back of the head, his brains splattering on the wall behind him. Now Sam was on the ground. He managed to pull his cell phone and dial 9-1-1 but the shooting stopped. He crawled to the broken window of the old Victorian house and remained under cover until responding units arrived.

THREE

The responding units were Santa Rosa Police. When the coast was clear, Sam carefully stepped over the dead body of Arlene, who was in the wrong place at the wrong time.

"I need to speak to your chief," Sam said. "I expect we have some bad cops involved in this."

"What did you see?" Officer Stone asked.

"Not a lot," Sam said. "Whoever fired on me was using a silencer."

"How do you know you were the target?"

"Trust me, I'm getting too close to the truth. I expect the killer wanted me dead but missed when Arlene walked into the line of fire."

Stone offered to take Sam to the station and he accepted. At the Santa Rosa Police Station, Sam played the CD for Chief of Police Renee Ore.

"Holy crap," Renee said. "How deep does this run? If it includes Anita Moore, there is no telling."

Renee contacted the Santa Rosa Office of the FBI and requested an independent investigation. Sam turned the file and CD over to Chief Ore and waited for the FBI.

Chief Ore sat behind her desk and reviewed the Stanton file. Sam was sipping a fresh cup of coffee when Agent Falkner and Special Agent in Charge Murphy entered the office.

"What do you have?" Murphy asked.

"Take a seat. This may take some time, so try to keep up," Sam said.

Murphy sat down.

"Last week I responded to a crime scene at San Quentin, where four inmates killed two guards while demanding two inmates by the name of Stross and Stanton, who were also in San Quentin, only in a different housing unit," Sam started.

"The crew was led by an inmate called Borackus. When the guards went to get the two inmates they wanted, they discovered the two inmates were gone, escaped. You follow?" Sam looked at Agent Falkner. "You may want to take some notes, this gets a bit confusing." Falkner smirked.

"When the warden realized that Stross and Stanton had escaped and she could not use them to bargain with the inmates, she gave the order to take down Borackus and his crew. Borackus, Jones, and the other four were all killed in the operation.

"After three hours of photos and bagging the dead, the bodies were transported to the Marin County Morgue. Doctor Harris, the Marin County medical examiner and a personal friend of mine, is recorded on surveillance cameras starting to do her work, when all of a sudden the camera goes off and she's found dead, murdered inside the morgue, which was, by the way, locked from the inside. Five of the six dead inmates were gone. The last was left with some strange marks on his forehead in blood and made with the fingerprint of inmate Borackus."

Agent Falkner smiled.

Sam said, "Don't start with the smug smile yet, my friend, it gets way stranger still. I began an investigation of the two inmates who escaped, Stross and Stanton, and discovered something strange in the Stanton file. I noticed the prints found at the crime scene of Stanton belonged to Borackus as well."

Agent Falkner was now writing notes to try to keep up with the story.

"Days later I was called to a warehouse in the Presidio in San Francisco, where I discovered the body of Jones, only he'd been dead for two hours and not five days, like he should be. Later that night, I was called to a motel where we discovered the dead body of Borackus, also only hours dead, still before rigor sets in."

"Slow down," Falkner said. "I can't write that fast."

It was Sam's turn to shoot a sardonic smile.

"So I came to Santa Rosa to talk to Stanton's lawyer, and as you have seen and heard in the confession, it appears this Jacob Stanton was framed for his wife's murder by the Sonoma County DA, and may have even turned someone in my office. I'm not sure, but as you can see, I'm having trouble trusting anyone right now," Sam said.

"Inspector," Falkner started, "what is this all about? Why the cover-up?"

"That's a good question. I have been working with Doctor Ruth Springer out of Stanford University, an expert in the occult, and she seems to think it has something to do with a very old sword and its location."

"Do you have contact information on this doctor?" Falkner asked.

"I do, only not with me. You can call me at my office if you need more," Sam said.

"I would like to meet with you and your commander first thing in the morning to coordinate a task force between our agencies," Murphy said.

"Sounds good to me," Sam replied. "However, who is going to arrest Rankin?"

"We have him in custody," Chief Ore said.

"Can I have a word with him?" Sam asked.

"He's not talking, he's waiting for his attorney. We have charged him with conspiracy so far. Do you think he's the one who took a shot at you?"

"Nope, the guy that shot Stoll and Arlene is not a milquetoast lawyer. He is either a crook or a bad cop."

Sam was taken back to his car by Agent Murphy. The two continued to discuss the strange happenings surrounding the case. Murphy was visibly intrigued.

***

"Don't Stop Believing" blasted from Sam's phone.

"Inspector Jericho."

"Sam, it's me," Ruth said.

"Ahhh, so nice to hear your voice, especially after my afternoon," Sam said as he walked into the hallway seeking privacy.

"Are we having dinner tonight?" she asked.

"I would love to," he said. "I have a terrific place in mind. It's called The Dead Fish, under the Carquinez Bridge. You know it?"

"I do," she said. "Pick me up at seven?"

"I'll be there." Sam put the phone in his shirt pocket and went over the events of the day in his head. He tried to piece them together so they made sense. What bothered him more than anything was the thought that Sergeant Morales could be dirty.

FOUR

Sam pulled into the parking lot of the office. Morales was not there. He dialed the cell number and made note of the time, 4:15 p.m.

"Sergeant Morales."

"John, Sam. Where are you at the moment?"

"Hi, Sam. I'm at San Quentin getting background on Stross and Stanton."

"Good, stay there, I'm on my way."

"OK, Sam."

Sam did the math in his head as he drove to San Quentin. It was possible for John to have shot at him and make it to San Quentin by now if he had rushed; but if he had been at San Quentin for any length of time, he could not possibly have been the shooter. Sam pulled up to the East Gate and showed his ID.

"Go right ahead, Inspector Jericho. They're expecting you at the warden's office."

"Officer Johnson, is it?" Sam asked the gate officer. "What time did you come on duty?"

"I'm on a double, I started at 0600 and will get off at 1000 tonight."

"Do you keep a log of when outside law enforcement arrive on grounds?"

"Yes, sir, we do."

"Can you tell me when Sergeant Morales came on grounds?"

"It was 1415 hours," Johnson stated.

"Thank you so much," Sam said and drove up to the warden's office.

OK, so he was here when I was being shot at, that is a good thing, Sam thought. Warden Windom and Sergeant Morales were reviewing the files of Stross and Stanton as Sam entered the room.

"Look at this, Sam. They dug a hole in the back of the cell and climbed through the plumbing chase to the roof," Morales explained. "Then they used a key to open the lock on the roof gate, then over the wall to the lower yard. Here is where it gets a little scary. Evidently there was an unsecured tunnel that reached to the bay, nobody knew about it."

"It appears they knew this prison better than we did," Warden Windom admitted.

"The prison clothes were found covered in blood and floating in the bay," Windom explained.

"Sharks?" Sam asked.

"That's what they want us to think," Windom said.

"Warden, I don't know about Stross, but it looks like Stanton was an innocent man," Sam said. "I'm working with the FBI, but it appears Stanton was framed for the murder of his wife."

"FBI?" Morales asked.

"Yes, we'll be meeting in the morning," Sam explained.

"Our team will all be taking the polygraph test first thing. We may have a rat in the corn patch."

"Really?" John asked, more to himself than to Sam.

"I have one more stop to make, then I need to grab a shower before my date tonight," Sam said.

"What is your next stop?"

"Well, funny you should ask, because it really is not a stop at all. They're here."

"Who?" John asked.

"The press," Sam said. "I don't want to be killed before I tell what I know."

Sam walked out the east gate of San Quentin to a bank of microphones facing reporters from every Bay Area television station, as well as Sacramento and the Associated Press.

"Inspector, what can you tell us about the escape?" one of the journalists asked.

"I'm glad you're here. This appears to be more than just a prison escape," Sam announced. He went on to tell of the shooting earlier and his joining forces with the FBI, and even his theory of foul play within the District Attorney's office. Sam was careful to tell about how he'd prepared and mailed a brief to the Attorney General's office and how he had concrete proof of the framing of Jacob Stanton. Hell, by the time Sam was done, anyone remotely close to the issue better be running for the hills. Sam made it clear he had nothing hidden that he would take to the grave if he were to meet an untimely demise; thus, perhaps dissuading any attempts on his life.

FIVE

That night he took Ruth to an excellent dinner at The Dead Fish.

"I saw you on the five o'clock news today," Ruth said as they waited for their drinks to arrive. "Someone tried to shoot you today?"

"I think I convinced them that I have no secrets, so maybe they have changed their mind about taking me out."

"I heard what you said about the Sonoma County District Attorney. She must be upset."

"I expect so. The FBI and the Attorney General's office is talking to her tonight. She may be resigning by tomorrow morning and by noon, she may be in county lockup," Sam said.

"What about Stanton and Stross?"

"Their clothes turned up in the bay covered in blood, perhaps sharks, or maybe the big Larkspur Ferry boat hit them with their big screws."

"Stop! You'll spoil my dinner with talk like that."

Sam did stop. He looked long and hard into her eyes. He thought he would never love again after his last divorce, but perhaps he had never been in love in the first place. He really didn't remember feeling about anyone like he did about Ruth, and not just because she was so beautiful; she was smart, and he didn't have to think to be with her, it all came naturally. She gave him a smile and he took a kiss.

Chapter XX

Abigail's Ladder

ONE

As the riders came over the mountain, they could see a mother and daughter playing in the field. Jake felt his heart warm as he got closer to home. It was home, wasn't it? This was where he spent time with his wife, child, and grandfather; this was where he and his brother Stephen trained, laughed, and cried. There was his barn and stable where Pylon, Brandy, and Rainbow lived. This was where Jake built the wishing well in the front yard for Abigail to toss stones in when she missed her daddy. It was home.

Jake could not imagine another place where he would feel the closeness of family and love, even more so than their place on the other side where Jake was offered a second chance. This was where he belonged. He had come to love his favorite chair and Conchita, the family pet. She was more than a pet, she was a member of their family. But somewhere inside where he didn't wish to go was the truth: the truth that this was not his home at all, the truth that one day this would end and Teresa and Abigail would go to a place he could not follow, beyond Sion, where Teresa had visited and where *she* considered home. Jake knew the time here at the ranch was growing short; soon he would no longer be with Teresa when he closed his eyes and slept on the other side.

TWO

As they drew closer, Abigail and Conchita came to meet them.

Abigail yelled, "Daddy! Daddy!"

Conchita yelled the same thing. Jake reached down and pulled Abigail and Conchita onto the saddle. Conchita moved to Jake's shoulder, putting her little tail around his neck. Her tiny hands held Jake's hair as they rode to the barn.

"I've got the horses," Daniel said.

"Let me help," Stephen added.

Jake took Abigail and Conchita into the house.

Teresa met him at the entry with a sweet kiss and warm hug.

"Daddy's home," Conchita said in her funny voice and they all cracked up. Jake gave her a scratch where he knew she loved it and she hugged his neck.

"How was your trip?" Teresa asked.

"Necessary," Jake said. "Samuel sends his regards and this." Jake handed Teresa a closed leather purse.

"What is inside?" she asked.

"I have no idea. I'm not a sneaky snoop like you, my dear." Jake smiled, remembering sticking his nose in a basket of 300 foreskins. Teresa opened the purse and took out a note and five small, smooth stones. The note from Samuel read:

Dearest Teresa,

You know time is running short, and soon you will return home with Abigail. Jacob is fearful of losing you. God has a plan for Jake and his bloodline. Pray for him that he opens his heart to the will of the Lord and embraces it. It will be a bitter taste to lose you and Abigail at the same time; the Lord has allowed for limited contact for you and Jacob because of Abigail. The stones are for the wishing well. Give them to Jake and tell him to use them wisely, as they're all that I have. When the time comes and you return home with Abigail, Jake can use the stones to call you back for a time. They represent a ladder, if you will. I expect we'll call it the Ladder of Abigail, as her love and desire is what made the stones possible. Jake must know, when the last stone is used, the ladder will close forever. This is the will of our Lord. Time is short: you pick the moment to tell Jacob and Abigail. I'm sorry, my child, but you have the burden of revealing the news to your loved ones. May God's peace and blessings be upon you.

"What did the prophet send you, my love?" Jacob asked.

"Please don't be angry with me, but can we discuss it another time?" Teresa said, with tears in her eyes.

"Of course, sweetheart. Nothing bad I hope," Jake replied, and left it alone.

Jake knew in his heart it had something to do with the end of their home at the Crossing. That night, Teresa prepared a special meal for the family. Aaron and Uncle Lester joined them.

"I hear you visited the prophet again, Jake. Did you get a view of any lumpa?"

"You know, I'm beginning to think this lumpa creature is like a snipe, all talk and no show," Jake said with a big grin on his face.

"Keep thinking that, my brother. We shall see what you look like when you run into one," Stephen said. "Tell him, Daniel."

"Stephen is right, they're not nice. The last one I dispatched was about the size of a horse and had a twenty-foot wingspan," Daniel said.

"What's a lumpa, Mommy?" Abigail asked.

"Nothing, sweetie. The men are talking about things beyond the ranch, nothing for you to fear," she said.

THREE

After supper, Jake and Abigail took a walk on the path they'd made leading to the wishing well. Conchita followed at her heels, as usual.

"I have some smooth stones in my room, Daddy. I'm saving them for when you go back to work," Abigail said.

"Stones," Conchita said, and tossed a small stone into the wishing well. Then she looked down the hole and heard it plunk into the water. Jake smiled and picked up Conchita. He gave her a scratch and she closed her eyes in pleasure.

"Can I wish for you to stay forever?" Abigail asked.

"You could, honey," Jake said. "But Daddy is doing work for the Good Shepherd and he must travel far away to do the work. Do you understand?"

"I think so. Like when Moses traveled far to do God's work?"

Jake smiled. "You're so smart! How'd you get so smart?" Jake tickled her and she laughed and squirmed.

Conchita started jumping up and down and yelling, "Jake, stop! Stop, Jake!" as Abigail begged for him to stop tickling her.

FOUR

The next day was exceptional. The sun was warm, and the smell of jasmine filled the breeze. Jake and Teresa took Abigail to their tree, the one where Jake had carved their names into the bark. Today Jake carved Abigail and Conchita's names into the tree.

"What do you want to tell me?" Jake asked.

"Why do you ask? As if you can't read my thoughts," Teresa said. Abigail was playing close to the tree with

Conchita. "Today is our last day at the ranch and you know it."

Jake looked into her tear-filled eyes. "I didn't know that. It's not fair! I can't live without you. And how can I live without Abigail?" Jake looked at his little girl playing with Conchita. "Where will you go?" Jake asked.

"We'll go home, Jake. Beyond Sion is a place I cannot describe. I'm hurting inside at the thought of leaving you, but it's home." Tears fell from her eyes and traced her cheeks.

"I wish you could see and understand. We are going with him, the Good Shepherd, to a place where we'll never cry or be sad or hurt," she explained. "Where creatures like the one who terrified our little girl are expelled."

Jake could see her heart breaking as she told him, "I love you, Jake. We left you something in your bag. Please don't worry about us, we're in a safe place." Jake marveled as the clouds seemed to rest on the ground around his family.

"I love you, Daddy," Abigail said, and then she joined her mother on a staircase that appeared from nowhere; Conchita, too. One last embrace and they were walking up a staircase into the clouds; it was like a dream. Teresa was now holding Abigail, and Conchita was on her shoulder, ascending higher and higher in the sky. Soon they were out of sight.

Jake turned to look at the tree where their names were carved. He awoke in his room on *Delilah's Secret*; the ship was powering through the ocean. He got out of bed and walked out onto the balcony of his suite. Stephen was on the balcony next to him, looking into the night sky.

"They're gone," Jake said.

"I know," Stephen said. "Are you OK?"

"I think so," Jake said. "I actually think I'm OK."

FIVE

Jake walked back into his room and went to his leather bag. He found a note and a small marble bag with five smooth stones inside. The letter from Samuel to Teresa was in the small bag with the stones. Jake read the note from Teresa.

My dearest Jacob,

If you're reading this, Abigail and I have gone home. Words cannot express my love for you, and I can only imagine the pain you're going through. Whoever said, "It's better to have loved and lost than never to have loved at all," has never gone through this kind of separation. I would never leave you, my love. I believe you're someone special, with a purpose far greater than only a husband and father. Your destiny is to help others, more than we'll ever know. I feel lucky that we had the time together at the Crossing; nothing on the other side can come close to the love we shared at our ranch. I'll always keep you in my prayers and will raise our daughter to know the kind of man her father is. Until the day we meet again on the other side, I hold you in my heart.

Love Teresa, Abigail, and Conchita

Jake felt the tears tracing the lines in his face as he read the letter. He said a small prayer and returned to the balcony to watch the night sky with Stephen.

"You will see her again," Stephen said.

"I know, I'm good."

"Jake, you need to have your head all the way in this now," Stephen said.

"I know. I expect I should be shattered, but I have felt something preparing me for this moment ever since I first met Teresa in Dreamland. I'm blessed to have had the time at the Crossing with Teresa and Abigail, even Conchita. But it seems we were on a schedule and the time for us has ended." Jake wiped the tears from his face that were flowing as he talked. "I have five visits left, and I'll make them count."

Stephen gave Jake a look that called him to arms. "I need you here with me, Jake. I feel we shall be in battle very soon, and we'll need to be ready for Zoltar and his army. We only have two days in port to prepare."

"Funny you should say that, my friend, as I was about to tell Captain Cook to set a course twelve degrees south by southwest so that we'll be on course to the island."

"Very good then, 12 degrees south by southwest," Stephen repeated. "See you on deck."

Jake dressed and met Stephen on the bridge with the captain.

Cook was programming in the new course. "How can you be certain this is the right way?"

"I know it is, like I know there are seventeen billion stars in that solar system you call Uribe, and think it's only known by the crew who mapped it. Shall I name them?" Jake asked.

"No need, I'm a believer. I'm also the only member on this boat who knew about Uribe—until now," Cook said.

"This course will lead us to Opole Island. We expect to encounter some hostility not long after we reach port. The time has come for everyone to be on their guard," Jake warned.

"We sleep in shifts," Stephen said. "I want Liea, Daniel, you, or myself awake at all times."

Jake pulled the crystal from his bag and gave it to Stephen. "Keep this on your person. You will present it to Zoltar when the time comes. We should be in port in three days. I'm not sure, but I think we're there for at least two more days before we meet Zoltar."

"You're right, Jake, I make it five days before we encounter Zoltar," Stephen said. "But there is something else, and I need your understanding on this."

"Say no more aloud," Jake said. *"You are going to tell me we have a spy among us, someone in league with Zoltar,"* Jake said telepathically.

"Daniel, are you there?" Stephen called.

"I'm here," Daniel said telepathically.

"What do you know of a traitor on the ship?"

"Only that I'm not the only one who feels it," Daniel said. *"I have felt it from the time we left San Francisco. I only thought I was being too sensitive."*

"Never think that," Jake said. *"Let's try to find the deceiver before we reach Opole Island."*

The three decided to split up and search the ship. They would attempt to reap the minds of the crew and expose the traitor; time was short, and they knew it. The plan included meeting back at Jake's room in two hours.

Jake was the first to return to the room, then Daniel, and finally Stephen.

"Any luck?" Jake asked.

"Negative. I don't get it," Daniel said.

"We met with every crew member, plus Tony and Ron," Stephen said.

"This is a big ship with lots of places to hide. Maybe it's one of the coast guard searchers we're missing, a stowaway," Stephen continued.

"One way to find out," Jake said. "I'll call Officer Reynolds. If anyone can find a stowaway on this ship, it's him."

SIX

Reynolds met them at Jake's cabin and listened to their suspicion of a possible intruder; he led them to his office and activated the motion detector security system.

"If we have an intruder, this will expose him," Reynolds said. The screens could locate every person aboard the ship.

"Nothing," he said. "You must be sensing something that is not there." But the feeling of deception was heavy aboard that ship and despite every effort to relax, nobody slept well.

SEVEN

The next morning as they dressed for breakfast, Liea picked up the crystal Stephen had set on the chest of drawers and held it to the light.

"It's beautiful," she said. "What is it?"

Stephen often forgot that Liea was only aware of what he told her. He had loved her for ten years, but she was mortal, and asleep to what happened in Dreamland or at the Crossing, or in this case, the Grasslands.

"That, my dear, is the key to the map," Stephen explained. "When placed on the rawhide map at high noon, the sun will shine through and expose the location of . . ." He trailed off as he heard Jake calling.

"What is it?" she asked.

"It's Jake," he said. "I have to go." Stephen took the crystal from Liea and ran to the top deck.

"It's Opole Island," Jake said. "This is where we stop."

As the ship made its way into the large port, Jake could see natives offloading another ship and wondered what was in the sacks they stacked on the dock. Others were leading mules to carry the sacks to the village. *Food perhaps*, Jake thought.

Captain Cook pulled in close and the crew tied the ship to the dock. Then they headed to the third floor where the gangway was located.

Chapter XXI

The Press Release

ONE

After releasing the news about the framing of Jacob Stanton for murdering his wife, the corruption in the Sonoma County District Attorney's office, along with the attempt on his life resulting in the murder of a lawyer and his secretary, Sam felt safe. He thought, *The rats in the corn are about to be rounded up if they stick around.* However, he may have been oversimplifying the intelligence of these particular rats. Perhaps they were too stupid to run for the hills. Perhaps they were just pissed enough to kill him for making their life difficult.

Sam returned to his home that night and noticed that Rusher was not around.

"Rusher!" Sam called. Nothing. Sam pulled his gun and walked to his front door; it was open, and appeared to be kicked in. "Don't Stop Believing . . ."

"Inspector Jericho," Sam answered.

"Where are you? We've got another body," Morales said.

"Really? Where?" Sam asked.

"City morgue. When can you get here?"

"Ten minutes, see you there." Sam closed the cell phone.

"Hey, Sam!" Judy Crossman, his next door neighbor, called. "I have Rusher in my backyard. He jumped over the fence and was running all over so I put him in my yard with the high fence. I didn't want to put him in his yard because now he can jump over."

"Thank you, Ms. Crossman," Sam said. "Would you keep him until I get back?"

"No problem, Sam, he can't jump over my fence!" she boasted.

Sam's next call was to Agent Murphy at the FBI. He explained he was on his way to the Marin City Morgue. He anticipated he was being set up by Sergeant John Morales.

TWO

When he arrived at the morgue, Sam approached from the south side and parked his car a block down the street. He saw two unmarked cars—Crown Victorias with tinted windows and tall antennas—coming from the other direction.

Feds, Sam thought. *Can they be any more obvious?*

When the first agent entered the building, a blast that shook the city block tossed Sam backwards into a juniper bush.

"Holy crap!" Sam yelled as a secondary explosion took out the morgue and three vehicles driving by, as well as the two fed cars. A giant fireball and mushroom cloud was all he could see. *They must have wired the door,* Sam thought. *Well, the theory that I'm out of danger just blew up.*

Sam got into his car and drove to the office. His commander, George Redman, was walking out as Sam approached the building.

"Sam, where have you been? Sergeant Morales was looking for you," George said.

"Oh, he found me, sir, and set me up."

"What? Let's talk," George said.

Sam had his gun in his hand. "Sorry, George, I'm not sure who I can trust at this point. This is the second time today someone has tried to kill me. I'm not going to give them a third crack at it," Sam said, waving his boss to go back inside the building.

"You don't think *I* had anything to do with it?" George said.

"Right now I don't trust anyone. Let's go to your office," Sam said, and pointed the way with the pistol.

As they walked, Sam opened his cell phone and pushed redial.

"Agent Murphy, it's Sam. I'm sorry to report your responding agents were killed in an explosion at the city morgue. Come on down to my office, I'm with George Redman, my commander. We're trying to figure out who is trying to kill me."

THREE

Within an hour, the Marin County Sheriff's Office was swarming with investigators, FBI agents, the press, special investigators from the inspector general's office and the Department of Justice, along with a mob of city and county employees.

Sam was exhausted. However, he was the first to pass the polygraph exam for the investigative task force looking into the corruption in the Sonoma County District Attorney's Office.

Next was FBI Agent Murphy. Sergeant John Morales was nowhere to be found. An all-points bulletin was released identifying him as a person of interest in the explosion at the city morgue and death of four FBI agents. Sam was pleased to see that Commander George Redman passed the polygraph exam. Almost all of Sergeant Morales' unit was absent from work on that day. The two who showed up refused to submit to the exam and were placed on administrative leave pending an internal investigation.

The team assigned to follow up on the investigation into the escape of Stephen Stross and Jacob Stanton was led by Inspector Sam Jericho, Special Agent Jack Murphy, and Special Investigator from the State Attorney General's Office Mike Gonzalez.. The team also included Doctor Ruth Springer, on loan from Stanford, Brad Conner from US Marshals, and Emily Salazar from Homeland Security.

The inspector from San Francisco was Callahan. Every member of the team was given a polygraph and cleared by internal affairs before being assigned. Jack and his agents started with the Sonoma County District Attorney and issued warrants for Inspector Gary Carter and Sergeant John Morales. A special detail of Sacramento police officers were assigned as undercover security for the team and their homes.

Governor Grey Davis called Sam and offered any assistance he needed. Sam did ask for three executives from the California Department of Corrections and Rehabilitation, specifically retired wardens Scott Bradshaw, Timothy Levin, and Linda Diaz. Sam felt they had a stellar team to expose the corruption and find the escaped inmates. The headquarters for the task force was located in a building in Larkspur Landing. For the first week the team met every morning at 0800 hours and shared information and provided status reports.

FOUR

Sam and Ruth drove to Santa Rosa the following Monday to have lunch at Sam's favorite Chinese restaurant on their way to meet with Sherri Alexander, the sister-in-law of escaped convict Jake Stanton. After lunch, Sam and Ruth drove to Sherri Alexander's home.

"Welcome, Inspector Jericho. I was wondering when you would be back to see me," Sherri said.

"Ms. Alexander, this is Doctor Springer, she's working the case with me. Have you heard from Jake?"

"Nope, he has not called or contacted me in any way. The news reports say they were killed in the bay by sharks or a boat. Why do you think Jake made it?" she asked.

"You and I both know he's alive. He may outlive all of us," Sam added.

"Inspector, I told you I know nothing. Would you like some coffee?"

"I think that would be good right now," Sam said.

"Doctor?"

"Yes please."

The phone rang and Sherri ignored it.

"Aren't you going to answer the phone?"

"I'm sure it's not important," Sherri said, and got some cups for the coffee.

The machine answered, "Hi, this is Sherri. Leave your name and number at the beep."

"Sherri, it's Jake. I just wanted to let you know I'm OK. The cops will likely come to see you and ask about me. Feel free to tell the truth. You know I'm innocent. They were not going to let me out so I left"—Sherri ran to grab the phone and Sam told her to let it be—"I'm so sorry you had to go through so much drama because of this and I promise I'll clear my name. I pray every day for you and your mom; one day we'll be together again. God has assured me Teresa is in a better place. I have so much I want to tell you, but now is not the time. Love and miss you, sis, take care."

Sherri looked at Sam and shrugged. "That is the first call I've received. I'm happy he's alive and I hope he finds a happy life," Sherri said.

"Sherri, we think Jake is innocent as well. I have evidence that he was framed for the murder. The killer is dead; however, we can't prove he was the one who did the killing," Sam explained. "What we're having trouble with is the reason for the crime. We think Jake knows where a rare sword is located, and some very bad people want the sword, so he's in grave danger. If he calls again, please try to convince him to turn himself in. I can help him. Here is my number again."

Sherri pointed to the refrigerator where Sam Jericho's card sat beneath a banana magnet.

Sherri poured coffee for Sam and Ruth.

"I'm so sorry for your loss," Ruth said.

Sherri watched her checking out a photo of the twin sisters standing side by side with Jake in the middle. Sherri noticed the look of compassion in her eyes.

"Thank you," Sherri replied.

"I can't tell you apart in the photo."

"I'm the pretty one," Sherri said with a smirk.

Ruth returned the good cheer. "This coffee is awesome."

"I know, I grind it fresh at Raley's Supermarket," she said. "It's hazelnut."

"Hmmm, smells good." Sam sipped the coffee and joined in on their conversation. "Sherri, you know Jake will call you back, and now you know I think he's innocent. Tell him to call me, this is important."

"I'll tell him if he calls. But I want Jake to be safe. It seems many are trying to frame him and kill him. I think it's disgusting how they railroaded him and tossed him into prison." Sherri looked into Sam's eyes. "They lost everything; Jake lost his home and everything he owned to defend himself against crooked lawyers and cops, and it makes me sick. I would like to think you're for real."

FIVE

Ruth and Sam finished their coffee with Sherri and started back towards Marin County.

"Amazing," Ruth started.

"What's that?"

"That she has stood by Jake through the murder of her twin, and all these years in prison."

"You know, I thought that very thing as I left Ms. Alexander's place the first time," Sam said. "I saw you checking out the photos on the wall. She was never called to testify. In fact, none of her family supported the prosecution."

"That strikes me as odd. How did the prosecutor get the conviction?" Ruth asked. "I mean, I know they were dirty, but surely a jury of his peers would have seen something."

"Unless the son of a bitch fixed the jury." Sam had his flip phone out and speed dialed the task force. "This is Sam. We need to widen the net. Let's reach out to the jury and the judge, also the appeal judges in this case. I want bank records, transactions, anything you can think of. I want these guys to know we know they're dirty. Only offer immunity to two of them for their testimony. I want them to flip fast and hard."

When he put his phone away he looked at Ruth. "You know, you would have made a good cop. Did I ever tell you that?"

Ruth smiled and batted her beautiful eyelashes. "Flattery will get you everywhere."

SIX

By the time Sam and Ruth made it back to headquarters, Murphy had flipped two jurors and a judge; that was enough for him to build a case.

"Who has the kind of money to buy judges, lawyers, and juries?" Ruth asked.

"We're talking big-time organized crime, that's for sure," Sam said.

"I knew the twelve instruments were valuable," Ruth said. "I'm amazed I'm witnessing the acquisition of them. This will not stop with the Sword of Goliath, you know that."

Sam looked at her.

"It will continue far beyond the sword," she said.

"That's why you're on this team. I need to know everything you can teach us about the twelve instruments. This team has jurisdiction to cross state and international lines if need be, but we're determined to get whoever is behind the conspiracy," Sam continued.

"It would sure help if we could get in touch with Jake Stanton. I'm sure he would know a lot about what we're up against," Murphy said as he walked in on their conversation.

"Perhaps we should reach out to him," Sam said.

"We can offer immunity and safekeeping, but first we need to find him, and hope we're not too late," said Murphy.

"According to this book on the twelve instruments, it suggests the location will be hidden in the subconscious. We don't even know if they know where the instruments are, or how to locate them," Ruth added.

"One thing is certain; Jake Stanton is smart enough to break out of a hundred-fifty-year-old prison, so he will likely be hard to find. But what about the other guy? What do we know about Stephen Stross?" Sam asked.

"Not a lot," Murphy said. "We have had two detectives on him for two days now and this is all we got." Jack dropped a thin folder on Sam's desk. "As of 2006, we have no record of Stephen Stross. About the time Jake Stanton was sent to prison, this guy comes out of nowhere. He robs four banks in six months; we connected him to the crime with surveillance tapes. He was picked up outside his girlfriend's house and sent to jail for using a gun. The district attorney found a way to strike him out and send him to prison for hundreds of years. However, he's one of the cases our corrupt DA prosecuted herself, so he has a good chance of getting off. We never found the money. His girlfriend won a case against the FBI for harassment. Other than the conviction by the Sonoma County DA, he's as clean as they come. We're currently trying to find him through his girlfriend. However, she has a temporary restraining order on the feds."

"Tell me about his girlfriend," Sam said.

"Not much to tell. She won two million from the feds in the harassment and civil rights violation, something about some illegal wire taps," Murphy added.

"Really?" Sam's eyebrows went up. "So do we still have the tapes from the taps?"

"We do. Nothing we can use in court, but this box is full of CDs with conversations marked on them."

Murphy pulled a box from under his desk. Sam started looking through it; he was muttering to himself as he looked. "Hmm, boyfriend," Sam muttered, and took out a CD and placed it into his computer and listened.

"When can I see you?" Liea asked.

"I'll pick you up at six," a male voice said. "I can't wait to see you. I was at the courthouse most of the day. He will likely lose his appeal. I think I'll have to go in to wake him, there is no other way," he continued.

"Maybe you can write him and then visit him," Liea said.

"That will take way too long. I think Zoltar is getting close to him and I must get to him first," the male voice replied.

"There must be a better way than getting arrested," she said.

"I'm watching the house, it won't be long now," he answered.

"Sounds like this guy was trying to get arrested and tossed into prison with Stanton," Sam said.

"It makes sense," Ruth added.

"Do we know where the girlfriend is now?" Sam asked.

"She's gone. She has not been to her home in weeks. Also, she got a passport last month," Murphy announced.

"Well, let's try to use that. I need a warrant for her home, and bank records," Sam said.

Murphy grabbed his coat from the hook near the door and headed out. "Let me see what I can do."

Sam looked at Ruth. "You know, we have been given a lot of support on this. I wonder if we can use the government's surveillance tapes from the Homeland Security satellite. The Office of Homeland Security has a view of San Francisco along with LA, New York, Chicago, and Atlanta that I know of. I wonder what the night of the escape from San Quentin looks like."

"You know someone at the Office of Homeland Security?" Ruth asked.

"Actually, I have a friend in the White House who owes me a favor."

"That sounds like a pretty big favor," she added.

Sam picked up his phone.

"Bill, Sam Jericho. I have a big favor to ask." Sam spent the next twenty minutes explaining the sensitivity of his assignment; his friend sent him to meet some friends at the San Francisco Office of Homeland Security.

SEVEN

On the drive into the city, Ruth asked Sam how watching a video of Jake and Stephen escaping from San Quentin could help them in their investigation.

"Would you rather be sitting in the office or doing something? That's the way it goes sometimes with police work; sometimes you just need to shake the tree and see what falls out."

Chapter XXII

The Deception

ONE

As the ship opened the gangway at the port on Opole Island, Jake and Stephen decided to go into the village and have a look around. Liea and Daniel, along with Tony and Ron, joined them.

"What do you expect to find here?" Liea asked.

"I don't know, my sweet, but it's a beautiful place, don't you think?"

It was quite beautiful; it reminded Jake of Hawaii. *Not a lot of white people around,* Jake thought. The population seemed to be Pacific Islanders.

"I have never heard of this place," Tony said.

"That's because it's not on the map," Ron responded. "We have gone through a doorway and we're on another plane. Look at your watch."

Tony looked at his Rolex that could tell time in three time zones. It was running forward and backward, unable to make up its mind which way to run; first 10:00 a.m., then 6:30 p.m. Tony tapped his watch and put it to his ear. "This watch cost forty-seven thousand dollars," he said.

"We're on the other side of that watch and in a different *when,*" Ron said.

The town is little more than a village, Jake thought. It looked a lot like the Bodega Village at the Crossing. The small church was much like the church at the Crossing. Then there was the country store with the large porch and the rocking chairs. Jake felt like he was at home; he sat in one of the rocking chairs and relaxed.

Liea went inside the store and Stephen sat with Jake. "What's on your mind, my friend?"

Jake gave Stephen that we're-about-to-be-in-some-drama look with his ice-blue eyes. "I feel deception, Stephen, stronger than when we were on the ship. Do you feel it?"

"I do, Jake, but for the life of me I know not where or when it will occur."

Jake and Stephen went inside the store and looked at the goods; the shelves were filled with fine clothing, precious stones, fruit, and interesting food from the island. They inspected some books on the shelves, and Jake chose a book of maps as they left.

TWO

The landing party ate their evening meal in town. They drank wine and dined on pork and pineapple. The natives were kind to them and shared stories of other vessels that had visited the island. Daniel asked if anyone with a rawhide map had passed through but the natives could not remember.

It was Tony who felt the first sign of the enemy approaching; they were far from the ship and carried small arms. Tony and Ron wore nine millimeters on their belts and carried AK-47 assault rifles. Stephen and Daniel also had a sidearm, but Stephen was carrying his sling and sword. Jake had his sword, as well as the dagger he'd used on Borackus and Slowpoke; it was the only weapon effective against the immortals that traveled with Zoltar.

Time was drawing short; Jake and Stephen felt confident they would be victorious after they had visited Samuel. But Samuel also told them to be on their guard. The enemy would be delivered into their hands. However, Stephen felt something was very different than in the dream; the deceiver was intending to surprise them.

Suddenly, darkness fell upon them. Tony and Ron went for their guns, but Zoltar attacked with the speed of the wind. He stood in front of the landing party and demanded the key to the map.

Stephen stepped forward; he reached into his pocket for the crystal but it was gone. Zoltar shrieked, and the sonic sound of anger drove them backward. Tony and Ron opened fire with their AK-47s but the bullets had no effect on Zoltar. The spears and arrows from the creatures behind Zoltar flew like in Stephen's dream. Tony was struck in the legs and chest, causing him to drop his rifle, then another arrow to the head took his life. Ron watched as his brother died, then the arrows found him as well; one in the neck killed him. Both men died a painful and sudden death. Jake was confused. *How? They are immortal, as am I*, he thought. Then it came to him and he understood. *The Bow of Jonathan, it is enchanted, and they have it!* Jake turned red with anger and pulled the dagger.

He took a defensive posture facing the green goon.

"Where is the key?" Zoltar screeched with a sound that made Stephen and Jake's teeth hurt.

"I have it, my lord!" a familiar, sexy voice came from behind Stephen. It was Liea.

Liea, the beautiful. Liea, the innocent. Liea, Stephen's love.

Stephen's heart sank. In a state of shock, all of the fight left his body and he stood with his mouth open in disbelief.

"No! What are you doing, Liea?" Stephen yelled, with tears filling his eyes.

Jake stepped forward and grabbed Liea as she was crossing the dirt road to Zoltar, his dagger at her throat.

"No, Jake! I love her!" Stephen cried. Jake looked back at Stephen, paused, then pushed Liea towards Zoltar and she ran to the monster.

Stephen fell to his knees when Liea hugged the monster.

"I have the key, master. I can join the immortals. Have I served you well?" she asked the smelly green monster.

Stephen was destroyed, and Jake feared the worst for his friend. He put himself between Stephen and Zoltar and loaded his sling. Zoltar took Liea in his arms and went to the air with lightning speed; the rest of his army followed. Jake fell to the ground and embraced Stephen.

"Why? Why would she do it?" Jake held his friend as he wept.

Stephen and Jake embraced in the middle of the dirt road for a long time. The response from the ship was quick, but far too late. Captain Cook and his response party respectfully collected the bodies of Tony and Ron, faithful companions struck down in the prime of their life by evil creatures condemned to hell's sulfur at the end of days.

There was a sincere feeling of sadness, loss, and deception among the crew. Jake and Stephen seemed blinded by Samuel's interpretation of Stephen's dream that clearly indicated they would be in the port of Opole Island two or more days before any enemy encounter. But who could have guessed Liea was working with Zoltar? What spell did the monster cast on her to deceive her?

Ten years of trust, ten years of sharing truths and walking in the light; Liea had encountered the Good Shepherd in visions and walked in the knowledge of righteousness and with the purpose of defeating the enemy. *How long was she with this abomination? How long had she been plotting against me? And why?* Stephen thought as he agonized over the loss of his love.

THREE

They'd met innocently enough. Stephen was led to Liea by Michael. She was only nineteen at the time and struggling with a drug addiction. He was a visitor to her church. She was a full-time student at Sonoma State University and worked in a coffeehouse to pay the $300.00 monthly rent for the cottage behind the church.

She had recently separated from the boyfriend who made his money dealing heroin. She was a prisoner to the drug herself; first she took the drug to maintain her slim figure, but like a deceiver, the drug took her prisoner, and she stayed with the abusive boyfriend to feed her habit. Only when she surrendered and embraced the Good Shepherd did the addiction cease to rule her life. Stephen was there when she was struggling to be free from the haunting nightmares the heroin brought. He was not judgmental, he was not a holy roller or a square; rather he was kind, strong, and mysterious. She was swept off her feet; the horror of her young adult life was finally over. She thought she would never get past the grief of losing her parents in a car accident.

At age 16 she was taken to an abortion clinic by her high school gym coach, who told her he would always be there to mentor her, never mind that he was the father.

Stephen gave her another chance, a chance to start over, to be a part of something good and righteous. He never thought she would betray him. Over the years of planning the mission of the Alliance she was not left out; she was an active participant in all aspects of the plan. Liea was trusted with secrets even certain Shaddai were not aware of. She was the contact in San Francisco. Liea and Daniel were at the other end of the homing pigeons sent by Stephen from San Quentin. Even before San Quentin, Liea was the architect of the bank jobs that led to the planned arrest, which allowed Jake to escape from San Quentin.

Stephen could not imagine how they could have been closer; marriage was out of the question, he being immortal and she mortal. She was there every weekend in the visiting room at the county jail and then San Quentin. He shared everything with her, which is to say everything he could. Everything except the one thing she desired the most, and now he thought he understood what that was. She wanted be a part of the bloodline. She also wanted the immortality that went with the select few who ate from the tree of life.

How many years had she watched his birthday come and go and he not show a day of aging? She was nineteen when they met, nineteen, and now on the threshold of thirty years, the year when most women begin the decline into old age. She was gorgeous; even now she didn't look a day over twenty-five, but she knew what was to come. She watched what the last ten years of the earth's gravity had done to her once very firm breasts. She only weighed a hundred fifteen pounds but remembered what it was like to weigh a hundred and five.

She was starting to see the telltale signs of aging, something Stephen didn't give a second thought about. The fountain of youth was something he took for granted, and she hated him for it. The envy grew as each year she watched herself age and him not change at all. Stephen was blind to her envy; he had no idea that something so fundamental would destroy them. Now, like a scolded puppy, he lay in the dirt with his friend, hearing again and again the warnings and lessons provided by Samuel. His voice was loud and clear in Stephen's head, "On your guard." Pride was what had destroyed Morning Star! *Pride has caused the fall I have sustained this day!* Stephen thought. And what of the lives of the innocent guards Borackus took in San Quentin? Was their blood not also on his hands? Had he even given this a moment's thought?

How much of the plan had been lost because of his blindness?

Stephen remembered everything now; his big mouth exposing the critical details of their plan and only hushed by chance. She held the crystal in her hand and asked for the details, the key from Samuel, the one that would lead the deceiver to the island of Icarus, a land that would turn an immortal to mortal simply by breathing the air, and he would have blabbed this to his beloved were he not interrupted by Jake and his call to the deck at the sight of the island.

Yes, he would have told her, and she would have taken this information and traded it to that monster for a never-to-be-fulfilled promise of immortality. Stephen knew this now, as sure as Tony and Ron lay dead on this side and began their time at the Crossing. And his once-blind eyes now saw what Michael and Samuel were trying to show him all along.

Jake stood and offered his hand to Stephen, the student offering help to the teacher, and as painful as this lesson was, it was just that: a lesson of pride and arrogance, the lesson presented to all creation—one of the seven deadly sins that was now branded on Stephen. The teacher accepted the hand from Jake and got to his feet. They walked back to the ship without saying a word. They both reflected on the events of the afternoon.

The deceiver was on the ship the whole time; hiding in plain sight, no glow above her head to tell what spirit she carried. The monster would surely kill her when he learned the key would not take him to the sword. Moreover, the map would lead all that followed to a land that weakens them to that of a mortal. Liea had returned to the prison that once held her. She'd squandered the second chance she had at paradise. Stephen would likely see her near the Grasslands to the east of the Crossing. That is as close as she would ever get to Sion or ascending to heaven. She embraced evil and chose to follow the enemy, but Stephen would never be able to forget how he lived in her presence. Was it his pride, arrogance, or foolishly taking his life for granted that led her to that choice? Likely not, but he would always carry the question, like a fatal scar on his heart. And it would be cold, and it would not heal.

FOUR

Back on board *Delilah's Secret*, Captain Cook called a meeting in the war room for all hands except Communications Officer Sandra West and Security Officer Timothy Reynolds, who were on watch. Executive Officer Darrel Armstrong sat to the right of Captain Cook at the circular table in the war room. Next to him was Navigator Julia Rhymes, then Chief of the Boat Duncan Jones, then Commander Galloway, followed by Engineer Raymond Brooks and Seaman John Wesley. Seamen Windy Butler and Frank McKinney were also present, along with Daniel, Jake, and Stephen.

Captain Cook addressed the group, "We're a force of fourteen Shaddai, all sworn to the El Shaddai Knights dedicated to locating the twelve enchanted instruments. The Alliance currently holds three of the twelve instruments, and the dagger is with us on this mission. We now suspect the enemy has the Bow of Jonathan and used it to slay Tony and Ron McNabe. The world is a lesser place with them crossing over.

"We're traveling to the land of En-Dor where a witch, who is also immortal, is hiding the Sword of Goliath. We were deceived by a woman, Liea, whom we loved and trusted. We don't know how much of our mission has been compromised. We have to assume she has told Zoltar of the witch and the sword. The enemy is aware of En-Dor and has a map that he believes will guide him there. When he learns he was tricked, he will attack with a vengeance. We must be ready.

"Two of us will always be on watch, and we'll use every means to conceal our wake and path. We must trust each other with our lives; we'll open our minds to each other. Together we'll marry in one mind and one direction. The night has revealed that we all wear the halo of the holy.

This ship is off limits to the spirit of the Grigori. We shall pray a binding of entry of evil.

"When we draw close to En-Dor, we'll likely experience temptation and witchcraft designed to deceive us. Our secret weapons will be mirrors; first capture the image of a witch in the mirror, then destroy the mirror and kill the witch. Jake will be armed with the Dagger of Moriah and will use it when necessary. If you have questions or concerns, speak at the table and we'll hear you."

It was Stephen who stood first. "I have sinned. I have let pride and arrogance corrupt our mission. I beg your forgiveness. My sin has placed all of you in danger."

Some low talking, and then it was Windy Butler who spoke next. "We all know the risk. We're sworn to this mission, and we all fall short at times. You're a great leader, Stephen; never think you're above mistakes. Shaddai are of the line of Seth, also of Adam, and born to sin. We trust you with our lives."

Tears welled in Stephen's eyes and his lips tightened into a thin line.

"With the help of the Good Shepherd I shall try to remain humble in the future."

The rumble of low talk raised, and then clapping of hands and boot stomping brought the meeting back to a positive note.

Jake talked next. "This morning, the location of the sword was revealed to me. I expect we'll be in En-Dor in two days. I have provided Julia the direction of the island and we're moving at full speed. We'll dock at a port on the south side of the island; the evil toads that inhabit the place will be in their holes. Reynolds has programed our rockets to blast the holes to bits, and this will drive our enemy to the open, where we'll engage."

The chief of the boat, Duncan, spoke next. "I'm blessed to serve with this crew. I'll gladly die fighting the good fight. I would suggest we remove the dresser mirrors in the rooms to use as weapons. Our teams should be three to a crew; two to hold the mirrors, and one to fire the death shot. Crews of three can carry ten mirrors at a time. With five crews we can kill fifty witches."

Next was Captain Cook. "I like the plan. It's sound, and I don't expect fifty targets in En-Dor; at best I expect ten. This number is consistent with the amount of intel we have on the place."

Stephen stood again. "The captain is right; the number will likely be under ten. The plan is sound. I would offer one last suggestion, and then we retire this meeting. Our victory will depend on the blessing from the Good Shepherd. Let us all pray."

The crew joined hands in the war room around the table and prayed that their journey would be blessed. Stephen ended the prayer with, "Not my will, but thine, be done."

As the crew reported to their posts, each was visited by the spirit of the Shaddai.

Chapter XXIII

The Task Force

ONE

The drive to the city was slow; traffic was hectic, and Sam wondered what Ms. Ruth Springer was thinking about.

"Penny for your thoughts," Sam said.

"A penny? Really? A penny, that's the best you can do?"

"It's an expression."

"Pretty cheap expression," she said with a cute smile.

Sam was smitten. He was in his zone with his work, a big case with lots of excitement and now her, this beautiful, intelligent woman, and she seemed to like him. *It doesn't get any better than this,* he thought. He searched his mind for that smart question that would camouflage his simple mind. "The book on the instruments; we never finished going through the importance, as I recall. When we decided the wounds on the two bodies were likely done by the Dagger of Moriah we rushed out of the restaurant."

"I remember, we were nearly done, but I'm happy to go into detail on anything you find interesting."

"Well, we're seeking individuals who are after the Sword of Goliath, so maybe that should be our focus. Sometimes the strangest things lead us to what we're after."

"Okay, the boy David reported to the front lines of the battlefield between the Israelites and the Philistines to bring news to his father, Jessie, about his older brothers, who were soldiers in the king's army. When David heard the voice of Goliath mocking the God of the Israelites, he became angry and offended that their army would endure such insults. David voiced his objections to the soldiers at the front line, who threatened to shut him up, and asked who he thought he was to speak such objections about the king's soldiers. David's brothers interceded on his behalf and explained that David was a mere shepherd boy trusted with guarding his father's sheep and meant nothing by his contempt for the soldiers," Ruth said.

Sam gave Ruth a smile. "This is a different version than the one I got in Sunday school."

She returned the smile and continued, "But David took his objections to the king's tent and actually won an audience with King Saul. King Saul was sick at the thought he had no champion to fight the Giant, and that he himself trembled at the thought of going up against Goliath. Saul was famous for being head and shoulders taller than any man in Israel until he came upon the Philistines, Grigori, who was the offspring of a forbidden relationship between Angels and the women of earth. David recognized God's repulsion for such a being and told the king a story of his days watching over his father's sheep, and how God blessed him on two separate occasions: once when a lion attacked the flock and David killed the lion with his sling, and again when a bear came against the sheep, and he killed the bear as well. David was a man after God's own heart, and also of strong faith. He believed God would deliver the lion and the bear into his hands and it was so.

"David told the king, 'Let this Philistine be as that lion and as that bear, and let the God of Israel deliver him into my hand this day.' King Saul was ashamed he had lost the faith this boy was showing and after much discussion, he agreed to let David represent the army of Israel. David left the tent of King Saul. He stopped at the dry creek bed and picked five smooth stones for his sling.

"The Giant Goliath laughed at the sight of David. He continued to insult the king and his God, and Goliath only stopped laughing when the boy spoke. David rebuked the Grigori and cursed him for offending the Lord God Almighty. The Giant became so angry that when he threw his javelin, his anger caused it to fly wild. Goliath then took up his shield and sword and approached the boy. David announced in a loud voice as he positioned himself for using his sling, 'You come against me with sword and shield and spear but I come in the name of the Lord God Almighty, whom you this day have defied.' David released a stone from his sling and it struck the Giant in the forehead and lodged there. The Giant went down and David was on him. He took the Giant's sword and used it to separate the Grigori's head from his body. David put the head on the end of the Giant's spear and presented it to the Israeli Army, who watched this contest in disbelief. Then the Israeli Army attacked the Philistines and won the day. David took the Sword of Goliath to King Saul as a gift. Saul made the sword his own and used it against the Philistines for many battles."

Sam appeared truly interested now.

"As time passed and the Legion of David grew, King Saul became insane and paranoid. He thought the people would remove him as king and replace him with David. On an eerie night following the death of the Prophet Samuel, King Saul, who was again preparing to fight the Philistine Army, had his squire seek out a witch, or soothsayer, to give him counsel. He went to the woman and had her call up Samuel from the grave. Samuel told Saul he would die the next day. Saul left the cave depressed. The next day in the battle, the archers found the king. He was mortally wounded by an arrow. The king then fell upon the sword and committed suicide."

Sam smiled. "This you have memorized? You're a regular walking Sunday school class."

"You asked for details," she said, grinning.

"I suppose I did. So, tell me if you know where the sword is now."

"That is a good question. I'm sure it's in one of the sand countries near Israel—or perhaps not. Perhaps it has moved like the land of Nod or the Garden of Eden or is under another name. Some say it's in the land of Babylon or Persia, known to us now as Iran. Others say it has shifted dimensions and is more of a when question than a where question."

Sam raised his eyebrows. "Time travel? Are you suggesting time travel is possible?"

Ruth gave him a sour face. "I don't think I said that, but some do believe places like Paradise and Purgatory are in other dimensions and time is different there."

TWO

Sam turned in to the parking lot at the building where the Office of Homeland Security occupied the entire twelfth floor. Once inside the lobby, they were met by Dave Guthrie. Dave was the chief of the watch and took them to the viewing room.

The room was enormous, and almost like a movie theater with stadium seating. The control booth was at the top of the seats and could project the image recorded on the giant screen for a large audience. Sam had called ahead with the date and time they were interested in.

While on their way, a group of three analysts had prepared what they were likely looking for. Ruth and Sam sat near the control booth as the analysts booted up the section of recorded information prepared.

Sam looked at Ruth. "Can I count this as a movie date?"

She blushed and punched him in the arm. The lights were lowered and the movie started. The first scene was of San Quentin at night. Two men were making their way across the rooftop of North Block and then down to the lower yard. It was as if they were watching a movie filmed by an overhead camera; it had everything except sound.

Were the officers in the towers blind or asleep? Sam thought as he watched the two cross the yard in some fog with no problem. They had on what looked like backpacks made from yellow raincoats. They lifted the rusty steel cover to a tunnel. The angle changed, and they could see where the tunnel emptied into the bay. The two escapees each blew up a makeshift rubber boat and they simply kicked out to the buoy marking the channel for the Larkspur Ferryboat.

"Right under Tower 4," Sam said. *How did they get on that boat?* he wondered.

"Look!" Ruth said. "What is that dragging beside the boat?"

It was cloth ropes, like bungee cords with great loops made to withstand tension and they were picking up the escaping inmates. Within minutes of connecting with the lifts, both men were aboard the boat.

The movie showed the clothing and blood being dumped by a man in a white coat. The coat was white with a red stripe, like a diving symbol. The next angle was the disembarking of the passengers.

"The coat was what the analysts closed in on to identify the escaping inmates," Guthrie said. "There were four in the landing party, one female and three males."

"This is incredible," Ruth said. "We're watching this from space?"

Sam gave her a wink in the low-lit room.

"They get in a truck here, and it takes them to Chinatown," Guthrie said.

"It's difficult to see, but we think they go into this old hotel. We are checking footage to try to identify where they go from there. We have no cameras that have a view under this canopy so it could be a while to find where they went from here."

The lights came up and Sam stood to thank Guthrie and his team.

"You have answered a lot of our questions already," Sam explained. "Can I get a copy of that footage? I would like to share it with the task force."

"We have a package for you already prepared, complete with the timeline report and some projections of where they may have gone," Guthrie explained.

"We can't thank you enough for everything." Sam and Ruth took the bag Guthrie and his team had prepared and left the building.

THREE

"Can I ask you something?" Ruth said when they got back in the car.

"Is it personal?"

"I think so." Both were clearly flirting with their best game.

"Okay," Sam said. "I'm prepared to reveal my soul to you now, my dear."

"What is the story with the Journey ring tone?"

The blood filled Sam's cheeks. He was prepared for anything but this. It wasn't enough that he had been busted more than once with the ring tone by her; he really intended to change it. It would have only taken a moment. But now, here he was on the hot seat, and must explain why Steve Perry bellows the cry of "Don't stop believing" every time his phone rings.

"I can explain, ahhh, well . . ." Sam stopped, took a breath, and came clean. "I was on a stakeout and bored out of my mind. I was going through the options on the new cell phone and I came across songs that reminded me of when I was in high school. I was dating Suzy Koop, she was my first love. On our first date we went to see

Journey. She loved that song and in my bored, lonely moment, I loaded it. I meant to change it but I always forget."

"Why is that an embarrassing thing for you to share, Sam?"

"I don't know. I guess I thought it made me appear a bit pitiful or desperate."

"Don't Stop Believing" the phone cried. Sam rolled his eyes. "Inspector Jericho. Yes . . . really? Call me when he gets in. Thank you." Sam closed the phone with his chin.

"They got John Morales. He was in Mississippi, he has a brother there. They're bringing him back tonight." As they got closer to the marina and the houseboats, Sam pointed out his home.

"You live on a houseboat?" Ruth asked. "I would love to see it."

Sam crossed three lanes and exited the freeway.

"I'm glad you said that. I wanted to stop and check on Rusher. He's in the neighbor's yard and I have not been home since someone kicked in my door."

"Someone broke into your home? Did they take anything?" Ruth asked.

"I am not sure; I was called away before I could check," Sam replied.

Sam entered the home with gun drawn while Ruth waited in the car. He checked it out from top to bottom to ensure it was safe and holstered his weapon before returning to the car and asking her to come in.

Ruth thought the place was exceptionally clean for a man living alone. Sam decided the intruder didn't enter after kicking the door open; perhaps he was persuaded to stop by Rusher. Sam poured some wine while Ruth used the restroom.

"Your wine is on the counter!" Sam yelled so Ruth could hear him. "I'm going to get Rusher and bring him home."

She took her time in the restroom, freshening up and checking her makeup. Sam got Rusher and put him in the house. Ruth was breathtaking as she crossed his cream-colored carpet in her bare feet.

She picked up the wine glass and took a sip. "Give me a tour."

Sam extended his arm. "This is the living room. That's my chair where I watch the Forty-niners play when I don't have to work on Sundays."

They walked to the guest suite and Sam showed his gun locker that took up nearly half of the closet in the room he used as his office.

"This is what I spend my money on." He opened the safe and showed off his gun collection. It included multiple handguns and rifles, but Sam was especially proud of the antique .45-caliber revolver with the sandalwood grip.

Then they went upstairs. "This is where I sleep," Sam said.

"Is that a hot tub in your room?"

Sam was sipping his wine and she turned and met his eyes. The kiss that followed was so natural. Sam loved kisses, but this was amazing; she was soft and beautiful, and kissed with the most sensual lips he had ever encountered. Sam felt like he did after that Journey concert when he kissed Suzy Koop, only better.

The passion was mutual. They pulled and tugged at each other's clothes while kissing, and then accommodated each other's hand gesture requests until they were both in their underwear.

Sam picked her up and carried her to the bed. He laid her down gently and she pulled him on top of her. He cupped her breasts and kissed her neck; she was burning under him and compelled him to continue.

He obliged her and she kissed and bit his neck. Like a first-time lover he concentrated until he was certain she had reached her orgasm. Then with long, slow body motions he joined her in ecstasy.

They laid naked, holding each other and breathing hard for a long time before returning to their wine and then firing up the hot tub. They enjoyed a long session of lovemaking, neither questioning the other about safe sex. Sam had no condoms, as he rarely spent any romantic time with anyone here. Doctor Ruth Springer had a similar story; the issue never came up, and they decided to risk it all on each other. It would be three months before this issue was discussed again. For now, it was a magical moment, and one that would be held sacred between them.

FOUR

It was the house phone that woke them. Sam checked the clock and noted it was 4:30 a.m.

"OK, I'll be there in about a half-hour."

Ruth sat up in bed and Sam kissed her.

"They just brought in Morales, I have to go to the office. You're welcome to stay and sleep, this will only take a couple of hours."

"I want to go too, then you can take me to my car. Can I share the shower with you?"

Sam was enamored. "I don't want you to go home, I want to spend the day with you."

"I want you to take me to my car because I left my cell phone there. I'll drive here after we go to the office."

Sam felt his heart glow. "I like your plan, let's get that shower."

They had just enough time to make a happy ending to the shower, then they rushed out the door and were on the 101 to the office.

"Don't stop belie—"

"Inspector Jericho." Sam was quick on the answer; Steve Perry didn't have a chance to finish bellowing the opening to his song. The caller was a wrong number. Sam handed the phone to Ruth.

"Would you be kind enough to change the ring tone please?"

"I like the one you have," she said.

Sam just shot her a look that said, no way.

"OK, I'll pick a song that is special to me so when you hear it you will think of me."

The whole thing was kinda high school but their love was fresh and new, so what the hell. Ruth went through the list. She settled on a song from ZZ Top, it was called "Gimme me all your lovin'."

"I'm choosing a ZZ Top song so you will remember me every time it rings."

FIVE

Morales was sweating bullets in the interrogation room. Sam wanted to go in and confront him, but Murphy was smart enough to know his presence in that room would damage the case. Sam would have to settle for watching from the observation room. Morales must have known he was on the other side of the glass, his eyes kept darting to the mirror when questions of Sam and the attempts on his life were raised.

"None of you understand; the world is quickly coming to an end!" Morales said. "I was working with two individuals who cannot be killed. They are immortal.

Marshal Raven is from the bloodline of Angels, you don't understand!"

The two interrogators were ready to contact a mental health interrogator because this guy was clearly a nut job. Ruth and Sam watched from the viewing room and hung on his every word.

"Jack, what about Doctor Springer? Can she ask him some questions? She's an expert on the occult and knows about the Angel stuff he's talking about," Sam said.

Murphy considered it.

"Well, he has not tried to kill you, so we have no conflict of interest. Go ahead."

Ruth took a couple of deep breaths. "I'll give it a shot."

Murphy and Ruth entered the interrogation room.

"Hi, John, how are you doing?" Ruth said.

"How do you think I'm doing? I'm being accused of attempted murder against one of my best friends. I would never try to kill Sam!"

"Can you tell me about the Grigori you were working with?"

"I was contacted by Anita Moore and told to talk to Marshal Raven and Eric Johnson. They introduced me to the whole Grigori thing. They're both immortal, and proved it by taking a gunshot to the heart. They work for an Angel they called Zoltar and he's all powerful. Anita offered me an inspector position to lead these guys around and give them information on the Stanton case!" Morales bellowed.

"When did you give them the information?" Murphy asked.

"Day before yesterday. Then I saw my name on *America's Most Wanted* and got scared. That's when I ran."

Ruth shot a look at the glass. She was thinking about Sherri Alexander. She left the room. Sam was outside the door.

"Let's give Sherri a call," Sam said. It was about seven in the morning, but the calls were going right to voice mail.

"Let's go. I hope she's OK," Sam said. They grabbed their coats and headed for the car.

Chapter XXIV

The Land of Icarus

ONE

Liea was in flight with her new friend. The ground disappeared beneath her as the winged Zoltar traveled to the *Ichabod* and landed on deck. The monster left Liea with his servants, Eric and Marshal. He presented the map and key to his servants, who included his twenty trusted soldiers he considered faithful. Now a woman had joined them, Liea, the deceiver of Stephen, her beloved. Her heart had been turned to stone. Marshal and Eric, both lieutenants in the service of Zoltar, were handsome men of renown in her eyes; they were instructed to entertain Liea while Zoltar and the other monsters went below deck to rest.

The ship was three stories high, with engines as well as sails. The *Ichabod* was black, with black sails and a flag announcing her name. Liea was rewarded with a master suite on the *Ichabod*, but what she wanted, what she craved, and what she had to have, was immortality. After all, did she not assist them in obtaining the secret map and key to take them to the sword?

The evil bat-like Angels who traveled with Zoltar were strong and powerful. Liea was blind to the gruesome appearance of the monsters. When Jake faced this army and when he looked upon them he saw them for what they were; their skin was green and their eyes were yellow, they were naked and had webbed wings and long tails. Their teeth were like those of a shark, pointed and jagged and ugly. The odor coming from the monsters was like rotten flesh. But Liea didn't see this; she saw power and gifted creatures who could take flight in the blink of an eye.

Marshal sat across from Liea in the master chamber at a glass table filled with a mound of cocaine. As she snorted the coke into her nose, her body cried out and ached for lustful sex, the kind of sex she watched on the triple-X videos when she was with a different kind of monster. Liea was home. She wanted the strongest bull in the pasture, and her animal instinct was made real.

Marshal and Eric had their way with her over and over while they drank whisky and powered up loud heavy metal music. She didn't sleep. By the second day, she was back to the heroin. The needle in her arm was like a long-lost lover returning to embrace his prisoner. She was his faithful servant and she missed him; her master understood her. The seven deadly sins that Stephen preached about became her new idol; she wanted to experience all of them and stand naked in the dark and worship them. She'd become a complete reprobate who no longer believed wrong was wrong as she embraced the deceiver. Liea didn't know that the monster she had joined had no intention of granting her wish to taste the tree of life. Zoltar told her the glowing fruit was with the sword and she would be able to partake and become immortal like him. Liea was lost, more than she would ever know.

Eric studied the map; he was the smarter of the two lieutenants and was focused on the directions written in angelic script. The crystal must be placed on the left section of the map at noon and the sun would do the rest; a reflection would provide the final destination and hiding place of the sword. They had no reason not to trust the map; after all, it had guided them to Opole Island, along with a little help from their spy, Liea.

"Why is the sword so important?" Liea asked.

It was Marshal who answered the woman. "You're so misguided, my little flower. You burn for sex and drugs and the freedom to indulge yourself. Only the enchanted instruments can save our way of life. Only when the last do-gooder is dead can we rejoice and live in anarchy as we wish."

Liea smiled and tried to look like she understood what he was saying.

"Your boyfriend will never stop hunting us or leave us to live as we wish, so we'll kill him and all like him."

"We'll try," Eric said. "The bastards killed Slowpoke and Borackus, and they will not stop until we're also dead. Our kind has chosen freedom, survival of the fittest, and the right to do what we want, when we want. We can become gods," Marshal explained to Liea.

Liea asked about the city of freedom she was told of by Zoltar. Eric explained that the City of Nod was where they could rest, with no worries of interference from the Alliance. Even though the garden was sacred ground and open to a chosen few, Nod was guarded by the Angels who protect their inherent right to be free.

TWO

It was 12:04 p.m. when Eric decided he had the exact location of the Sword of Goliath. "I have it! It's in the East."

Marshal ordered the pilot to set their course.

"I expect we'll reach it in less than a day," Eric said.

They celebrated; day and night, the party never ended. Booze, drugs, music, and sex.

The next morning, Liea was the one to see land first. She woke Eric and Marshal; they stood on the deck and used binoculars to check out the island's white sandy beaches and rich vegetation.

Zoltar and the others came up on deck and then took flight over the island; when the ship was in port, the wicked Grigori came ashore. They made their way through a normal enough looking town. *It's like a town from an old Western*, Liea thought. The broad sidewalks boasted stores selling canned goods, baskets of fruit, hanging salami, and salted meats, as well as all manner of baked goods.

There were a few saloons with batwing entrances, horses tied to hitching posts, a large livery stable and a blacksmith shop. A lumber mill was powered by a waterfall. The people of the town were unarmed and dressed in jeans and shirts; most wore boots, but Liea saw some women wearing laced knee-high shoes, the sort you might see in houses of ill repute.

Then there were the others, still human—at least they looked human—but very large. Some dressed like priests, with black robes and hoods. Others were wearing armor, like soldiers from a Roman movie, Liea thought. No, not like Romans, like Vikings. They were like giant Vikings, and they carried swords and shields. The townspeople were checking out the newcomers.

"According to the map, the sword is in a temple at the east end of the village," Eric said.

Within moments they were at the temple gates. Large Viking-looking men guarded the temple. They were armed with swords and flaming arrows.

"Who is your king?" Zoltar barked at the Viking guarding the entrance to the temple.

"We're led by no king, we're led by the council," he answered.

"Who speaks for the council?" Zoltar asked, clearly becoming impatient.

"His name is Jedidiah. He has been called and is coming now."

The gate opened and an old-looking Giant walked out. He was head and shoulders taller than any other Giant around the temple. He wore a helmet with horns on each side, and his mustache was longer than his large caveman chin.

"Who are you, and what is your business here?" the Giant asked.

"I am Zoltar, and I'm seeking the Sword of Goliath."

Zoltar watched as the mustache raised on the sides of the Giant's face. He was smiling; something struck him as being funny. Zoltar was becoming furious.

"Why would you seek the Sword of Goliath in the land of Icarus?" the Giant asked.

"Icarus? Not the land of Icarus." Zoltar took flight without saying another word, his soldiers following.

"You fools! What have you done to us?" Zoltar screamed from high in the sky.

The travelers returned to the boat; they were dumbfounded by Zoltar's behavior.

"What is it, master?" Marshal asked.

"We have been tricked! The land of Icarus is the place of dead men's bones. The woman has trapped us. This land is said to change immortals into mortals. This is where Angels come to die, you fools!" He was beyond furious. "Where is the woman?"

Eric brought Liea to the monster. She was trembling. All thoughts of living a long and happy life had vanished, and now she only wanted to escape this single moment. Her twenty-nine years flashed before her eyes: her lovers, her family, her lies and deception, like a slow-motion replay of a life filled with self-centered choices. Even when she was with Stephen, her jealousy and envy were her defining moments, and now she was the weapon, or the vessel, of destruction. Even in her betrayal she'd served the Alliance. The irony of the whole thing was beyond her comprehension. In her selfish desire to betray her beloved, she has done him a great favor: the army of Zoltar has been exposed to Icarus. She was in tears, and held by her hair before Zoltar. She saw him now like Jake did: he was green and had yellow eyes; but the odor—*Death,* she thought. *He smells of death.*

"What have you done, woman?"

Liea looked into the eyes of the monster and tried to remember Stephen's love.

"I have deceived the one I love," she said with a shaky voice. "I have myself been damned."

The monster used his long and razor-sharp fingernail to open her up in the mid-section, her intestines spilling out and hanging in front of her while thick, dark blood flooded the deck. The next move was as quick as light-speed using the same nail to open her neck, causing arterial spray to paint his bare green chest before she pitched forward at his feet.

"She's dead," Marshal said, and the same judgment was taken against him. He died like a mortal man, slow and painful, in this cursed land of dead men's bones.

Eric mustered the courage to speak. "We're mortal," he muttered as he watched the quivering body of his peer bleeding out on the deck next to the woman.

"Indeed, we're all as mortal as a monkey or a man. You're all dying at a rapid pace. Each day you live is the same as a man's year. In a month you will all likely be dead. Because of this woman, you and the rest of your crew are cursed to die a death of accelerated aging."

The lips of the monster pulled back into an evil grin, exposing his shark teeth.

"Is there no hope of escaping this death, master?" Eric asked, now grasping the seriousness of the situation.

"The only hope is the witch who guards the sword; it's said she has some glowing fruit of immortality."

Now First Lieutenant Eric Johnson was commanding the *Ichabod* as Zoltar and his army returned to the sky to backtrack to Opole Island in hopes of picking up the trail of *Delilah's Secret*. The ship had three days' head start and their trail would likely be a cold one.

THREE

In a hut of mud with a roof of straw in the land of En-Dor lived a woman. This woman was more than three thousand years old. The woman found favor with Morning Star, the most powerful Angel on earth, as she made him her god and master. Morning Star blessed the woman with immortality for her service and worship. It's said he provided her with a basket of fruit from the Garden of Eden gathered by the serpent. This woman dwelled with four eunuch servants, descendants of Cain and older than the woman herself.

The servants were dressed in leather armor hidden beneath large brown hooded robes that tied at the midsection. Each of the goons carried a sword and a dagger concealed in his robe. The woman was dressed in a black robe with a large black hood; her face remained hidden in the shadow of her hood.

Outside the hut was a moat and a gatehouse with a footbridge leading to the dwelling. The gatehouse remained locked and guarded by one of the servants at all times. The woman sustained herself by telling fortunes to the visitors from other dimensions—or other whens—and occasionally to the wealthiest dwellers in the land of En-Dor. The people of En-Dor knew the woman to be a witch; not just any witch, but the oldest witch that ever lived. Her practice of her craft had made her a legend in her own time.

The woman began her craft when she was very young and serving in the house of a general in the king's army. The young woman boasted she had inherited her mother's gift of calling upon the dead and bringing their spirit from the Crossing. Her boasting nearly got her killed, as her craft was forbidden in that day. The woman only escaped death because of her master. She hid in a cave and for years she would only perform her craft to those she trusted. Then one day she was called upon to serve a man she didn't know. He was a rich man and paid very well. The man was asking for her to call up the spirit of a man of God, the spirit of Samuel the prophet. The woman feared for her life but did as he bid her just the same.

During the ceremony, the witch learned that the man was the king, the very king who put to death all those who practiced witchcraft and soothsaying. The king promised that if she would do this one thing for him, no harm would come to her. The witch completed the ceremony, and the spirit of the prophet appeared. The spirit told the king he would not live to see another day. The king left the cave and the woman followed him back to where his army had camped. She remained at a distance and when the king was wounded by an arrow, she watched him take his sword out and fall upon it. The woman then took the king's sword, as she knew the sword held power. It was the sword of the Grigori Goliath, and could kill the immortal. The four priests who protect the woman were a gift from Morning Star, or Satan.

FOUR

Each day the four priests processed the visitors who wished the service of the woman of En-Dor. Four each morning and four each afternoon came through the gate and crossed the small footbridge to the hut of the woman. At the gate, two priests searched each guest. The search included removing their clothing and submitting to a body cavity search. The visitor was then provided with a robe and slippers to wear inside the dwelling. No weapons, no bags, no possessions of any kind were allowed past the gatehouse. The woman could see and tell the future of all—except her own. She was blind to her own destiny.

In the dwelling was the parlor; it was very dark. The room had a circular table and three chairs. On the walls were the candleholders, the only source of light except the two candles on the table. The place smelled of mold and spices, like a cellar in a very old building.

The parlor led to an arched hallway on the left, with doors both on the left and the right. The other archway led to a kitchen with a potbelly stove. The dwelling had no windows and only one door leading in or out. The old woman stood over a large pot chanting her spells; she added sharp root to the boiling brew, then reached into a basket and picked up a snake. She spoke more words and the snake opened to her and the fangs dripped into the pot. She returned the snake to the basket and cackled with a laughter that would cause one's flesh to want to crawl off the bone. More words were spoken and she sprinkled some sage into the brew. Then she took a wooden bowl and filled it from the pot. She walked to her high-back chair where she sat and sipped from the bowl.

Speaking to an empty chair across the small ironwood table, she said, "How nice it is for ye to visit." She cackled. "From whence do ye come this time?" She waited and drank. "And how will I know it?"

She seemed very interested in the empty chair, and if the goon didn't know better, he would have thought she was speaking to someone sitting in that very place. The priest had seen this before, and knew better than to interrupt her when she was entertaining a guest. The large gorilla in the priest robe turned on his heels and went back to the gatehouse to tell the would-be client the woman would not see her today.

"Come again tomorrow, and mind you, bring the gold pieces with ya," he grunted.

Chapter XXV

Nod

ONE

Stephen felt a sharp pain in his stomach, then moments later, in his neck. "She's dead."

Jake turned and looked at Stephen's tearing eyes.

"Liea is dead. Zoltar killed her, and she's dead. I felt it in my gut, then in my neck. She was thinking of me when she died."

Jake put his hand on Stephen's shoulder. "I remember a time when you helped me deal with my loss of Teresa," Jake said. "We were in West Block at San Quentin, and I could not sleep. I wish I could return the favor, my friend."

Stephen regarded Jake with a painful smile. "I remember. Thanks, Jake. I'll be OK. The Bible tell us that God works all things for the good for them who love him and are called according to his purpose. It's going to be all right."

Jake smiled back at Stephen, mostly in amazement at his strength in this time of loss and betrayal.

TWO

Jake popped his head into the ship's second command center. "Get the crew and meet me in the war room," he said to Captain Cook.

When Stephen and Jake entered the war room, they were pleased to see Daniel and Cook already seated at the round table.

"We'll be arriving at En-Dor in less than a day," Jake explained. "We need to go over our plan again and start preparing."

"Daniel, you will be entering the witch's dwelling as a paying customer." Jake explained.

"How will I dress? Shall I enter in these clothes?" Daniel asked.

"I think not," Stephen said. "I like your style, Daniel, however, she's accustomed to wealthy travelers, and will become suspicious if you enter dressed so commonly. And you need to carry her preferred method of payment, gold or diamonds."

"I thought about how you should dress," Jake said. "You're about the same size as Tony. You can take what we need from his wardrobe."

"I agree," Stephen said. "In a way, I feel he and Ron remain with us in spirit. From the vision, we know she has between four and six goons we'll have to dispatch, and immortals are hard to kill. However, the guards with her have a vulnerable kill spot that will take them out. The weak spot is the base of the neck, both front and back. The front is a very difficult target because of the size, so better to focus at hitting the back of the neck. Bullets, swords, and daggers are all very effective on them. Hit the base of the neck and they will fall paralyzed to the ground; alive, but fundamentally disabled."

"What about the witch?" Daniel asked.

"She will be a much harder challenge," Stephen said. "She has not survived this long by being stupid. I expect, however, she would not have survived this long if knowledge of her having the Sword of Goliath was out there."

"How do we know she still has this sword?" Reynolds asked.

"Good question. Jake, you want to take this one?"

Jake stood up. He looked into the faces around the room, something familiar in each one of them; his brothers and sisters, all descendants from the bloodline of Seth, his bloodline. Sure, each was from a different branch, or even several branches over, but all related; unlike Liea, who was not of the bloodline, but was trusted as a member of the Alliance. Here were the Shaddai, some of his family, and with him in the quest to retrieve the Sword of Goliath.

"This is important, so hear me well." Jake ran his fingers through his loose hair and began. "About three and a half years ago, I was living a happy life as a building contractor. I had never killed anyone, and except for a few moments as a child, I had never raised my hand against another and drawn blood. I had a strange dream about a sword. It meant nothing to me, just a crazy, unexplainable dream. I had no idea my wife and unborn child were to be murdered because of that dream. The enemy had my wife killed and framed me for the crime.

"The enemy knew the location was with me before I knew it myself. I understand his plan was to torture my wife in my presence to force me to give it up, and I would have in a moment to save Teresa. I was at my lowest low; I was serving a life sentence without any chance of parole when I met Stephen."

Jake looked at Stephen and regarded him with a smile.

"In a jail cell, Stephen woke me to my true calling. I was astounded beyond words the first time I visited the Crossing. I was blessed with months at our ranch at the Crossing with my wife and little girl. At the Crossing, Stephen taught me the way of the Shaddai.

"While in prison, my body reached the age of 94 years before I was able to visit the garden. Every day from the moment Stephen awoke me, the light has become brighter and brighter, and I could feel I was getting closer to knowing where the sword was located. It was at the Crossing that we traveled to seek Samuel's wisdom.

Samuel interpreted my dream and explained that the sword was in En-Dor with the witch. Even so, En-Dor is located in another dimension, and directions on how to get there were unknown. We were at sea on this voyage when the latitude and longitude was revealed to me and the ship was put on course. Faith is what is leading us now. We have done all we can do, and now we must stand and be true."

Jake's eyes welled with tears as he spoke from his heart.

"We're all from the bloodline of Seth. We're likely from different whens; however, together we have set out to redeem the sword, a simple talisman, but we're walking in obedience."

Jake sat down and the room applauded his story; they clapped their hands and stood up to show respect and unity.

Stephen was next to speak. "I expect when we arrive in En-Dor, we'll encounter evil like we have never experienced in the past. Our plan must be flawless, so let's go over it again. We have a crew of fourteen, and our kind has battled legions with fewer in the past. Surprise will be on our side. Tim Reynolds will control the attack from the ship only after we have determined we have no other choice than to break cover."

Stephen went to the dry erase board and marked the course of attack. "The first of the landing party will include Jake, Daniel, and myself. Next will be our cover group, Julia, Duncan, Francis, and John. They will seek elevated positions and provide cover to the four corners of our target. Ray, Frank, and Windy will bring in the secret weapon, and then stand by for the attack command. After we step foot on land, we communicate through telepathy only. If someone tries to speak to you, speak in Shaddai so they understand nothing. The captain and Tim will remain on board and fire any necessary long-range weapons our team paint with lasers."

"I expect all members of the landing team will carry laser markers," Tim added.

"The secret weapon, the mirrors," Wendy said. "It will likely take all available to carry one as we enter."

"I agree," Jake said. "We determined it will be in our best interest to carry as many mirrors as we can into the dwelling. If we can catch the witch off guard and get her reflection in time to destroy the mirror, Samuel seems to think it will destroy her. Stephen will go for the sword, and I'll cover him with the Dagger of Moriah," Jake said.

"The sword is in her bedchamber in a pit beneath a trunk. Don't bother trying to remove the trunk, it's bolted down. We must break the lock and open the trunk to enter the pit. We should expect snakes in the pit where the sword is. The latest vision seems to indicate the sword is buried under the snakes," Jake continued.

"Snakes?" Stephen asked. *Why did it have to be snakes?* He looked as if he was about to lose his lunch. "I hate snakes!" Stephen said.

"Steady, brother," Jake said, trying not to laugh

"I think we're as ready as we'll ever be," Captain Cook said. "If you're on watch, report to your post. Everyone else, the master dining room is ready for the evening meal."

THREE

After the meal, Jake and Stephen took a walk on deck.

"We have come a long way, amigo," Stephen said.

Jake smiled. "We sure have. What are we forgetting, Stephen? I think . . . like with Liea, we're missing something."

"Perhaps we are. I can't think of anything. We have come to the threshold of our quest, and all we can do now is trust in him who sent us and stand true."

FOUR

Both Jake and Stephen were asleep the moment their heads hit the pillow. Jake found himself responding to Stephen, shaking him awake. He was in his bed at the Crossing. The smell of bacon frying in the kitchen called to them. For a moment he thought he was with Teresa and Abigail, then as quickly as the thought came, he knew they had ascended. This was his home now. Jake and Stephen were delighted to see Hector's wife, Lucy, preparing breakfast.

Aaron was in his chair smoking his pipe and talking to Tony and Ron. Following kind words and embraces, Tony and Ron explained they were happy at the Crossing.

"We now know the enemy has the Bow of Jonathan," Tony said. "It was a hard way to learn that little factoid," he continued.

"What happened in the village on Opole Island?" Ron asked.

Stephen's head dropped in shame. "It was Liea. She was working with the enemy and betrayed us. The creatures knew we were there and knew about the key to the map. The silver lining is that the map they're following will lead them to the land of Icarus."

"Even as mortal beings they will be extremely dangerous," Jake added.

The men went over their plan to attack the witch at En-Dor with Tony, Ron, and Aaron.

"The plan seems good," Aaron said.

"Have you considered that the army of Zoltar will likely be following your back trail?" Ron asked.

"That is a good point," Jake said. "With the goons in En-Dor and Zoltar following our trail, we could find ourselves boxed in."

"I have thought about that," Stephen said. "I would like to visit Samuel and seek his advice on the matter."

"I thought you might," Aaron said. "Daniel is saddling the horses.

FIVE

Jake felt a sadness wash over him as he walked to the stables and passed the wishing well he and Abigail had built stone by stone. As Jake entered the barn, the familiar aroma of oats and hey added to the nostalgia. Pylon was happy to see Jake and regarded him with a hardy neigh as he tossed his head up and down with excitement. Jake had brought him an apple and used his pocketknife to carve the fruit into bite-size pieces for the horse. Pylon enjoyed the treat, and rewarded Jake by rubbing his head against Jake's arm and side. Jake was obliged to scratch the horse between the ears and Pylon closed his eyes in pleasure.

Jake examined the weapons rigged on the saddle, including a short bow with a quiver of arrows, a sword, and two daggers. The men mounted their horses and started across the meadow to the northeastern mountains. Jake noticed snow on the mountains and thought it not just remarkable but beautiful as well. When the men reached the point where Jake always looked back at the ranch, they stopped and surveyed the view.

"I miss them," Jake said.

"I know you do, and I miss them as well. But know they're in a far better place and be at peace," Stephen said.

"I know you're right, but I miss them just the same."

Daniel pulled his short bow and nocked an arrow.

"On your guard, Jake!" Stephen yelled, and they pulled their bows and selected an arrow.

"What is it?" Jake asked.

"I'm not sure," Daniel said. "I thought I heard something."

Suddenly a loud screeching sound broke the silence and the horses reared in terror, causing the men to nearly fall to the ground. Daniel released his arrow and the sound returned, only this time pain was heard in the screeching roar. Fire lit the trees next to Stephen and Jake as Daniel was nocking a second arrow.

"It's a lumpa, and he's mad!" Daniel said. "Watch the horses."

The men quickly dismounted, and Jake tied the horses to a shrub opposite the fire.

"Take him, Daniel!" Stephen said, running to his side.

Both men released their arrows that found their mark. The wounded beast broke cover in a flanking maneuver and started for Jake.

The creature was about the size of a large horse, with red eyes and pale, mint-green skin. He was on his hind legs, charging Jake with jagged shark teeth and razor-sharp claws like a bear. A set of bat wings were folded, allowing the creature to navigate the thick brush in the forest. Jake took a breath and found his target. When he released the arrow, it buried deep in the creature's heart, causing death before the lumpa hit the snow-covered ground.

Daniel and Stephen followed the red snow around the burning tree and saw the lumpa lying dead at Jake's feet.

"I thought you said the lumpa only come out at night!" Jake said with eyes so wide you'd think he saw a ghost.

Stephen smiled. "Only in the summer months."

"I should have warned you that during the heat of the summer, lumpa rarely leave the coolness of their deep caves where they can escape the summer heat. During the cooler months they're very alert and territorial. You did good, Jake; your first lumpa kill. Now you must eat the animal's heart."

"What?" Jake exclaimed, disgusted.

Stephen used his dagger and opened the beast up and removed its heart with the arrow that had gone right through it.

Stephen handed the arrow to Jake and smiled. "Well, go ahead then, before it gets cold!"

Jake just looked at the bloody lump about the size of a football. His nose wrinkled as he moved it close to his face to give it a sniff; it stunk like sour milk and copper. Jake closed his eyes and was moving the rotten hunk of bloody flesh to his mouth when Stephen batted it from his hands and began to roar with laughter.

Daniel joined him and pointed a finger at Jake and said, "You were actually going to put that nasty thing in your mouth!"

Jake felt the blood fill his cheeks and he dropped his brow in anger.

"Come on, Jake," Stephen said. "It was simply a joke."

Jake could not help but smile, and the smile turned into a laugh. He knew what it must have looked like to them and it was kinda funny; only he thought it would have been funnier if the joke was not on him.

"Payback is a bitch, Stross!" Jake said. "When you least expect it, you'd better expect it!"

When the men tossed enough snow on the flaming tree, Stephen knelt to the dead beast. He used his knife and opened the throat of the lumpa and cut loose a strange tube-looking organ.

"This is the part the wizards hunt lumpa for," Stephen explained, and rolled it up in a piece of rawhide, then placed it in his saddlebag. Next he took the claw from the right hoof of the creature and removed it.

"Be careful with this." Stephen handed the claw to Jake. "It's a nice trophy, but very deadly. The claw of the lumpa carries a poison; we'll take it to Samuel, he knows how to make it safe."

Jake carefully took the claw with a piece of rawhide and placed it in his saddlebag.

"We're losing daylight; we need to get out of these woods," Daniel added.

SIX

The snow was about twelve inches deep in the Grasslands and the horses were enjoying the cool weather and soft snow beneath their hooves. Samuel, as usual, was working in the stables. Daniel, Stephen, and Jake dismounted and were leading their horses into the barn.

"Hello, my children!" Samuel said. "How nice it is to see you. Come inside the house when you have tended to your horses. I'm preparing roast hoggal with baby potatoes and fresh corn. Let us break bread and celebrate your safe travel."

Stephen removed the saddle from his horse. "We ran into a lumpa on our way to your home, Your Grace." Samuel's look deflated, and he gave a look filled with questions about details from the encounter.

"No injuries? Thank the Lord," Samuel said.

"No injuries, and we have brought with us the breath box and a claw," Stephen said as he brushed his horse after removing the saddle.

The men fed the horses and entered the house with the prophet. Samuel brought out his famous homemade wine and they sat around the large table in the front room.

"Tell me everything about the lumpa," Samuel said. "I have not seen one for years, but I rarely leave my home these days."

Stephen took a long drink from his wooden cup. "Liea betrayed us, Your Grace."

Samuel looked dismayed. "Yes, I know, my child. She's staying in Nod, east of the Grasslands. I understand she's with Mordred, a very wicked wizard who has promised to give her a life after the gathering of the enchanted instruments. I'm afraid Liea is a lost soul, Stephen. She spends her time seeking bitter root to grind and smoke. It's a serious drug that causes her to sink deeper and deeper into a nightmare."

"I have heard of the root," Daniel said. "It sends the user into dark dreams filled with hallucinations."

The pain and sadness in Stephen's face was obvious. Even though she'd betrayed him and set them up for death, he found himself feeling sorry for her. Stephen remembered when they first met; it was love at first sight. He would do anything for her, and likewise she loved him like no other.

"I want to see her," Stephen said.

"Are you crazy?" Jake exclaimed before realizing his faux pas.

Stephen looked up at Jake with eyes welling tears and said nothing.

"Stephen, Nod is filled with evil wizards and fallen Angels; they would dismember us before we made it through the gate, and then what? We find Liea so she can help her new friends tear us apart and beat us with our own limbs?" Jake explained a bit more gently.

Stephen said nothing as he looked at Jake.

"He's right, my son. To visit Nod is to invite torture and death, and in that order," Samuel said.

"I understand, Your Grace. I just need to ask her why she did it. I know she loved me, I know it." Stephen's voice was breaking as he talked.

His hurt and sadness were painful for Jake to watch. He wanted Stephen to find closure on the matter.

"I'll go with you," Jake said.

Stephen looked up at his friend. "I can't let you do that; you're too important to the mission. I'll go alone."

"We'll all go," Daniel said. "I always wanted to see what was behind the walls of Nod."

"It's a mistake, my children," the old man said. "Nod is as evil as Sion is holy. To even get near it is to invite sin into your heart."

"Bless us, Samuel. Bless each of us so we don't fall into temptation," Jake said. "Pray that God will deliver us from the evil temptation of Nod."

"If I cannot persuade you to stay away from the place, then you may as well make the trip useful. When you enter the palace, you will see their talisman holders for the twelve instruments. As you know, we have three of the twelve, and we know where the Sword of Goliath is. Look into the placeholders and determine if the enemy has captured any of the instruments."

Jake looked at Samuel with a questioning expression. "And if we see instruments?"

"Do nothing!" Samuel exclaimed. "We are not prepared to begin a war on their ground, in their house. Simply observe and report. When the time is right, we'll strike. Now, come, my children. Kneel here before God and clear your minds. I'll say a prayer that God helps you resist the temptation of Nod."

When the men were blessed by the prophet, they returned to their seats at the table.

"Zoltar has likely been to the land of Icarus and is no longer immortal, and his Grigori are likely aging rapidly. However, this is not the last we'll see of Zoltar; he's still a very dangerous monster," Samuel said. "I have something for you; it will assist in your visit to Nod, and perhaps it will help when you face the woman of En-Dor. It has not been used in many years and has been with me."

"What is it, Your Grace?" Jake asked.

Samuel made his way to a trunk in the corner of the front room and brought out a coat; it looked very old and worn and had many faded colors on the sleeves and in the lining.

Jake studied the coat and was amazed when the old man put the coat on; they all were. Samuel was gone! He vanished right before their eyes.

"Well, what do you think?" the voice said, seeming to come from midair.

"Where are you?" Jake called, and reached towards the voice, but felt nothing.

"I'm here, my son," the voice said.

Jake moved quickly, clutching the fabric of the coat. Samuel removed the coat and it appeared in his hands as he blinked into vision.

"That is something. How does it work?" Jake marveled.

"The coat is activated by body heat. It will render the wearer invisible. I traded for it with a wizard, many years ago."

"What did you have to give up for such a magnificent instrument?" Jake asked.

Samuel smiled. "The wizard was seeking directions and food when we met on the path in the woods. I tried to refuse the coat, but he would not hear of it. He insisted I take it for the kindness I showed him."

Jake took the coat from Samuel and was trying it on.

"It worked splendidly for hunting hoggals," Samuel said.

Daniel and Stephen laughed at this. Jake faded to invisible as he buttoned the coat closed around him. What was even more impressive was that the sword Jake was wearing was also invisible.

"How is it possible we're not able to see the swords and other things Jake is wearing?" Daniel asked.

"The coat, once activated, will cover the host and anything the host touches. It is really quite remarkable," Samuel said.

"I should say it is," Stephen agreed, still amazed.

Samuel smiled big. "Watch this," he said with mounting excitement. "Jake, come and take the hands of your brothers."

For a moment, nothing, then Stephen and Daniel blinked once, then twice, then they were out of sight.

"Excellent!" Samuel said, now laughing with excitement.

Jake released his friends and removed the coat. Instantly they blinked back into view.

"Samuel," Jake said. "May I ask you something?"

"Yes, my son, anything. Anything at all."

"Each time we come here you send us away with something remarkable. You gave me the bag that can carry items from the other side, a map that caused the enemy to believe it was the map to the sword, then a key to the map, then the water from the birdbath, the book of the Crossing, and now this incredible coat."

Jake held Samuel's eyes with his own. "Why did you not simply give the items all at once? Why the piece by piece?"

"That's easy. I wanted you to keep coming back. I like your company." And that was it, Samuel poured the wine.

As the men dined, Daniel was first to break the silence. "So what can we expect in Nod?"

Samuel poured more wine. "It has been ages since I have visited the city; however, you can expect to see evil at its worst."

Jake and Stephen were watching the old man as he searched his mind for the words.

"The only positive thing about the city is they have no young ones. That is, they have no children; only individuals who made a conscious decision to reject righteousness have been exiled to Nod."

Stephen's head dropped and he looked at the floor.

"Liea will be with Mordred in the palace near the Fright River. I believe your best efforts can put you in the palace if you travel by way of the riverbed. Only the wall posts will be able to spot you and if we have a fog, you should be safe," Samuel explained. "Getting back may be another matter altogether. The coat is your best defense."

The men finished up and planned to move out after a few hours of sleep.

SEVEN

It was Daniel who woke up Jake. Stephen was already saddling the horses and rigging them for silent movement, a craft practiced when moving in enemy territory. Jake quickly dressed and followed Daniel down the corridor. It was extremely dark, and the coolness in the air reminded Jake of early morning chow release at San Quentin.

The light in the barn lit a path in the dark, moist fog.

"We must get to the river before daybreak," Stephen said.

The men set off into the darkness east toward Nod and heard strange noises in the black, wooded areas.

"Keep to the path," Stephen said, "and mind your horse. The animal will quicken to the danger first and tell you what to expect."

Well that's comforting, Jake thought as he bent forward and patted Pylon's neck. He was a great horse. Jake found that Pylon seemed to know what he was thinking before he could give the command.

"Steady, old boy. Nothing to fear but fear itself," Jake whispered in the ears of Pylon. The horse turned his ears to Jake and welcomed any comforting words he may have. The path was well traveled, and it was relatively easy to tell when a horse's hoof strayed off into the soft soil covered with dried leaves making a distinct, crunching sound.

The men kept the talk to a whisper or used telepathic communication as they moved through the darkness. The sound of the river told them they were close.

"Better dismount here," Stephen said. "We can use the river to enter the city; the water flows under the wall."

The men tethered the horses safely and tried to walk quietly but the dried leaves and twigs were loud under their feet. If it were not for the sound of the river, they would surely have been discovered. As they approached the wall of the city near the river, Jake took the coat from his pack and put it on; the river was low enough that the men were able to walk under the wall on dry land. Once inside the city, the men held hands to ensure they were not seen.

The city appeared to be one big party; the streets were lined with booths and large signs inviting all sorts of sexual taboos. The women walking around in the plaza of the palace were nude and gorgeous. Jake caught himself looking, and then remembered what Samuel had told him about temptation and pushed the impure thoughts from his mind.

"How will we find her?" Daniel asked telepathically.

"Samuel said she would be with Mordred in the palace. Let's take a look," Jake replied.

The men entered the parlor of the palace and moved to the stairwell. The building was magnificent, all marble and cherry wood. The statues included winged men with spears, and others on horseback holding swords. The ceiling was at least sixty feet high, and about halfway up were giant shelves with large, gold markings. Each shelf included a glass case with a picture of an object inside. There were twelve shelves, one for each of the twelve enchanted instruments, and all were empty.

Up the stairs and down the first corridor, Stephen carefully opened each door and looked inside.

The third door Stephen encountered was locked. He went into his bag and came out with a paperclip; he judged the object by how it felt, as sight was not an option, still being invisible.

"I'm going to pick the lock, be on your guard," Stephen said. Within minutes Stephen was pushing the door quietly open. Inside was a bedchamber, and on the bed, asleep, was Liea.

"I'm going in alone; you two stay here and let me know if someone comes."

"Be careful, brother," Jake added, and then let go of Stephen's hand.

EIGHT

As Liea opened her eyes, she saw Stephen fade into view.

"Impossible! You can't be here. Impossible!" Liea said, eyes wide in surprise.

"I'm here, Liea. I had to see you. I had to talk to you."

Liea looked at the floor in shame. She could not face him, not after what she had done to him; the lies, the betrayal, and for what? Only to be betrayed herself.

"Why did you do it, Liea?" Stephen asked.

"I wish I knew," she said. "I truly wish I knew what I was thinking when I let that monster close to me."

Liea fell back to the bed in a sitting position, hands covering her face as she welled up tears for effect.

"He said I was going to live forever, never get old, never lose my youth . . . like you. I watched you celebrate a birthday every year for ten years, but you look as young as the day I met you. I wanted that. Can't you understand I wanted to be pretty?"

Stephen reached down and pulled Liea up to her feet. "You were always pretty, Liea. You didn't look a day over nineteen up until the moment you betrayed me."

Liea looked into Stephen's eyes and knew he was telling the truth. She could see the pain behind them and for the first time realized she had broken his heart.

"I'm sorry," Liea said.

"Me too," Stephen replied.

"Take me with you, Stephen. Get me out of this awful place, I'm begging you. It is worse than death. Take me with you."

"I'm sorry, Liea, I can't do that. You're not able to leave this place. You have surpassed repentance and seen this place. You have no faith and with no faith, you cannot be saved. Good-bye, Liea."

As Stephen turned to exit the room Liea began screaming, "Intruders! Help! Intruders! Come quickly!"

"Are you there, Jake?"

"Right next to you. Give me your hand."

A great look of surprise washed over the face of Liea as she watched Stephen vanish in mid-stride.

"What is it?" the thug answering her call asked.

Liea turned back towards the bedroom and collapsed on the bed, realizing she was damned, and nothing could be done about it.

Chapter XXVI

Unmasking Evil

ONE

Sam and Ruth were speeding north on the 101 with red and blue emergency lights flashing. Cars were pulling aside and letting them through. The forty miles was completed in less than twenty minutes. Sam noticed a strange SUV next to the house, as well as Sherri's car in the driveway. Sam ran to the door with his gun drawn.

While standing to the side of the door he pounded and called aloud, "Ms. Alexander, are you in there?" He pounded again. "It's Sam Jericho with the Marin County Sherriff's Office. Open the door please!"

Suddenly the door exploded with two six-inch holes at about chest height. Sam ducked and then peered through the hole. He could see Sherri tied to a chair facing the door and behind her was a dark figure with a double-barreled shotgun. Sam could see smoke coming from both barrels.

The voice that spoke next was that of Arnold Beans, a wicked little man who served Zoltar. With him was his partner, Gerald Rodgers. Both were investigators in the Sonoma County District Attorney's Office.

"We want Jake Stanton," Arnold said. "If you want to see this one alive, you will oblige us. Where is Jake Stanton?"

Sam was flabbergasted at the idiocy he was dealing with.

"What makes you think I have a clue where Stanton is? I would love to find the man! He escaped from San Quentin and we have about a hundred men looking for him, although I expect there are a lot more like yourself looking as well. So what do you say we put down the guns, have a beer, and talk about where the son of a bitch is, eh?"

Two more thundering reports from the shotgun and splinters from the door flew and landed in Sam's hair and on his shoulders. Sherri screamed in horror. Sam was heating up with fury and yelled at Arnold, "What the hell are you shooting at me for?"

About that time, from around the side of the house, Gerald popped up and started firing his nine-millimeter automatic at Sam. His shots were wild, and Sam took a moment to put the man's head in his sights and with one shot, ended Gerald. A small hole appeared on the forehead of the balding man and he pitched forward and landed in a kneeling position, his head bowed as if in prayer with his arms at his sides. And there he stayed, neither breathing nor falling from his knees, dead.

"Let her go," Sam said. "Let her go and you will live to stand trial. Harm her or refuse me and I'll kill you."

"You're not giving me orders. I'm only going to say this once; get in your car and leave or I'll kill this woman!"

Sam heard something in Arnold's voice, something that told him he was talking to a man with nothing to lose. Arnold, like many others in law enforcement, would rather die than go to prison.

"Okay, you win, I'll go. But you leave the woman."

"You don't give orders!" Arnold yelled. "I'd better hear that car start up and drive away or I'll kill her. You have two minutes, now go!"

Sam went to the car and told Ruth to drive away. Arnold had no clue she was there; he would expect Sam to be alone. She slid to the driver's side and Sam opened and slammed the car door, then she started the motor and the car rolled out of the driveway.

Sam creeped around the SUV and positioned himself to receive anyone coming from the house. He could hear Sherri crying and Arnold shouting orders. As Sherri came out the door, Arnold was pushing her. She fell down the steps and laid on the ground. Arnold was frozen at the sight of his partner still in the kneeling position, only now he had a red shirt from the blood that spouted from the small hole in his forehead.

Without warning, Sam fired a shot from his .45 with his special hollow point bullets, removing Arnold's gun arm still clutching the shotgun. Arnold rocked sideways, then returned to the position he was in, looking at his arm on the ground holding the gun. The fingers on the arm were shaking, and Arnold could see his academy ring reflecting the sun in his eyes as he stared at it in shock. Next he looked at the stub hanging from his shoulder and let out a scream like a five-year-old who had just stepped on a rusty nail.

The birds in the nearby apple tree joined him in his cry as they took flight at his scream. Blood was pulsing from the wound. He tried in vain to use his other hand to plug the hole; the result was like putting a thumb to a garden hose and spraying in a wild direction.

Sam was quick to remove his belt and walk to Arnold. By now Sherri had moved to a safe distance and watched from under the eave of her garage. Sam wrapped the arm with his belt and pulled it tight. Arnold was still crying like a child.

"You shot my arm off!" Arnold cried.

"Yes, well, my loads will do that," Sam replied in an indifferent tone.

"You shot my arm off," he repeated.

"You said that already and I agreed. Now tell me, what are you doing up here bothering Ms. Alexander?"

"We were sent to get her so we could trade her for Jake Stanton. Ms. Moore wants him bad. She's not going to like that you killed Gerald and shot my arm off."

"No, and I expect you didn't much like it yourself."

"I didn't."

Sam's cell phone started playing ZZ Top's "Gimme me all your lovin', all your hugs and kisses too!"

"Inspector Jericho."

"Sam, it's me, are you OK?"

"I'm fine, come on back."

Sherri was moving towards the door back into the house.

"Are you OK?" Sam asked.

"I will be," she answered.

Sam dialed 9-1-1 for an ambulance.

TWO

When the ambulance arrived, Arnold had passed out from the loss of blood. Sam and Ruth were in the kitchen talking to Sherri. The paramedics loaded Arnold onto the litter and were about to leave. Sam stopped them to retrieve a plastic trash bag with ice and one right arm from the freezer.

"Not sure if you can put this back on but I kept it fresh just the same."

The paramedic took a look in the trash bag and grimaced. *It is turning out to be an eventful day,* Sam thought.

"What did the men want with you?" Sam asked.

Sherri was sitting on one of her bar stools sipping a cup of coffee and trying to gain her composure. "They wanted Jake. I told them I had no idea where he was but they would not believe me."

"Did they say why they wanted Jake?"

"Yes, something about a sword. They thought he knew where an old sword was hidden."

Sam scratched his chin and thought for a long moment. "Do you have somewhere you can go, someone you can stay with until this all blows over?" he asked. "I know you will not have trouble from Arnold and Gerald, but they may have comrades, and I want to know you're safe."

"I suppose I can go to Seattle and see my cousin. How long do you think it will be?"

"I can call you when it's safe to come home, but you're not safe here now."

Sherri agreed to leave town in hopes of avoiding further contact with men seeking Jake.

THREE

Ruth and Sam took the scenic route back towards San Francisco on the coastline highway. The fog had lifted and the sun had brightened to a beautiful day.

Sam called the office to see if Murphy had any new leads.

"Murphy," the voice on the other end of the line answered.

"It's Sam. I'm on my way back to the office. Let's get everyone in a room, I want to discuss where we are and what direction we need to go next."

"Will do, Sam," Murphy said.

It was about two o'clock when Sam and Ruth entered the conference room. Murphy and the rest of the task force were already seated. Sam went to the front of the room and addressed the team of about forty individuals.

"For the new folks on the team, my name is Sam Jericho, and this is Dr. Ruth Springer. I wanted to get everyone in a room so we had a chance to compare notes and determine the best direction to take this investigation. First and foremost, what we know . . ."

Sam started writing on the whiteboard with the red dry erase marker.

"Jacob Stanton and Stephen Stross were both serving a life sentence at San Quentin and successfully escaped last week without a trace. I have since had an opportunity to look into the crime of Jacob Stanton and found discrepancies and possible corruption in the Sonoma County District Attorney's Office, and even within the Marin County Sheriff's Office. It's not yet determined how deep the corruption lies, and that is why you see a multitude of law enforcement agencies represented on this task force. We're made up of agents from the FBI, US Marshals Service, the Office of Homeland Security, Marin County Sheriff's Office, Office of the Attorney General, Internal Affairs, CDCR, and even Dr. Springer, who is on loan from Stanford University. This task force is assembled with three major objectives."

Sam wrote on the board: 1. Investigate the corruption within the agencies, 2. Locate the escaped inmates from San Quentin, and 3. Investigate the murder of the Marin County Medical Examiner and determine what happened to the bodies from the city morgue.

Sam continued, "FBI Special Agent in Charge Jack Murphy has run a preliminary investigation on some of the players, and determined a circuit judge and several jurors were involved in a conspiracy to set up Jacob Stanton. In addition, my own Sergeant John Morales was arrested for participating in the attempt on my life and obstructing justice."

Sam turned and faced the team. "Trust is not something we're giving for free at this point, it must be earned. Each and every one of you have undergone an extensive polygraph test to be a part of this team. We're going to be very close from now on. Some of you may be approached by the ones we'll be investigating and actively recruited to swap sides. That's why we'll be giving you additional polygraph tests to ensure this team remains pure. Make no mistake about it, the corruption thus far has reached the highest levels in our justice system and we expect to obtain indictments for some elected officials before we're done. Your background will be exposed, so if you have a skeleton, best to come clean now."

Sam walked back and forth in the front of the conference room, stopping on occasion to look into the faces of the team members as he made his points.

"I expect this investigation to get pretty messy before it's done. What we have thus far is a theory. We believe Jacob Stanton was framed for his wife's murder and sent to San Quentin by the Sonoma County DA's Office, and also an organized crime boss by the name of Jessie Borackus and other members of a religious sect who worship or follow a leader called Zoltar. Now I know that sounds a little strange, but we have reason to believe this is a fairly solid theory. We think the followers of this Zoltar are trying to get at Jacob Stanton, believing he has some special knowledge of where their religious artifacts may be located.

"According to our investigation, this Borackus was sent to San Quentin by the Sonoma County DA and was in communication with the DA while in prison. We have cell phone records indicating he was calling DA Anita Moore while housed in the institution's reception center. Borackus was killed in a hostage situation in the prison, and later was one of the missing bodies from the Marin County Morgue. At a separate location, a motel in San Francisco, his body was recovered under strange circumstances.

"We have very little on Stanton's accomplice, Stephen Stross. He wasn't even on the map until he was arrested for bank robbery earlier this year. We have no record of his birth or any other hints he ever existed prior to his conviction for the bank robbery."

Sam took a moment and drank from his water bottle, then went back into his narrative. "According to the trial notes, it appears the attorneys worked out a plea bargain with the three strikes law, almost purposely inserting him into Jacob Stanton's cell at San Quentin. It's all very strange from start to finish; however, the two seem to have successfully broken out of San Quentin using information that only someone who knew the building plans of the prison would know. The building plans from San Quentin burned in a courthouse fire in 1860." Sam took another drink from the water bottle.

"Even the county records of the retrofit project of the prison from 1971, following the 1969 earthquake, make no mention of the tunnel system used in the nearly flawless escape. I say *nearly* flawless based only on the satellite images captured by Homeland Security. Were it not for that, the escape would have proven perfect, right down to the clothing found in the bay indicating a possible shark attack. The images we have seen indicate the men made it to a hotel in Chinatown. The rest is inconclusive."

Sam finished his water. "I expect we'll execute warrants very soon on Ms. Moore and the judge. Until we do, I don't want to hear about this on the five o'clock news because someone in this room leaked information. I trust we keep what is said in this room among the people on this team. Any questions?"

A short, blond lady with an FBI coat asked the first question. "Excuse me, Inspector, but can you elaborate on the nature of Ms. Springer's expertise and how it will benefit the team?"

Sam was suddenly caught off guard. Had he somehow exposed their relationship with a look or a gesture? How inappropriate and downright hellish to become romantically involved with a team member and then be exposed!

"Ah, yes, Dr. Springer is an expert on the occult and the type of supernatural occurrences this case has. I'll let her speak, as some of the evidence we found is right up her alley."

Sam looked at Ruth with red cheeks. "Doctor."

Ruth stood and walked to the front of the room.

"Thank you, Inspector Jericho." Ruth pulled on some wire-rimmed glasses but they took nothing from her beauty. She was a stone fox. Most of the men in the room were drooling at the sight of her, a natural beauty with a rock-hard body and dark hair. *But that caboose*, Sam thought. Never had he seen such a nice ass.

"I was telling Inspector Jericho that we at Stanford have seen this type of ritual killing or wounds only in books related to the twelve enchanted instruments, one being the Dagger of Moriah."

Ruth held up an eight-by-ten photo of a dagger with a gold handle and jewels inlaid in it. "This is an example of the weapon we believe caused the wounds on at least two of the bodies from the Marin County Morgue."

Ruth passed the photo to the people in the first row.

"The dagger is believed to be the one Angel Gabriel took from Abraham on Mount Moriah when he raised it to slay his son, Isaac."

A low rumble among the listeners caused Ruth to clear her throat before continuing. "This dagger, along with eleven other enchanted instruments, are the objective of a subculture called the Shaddai, believed to be from the bloodline of Angels who bred with humans thousands of years ago."

Again the low rumble, along with some giggles from what sounded like the ladies in the back row.

Ruth pushed her shoulders back and continued. "We have reason to believe the angelic beings have superhuman powers, and some are believed to be immortal."

Now hands began shooting up all over the room. Ruth pointed to a tall FBI agent standing against the wall.

"My name is Bret McDonald. I have worked for the FBI for twenty-three years. Are you saying we're dealing with monsters or aliens of some kind?"

Ruth took a breath. "Look, I don't expect to convince you or anyone in this room of the supernatural. I don't believe this to be the time or place for such a discussion. I have a published report on the Shaddai and the twelve enchanted instruments; you're welcome to read the report. Once you have done so, I'll be happy to answer any questions you have on the fundamental possibility of other intelligent life forms sharing the planet with us. I'm simply here to help your investigation if I can."

As she spoke, the hands went down one by one until only the short, blond lady with the FBI coat was left with a raised hand.

"Yes?" Ruth pointed at her.

"My name is Angela Callahan. I want to thank you for your assistance and ask where I can read the report on the Shaddai you mentioned."

Ruth smiled. Others were taking out their pens and pads as she spoke. "You can go to the Stanford Research Center website at www.Stanford@SRC.ca.gov and type in Dr. Ruth Springer, and you will see a page of published reports explaining everything we know about the Shaddai and Angel studies."

Ruth felt relieved when nearly every member of the team noted the website on their pads.

Sam walked back to the front of the room.

"Thank you, Doctor Springer."

Ruth smiled and took her seat. Next Sam motioned for Agent Murphy to come forward.

"Most of you know Jack Murphy. He is going to divide the task force into strike teams with specific assignments for this investigation. Some of you will be working on the prison escape, others will be assigned to the murder investigation team, and the rest will be working on the corruption ring we believe has infected all of our agencies. We'll be meeting three times a week to brief and organize arrest warrants. Any questions?"

Seeing no raised hands he said, "I'll leave you in the very capable hands of Agent Murphy."

Sam walked out the side door, followed by Ruth.

They walked saying nothing until they were in Sam's car. Sam opened and closed the car door for Ruth and then slid into the driver's seat.

"Oh my God," Ruth said, looking at Sam.

"I know," he said. "I almost died when that woman asked me what your contribution to the team would be."

Ruth smiled and punched Sam in his shoulder.

"Ouch!" He smiled.

"Take me to my car," she said.

"I don't want you to leave," Sam said.

"I'm going home and taking a shower and changing my clothes, but you can come if you want," she said with a come-hither look.

"I'm right behind you," Sam said.

FOUR

Sam followed Ruth to her home in the Marin foothills. It was only about a ten-minute drive from his houseboat. He was impressed as soon as he hit her steep driveway and noticed the white Victorian house with the large porch and bench swing. The garage door went up and she pulled inside and closed the door.

As Sam parked, she exited from the side door and met him on the porch. She embraced him and they kissed for a long moment.

Ruth removed her keys from her purse and opened the door. Sam was pleased to see the house in impeccable order. As he walked on the cherry wood floor entry, he stopped to remove his shoes.

"We don't take off our shoes in this house," she said.

Sam smiled and followed her to the front room. He was inspecting the pictures and paintings on the walls of the entry and hall. As in her office, she had artwork related to her Angel studies.

"The tomb of Zoltar," Sam said as he pointed to a large painting on the wall.

"Very good," she praised.

Sam noticed the beautiful antique furniture.

"This place looks like it belongs in a magazine like *Better Homes and Gardens*."

Ruth smiled. "It was featured in the October edition of the *Marin House Digest*."

"Wow!" Sam exclaimed. "How about the nickel tour?"

She took his hand and led him through the large parlor and arched doorway.

"My home office."

Sam was impressed with the dark wood desk and bookshelves on all four walls from floor to ceiling, all neatly lined with hardcover books. The office had a leather couch and loveseat with a matching coffee table. The window was in the middle of the bookshelves and included wooden blinds so the room could be rendered dark in the daylight hours. The room was lit with a chandelier and desk lamps. The light switch also controlled two wooden ceiling fans from the high ceiling. Behind the desk in the bookcase was a hidden doorway leading into the master bedroom.

They went through the passage and Sam was amazed at the large master suite with a bed so high one needed to use the stepladder to climb on. The room included a large walk-in closet and an incredible bathroom with a claw-footed free-standing tub.

"This is the guest room," she said.

"The guest room?" Sam said. "I thought this was your bedroom."

Ruth smiled again. "Nope, I sleep upstairs. Come this way."

Ruth took his hand and they exited the bedroom through the traditional doorway, leading into a hall with several doors that opened into additional guest rooms and the office. They were all very nice, and all with private bathrooms. The hall was long, and the art on the walls was magnificent.

"This way to the kitchen," she said as they entered the kitchen through the hallway and white batwing doors.

Sam noticed a large industrial stainless steel eight-burner gas stove with three ovens under and two ovens over. In the center was a Jenn-Air indoor barbecue, with a hood containing hooks where copper-bottom steel pots and pans hung. To the right was a six-stool eating bar with glass-faced cabinets above and below. To the left was a large dining table that would easily seat eight. The kitchen was surrounded with beautiful granite countertops and two large stainless steel refrigerators. Next to the refrigerators was a door leading into a sub-zero walk-in cool storage room and attached pantry. At the end of the granite countertop was a large butcher-block table with a shelf filled with knives, each in a special slot and all with matching pearl handles. The other side of the kitchen also had the white batwing doors and behind the large dining table was a glass slider leading to a large covered porch with another table for outside dining. Through the batwing doors was the second dining room with a large table that would easily seat nine chairs on each side of the cherry wood table and one at each end. The table was the centerpiece of the dining room, and matching china hutches were on either side against the walls. As they passed by the table and walked under the arched doorway like the one leading to her office, they were in what she called the media room. It was every bit the size of the room she called the parlor and contained large, comfortable couches with matching recliners in front of the seventy-two-inch flat screen television with hidden surround sound in the walls and ceiling, as well as the furniture.

The next room was the living room, followed by the family room. The cherry wood floors were in every room except the living room with the plush, white carpet. The family room was attached to the parlor, and Sam found they had arrived to the place where they'd started. This time they went to the right of the parlor to the staircase that circled upward to the second floor. The second floor had another four bedrooms, all with their own private bathrooms and all with queen-size beds. Each room had a name, as did the four downstairs. The name was on each of the solid wood doors. Downstairs were colors, like The Red Room and The Green Room, and on the second floor the names were of trees, like The Cottonwood Room and the Bull Pine Room. Each of the rooms had a theme matching the name on the door; the artwork in each of the second-floor rooms was of the trees they were named for. The staircase to the third floor was next to an elevator door. They took the elevator that led to the third floor, and also to the first floor, only the first floor door was hidden behind a large mirror and looked virtually undetectable until the doors opened.

The third floor was her master suite; the nine-bedroom Victorian mansion was almost like a small hotel, and the master suite was incredible. The suite included a large sauna, hot tub, sitting room, and small library. The bathroom was all river rock and old stone, with multiple shower heads and a waterfall that emptied into an indoor heated pond with water jets to make it almost like a small swimming pool. The plant life in the room made it look like a tropical rain forest. Sam felt completely relaxed in the room and took her again in his arms and kissed her for a long moment. Ruth tugged at his clothes and they were disrobed in no time. Ruth took his hand and led Sam into the heated indoor pool and they swam together and made love in the water. From the pool they stepped into the shower and made love again. By the time they made it to the king-size bed they were exhausted. They lay in each other's arms until sleep took them.

FIVE

ZZ Top blasted "Gimme all your lovin', all your hugs and kisses too! Gimme all your lovin', don't let up until you do!" indicating Sam was getting a call. His pants were in the bathroom so he slipped off the bed while Ruth was still asleep to answer the phone.

"Inspector Jericho," Sam said. The connection was bad and Sam could hardly understand what was being said, but he didn't hang up. He kept trying to listen and could hear what sounded like an ocean and a voice together. He thought he heard Jake Stanton before the phone went dead.

Sam put the phone on the nightstand and slipped back into the bed next to his beloved. He lay awake for a long time, staring in the darkness, thinking about the case.

Why was Stanton so special? Why was his wife Teresa murdered? Why did District Attorney Moore want Stanton so badly? Sam decided the next move would be to get some of the answers to these questions, starting with Ms. Moore. With this in mind, the darkness took him and he slept.

Sam was still sleeping when Ruth came out of the shower with her hair in a towel and wearing nothing but a smile. Sam returned the smile.

"Why are you up so early?" he asked.

"Early? It's almost nine o'clock," she replied, and jumped onto the bed. She moved to kiss him and he rolled off the bed away from her and went to the bathroom.

"There is a new toothbrush in the second drawer," she said. Sam pulled the second drawer open and noticed a basket with about a dozen new toothbrushes still in the box.

"So, am I but one of your many boyfriends who may need a toothbrush?"

"Don't be an idiot!" she said. "I bought the Costco box for myself and it held twenty in the box. I like to change my toothbrush about once a month. Don't you?"

Sam thought about it; he must have had his toothbrush for at least a year. "Ahhh, yes, I was only kidding, I do the same thing." He made a mental note to buy some toothbrushes for his own second drawer.

"Do you want me to toss your clothes in the washing machine?"

"Can't wait, gotta run," Sam said. "I'll stop at the boat and change, but I'm going to meet with Jack and get the warrant for Ms. Moore today."

Ruth walked into the bathroom as Sam was rinsing his mouth in the sink.

"When will I see you again?" she asked as she walked up from behind him and took him by his business below.

Sam turned and they kissed. She was still only wearing a towel on her head. Sam came alive again and turned her around and they made love. It was incredible once again as they reached climax together, her towel now tossed to the floor, her long hair spilling over her face as they finished.

"I have to go, I'll call you this afternoon. I want to cook dinner for you tonight," he said.

"And he cooks, too?" she said from under her damp, dark hair. She went up on her toes and kissed the corner of his mouth and then they dressed.

SIX

Sam met Jack Murphy at the station. He had District Attorney Moore in the interrogation room with her lawyer.

"I don't suppose she's going to confess with Shapiro sitting in there," Sam said.

"We shall see," Jack replied.

Jack and Sam entered the room where Anita Moore and her lawyer were sitting on hard plastic chairs around a small, round table.

"Good morning, Anita," Sam said, and took a seat across from them.

Jack took the last vacant chair.

"Good morning, Sam," she said.

"So, what can you tell me about the Stanton case?" Sam started with a smile. She regarded him with a sour look.

"You know how this works, Sam. I have a lot I can give you; however, I want a deal."

"What kind of deal did you have in mind?" Sam asked.

The skinny lawyer went into his briefcase and pulled out a brief about six pages deep. It was a document indicating District Attorney Moore would resign her position and serve no more than three years in prison for the false prosecution of Jake Stanton. In exchange, she would cooperate with the investigation into the attempted murder of Inspector Jericho and the ongoing attempted murder of Jake Stanton and Stephen Stross by unnamed individuals as yet, however, not limited to state officials and politicians.

"This looks awfully legal and official," Sam said. "Give me a moment." Sam took the document into the task force executive office and called Sally Unger, the chief of staff for Governor Davis.

"I'm scanning in the document now, Sally. Take a look and let me know what, if any, authority I have to cut a deal." Sam pushed send on the computer while still on the phone.

"I'm reading it now, Sam," Sally said. "I talked to the governor and the state's attorney last night and was given some guidelines. We were even thinking of offering Ms. Moore immunity for cooperation, and this looks like it meets the criteria we would want."

Sam could hear some conversation in the background as he waited.

"Looks good, Sam," Sally said. "Go ahead and make the deal. This says we can prosecute her fully if we don't find what she has to offer satisfactory, and I can see no downside."

"Thanks, Sally, I'll keep you posted."

Sam hung up the phone and went back into the interrogation room, followed by Jack.

"I have authority to sign this so let's see what you have." Sam signed the document and handed it to the skinny lawyer.

"Okay," Anita said.

"Wait!" Jack said. "Let me get the tape started." He pushed the record buttons on the machine. "The date is Thursday, December 7, 2006, and the time is about 0930 in the morning. My name is Special Agent in Charge Jack Murphy, assigned to the Santa Rosa office of the FBI, and I'm with Inspector Sam Jericho of the Marin County Sheriff's Office. Inspector Jericho is leading the investigation of the conviction of Mr. Jacob Stanton and subsequent escape from San Quentin State Prison. In addition, Inspector Jericho is investigating the murder of several prison staff and the Marin County medical examiner. The investigation has uncovered the possible corruption of elected officials, law enforcement officers in the Marin County Sheriff's Office, Sonoma County District Attorney's Office, as well as the FBI and other agencies. This is the interview of Ms. Anita Moore, Sonoma County District Attorney, who is represented by counsel, and who has agreed to cooperate fully with the investigation. Ms. Moore, you understand you have the right to remain silent, and anything you say can and will be used against you in a court of law?"

"Yes, I do," she said.

"You have exercised your right to have your attorney present during this interview?"

"Yes," she said. Sam looked at the skinny man with beads of sweat pooling across the brim of his nose.

"And your name, sir?"

"My name is Nathan Jones, and I'm counsel for Ms. Moore in this matter."

Sam turned his gaze back to the woman who was turning whiter than snow by the second.

"Ms. Moore, what can you tell me about the prosecution of Mr. Stanton?"

Anita moved closer to the microphone and looked down. "I was acting on behalf of Tomas Ratliff and Francisco Escobar."

Sam gasped. "I'm sorry, did you say Senator Tomas Ratliff, the president of the State Senate, and Speaker Escobar, the Speaker of the State Legislature?"

"Yes," Anita said. "About three years ago, Senator Ratliff invited me to dinner at the Seafood Peddler in San Rafael and I met him and Speaker Escobar, along with another man. The man was dressed in black and looked pale as wax. They called him Zoltar, and treated him as if he were royalty."

Anita flipped her long hair behind her shoulder in a nervous manner. "The man in black said very little during the meal; most of the talking was done by Senator Ratliff. I was given a briefcase filled with money." She looked down at the floor. "It was more than six million in cash." She looked up again and held Sam's stare with her own. "It was the most cash I had ever seen in my life."

Sam was drinking it all in.

"Senator Ratliff said the money was mine. I needed only to arrest and prosecute Stanton for the murder of his wife." She broke off her gaze and looked back at the floor. "I noticed two other men in the restaurant. They were the same two men who had been following me for the past week. He was the real killer of Mrs. Stanton, I even had his fingerprints. I wanted the money and most of all, the power Ratliff and Escobar were offering. I'm ashamed of my role in the crime." Anita Moore looked truly sad.

"Tell me about Sergeant Morales," Sam said.

"I received a call from Ratliff about a week ago. He said you were getting close to cracking the case. He told me to offer Morales an inspector position and five hundred thousand to stop you. I never said kill you, only stop you. He could have simply burned your evidence or sabotaged the investigation." She began to cry.

"A woman died that day, the receptionist. Her name was Arlene."

"I know, I'm so ashamed and sorry."

"And what about Sherri Alexander and the goons who tried to kill her?" Sam hammered.

"They were sent by Ratliff to try to locate Stanton. The whole thing is about Stanton and an old sword that he supposedly knows the location of."

"Did you hear Ratliff or Escobar talk about killing anyone?"

"Yes, I did better than that, I have a tape of the whole thing." Anita took a small tape recorder from her purse and handed it to Sam.

Jack took the recorder and turned it on. "I want you to have that sergeant who works for Jericho to call me. He's blown, but I want him to kill Jericho." Sam stopped the tape; it was Senator Ratliff all right.

"Tell me about Albert Stoll and the killing that took place in Santa Rosa."

"That was Gary Carter. He's an inspector assigned to my office. He was working directly for Ratliff and Escobar. He met with them more than I did. The only reason I was brought in was to send Stanton to San Quentin. They thought prison would loosen up his lips and he would tell where the sword was, but he never did. After about three years they sent Borackus in to get the information."

Sam gave her a stern look. "Why are you telling us now?"

"Sam, I'm terrified. Carter has been missing. Everyone who knows anything about this case is dropping dead. Now that Borackus is dead, I know they will try to kill me; my life is in danger. Zoltar is horrible. I know he will silence all who know anything about his plan." Anita was weeping.

"Well, get comfortable. You will be waiting till all of this has been transcribed and signed before we put you in custody." Sam and Jack walked out of the room and back to the office.

"I can't believe Senator Ratliff and Speaker Escobar are behind this. This just got a whole lot more complicated. We need to call Sally," Sam said.

SEVEN

Sam was putting the final touches on the chicken meal he'd prepared. It was not the traditional boil-broil BBQ chicken dish. He actually cooked four chicken breasts on low in the oven, removed two of the breasts and chopped them into very small pieces, mixed it with the special stuffing mix and spices he'd created, and stuffed it back into the other two breasts after slicing them in half. Then Sam returned the dish to the oven with a splash of lemon and some crushed pepper. Also he prepared twice-baked potatoes and fresh asparagus in garlic olive oil. He opened a chilled bottle of Kendall-Jackson wine and he was ready to serve.

Sam heard the car door shut. Rusher was at the door to greet his lady friend. The bell rang as he was lighting the candles on the dining table.

"Rusher, down," Sam ordered. Rusher walked to his bed and laid down with his head on his paws.

"Hello, beautiful," Sam said. Ruth smiled and handed him some flowers.

"Yum, what smells so good?" she asked.

"Well, it's my attempt at stuffed chicken breasts," he said, taking her coat and placing it on the hook in the mud room. Rusher looked up from his paws and regarded her with a tilted head.

"Ahhh, how cute. Hello, Rusher."

Rusher looked at Sam and he nodded his head. Rusher walked to Ruth and let her pet his head and scratch his neck. He even leaned into her touch and made a growling sound of pleasure as she bent and pulled his thick fur.

"Rusher, down," Sam said in a low voice. Rusher immediately walked back to his bed and resumed his position with his head on his front paws. Ruth had never seen a more obedient dog.

"You can wash in the sink," Sam said as he went to the 1970s stereo and put on a record from his collection. It was Journey. Ruth looked over her shoulder and smiled. Sam returned her smile and they sat at the dining table to enjoy the meal he'd prepared.

Chapter XXVII

Zoltar and the Witch

ONE

Zoltar and his army left Captain Johnson on the *Ichabod* and took to the air. He determined that the back trail of *Delilah's Secret* was leading to En-Dor. Zoltar had heard of this place many times in the past. He knew of the old woman and her dark craft. What he didn't know was where the Sword of Goliath was. He had no idea the witch had kept this secret all these years. Even now he didn't believe the old hag had knowledge of the sword; he believed the old woman would have surely sold any information related to the sword by now if she had it. She was filled with greed; gold and gems were her gods.

As the wicked army of forty fallen Angels, what is commonly known as a legion, flew east over unnamed waters, Zoltar led with his sword drawn. The legion was now mortal and vulnerable to an attack.

As the legion arrived in En-Dor they employed their cloaking device, rendering them with the appearance of the indigenous population, or humanoid. The legion divided into three groups led by a master Angel in each group. Zoltar gave orders to the master Angels to remain at the ready but infiltrate the pubs and bars seeking any intelligence about the sword.

Zoltar and Derrick, his new second in command, decided to visit the old woman to see if she still had the glowing fruit and any knowledge of the sword. The sun was sinking into the western skies, casting long shadows of the tall human-looking monsters in dark robes with waxy white skin as they traveled up the old road towards the witch of En-Dor.

It was nearly dark when they reached the gatehouse of the old woman. Two goons stood at the gatehouse guarding the entrance of the old woman's hut. As Zoltar and Derrick approached the eunuchs, they drew their swords.

"Nay, friend, put away your iron. We're friends of the old mother who lives in yonder hut."

The eunuch held his ground and extended the sword in the direction of Zoltar, who now looked like a waxy, tall white man with dark, shoulder-length hair in a hooded robe.

"She's not taking clients this late in the eve, mate. Come back on the morrow if ye would see the woman of En-Dor," the goon said in a pirate-like voice.

"You don't understand, mate! I am Zoltar, brother to Morning Star, and I demand an audience with the old woman *now!*" The hood fell back to his shoulders, revealing a face filled with fury and dark-yellow eyes, almost like a snake. The eunuch stepped backward and nearly fell down in his confusion.

"Forgive me, master, for I didn't recognize you in the robe." The eunuch went to one knee and set his sword on the ground.

"I shall announce you to the old mother. Please follow me, master." He rose and put his sword away. He led Zoltar over the footbridge and into the hut.

"Please sit, master, I'll summon my lady."

Zoltar and Derrick stood in the dark, dank parlor waiting for the witch. In the room was a table with three chairs. The lighting was from wall candles and two table candles. Baskets filled with sharp root and spices, vegetables, and fruit hung from the ceiling. Zoltar could not see any glowing fruit in the baskets.

"Zoltar, brother of Morning Star, in my home. To what do I owe this great honor?" the old witch cackled as she entered the parlor from behind them where no door was visible.

Zoltar and Derrick spun around, clearly startled.

"Nay, old mother, 'tis I who am honored to be in your presence," Zoltar responded. "This is my captain, Derrick. He bids you long life and many blessings, old mother."

"Enough of the niceties, for they're unbecoming to both our natures. Why have ye come to En-Dor?" the old witch scowled.

"At last, words of comfort, and aye, the niceties are sticking in both of our throats like poison. We are here for two things, Witch; glowing fruit, and the Sword of Goliath!" Zoltar spit back at the hag.

They were looking each other up and down as two wildcats might do when territory was an issue.

"But why do ye seek the glowing fruit, and what would I know of this sword?" the hag said as she moved closer to the wall.

"Don't provoke me, Witch. I would have the fruit and any knowledge of the sword, and I would have them before you speak another word."

"Master, I need some time! I don't have the fruit in the hut and I must inquire about the sword. Is there a reward attached to either?"

Zoltar was not able to remain in his current appearance. His anger weakened him and he came out of the robe, standing nearly ten feet tall, green batwings spread and now speaking from a mouth filled with razor-sharp teeth.

"Curse you, woman!" he screeched, and his clawed hands went to her scrawny neck. But nothing was there; his hands passed through her as if she was simply being projected from a three-dimensional movie projector.

"Blast ye, Witch! Where are you?" Zoltar was moving around in the hut, tossing tables and chairs in anger.

"Take control of your temper, Master Zoltar! I'll get ye what ye wants. Take control and be at peace, master, for I am but an old woman at your service. Come back at first light and ye shall have the fruit. Also, I can provide ye the sword, as I believe it's in the city of En-Dor. Only I'm a poor old woman and the forces who have the sword are asking a chest of gold coin be given over for the sword location. Can I tell them ye will pay the bounty?"

"Aye, say true, Witch. I and my legion will give over the chest, only it will not be at first light. My ship is on the way to En-Dor. The *Ichabod* will be arriving any time now."

"Excellent, excellent," the witch said, and cackled louder than before. "Can I offer ye my hospitality while we wait for your ship?"

"Nay, old mother, we shall return when the ship arrives. Have ready the sword and the fruit that glows."

Two eunuchs walked into the parlor as Zoltar and Derrick were leaving. Zoltar once again appeared as a large, wax-like human with a white face and long, dark hair.

Zoltar joined his legion in the city at the Travelers Nest Hotel. The forty strangely large men were a sight at the bar where they sat drinking whisky and shooting dice. They had no idea *Delilah's Secret* had made port on the south side of the island, and Jake and Stephen were preparing an attack on the witch of En-Dor.

TWO

Very early the next morning, Stephen and Jake deployed the landing party; Daniel was the first off the ship and moving toward the hut of the witch. In his bag were gold coins and gems. Next were team members Windy, Darrel, Tim, and Julia; they were armed with laser targeting devices and weapons.

Captain Cook and Chief of the Boat Duncan took up positions in the ship's weapon control booth where they could monitor the landing party and watch their progress through the mini cams on their heads, as well as their chests. Each camera was assigned to an individual and fed to a monitor with the name of each team member.

Commander Galloway led Brooks and West, with a stack of mirrors, towards the staging area outside the witch's hut. They remained at the ready, awaiting the attack command when they would storm into the hut and place the mirrors. Stephen and Jake, dressed in jeans covered by priest's robes, made their way up the path towards the witch's hut. The fog was lifting from the pond near the moat like steam from a hot plate. The same mist arose from the moat surrounding the hut.

Daniel approached the gatehouse and was met by two large eunuchs. "Morning! Is this the place of the old mother who can tell a fortune in exchange for gold coin and gems?"

The large eunuch in the hooded robe stepped towards Daniel. "Let me see the color of thy metal, stranger, and perhaps we can accommodate ya."

Daniel reached into a large leather purse and brought out two smaller rawhide bags. He tossed them to the eunuch, who inspected the gold coins and then the gems. His eyes grew wide at the sight of the riches. Never had he seen such fine gold and gems.

"I have more if you like. I seek a reading from the old mother of En-Dor."

The eunuch regarded Daniel with a greedy grin. "Aye, we should be able to help ye, stranger." He motioned for Daniel to enter the gatehouse. Daniel walked inside and the door shut behind him.

"Jake, can you hear me?" Daniel asked telepathically.

"We're right behind you, Daniel. As soon as you enter, tell us what you see."

"We must search ye for weapons, friend. Disrobe." This was a bit surprising to Daniel, but he had nothing to hide, so he complied. The eunuch made him open his mouth, lift his arms above his head, and even bend over and pull apart his cheeks. At the end of the search, he handed Daniel a robe and some slippers.

"Your belongings must remain here and will be returned as ye exit," he said.

Daniel walked over the footbridge and entered the hut. It was dark, and smelled of spice and burning onions. *"Jake, I'm in the parlor of the hut. It's very dark. There are no windows, only candlelight. The room is large, perhaps a thousand square feet, two hallways on the northern wall, no other doors."*

THREE

At the Travelers Nest Hotel, about three miles north of the witch's hut, Zoltar was waking and stretching in the large suite on the thirteenth floor. He called for Derrick to join him in the roof garden for breakfast.

"Where is the legion?" Zoltar asked.

"Camped about a mile north, with the exception of the sentries outside your door and the two we sent this morning to watch the old hag's hut. They are walking so as not to break cover and reveal their wings."

"Good," Zoltar said. "And the *Ichabod*?"

"We expect her soon, master."

Zoltar walked to the edge of the roof garden and looked out to sea. "Any news of *Delilah's Secret* or the Shaddai?"

Derrick dropped his head. "Nothing new, master."

"They must be coming here. Where else could their back trail be leading? It must be En-Dor," he said with a confused look on his face. Zoltar appeared to be thinking of other areas the ship could be traveling. "It must be En-Dor!" he said again.

"Agreed, master."

The two walked to the table and sat down to dine on raw meat and snakes still alive in small glass containers. Zoltar removed the glass top and reached his long fingers into the container and pulled out about three snakes, all at least ten inches in length, and pushed them into his mouth. The snakes were biting his hands and even the side of his face as he devoured them. Zoltar seemed pleased the snakes were lively as he ate them.

FOUR

Jake and Stephen were in position, the cover team was in position, and the team with the mirrors was in position.

"Good day, traveler," the hag said as she seemed to appear through the solid wall near the entrance.

"Pardon me, old mother," Daniel said as he turned to her. "You surprised me appearing from no door."

"Ye come for my craft, ye bring cold coin and gems; what would ye have in return? For I shall not tell of my magic, only use it to tell ye's future, traveler."

Daniel determined the vision in front of him was not the woman in the flesh; she seemed to be a vision rather than flesh.

"Jake, I'm still in the parlor. The hag in front of me is not the witch in the flesh; she's close, however."

"Come, traveler, sit down," the witch said as she motioned towards the table and chairs.

"It's customary to bow and kiss your hand before accepting your hospitality." Daniel moved close to the witch and went to a knee, and before she had time to react he had reached for her hand, only to see his hand pass right through hers.

"What is this?" Daniel exclaimed. "Are ye not flesh? Where is the old woman of En-Dor, for I have paid the bounty to see her and not this aberration!"

Daniel was on his feet and moving towards the kitchen, where a large pot was sitting over a fire pit under a rock chimney.

"Alas, stranger, ye must sit and stop moving about my dwelling," the witch said.

Two eunuchs entered and moved toward Daniel. "Have a seat, friend," one of them ordered.

"Ye took my bounty; I would see the old mother and not a ghost of her, or lead me out and return the gold and gems."

"Nay, not so fast. Ye have paid, and so ye shall see me," the witch said, and walked in from the hallway on the right.

"Jake, she's here, and she entered from the hall on the northeastern wall, likely the bedchamber with the chest."

Daniel went to a knee and took a cold hand that looked and felt like that of a dead person. It was clammy and made Daniel's skin crawl; gooseflesh appeared on his arms and the back of his neck.

"Old mother, I have come to inquire of my dead lover, Liea. I need to tell her I miss her and love her. Can you call her up for me?"

The witch considered the request. "Aye, stranger, I can call her up, but ye must tell me ye's name and when she died."

"I'm Stephen, son of Anthony, and she's Liea, daughter of Kaden. She died a week ago today, and could not be located at the Crossing. I have been to all who practice the craft and none could reach her or call her up."

"Ye have come to the right place, my child. I'm Tabatha, the all-knowing mother of En-Dor. Sit and let me wake her for you to see."

Daniel sat at the table. The two eunuchs positioned themselves behind him and the witch sat across from him. The witch passed her hands over the table and a glass ball appeared in the middle of the table between them.

"This is the glass eye of Tabatha. It sees into the hereafter and even the yet to come," she cackled.

The sound of her voice made Daniel wish to run for the door; instead, he reached out to Jake.

"She seems to be going into a trance, I recommend we move quickly!"

"Hit the deck, Daniel!" Jake said.

Daniel went to the floor as a thunder crack sound shook the hut and the ceiling opened up, revealing blinding daylight. The witch screamed as if she were being burned by the sun and the eunuchs rushed to protect her. From his place on the floor, Daniel could see the black robes of the witch and two large goons standing over her, then another thunder cracking sound and the tops of the back of the heads of the goons evaporated into thin air, causing blood to spray and spill. The witch screamed, and Daniel could see a dozen witches appearing all around him, but they were nothing more than reflections of the witch cast by the mirrors carried by the Shaddai attack team.

It was Jake who reached her first; Stephen was right behind him. She was changing from an old woman into a goat in an effort to escape. Jake took hold of the hideous creature with a goat-looking face and human arms and legs. He took the Dagger of Moriah and drove it into her neck, causing blood to spray and her cry to turn even more animal-like and desperate.

The goat head flashed and she was again the hag, now on the floor, dead. Jake and Daniel moved towards the bedchamber. The room was dark, lit only by a single candle.

Daniel pointed his laser at the corner of the ceiling. "Cook, target painted, fire."

The mortar from the ship opened the ceiling of the bedroom and daylight spilled into the room. Jake could clearly see the trunk at the foot of the bed.

Stephen used his sword to break the lock and they pulled open the lid. As daylight spilled into the cellar below, the snakes moved toward the darkness of the corners.

Jake entered the large trunk and moved down the stairs till he reached the floor. He kicked several snakes away and picked up a cloth wrap and brought it up from the cellar. Stephen and Daniel were next to him when Jake unwrapped the shiny Sword of Goliath and laid it on the bed of the witch. The sun reflected the gems in the handle, and smiles appeared on the face of the men.

Jake took Stephen's sword and handed him the Sword of Goliath. "You carry it, my brother. You deserve to hold such a prize after all you have been through."

The smiles were quickly washed away as shadows of giant bat-looking creatures were cast on the floor of the hut.

"To the ship, and Godspeed!" Stephen yelled, sword raised.

It was Daniel leading the retreat back to the ship. Stephen and Jake stayed back and moved to the canvas. Under the canvas were their bows and slings, also a small bag filled with stones from the Crossing, as the legion of bat-looking creatures gave chase to Daniel and the rest. Stephen and Jake were covering their back, launching arrows and very special stones at the fallen Angels, bringing them down like a fair day goose falling from the sky.

With each arrow launched and stone tossed another Angel fell to the earth with a loud thud. They were mortal; never before did so many Angels fall so quickly, with more than twenty on the ground dead, the others scattered, pulling off from their attack. Jake was looking for Zoltar as they moved through the tall grass, still dropping green batwinged monsters as they moved.

Jake and Stephen were about a hundred yards from the ship. Sandra turned and was struck in the neck by a flaming arrow fired by Derrick. Jake turned and saw Zoltar falling on him from the sky. When he made contact with Jake, the large monster crashed to the ground and a loud *snap!* was heard as his wing broke and the two rolled down the dirt hill toward the sea.

Jake pushed the monster off him hard and Zoltar stood up and faced him. Jake's mind raced back to the eighth grade when he faced Billy Parson. The stir inside him was stronger than ever; he wanted to tear the monster to pieces, and Zoltar could see this blazing from Jake's ice-blue eyes.

Zoltar tried to take to the sky and escape, but the broken wing didn't permit this. Next Zoltar went for the bow in the dirt and Jake made no attempt to stop him. He finally had him right where he wanted him: big, scary Zoltar abandoned by his magic and superhuman powers now armed with a manmade bow and arrow.

Jake felt a smile trying to surface and resisted.

With his arrow nocked, Zoltar pulled the bow. Jake heard fear in his voice when Zoltar commanded Jake to back off.

"Not likely, Zoltar. You attacked me, you murdered my wife, and now is your time of reckoning. The Good Shepherd brings you what you have sown in all your years," Jake said.

"Stop! I'm Zoltar, brother to Morning Star, and I command you to halt your aggression towards me." Zoltar released the arrow. Jake snatched it from midair with one hand and snapped it as he moved closer to the monster.

"Now you pay for the evil you have done!"

Zoltar grabbed Jake with both hands around his throat and picked him up off the ground. Jake reached behind his neck and pulled the Dagger of Moriah from a holster between his shoulder blades and pushed it into the neck of Zoltar. The monster dropped Jake and looked confused as death began to take him.

"Hurts, ahhh, hurts," the monster said with what he had left of a voice.

More than the pain, Jake could read the fear in his eyes.

"For Teresa and Abigail, you unholy creep." Jake pulled the dagger from Zoltar's throat and stuck it into his heart. The monster's eyes went to the dagger and then met Jake's.

Jake was pleased to see that the fear and pain was still there, only surprise was the winning emotion in those eyes.

"You're mortal, and now you die."

Zoltar fell to his knees, blood spraying from his neck and pulsing from his heart. Jake looked back at Stephen and motioned for him to come forward. Stephen drew the Sword of Goliath. Zoltar's eyes widened at the sight of what he had coveted for so long. Stephen buried the sword to the hilt into the chest of the monster, who again looked down at the now two enchanted blades buried in his flesh. His final look told Jake he died afraid. Zoltar pitched forward and breathed his last breath.

Jake and Stephen stood over the body of Zoltar and looked up. The remaining Angels fled. Daniel and Windy had come for Sandra, who lay injured. Jake looked at Stephen and was pleased to see the smile starting to form at the corners of his mouth. Something in the wind was like a warm spirit of victory blowing among the Shaddai.

FIVE

When all were aboard, *Delilah's Secret* moved slowly from the port and a course was set for San Francisco. Jake and Stephen went to the sick bay to visit Sandra, who had suffered a neck wound in the battle. However, she was healing nicely, and would make a full recovery.

With the Sword of Goliath and the Dagger of Moriah in the ship's safe, Jake and Stephen shared a moment of peace and satisfaction. It would be a long journey back to San Francisco and there was no need to rush.

SIX

Jake made his way to the ship's communication room and made a phone call.

"Inspector Jericho."

"Hello, Inspector, this is Jake Stanton. I understand you're looking for me."

At first Jake thought he'd lost the connection.

"I'm in no mood for jokes. Is this really Jake Stanton?"

"It is, sir, and I would like to meet you and turn myself in."

"Jake, if this is you ... oh, man, if this is really you, I expect you will not be in custody long. In fact, I expect we all owe you an apology; not just for taking your freedom and sending you to San Quentin, but for prosecuting you in the first place. When can we meet?"

"Well, at the moment I'm on a ship, and likely in a different time zone. It's only because of the vessel I'm traveling on that I can even call you. I'll be back in San Francisco in about ten days. May I buy you a cup of coffee?"

"Yes, you may, and later, I'll buy you a beer. We have a lot to talk about. I'm so glad you called."

"What about Stross?" Inspector Jericho asked.

"If it's all the same to you, I would rather not discuss Stephen Stross. Regarding everything else, I'm at your service. Only with Stross, I would like to reserve our conversation for another time."

"I suppose that's fair, Jake."

"I'll see you in about ten days. Call me when you get close so I can ensure we have any and all of your enemy concerns under control."

"Sam, I have already taken care of my enemy concerns. I'll call you in about ten days. Take care."

"You too, Jake."

When Sam hung up the phone, a large smile appeared on his face. Ruth gave him a look and then a victory kiss.

Stephen walked into the communications room on the ship. "You called Jericho, didn't you?"

Jake nodded.

"Well, he will be glad to see you when we return."

"I do believe you're right."

"I'm exhausted," Stephen said.

"I'm going to sleep for as long as I can."

"You deserve some rest, my brother. I'm going to do the same."

SEVEN

Jake lay in his bed looking at the ceiling, thinking about the battle with the witch and Zoltar. He reached into the drawer of his nightstand and pulled out a small, smooth stone and held it in his hand until sleep took him.

When Jake opened his eyes he was at the Crossing. Teresa was kissing him. Tears welled in his eyes and he held her tight.

"How long do we have?" Jake asked.

"We have eternity, my love. But what about Stephen and the talisman?" she asked.

"Let's make the most of the here and now," Jake responded. They made love all night, and then fell off into a coma-like sleep.

Jake felt the warm morning sun on his face but didn't want to open his eyes for fear he would be away from his beloved. As he slowly opened his eyes, his gaze was met by two tiny eyes looking back. "Jake home! Jake home!" It was little Conchita.

He sat up and Abigail yelled, "Daddy!" and pounced on him. "Daddy, you have to see it, look! I have a loose tooth!" Jake looked at his beautiful daughter and touched her loose tooth and tears once again ran down his cheeks. Teresa stood in the doorway with a cup of coffee in her white night dress. She looked like an angel. Jake didn't know how much time he had. In his right hand he held a small, smooth stone and he decided to keep it.

"I love you, sweetheart," Jake said to Abigail.

"I love you too, Daddy." She grinned, melting his heart.

Jake heard his grandfather, Aaron, in his mind. *"Much is given to those who serve, and much is expected."*

Jake decided he would take the path as it presented itself and go through the doors as they opened. He was at peace, but still, he felt the stir inside him; it was sleeping, but was there all the same.

The End

Afterword

by Anthony Jones

*It's with relief and sadness that I end Book 1 of the
Bloodline Chronicles. No doubt the story left many
matters unresolved. Inspector Jericho and his task force
were only beginning to close in on the politicians in
league with Zoltar and his followers. The Ichabod was
left steaming on towards En-Dor. Zoltar and the witch
of En-Dor are dead, and the Sword of Goliath is safe in
the hands of the Shaddai on Delilah's Secret. Jake was
left at the Crossing with his family on what he hoped
would be an extended visit.*

*With the sword, the Shaddai now are one step closer to
completing the talisman. I believe the Bloodline
Chronicles have many adventures remaining, and I'm
more than a little curious to see where the tale goes next
and how the story ends.*

*I think Jake and Stephen will continue to press on and
begin the hunt for the next enchanted instrument.
However, I hope to fall back and tell the story of
Stephen, and how he was awakened and set on the
quest back in 1827. I think Stephen's story is relevant to
the Bloodline Chronicles and will bring to light some of
the history touched on in Book 1. We know Stephen was
awakened at age 25 by David, his guardian, but we
don't know what happened to David or what happened
to Stephen's family; most importantly, we don't know
how the Holy Shaddai began.*

*At the Crossing, we meet many of Jake's family
members and even hear about Daniel's wife and her
eventual ascending beyond the Crossing. Teresa and
Abigail have come back to the Crossing at the end of
Book 1, and we know the Oracle Samuel told Jake that
Abigail was his bloodline and his destiny. I think we'll
meet up with Abigail in the future, perhaps several*

books ahead, because I think she's an important character and may even be the one who completes the talisman of the twelve instruments. I can tell you, some of the members of the Shaddai will likely fall before the twelve enchanted instruments are all gathered.

I have truly enjoyed writing this book. It's my first work and as such, I'm nervous as to how it will be received. Over the course of writing the book, I have enjoyed long discussions with friends who seem to think the story is unique and a subject matter they're interested in. Nevertheless, I'm reluctant to let it go.

I'm not interested in selling a masterpiece. At a minimum I would like the books I write to become a legacy to my children, and chronicle the stories from my mind during my time on this earth. I know I would love to have a book from my grandfather, Aaron, who died when I was a young man. That's right; I used Aaron as a character in this book as the grandfather of Jake. Also, I used the names of other people I know or from books I have read and put my own twist on them. That is the beautiful thing about writing fiction, you get to do anything you want: create places, and characters, and set them in motion to tell a story made up from personal experiences, or as far as one's imagination will allow. The Crossing started out to be a "dream place" I called Bodega Village, only it grew to several towns separating Sion from Nod, or the holy from the unholy, in a completely different dimension.

I hope readers will enjoy reading the story as much as I enjoyed writing it. I want to acknowledge Stephen King and his work on the Dark Tower series, as it was this series that inspired the Bloodline Chronicles. Even the name Jake was borrowed from Jake Chambers. Other names from King include Pylon, Rusher, and Dashane.

I expect Sam Jericho will be returning in Book 2, as well as Stephen and Jake. I still think the story of Stephen is a separate book, and the book Samuel gave Jake called The Crossing is important to the series.

In closing, I want to recognize my good friend, David Lewis, as he continues to encourage me to tell the story and acts as a wonderful sounding board for ideas. I'll be introducing the next villains with the help of David after killing off Zoltar, Borackus, and Tabatha, the witch of En-Dor. In the next book I expect Jake and Stephen to encounter Azazel and Semyaza, as they're expected to be released from Nether Gloom by a wicked wizard of Nod.

God Bless.